HEX

BROKEN PACT, BOOK ONE

HEX

ASH FITZSIMMONS

This is a work of fiction. Names, characters, places, and incidents are products of the author's imagination or are used fictitiously and are not to be construed as real. Any resemblance to actual events, locales, organizations, or persons, living or dead, is entirely coincidental.

Print Edition ISBN: 978-1-949861-75-4

Cover design by MiblArt.

www.ashfitzsimmons.com

CHAPTER 1

There is no nose so exquisitely sensitive as a troll's.

The boys of the Wild Hunt come close, but even they admit that the trollish sense of smell is peerless. An untrained troll can sniff out what a person standing across the room had for breakfast, and possibly dinner the night before, depending on his oral hygiene. A troll with a standard investigative agency background can track a scent trail weeks after it was laid and tell a subject's species, no matter how well he masks. (Well, with one exception, but my boyfriend's masking ring was a *weird* piece of work.) An exceptionally well-trained troll can smell toxins in blood and potions in the air, useful skills for a healer.

In sum, that old human rhyme about the blood of an Englishman? Accurate.

People of other species claim that they understand the troll nose, but there's a vast gulf between academic comprehension of how faint an odor has to be for a troll to miss it and the lived olfactory experience. Honestly, a troll can lose his sight and, with the exception of driving, still get around quite easily. The only person I knew who really *got* it was Annie Humphries: born human, then adopted into the Hunt, with all that entailed. A few weeks after her nose got its upgrade, I found her miserable at a Monday meeting after she took an unauthorized weekend jaunt home to Richmond, and she looked at me in dismay, having discovered the hard way that shopping at Yankee Candle was now tantamount to torture for her.

Scent is the sense most closely tied to memory, and at

least for trolls, it's the first to come online at waking. Which was why I didn't have to open my eyes to know that something was terribly wrong.

Tobacco. Not *good* tobacco, something cheap. Ash, mostly from the tobacco and its wrappings. Marijuana, too—and no, this wasn't good weed. The weird chemical note suggested a vape pen. Below that was the scent of mildew, not overpowering but present. Nearby was a source of garbage. I could pick a few easy components from the bouquet—eggs, turned milk, and something charred, probably cookies, judging by the hints of chocolate and vanilla and caramelized sugar—and a deeper sniff brought forth scents that pointed to a bathroom, astringent cleaners and cheap soap and traces of blood.

As the deep part of my brain ran its analysis, the higher levels rapidly began to retreat from sleep. This didn't make sense. My bedroom smelled of wood polish and detergent and the petunia in imported potting soil that struggled to survive by the window. I'd cleaned the adjoining bathroom on Tuesday, but there was no blood in the mix. And I *certainly* didn't have anything to smoke in my house. Sure, I'd experimented during my youth, but I gave all that up around the time that I took a job with the Division of Plants and Potions.

Then my nose identified a scent combination that made the rest of my mind jolt awake: gasoline mixed with motor oil.

The two were known in the Pactlands, the former for its inflammatory properties and the latter for use in machinery. But seldom did one smell them in conjunction, as the vehicles we owned were powered by spell-driven engines, cleaner and far less expensive to operate. That I was picking up on oil and gas together, and *strongly*, suggested I was somewhere outside the Pactlands—somewhere with human traffic.

The fuck?

My eyes shot open, and I immediately regretted it. My

head throbbed like I'd spent the night in a bar, and the bright light that hit them made me wince and screw them shut. Calling upon my resolve, I opened my eyes again and forced them to focus.

The light came from a streetlamp on the sidewalk at the end of the apparent alley in which I found myself. Easing my body upright, hoping not to puke from the headache, I blinked a few times and tried to make sense of my surroundings. I was sitting on a couch of some sort—no, a dirty chaise longue, perhaps someone's poolside castoff—that groaned and sagged dangerously beneath my weight. To my left was a trio of large trash cans, and as I turned right to look toward the street again, a white box truck rumbled by, belching diesel fumes. Glancing at the brick wall directly in front of me, I spied a metal door, its label barely visible in the light from the street: DELIVERIES.

In English.

Yes, I was definitely outside the Pactlands, but how?

I stood, trying to ignore the pounding in my skull, and staggered to the end of the alley to peer out. A two-lane paved street, though the configuration of the traffic lights hanging over the intersection suggested it was a one-way thoroughfare. One- and two-story brick buildings on either side, bunched up together, their plate-glass windows and signage indicative of shops and restaurants. Trees, actual *trees*, growing from holes in the sidewalk and rising above the buildings behind them, their leaves still green in mid-September. The shop on the other side of the road had decorated its door with a pair of smiling pumpkins— ceramic, not organic—and the banner stretched across its window proclaimed, HAPPY FALL, Y'ALL! in sparkly orange and red letters.

This made no sense. Still sleep-foggy, I returned to the chaise and carefully sat, then reached up to rub my face.

And then I felt my tusks.

Trolls, male and female alike, grow oversized lower cuspids, which protrude even when our mouths are other-

wise closed. They're useful in a brawl, and if they're sufficiently sharp, you can disembowel an opponent. But
they're not exactly *subtle*, and in no universe would one
ever mistake a troll for a human with a bad underbite.
Tusks aside, we're significantly larger, we only have four
digits per hand or foot, and we have far less hair. By troll
standards, I was considered a beauty, but since I was more
than eight feet tall, with a green complexion, the only way
I was allowed out of the Pactlands was with masking jewelry. I'd purchased a locket years ago, something I could
easily configure to my preferred mask instead of having to
remake it each time with an agency loaner. Because I over-
saw the Interdiction division, which occasionally necessi-
tated quick trips outside, I didn't remove my locket except
for bathing. Better to sleep with it on than to get to the
external portal building and discover I'd left it on the
nightstand.

I reached for my locket, intending to mask before anyone could come along and see me…but as I patted my
chest, I realized two things: I was wearing my pajamas, a
flirty little pink short set with a lacy camisole, and my locket was nowhere to be found.

Oh, this was *bad*. This was very bad. Best-case scenario,
I'd be fired; worst-case, I'd set off a panic, incite a mob…

A mob with *cameras*. Everyone carried phones, there
were cameras in pockets and purses and mounted on
walls…

I'd wind up in a government lab, perhaps…

Would they kill me? Interrogate me? If I pretended not
to understand English, could I protect the Pactlands from
discovery?

As my mind raced through the horrible potentials, the
delivery door opened with a squeal of metal hinges, and
out stepped a human.

She was unremarkable, as humans went: mid-thirties,
perhaps, around five and a half feet tall, and of average
build. Her blonde hair had been pulled back into a careless

ponytail. She wore a pale blue tunic top over black leggings, topped by a stained white apron, and in one hand, she carried a vape pen.

For the briefest of instants, relief swept through me. I knew her—that was Maya Mackay. She'd founded Mangia Due, the café in the DPP tower with the unexpected Italian name. Like her friend Annie, she'd been dosed with the novel Roulette potion nearly four years prior, and I'd evacuated them and the rest of the exposed to the Pactlands until we understood the effects. While the others had quickly been returned, albeit with altered memories, Maya and Annie had been kept back for their protection and ours—I mean, we couldn't just abandon a pair of humans who'd grown wings and antlers. I'd bought many a coffee (and a few beers) at Mangia Due when Maya was behind the counter, and as far as I knew, we had no quarrel with each other...

But that was before Maya was given the antidote to Roulette and the potion that allowed me to alter her memory. Much as I'd hated to do it, I'd removed all traces of her time in our pocket world, instead letting her believe she'd been in witness protection. She'd returned to her home and her life, wingless and safe—and considering her wide-eyed, slack-jawed expression, she was about to scream.

We stared at each other as I frantically tried to string together words that would keep her calm. I couldn't run, not unmasked, and I didn't want to hurt her...

Maya's face shifted, shock giving way to bemusement, and she planted her free hand on her hip as she absently tapped her vape pen against her leg. "Uh...hey, Chief," she said in perfect, if accented, Pactish. "Want to tell me why you're hanging out on our smoking couch?"

It was my turn to goggle, and my mouth flapped open once or twice in false starts before I managed, "*How*..."

She chuckled, her smirk visible even in the low light. "You know, I don't want to tell your research team how to do their jobs, and I'm sure they're great at what they do, but, uh...shouldn't they have had sense enough to wait until the potion that affected *every other potion* was cleared from my system?"

"They...I...I thought they did..."

"Obviously, they didn't wait long enough. Memory wipe was a bust." She shrugged, then said, "Good to see you again, but can I ask what you're doing here in your nightclothes? And, um, you're looking a little green, there."

"I don't know what's happened," I replied in a rush. "No idea how I came to be here, and my masking pendant is missing, and—"

"Okay, whoa, *whoa*," she interrupted, holding up her hands. "It's all right. Let's get you inside, huh?"

Disorientation fueled my panic. "I don't know...I don't remember..."

Maya tucked her vape pen into a pocket on her thigh, then crossed the alley and gripped my bare shoulders. "Calm down, Chief."

"This doesn't make sense, I—"

"Gentle Breeze," she murmured firmly, holding my stare, "I need you to work with me. Come on inside, I'm alone. You can't stay in the alley."

Against my will, my eyes began filming—a fear response, certainly, and I'd awakened enough by then to be terrified. "Maya, I—"

"We're going to get help," she insisted. "Come on in, and I'll call Annie. She'll take you home." With that, she gripped my arm and tugged, and I rose from the plasticky chaise. "That's it," she coaxed, "right this way. I've got coffee on."

Generally, I wasn't the type to lose control of my emotions. While I came from a farming family, my father's late father saw his share of combat in the days before the Pact, and my kin said that he and I were of one spirit. His tusk sat on my desk at work, safely encased in resin—my inheritance, far more valuable to me than any sum of money.

The gift meant that my grandfather believed in me, that he held me in esteem above the rest of my cousins—even those who left the farm for academia or to become healers—and that he thought I would bring honor to our clan. And to that point, I believed I'd done my part: a high-ranking position at DPP, the respect of my director and my subordinates, a house owned free and clear.

Shuffling behind Maya, trembling with nervous energy, surely wasn't what my grandfather had had in mind. Panic attacks weren't my style.

But this was different. I'd been outside the Pactlands on hundreds of trips over the last two centuries, and while I didn't fear the world beyond our borders, I had a healthy respect for it. But I'd always gone protected by masking jewelry. Now, for the first time in my life, I was outside and *exposed*, and every instinct was shouting at me to run.

Instead, I heard the door close behind me and forced myself to take deep breaths while I examined the building's interior. The space was overwhelmingly white and chrome, blotches that resolved into a kitchen—long metal counters, the door to a massive walk-in refrigerator, multiple ovens, an assortment of pots and pans hanging within easy reach. The scent profile suggested the recent presence of multiple humans, with notes of sweat and shampoo, cigarettes and alcohol, but clouding everything was the strong smell of baking cake, vanilla and sugar in a telltale bouquet that made my mouth water. The source appeared to be an oven halfway across the kitchen, and the oversized stand mixer still bore splashes of batter on its scuffed steel body.

So distracted was I by the olfactory assault of cake that I almost jumped when scratchy cloth landed lopsidedly on my shoulders. "Sorry," said Maya, "can't quite reach. I don't have any blankets around here, and a tablecloth is the best I can do…"

I straightened it and pulled it around myself like a thin shawl, and I followed her out of the kitchen and into what was obviously a restaurant. Tables of various sizes and configurations filled much of the space, though the bar along the side was lined with stools. The mural ringing the restaurant was difficult to make out with only the glow of the kitchen lamps to light it, but it seemed vaguely Mediterranean to me, a scene of gnarled trees growing along the slopes of gently rolling hills, dotted with shapes that might have been houses. "Here, have a seat," Maya coaxed, tugging a table out of the way to give me access to a padded booth. "I'll be right back."

Carefully, I lowered myself onto the bench, hoping I wouldn't break Maya's furniture, and hunched shivering beneath my tablecloth. The Pactlands was usually a temperate place, regardless of the season—magic is useful like that—and while the restaurant wasn't cold, neither was it comfortable for me in my skimpy pajamas.

A moment later, Maya returned, carrying a generously sized mug. "Try this," she said, pressing it into my hands.

Coffee, obviously, a scent I already associated with Maya, but as I pulled it closer, I picked up on the rest of the brew: splash of cream, one sugar, and a healthy pour of whiskey. I arched a brow at Maya, and she said, "Little Jameson in there to take the edge off. You look like you could use it."

She wasn't wrong.

I drank deeply, wincing as the hot liquid went down, and felt the familiar burn of alcohol at the back of my throat. Troll-strength brews were considerably stronger than those produced for species with less robust constitutions, but the whiskey was somewhere around eighty proof, and that was fine by me.

As I downed my coffee—which, in fairness, was more medicinal than anything—Maya pulled up a chair and joined me with her unspiked mug. "We're alone here, so take it easy," she said. "I came in early to get a jump on the weekend's baking."

Glancing past her, I noted how dark the world still was through the window facing the street. "What time is it?"

"Eh, five-ish. Sun won't be up until nearly seven, and the rest of the staff won't roll in until eight or so."

"Isn't that late for breakfast?"

She grinned. "We only do weekend brunch here. Monday through Friday, this is a lunch and dinner spot." Spreading her hands, she said, "Welcome to the original Mangia. How's Due doing, anyway?"

"Busy," I murmured. "I think there'd be a riot if the director closed its doors. You...remember it?"

"I remember *everything*," said Maya. "Including the cover story you gave me. It just feels like a movie I've seen too many times—like, I can quote it, but it doesn't seem real."

I sighed and lifted my mug.

"Not your fault. You did your job. Anyway, I'm glad it failed. Makes things easier on Annie when she stops in—she doesn't have to worry about slipping up with me."

"Annie knows?" I asked.

"Oh, yeah. So does Wylan. And before you get upset, Diriem's apparently very much aware of the situation and doesn't seem bothered."

The mention of the Division of Intelligence's director left me slightly uneasy, as usual. While I'd certainly met Diriem ti'Dana—hell, I'd stayed in his mansion—I hadn't worked closely with him, and I wouldn't have counted him among my friends. I'd helped train up his great-granddaughter, Rose, who by all accounts had him wrapped around her finger, and he'd never been antagonistic toward me...but farseers left me on edge, particularly those as talented as Diriem was. Maya, however, seemed blasé about the whole affair.

"But enough about me," she said, cradling her warm mug, "what's going on? Are you hurt?"

Briefly, I took stock of myself. "I don't think so...just a massive headache."

She put down her drink and quickly stood. "Stay put. Let me check."

I sat still while Maya inspected the back of my head.

Since the only hair I had to contend with was the tuft running over the top, she didn't have difficulty checking my scalp, and soon, after a bit of poking, she said, "No cuts that I can see, and nothing seems bruised. Does it feel like a migraine? A hangover? If it's hair of the dog you need, I've got plenty."

The phrase sounded nonsensical in Pactish, but I'd spent enough time in the outside world to know her meaning. "No, it doesn't feel like a hangover. I didn't drink a drop last night."

"Okay," she said, returning to her chair, "so let's start there. What happened?"

Though I was still somewhat disoriented, my panic flare was beginning to subside, calmed by the combination of a familiar face and quasi-Irish coffee. Too bad Maya wouldn't have a stash of pain potions on hand—my headache showed no signs of abating. "Uh…well," I said, "I left the office around six. Late meeting. Picked up dinner, went home."

"Which is…"

"Old Farm. I bought a house a while back."

Maya's brow furrowed. "That's…"

"Outskirts of Beukal. Suburb, really."

"*Ah*. I never had much reason to get out that way. Go on."

I paused, playing back my memories of the previous night. "So…right. Left the DPP tower, picked up dinner on the way, home before seven. I ate—"

"Anything weird? Adulterated?"

Having been the victim of potion-tainted pot, Maya *would* be sensitive to that possibility. "No, nothing unusual. There's a sandwich shop I visit a couple times a week— they've got this meat lover's option, and it's probably two pounds of cold cuts, so it's enough to keep me going. But no, I didn't sense anything off…"

"What?" she asked as my voice faded.

My internal emergency sirens having quieted a degree

and my higher functions having begun to come back online, I recalled my training and put down my drink. "Paper towel."

"Huh?"

"Do you have any? Or cotton swabs? Something clean and unscented."

She hurried into the kitchen and returned with a sealed roll of towels. "Here you go. Why do you need—"

"Just a moment, let me get a sample."

I ripped open the roll, pulled off a few, and swiped under my arms, behind my neck, over my chest, at the base of my spine—anywhere I could feel a hint of sweat—then stuffed the dampened paper under my nose and inhaled deeply.

I knew my own scent—I'd long since ceased to notice it unless I was in desperate need of a shower—and most of the odors I picked up on first sniff were the familiar notes of my perspiration and the soap I'd used the previous morning. I caught whiffs of my laundry detergent, which, though marketed as unscented, wouldn't qualify as such to a troll. I picked up on the usual signs of a meaty meal being metabolized and on the less familiar—and embarrassing—whiffs of my endocrine system's recent terror reaction. The ghosts of the cigarettes and vape cartridges consumed on the chaise outside. Even a hint of the alcohol and coffee that were just beginning to hit...

There. Faint, almost hidden by dinner and the stench of fear, was a metallic smell I'd committed to memory decades before as a trainee and come across only a handful of times in the field. Illicit growers and brewers went to considerable lengths to hide their operations, after all, and so an Interdiction agent needed to know the signs and effects of a variety of odd potions.

"I *was* drugged," I muttered.

"How do you know?" Maya asked.

"Here, smell the...never mind," I said, recalling my companion's limitations. "There's a sedative potion, a *strong* one, and as it breaks down in the body and is expelled, it has a distinctive scent. Metallic, but also a little sweet. It's hard to describe…"

"But it's in your sweat?"

"Oh, yeah." I put the wadded towels aside and sipped my coffee. "Fairly positive. I mean, it'd be better to confirm with a blood test, but that's not an option at the moment."

"Who would have drugged your *sandwich*?" she pressed. "And why?"

"That's just it—it wasn't in my food," I replied. "I'd have smelled it. So, how did I ingest it? Home by seven, ate dinner, did some paperwork, watched the late news…"

Maya grinned. "Stayed up to watch your boyfriend, eh?"

I rolled my eyes. "Annie told you?"

"You two were moving in that direction before I left," she protested. "Annie's just keeping me current."

Seeing as I had bigger problems that morning than the dissemination of news of my love life, I let it go. "*Yes*, I stayed up to watch him. I watched him long before we got together—he's great at what he does."

"I'm not criticizing," she said. "If my significant other were on TV, I'd probably tune in every so often, too."

"I still can't believe you bested the memory wipe," I said, and drained my mug in one long gulp. "You're okay, though, yes? We kept your affairs in order for you?"

"Oh, you did a great job," she assured me. "The restaurant's still open, my house was standing when I got back, and my car runs, so I'm not complaining. Things are more or less back to normal…though I did switch to a vape pen," she said. "Smoking pot directly makes me a little anxious these days, and since that's the exact opposite of what I'm going for…"

"I don't blame you."

She made a face. "But that's the last thing you remember? Watching Moonless Night?"

Shaking my head, I said, "No…I watched the news, and then I brushed my teeth and washed my face, and then I went to bed. I'm sure I fell asleep in a minute or two…and the next thing I knew, I was in your alley."

"Shit."

"Shit, indeed. So," I said, glancing around the empty restaurant, "think we could call Annie? I realize it's early, but under the circumstances…"

"She'll understand," Maya replied, and pulled her phone from her pocket. "One trip home, coming right up," she said as she tapped at the screen, then held the phone out between us and pressed the button to dial.

The call failed immediately.

"Huh," she grunted, and tried again…with the same result. When the call failed for the third time, she tried to send a text message, but it wouldn't go through. "Maybe there's a problem with Annie's phone," she mused. "Can you give me another number to call?"

"Sure. May I?"

She passed me her phone, and I gingerly poked at the screen, wishing I had my phone with me instead of the undersized thing in my palm. I started with Moonless Night, hating to wake him after his late shift but confident that he'd come rescue me.

The call failed.

My gut clenched as I redialed, making sure I'd input the correct number, but as before, I received nothing but a disappointed beep for my efforts.

Maya watched with concern as I then tried to call Syvin Deop, my counterpart on the Regulatory side. While she, unlike the Huntsmen in my life, wouldn't be able to simply teleport me out of there, I knew she'd jump in a car and come get me. Syvin was a faun, after all, and she understood as well as I did how dangerous it was for one of us to be outside unmasked. Besides, she was an early riser, and I suspected that the worst I'd do would be to interrupt her breakfast.

The call failed.

Trying to ignore my building dread, I pushed aside my pride and called my boss, Pateme ti'Tam. While I *knew* he'd be awake at that hour, I was reluctant to go to the agency director with a problem as severe and strange as my predicament was, especially as I was stuck in my pajamas. But my attempts to reach him failed just like the others, and I handed Maya her phone, flummoxed. "Maybe there's a problem with the phones. Maintenance or something," I said, trying to convince myself.

She frowned. "*All* of your carriers are down?"

"We only have the one."

"Mm. Maybe the problem's on my end," she said, squinting at the phone's screen, "but I've got bars. Here, come back to the office. I've got a landline."

As I followed her into the rear of the building, Maya explained, "Our internet package was actually cheaper with the landline, so I keep it on. Emergencies, you know? This way." She opened a scuffed wooden door, revealing a windowless space about the size of a trainee agent's cubicle, most of which was filled by a mismatched desk and chair. A laptop sat docked on the desk beside a white cordless phone. "Go ahead," said Maya, passing me the handset, "try that."

"Please," I whispered in Trollish, then dialed Moonless Night's number and held my breath.

The call failed.

"Whatever's wrong, it's in the Pactlands," I said, putting the phone in its base. "*Shit*. I don't suppose you have a secret method of communicating with Annie that you've been hiding from me, have you?"

"Afraid not," Maya replied, grimacing, then folded her arms and thought briefly. "Okay, we've got to get you sorted, but if the Pactlands isn't taking calls right now, then we've got to hide you until we can get word to Annie or someone. And you don't have a stash of masking jewelry hidden somewhere around here? Or, like, near the Oilville portal?"

"I wish," I muttered.

"Damn. Well, I'd take you back to my place to hang out, but my cousin and his family have been here since Tuesday."

"You're missing out on family time?"

She gave me a look. "Three kids under five. I'm *escaping* family time. They're leaving today, but not until after lunch, and I can't just lock you in the office until then. But..." Her face smoothed as an idea hit, and she snapped her fingers. "Rose's house."

"Rose ti'Dana?" I asked, taken aback. "She lives in Viratta—"

"*Now* she does, but when she was Rose Thorn, she lived in the West End, not too far from here. She still owns her house. *Nice* place. Puts mine to shame, but then I guess her parents bought it back in the nineties," she added. "Anyway, she gave me a spare key in case of emergencies, and the power and water are on. You could stay there for now—I'm sure she wouldn't mind."

As appealing as that plan was, I reluctantly shot it down. "Won't the neighbors be suspicious if there's sudden activity?"

"They've seen me around..."

"But you won't be there. And if some well-meaning neighbor thinks a squatter has broken in and calls the police..."

Maya's face fell. "Oh. *Ugh.* Yeah, no, I see the problem...so we go to Plan B."

"What's Plan B?" I asked.

"Annie's parents. They're out in the suburbs."

"Annie's *parents*?" I echoed, aghast. "If we were going to spring the Pactlands on them, then surely we'd start with a sorcerer. *Maybe* an elf. Going full troll from the start is a terrible idea—"

"They know," she interrupted.

I froze, startled into momentary silence. "Come again?"

"They know about the Pactlands," said Maya. "Annie and Wylan filled them in, like, two years ago. Around the time you sent me back."

Yes, Annie was young, but to be so cavalier about security... "Why on earth would they—"

Maya put up her hands to stop me. "It was Diriem's suggestion, so blame DOI."

Farseers.

"They've taken it all pretty well," she continued. "Annie introduced us a while back, and they're nice folks. Got a house out in the county, quiet neighborhood, bunch of retirees. I bet they'd be willing to help."

"You think so?" I asked dubiously.

She nodded. "You know a sorcerer from north Georgia who went on the run or something? They hosted her for a little bit."

Oh, I knew *exactly* who Maya was talking about. Jane Fortune was a baby pyromancer who'd taken down a Forum representative—her sociopathic grandfather, incidentally—been wooed to DOI, and was engaged to the last surviving member of Hall ti'Catama. Since she was also kin to the wife of one of my up-and-coming agents, I heard my share of the gossip. I'd known that she'd had to flee at one point, but I hadn't realized that her path had taken her to Annie's parents.

Then again, Jane had been raised outside, and so she was in large part culturally human. I shouldn't have been surprised that she'd have formed a relationship with another American expat.

Perhaps Annie's family had been told of the Pactlands' existence, but it was one thing for them to host a sorcerer, and quite another to ask them to take *me* in. Annie's husband was obviously inhuman, but he could mask—had he ever revealed his true nature to her parents? I couldn't very well ask Annie for the details that morning, and I could see a million ways that this plan could go horribly wrong...

But I was stranded in Richmond in my nightclothes, in

pain, coming out from a sedative potion, and feeling naked in more ways than one, and desperation forced me to override caution.

"If you think they'd be willing..." I said slowly, letting that hang.

"Can't hurt to ask," Maya chirped, and pulled out her cell phone again. "Probably a good thing I saved their number, eh?"

CHAPTER 2

I had mixed feelings when the call connected—relief, certainly, that the number was working, but also dread as it became undeniable that something was wrong with telecommunications in the Pactlands. Sure, the system occasionally had an outage, but those were rare and brief. Ever since the advent of the mobile phone, I'd never been unable to reach home—a lifeline when work took me outside.

But I only had a few seconds to dwell on the problem before the line opened on the other end, and a female voice said in English, "Hi, Maya. Is everything okay?"

Not a terribly high or low voice by human metrics, I thought. Middle-aged, perhaps a little froggy with the early hour. She had a light drawl, much like Annie's, and I could almost imagine the voice as an older version of my agent's. She sounded alert but concerned—unsurprising, all things considered.

"Morning, Maggie," Maya replied in kind, holding her phone between the two of us with the speaker engaged. "Sorry about the early call—"

"Oh, don't worry. Dave's been on a conference call with a customer in Paris for the last hour, so I'm up. What's going on, hon?"

She took a deep breath but kept her tone light. "Uh…well, I've got a situation here, and I could really use y'all's help."

"What's wrong?"

Maya glanced up at me, then turned her attention back to the phone. "So, um…someone from *Wisconsin* was dropped outside Mangia overnight. She thinks she was drugged, she has no clue as to how she got here, and her masking jewelry is missing."

I heard a brief silence on the other end, and then the woman—Maggie, rather—uttered a long, slow, "*Oh*. This missing jewelry, is it a real issue, or are we in need of, like, a hat?"

"No, ma'am, this is a problem," Maya stressed. "*Big* problem. We've been trying to call Wisconsin for a pickup, but we can't reach anyone there who can help, and this person needs to hide until we can get a lift home figured out. She's with me now, but I've got company at my house, and—"

"Is Annie not answering her phone?"

"Maybe it's just my phone," Maya said doubtfully, "but I think there's an issue on her end. Want to try to reach her?"

"Yeah, let me. She tends to pick up when Dave and I call. Back in a minute, bye."

The call ended, and Maya put the phone on the desk to wait. "Don't go far," she murmured.

I leaned against the wall, holding my tablecloth around me, and waited only a moment or two before Maya's phone rang.

She took the call on speaker. "Any luck?"

"No," said Maggie, who sounded perplexed. "I tried Annie and Wylan both, but nothing went through—not calls, not texts, nothing. I even made one of those video calls. Is that what happened to you?"

"Yes, ma'am. Every number failed. It might just be a network problem in Wisconsin, but—"

"That's not helping your friend there, is it?" she interjected. "Who's with you?"

Maya paused ever so briefly before answering the question. "Her name is Gentle Breeze," she said, using the English translation. "She's—"

"Annie's boss?"

"Exactly. I can vouch for her—"

"Oh, honey, don't worry about it. Annie speaks so highly of her…yeah, we can help out. Of course."

The knot of worry in my chest loosened ever so slightly at the unexpected warmth in her voice.

"You're sure?" Maya asked. "I hate to impose—"

"You can't schedule emergencies," said Maggie. "Dave's working from home today, and I don't have firm plans, so you're not imposing…" She cleared her throat. "Just one concern. She's, uh…larger, is she not?"

Maya gave me a quick once-over. "About eight feet, I'd say, and built like a linebacker."

"That's what I was afraid of. Can she fit in a car?"

I winced and wiggled one hand, and Maya caught my meaning. "Not well. She could probably scrunch up, but y'all don't worry about that. I've got an idea. We'll be out that way in a little bit, okay?"

"Sure, we'll be here. You drive safely, now."

Once Maya hung up, she said, "Maggie and Dave are sweet people. They'll take care of you until we can get you home."

I nodded, still unsure but resigned to the plan. "So…*Wisconsin?*"

"That was Annie's and my cover story, yeah? Witness protection in Wisconsin?" Shrugging, she said, "Just in case anyone unexpected was around on Maggie's end. It's our little code word."

"*Ah.*" Annie and Wylan might have violated a stack of security protocols, but at least *someone* was taking precautions. "How are we getting to them?"

She sucked her teeth. "So, my car's not really an option. You'd be miserable squished in there."

"I don't know, I've fit in some odd vehicles…"

"She's a 1971 Super Beetle. Restored," she added, misjudging my expression. "She's cute. Candy-apple red, runs like she just came off the factory line."

"Yeah…no, that's too small," I muttered. "I thought

you had a larger car—"

"The Honda died last year. Sorry," she said. "But I've got something better—I bought a delivery van for catering. It probably won't be the most comfortable ride of your life, but you'll be able to sit without curling into the fetal position. And there are no windows, so bonus."

"I've ridden in the hold of more agency Jeeps than I can count," I replied. "Sure, bring on the van."

She clapped her hands and pointed at me. "Boom. We're in business. Now, the van's parked down the street, so you stay here for a few minutes, and I'll be right back. Oh, and if any timers go off, just pull whatever's in the oven out, okay?"

With that, Maya slipped off into the predawn quiet, leaving me alone in the empty restaurant. I checked the ovens, then hunted around the building until I found the women's bathroom and flipped on the lights.

The gold-framed mirror was exceedingly unforgiving that day as I slumped to take a look at the damage. I looked paler than usual but puffy, and my eyes were sunken and bloodshot—not an uncommon reaction to the sedative I'd been slipped. My hair was greasy, and while my tusks were relatively clean, I'd have punched a man for a toothbrush. At least my pajamas appeared to be undamaged, though given how little the shorts and tank covered, they didn't do much to cover me at their best. I'd bought that set for my boyfriend's benefit, and while he appreciated the look, I'd found the pajamas surprisingly comfortable and wore them even when he wasn't around.

I'd never make *that* mistake again. By troll metrics, I was easy on the eyes, but that didn't mean I wanted to parade myself around with every curve and muscle bulge on display.

Especially not in front of a pair of humans.

But Maya's tablecloth didn't even make a proper wrap skirt, so I draped it over my shoulders, splashed water on my face, and availed myself of the facilities before she returned, rumbling up the alley with the scent of burned oil.

I peeked out the delivery door and found a white panel van idling by the trash cans. In the low light, I could make out the word Mangia painted on the side in a red slanted script, flanked by wine bottles and surrounded by a border of what appeared to be looping pasta. Maya cut the engine and climbed out of the front, then motioned for me to follow her to the rear. "Coast is clear," she said after peeking out at the street. "Hop in the back, okay?"

"You should get your engine checked," I said as I climbed inside. Besides the built-in shelving and a pull-down table, the back of the van was empty, devoid of so much as a seat belt.

"What's wrong with the engine?"

"Oil. Uh…is anything back here unsecured?"

"Nah. I'm sorry, it's not great—"

"Just try not to take the curves too quickly," I said, and sat with my legs stretched across the van, keeping the metal shelves within reach in case I needed to brace myself. "Okay?"

"I'll be careful," Maya assured me. "Let me pull a couple of things from the ovens before they burn, and we'll be off. I'll be right back," she promised, then closed the doors, throwing me into darkness.

When you find yourself in the back of a pitch-black van in your nightclothes, being shuttled to an unknown destination so that a frightened mob doesn't shoot you or worse, you have time to think about just how your life went wrong to get you where you are in that moment.

The van floor was cold, and the space smelled of the ghost of old dinners—garlic, sage, rosemary, cooking wine, tomatoes, onions, and meaty scents, not to be outdone by hints of sugar and butter and vanilla. *So* much vanilla— good vanilla, too, I absently noted as we bumped along. The Mangia Due crew were fine bakers, but I'd missed

Maya's creations. At least someone was getting to enjoy them. Beyond food, I could smell sweat and deodorant and a particularly noxious musky body spray that had to linger even for the wearer's virtually nose-blind colleagues, plus the plasticky odor of the van's liner and the engine scents of a gasoline-powered vehicle.

And humiliatingly, I smelled the lingering traces of my fear sweat.

Yes, I was afraid. I was woman enough to admit that truth, and it *bothered* me. I'd run into producers' labs and raided growing operations within and outside the Pact-lands—hell, I'd gone after a damn siren and almost gotten myself killed for my pains—and while a certain degree of anxiety and pre-operation jitters was expected, I'd seldom been deeply afraid. But this was different, the sort of scenario we discussed in training and tried to workshop over the years but honestly for which we didn't have a solid game plan. Bottom line, sorcerers were safe outside if they kept their heads down, and elves, with their inherent masking abilities, could get by in a pinch, but the rest of us were fucked. The best we'd been able to come up with was the obvious: hide and hustle to a portal.

Whoever dropped me outside—and I was still puzzling through *that*—had been either kind or lazy enough to leave me fairly close to the Oilville portal. I knew that one well; DPP's greenhouse was anchored outside in a rural area west of Richmond, and plenty of licensed—and unlicensed—growers had set up operations in the mid-Atlantic. Oilville was perhaps half an hour's drive from Carytown…but the portal wouldn't open unless I called the portal attendant on the other side, and if telecommunications in the Pactlands was indeed down, then I'd be stuck sitting in the woods. I *did* know the phone number— that was one we'd all committed to memory, just in case— but hell, at that moment, I didn't even have a phone.

Back in the day, matters had been simpler, as the portals would open if you presented a token and said the passphrase. The Portal Authority—at DOI's insistence—had phased those out in favor of live gatekeeping because too many tokens had fallen into unauthorized hands, and allowing tourists to go outside was a massive risk to us all. But the Portal Authority's staff not being the most scrupulous of the bunch, the portals continued to act as a sieve for those with sufficient funds to open doors and seal lips, and so the tokens wouldn't have made much difference, security-wise. I'd have given a tusk for a functional token right about then, but they'd all been decommissioned decades before, and any left in the wild were nothing more than useless trinkets.

As I ran through the variables and came up with no brilliant escape plan, I faced the reality that I was at Maya's mercy. Nearly four years before, I'd been the one who'd led a hastily assembled team to Carytown to investigate a suspected potion incident, and I'd made the call to pack the afflicted back to Beukal for quarantine and treatment. The site had been Maya's house, and we'd walked into the aftermath of a costume party gone horribly wrong. Thanks to a potion-tainted batch of marijuana that the ever-gracious hostess had shared with her friends, three people were dead, Annie had woken with a rack of antlers, and Maya had sprouted wings overnight. I hadn't been around when they woke in quarantine, imprisoned in the DPP tower until our research team could be sure they weren't contagious or in immediate danger, but I'd heard that the people responsible had received an earful from the director after the fact because no one had bothered to put an English speaker on shift until Rose threw a fit. That was probably the closest that Annie, Maya, and their friends would ever come to an alien abduction, and it had to have been traumatic, compounded as it was by the deaths of the partygoers. We'd altered their memories before sending them home—all but Maya and Annie, who'd been forced to stay for nearly another two years while the research team worked out an antidote—but still, we could have handled the matter better.

Perhaps this was the universe's way of evening the scales. I might have laughed if not for my knotted guts and throbbing head.

Maya wouldn't betray me, would she? I thought back over her time in the Pactlands, wondering whether she held a grudge. We'd housed her, given her money to live on, and loaned her a vehicle, and in turn, she'd created the best little café in any agency facility in the capital. Sure, Maya had been ready to go once her wings disappeared, but she'd made friends in Beukal, hadn't she? The kids she'd hired to run Mangia Due, some of the agents, the freaking *Hunter*—she wouldn't do anything to hurt them, right?

But what if she was playing the long game? What if our destination wasn't a house in the suburbs but rather the police department? If this ride grew suspiciously long, could I open the door from the inside and…what, jump out onto the Interstate? Expose myself to the other motorists? What if I jumped and a car hit me—would I be carted off somewhere for medical aid and intensive questioning or shot and buried in a shallow grave?

And why was I worrying about Maya when we were ostensibly bound for Annie's parents' home? They'd lost their daughter to the Pactlands, and then she'd bound herself to a man who was anything but human—and worse, she wasn't human herself any longer. Even if Maya didn't have hard feelings, could the same be said for the Humphries family?

I didn't want to cry. I willed myself to maintain my composure, clenched my teeth and took slow breaths until the urge subsided, but the feeling endured, bobbing just beneath the surface and trying to rise.

No.

No tears.

I was The Joy in the Spirit at the Scent of Rain on a Gentle Breeze, damn it, and I would *not* dissolve into a weepy mess. I wouldn't curl up in the back of the van and wait to be killed. If my fears were realized, then I'd go down swinging—and a desperate troll makes a *dangerous* opponent.

Stern pep talk aside, however, I still had no idea how I'd gotten out there. I'd have bet my life that I'd been drugged, but *how*? More importantly, by whom, and why? If I had an enemy who wanted me dead, especially an enemy savvy enough to break into my house without waking me, then why didn't he take one of the many far easier routes of offing me? Why go to the trouble of sedating me, driving me out of the Pactlands, and dumping me in Richmond? Nothing made sense.

And the phone numbers that wouldn't connect unnerved me more than I wanted to admit, even to myself. A system-wide outage would be inconvenient, certainly, but outages were generally fixed in less than half a day, and one of that magnitude would be an all-hands, no-sleep situation.

Had something happened overnight in the Pactlands? Power failure? Terrorist attack? Coup?

Was Moonless Night okay?

As my mind conjured a selection of increasingly unlikely but horrible scenarios, the van, which had slowed considerably of late, came to stop. Suddenly, the vehicle went into a crawling reverse, and I braced myself in the back. When it stopped again, I pulled myself into a crouch and stayed clear of the doors, avoiding a full fighting stance but preparing for the worst.

The engine died, and I heard Maya's door open and close. A moment later, she opened the rear doors and squinted into the darkness. "Chief?" she whispered. "You okay?"

Well, no guns yet. I stood, stooping slightly, and exited into the cool twilight.

Maya had backed the van down a driveway, and I found myself squinting out into a small yard, the grass still green and the surrounding trees in leaf. There wasn't much in the way of gardening that I could see, just grass, but the lawn was tidy and, judging by the smell, had been mown in the last couple of days and fertilized in the previous week. The driveway lay adjacent to a two-story white brick house—a rather ordinary dwelling, I thought, maintained but not ostentatious—and Maya had parked beside a closed garage. Peeking around the van, I saw neighboring houses similar in style to our destination, a few with a light or two in a window, but the street was quiet.

Remove the trees, and it might have been my neighborhood at that hour…well, if you changed the scent profile. The smell of gasoline engines lingered, as did those of an assortment of lawn and garden products, a bouquet of mulch and straw and fertilizer. As nothing but grass grew well in the Pactlands without substantial magical support, most of us didn't waste much effort on our yards, but I'd found that suburban humans were a different story, decorating their plots with trees and bushes and all manner of flowers, sometimes even vegetable and herb gardens. Glancing again into the yard behind the house, I picked up on the scent of apples and traced it to a tree at the back of the property. The notion of being able to step out the door of an average non-farmhouse and *pick food* had always struck me as bizarre, but there it was, a nicely laden tree ready for harvest.

We'd had that once, the elders said. Before the Pact, when our clans still lived outside, we'd put seeds in the ground and watched them come up with minimal tending. No magic needed—a good thing, as mine isn't one of the magic-wielding species. Of course, some of those harvests were never brought in because of human encroachment or the occasional clan raid, but land that gave fruit had been ours once—even if we'd held it with blood.

I'd never known those days. Having only seen my two hundred seventy-eighth birthday in the spring, I was still a youngling to many, not yet middle-aged. The Pactlands had always been my home, so while it was possible to hold a bit of nostalgia for a past I'd never experienced, I still found the idea of amateur backyard agriculture weird. My family's farm was leased from the Pact, regulated, and anchored to the outside world with magic, the last a necessary step to make the land more than a prairie. I'd never lived in a place where the soil simply *gave*.

"Coast is clear," Maya murmured. "No joggers. Come on, this way."

Holding my tablecloth around me, I hustled after her up a short cement walkway to the back door. Maya didn't bother knocking before she opened the door, revealing a mudroom. I did my best not to wrinkle my nose at the smells inside, as one wall was lined with pairs of boots and tennis shoes, all well-used and unequipped with so much as a single deodorizing insert. The rain jackets hanging on the wall above them and the umbrellas leaned in the corner carried a faint whiff of mustiness. Not a great deal of cross-ventilation in that space, I surmised. But I could make out other, more pleasant, scents as well: a floral perfume, the astringent notes of aftershave, and the unmistakable smells of bacon and coffee—*good* coffee, freshly ground.

"Maggie?" Maya called into the house. "Dave? We're here!"

Footsteps neared, and a woman in a pair of navy leggings and an oversized white shirt appeared at the other end of the mudroom. She was a little shorter than Annie, and her brown hair was a few shades lighter and streaked with gray, but I couldn't miss the resemblance to my agent.

Spotting us, she smiled tightly and motioned us inside. "Hey, there. Come on in," she said—to my shock, in drawled but serviceable *Pactish*. "Coffee's up. Are you hungry?" I must have gawked, as her smile warmed a degree. "It's okay, you're safe. Gentle Breeze, right?"

"Uh...yes," I managed.

"Maggie Humphries. This way, dear. Aren't you freezing?" She stepped back, giving us room, and frowned as I drew near and ducked through the doorway. "Good heavens, is that a *tablecloth*?"

"Working with what I've got," explained Maya.

"Well, we can do better than that. Go on in the den and have a seat," she told me, "and pull that afghan off the back of the couch. How do you take your coffee?"

"Black, please," I replied, frozen on the threshold of the kitchen. My body had primed itself for battle or flight, and this…well, this seemed unexpectedly welcoming, and I wasn't entirely sure what to do.

As if sensing my discomfort, Maggie softened. "Hey, now," she said, lowering her voice, "it's all right. We're going to get you home. It's just Dave and me here, and he's finishing his call in the basement, so don't you worry." She paused, then added, "It's nice to finally meet you. Now," she said, opening a cabinet, "are we thinking this or *this*?"

Her left hand held a standard-size human mug, while the right held one that was surely a novelty item, a mug that could have doubled as a teapot.

I chuckled awkwardly. "Wouldn't say no to the big one."

"That's what I figured. Go on, make yourself at home. Maya?"

"That smells great, Maggie, but I've got to get back to the restaurant," she said. "I'm sorry to—"

"*Hon*, no," said Maggie, slipping into English. "We're fine. I'll keep you posted, okay? And call me if you hear from Annie before I do."

With promises made, Maya departed, leaving me with Maggie. I carefully sat on the couch, wincing as I heard the supports creak beneath my weight, and exchanged the tablecloth for the plaid afghan. The two were about the same size, but the blanket was softer and warmer—and if nothing else, the Humphrieses' den was far nicer than Maya's delivery van, a cozy space with plush furniture, a fireplace, and a thick rug. They'd even hung a selection of what had to be family photos on one wall, and I suspected that the little girl with the brown pigtails and pink dress was Annie in the not-so-distant past.

This was not a situation for which I'd been trained. We'd learned how to interact with humans, of course—"carefully and as infrequently as possible" was the usual guidance—and I'd instructed my share of trainee agents in the art of getting by without getting shot on trips outside. I knew how to handle myself in public, grab a meal, rent a hotel room, even sweet-talk a cop into giving me a warning. But we didn't *socialize* with humans. We didn't enter their homes unless we were raiding them (and in those cases, we made the necessary memory adjustments to any witnesses). I tried to reassure myself that these were just people, basically sorcerers without the talent—hell, they were Annie's kin, and the kid was great—but I wasn't at my best that morning, and my discomfort only increased when an oddly dressed gray-haired man clomped up the stairs and poked his head into the den.

"*Oh!*" he said, catching sight of me, but recovered quickly and smiled. "Hey, there," he continued in Pactish. "Maggie sent me a note that we were having company, but I've been on the phone this morning, so I missed the details. Dave," he said, walking toward the couch with his hand outstretched.

I rose partway, gripping the blanket, and tried not to crush his fingers. "Gentle Breeze. I'm so sorry—"

"Wait." His smile widened. "You're with our Annie, right? DPP?"

"That's me."

"Well, isn't that something? Sit down, sit down," he urged, and called toward the kitchen in English, "Maggie, honey?"

"Coming!" she replied, and swept into the den, the giant mug cradled in both hands. "That should get you started, now," she told me, switching to Pactish. "Are you hungry?"

I took the mug gratefully, and then, forcing my frazzled brain to focus, said in English, "Thank you. Much appreciated. And this is fine, so..."

"Figured you understood, but I didn't want to assume," said Maggie, perching on a nearby chair. "And that afghan's not nearly enough. Dave, could you get the big quilt from the linen closet?"

"Oh, no," I began as he turned to leave, "it's—"

"You've got goosebumps," said Maggie. "Let's take care of that first."

She had, I realized, descended into full mothering mode, but frankly, I didn't mind a little fussing-over that morning.

As Dave headed upstairs and I sipped my coffee, Maggie leaned closer and asked, "Are you hurt?"

"I, uh...not really," I replied. "Nasty headache, but that's probably due to the sedative wearing off."

"Sedative?"

"Someone drugged me last night. I don't know who or how."

She made a face. "I'd say let's get you to a doctor, but..."

I chuckled weakly into my drink. "Better not."

"Do you want some painkillers? I've got aspirin, Tylenol, ibuprofen...not sure I know the Pactish for all of that—"

"Oh, I'm well acquainted with those. Wouldn't say no to a few aspirin, if you don't mind."

"Not at all." She returned to the kitchen, then brought me a small plastic bottle.

I shook out six pills into my palm and dry-swallowed them, then glanced back at Maggie in time to catch her surprise. "Our dosing is different. Pills, potions, whatever, the effect is considerably weaker on us. If you drank a troll-strength beer, you'd be under the table at best, probably sick with alcohol poisoning."

"Huh. Sorry, I didn't realize—"

"Don't apologize. You'd have no way of know-ing…well, unless Annie's said something." I paused for a bracing sip, hoping the caffeine would kick in. "How *do* you two speak Pactish, anyway? Did Annie bring potions home?"

Maggie shook her head. "No, nothing like that. She and Wylan had us over for dinner, and they didn't want to have to translate all night, so Wylan just…" She shrugged. "*Poof.*"

Well, that was only mildly terrifying. No one knew the precise limits of the Hunter's power, and I suspected Wylan preferred it that way. "So…you've been in the Pact-lands?"

"Just to the lodge. Met Wylan's family. He's a sweet guy, but between us, I don't know how Annie can live with that many men in one house. Oh, my *God*, the testos-terone," she said, softly laughing. "But that's not fair—they're always delightful when we visit. Now, I can't keep them all *straight* yet, but I'm working on it."

Okay, so they'd been to the Pactlands, or at least the Hunt's weird corner of it, on multiple occasions. As a rep-resentative to the Forum, Wylan should have understood what a security risk that created…well, perhaps in the ab-stract. At first blush, Maggie seemed almost harmless. I'd have to have a stern talk with Annie, but something told me that wouldn't stop the visitation; the Hunt had a *long* tradition of doing whatever it wanted, and the rest of us be damned.

"How often do you go over?" I asked, partly making conversation and partly digging for intel.

"Oh, we've only been a handful of times," Maggie re-plied. "The boys are a *lot*, and besides, I like to cook for the kids…uh, Annie and Wylan. He's not exactly a kid, but you know what I mean."

Seeing as I had almost two centuries on him, I still thought of him as somewhat of a youngling, but Maggie must have been a few decades her son-in-law's junior. Theirs had to be an odd relationship.

"Anyway," she continued, "I was hoping we'd get a chance to meet you someday. Maybe not *quite* like this, but…"

I frowned. "You were?"

"Sure. You took care of our Annie, and she thinks you're fantastic. I want to thank you, if nothing else."

"I, uh…I kind of abducted your daughter…"

"You didn't leave her here, and I can't imagine what she and Maya would have gone through had they tried to deal with Roulette in Richmond. That said, it'd have been *nice* to know what was really going on instead of thinking our baby was in witness protection," she added, shooting me a pointed look, "but I can forgive that. You did right by her, and we're grateful. So, don't you worry," she said as the staircase creaked beneath Dave's rapid footsteps. "You're safe here. Probably not the most exciting place you've ever been, but we're going to take care of you until we can get you home. All right?"

I nodded, swallowing as my throat tightened. "Thank you."

"Of course. And there you are," she said, motioning Dave into the den. "I thought maybe you'd been buried in a towel avalanche."

"Just had to do a little digging," he said, and unfolded the quilt in his arms to show me. "How's this?"

"Perfect," I replied, and wrapped it over the afghan. With my torso bundled in two layers of blankets, I was beginning to take off the chill, though my bare legs still protested.

Maggie gave her husband a brief, disapproving examination. "Were you planning to put on real pants today, hon?"

Dave, who'd dressed in a blue pinstriped button-down shirt, navy necktie, and baggy red knee-length shorts, swept one hand over his clothing as if showing it off. "You don't like the tie?"

"Not with the shorts you sleep in."

"Well, what Paris doesn't know won't hurt them. I hate Zooming with real pants on," he told me. "If they want a conference call before dawn, then they're only getting business from the waist up. So," he said, loosening the knot of his tie as he took a free armchair, "what brings you here?"

"Poor woman got drugged and dumped in Carytown," Maggie volunteered.

Dave's brow knit. "Drugged?"

"I can smell the sedative on me," I explained, "but I don't know how it got into my system. All I know is that I went to bed at home and woke in the alley beside Maya's restaurant. And now we can't reach anyone in Beukal or at the lodge, so..." With a sigh into my coffee, which really was smooth, I muttered, "I don't know what the hell's going on."

"Maybe there's a problem with your phone," Dave offered.

"Not mine—it's back at my house," I said. "We tried Maya's cell and landline, but no luck."

"Can't hurt to try another one. Now, where did I leave that...*ah*." He stepped into the kitchen and pulled his phone off the table, then smiled as he took his seat. "Let's see if we can get Annie on the line, eh?"

At least my nonexistent hopes weren't dashed when the call failed to connect. Dave looked bemusedly at the device, then at Maggie, who said, "Try Wylan. You've got his number programmed, right?"

He began tapping at the screen. "Mm-hmm."

"Nice to have an emergency contact," Maggie told me. "It's not like we're ever in any great danger here, but he insisted. I mean, you could probably do worse than having the Hunt on standby, right?"

The image that leapt to my mind—that graying, middle-aged couple calling down a pack of armed, mounted

Huntsmen on whatever passed for the local ruffians in the suburbs—made my stomach lurch. While Wylan and his brothers looked closer to human than I did, their antlers were a giveaway, not to mention their assorted weapons, eyeshine, and lace-up shirts and leather trousers. I'd seen the Hunt riding, and I'd have had a healthy respect for them even if I weren't involved with one of their number.

Unfortunately, the call to Wylan failed as well. Dave passed me his phone and let me try my colleagues once more, but I had no more luck than he'd had.

"Okay," he said, putting the useless phone on an end table, "so, what does this mean?"

"I don't know what to tell you," I replied. "We do have occasional communications outages, but never like this. Since Maya was able to call you, I think we have to conclude the problem is in the Pactlands, but I'm stumped." I paused for a sip of coffee, which was doing wonders to clear my head, then said, "You two are taking all of this awfully well."

Maggie chuckled. "If Annie's with the boys, she'll be fine. As for everything else...I mean, we've seen magic. Annie's told us about her job and some of her coworkers, so..."

"Not entirely a shock," Dave offered.

I grunted into my mug. "Well, all else aside, you're right about Annie. The kid's fantastic, and she holds her own. One of my best trainees, and she's doing well as an agent. Your daughter is...*low* on the list of people I'd worry about in a crisis."

They flashed brief smiles, and fleetingly, I wondered if my parents would have reacted in the same way had they sat down with my first supervisor. I knew they were proud of me, but since they still asked when I was moving back to the farm every time I visited home, I suspected the answer was *no*.

As I finished my drink, Maggie asked, "Do you want some more coffee? We've got plenty of grounds. Or food?

I was making breakfast when y'all got here. The bacon's in the microwave."

"Thanks," I said. "Perhaps in a..."

Something within me finally woke up. My mind had been spinning, but it had also been trying to piece together the previous night in the back of my thoughts. Suddenly, I had a flash of memory.

After a moment, I heard Maggie say my name, then focused to find her standing in front of me, waving one hand. "Oh, uh, sorry," I said, realizing I'd momentarily blanked on them. "I just remembered something from last night."

"What's that?"

I paused, closing my eyes and coaxing the details from the shadows. "It's not entirely clear, but I think I woke, and I wasn't alone."

"Woke at home?" she asked, returning to her chair.

I nodded. "In my bed. I didn't see anything, but I *smelled* something off. Uh..." The memory was patchy, but the longer I circled around it, the more it came clear. "Male," I murmured, parsing the scent profile. "A sorcerer. Nervous. His detergent—that's what woke me," I explained, opening my eyes again. "There's this brand that's meant to smell like pine, but it's wrong—too citrusy, too metallic. I hate that stuff, and his clothing reeked of it. *That's* what got my attention."

Dave rubbed his chin. "So...a man broke into your house last night, drugged you, and drove you out here?"

"Doesn't make sense, does it?"

"I don't mean to pry, but are you involved in some sort of high-profile case?" he asked. "Something that would give you enemies with resources?"

"Like that Silver fellow?" Maggie added.

She'd used the Pactish for his name, and I arched an eyebrow. "Annie told you about him, did she?"

"Her friend was all tied up in it, so she gave us the short version."

To be fair, Annie and Rose *had* been friends prior to their introduction to the Pactlands, and anyone who worked around the Virginians and Georgians knew they maintained an informal support network—probably to hear English and eat quality Tex-Mex, I assumed.

But I had more pressing issues than how much Annie was telling her parents about work. "No, I'm not involved in anything like the Silver take-down," I told them. "Not currently, anyway. Things are quiet in my office. I mean, my only firm plans for the rest of the week were dinner with my boyfriend Friday night."

That gave me a measure of comfort. Surely *someone* at DPP would notice my absence, but if they didn't, then Moonless Night would know there was a problem when I didn't show up in thirty-six hours. We'd made reservations at a place in the Edolis with generous portions and plenty of mountain charm, and so he was going to swing by my house and pick me up. That way, if the Friday-evening portals were unusually snarled, we'd be together…

The portals.

If this were indeed a temporary telecommunications outage, then the phone number for the external portals would be on the priority list to bring back online. Maya was busy, and I suspected that the Humphrieses didn't have a delivery van hiding in their garage, but if I walked to Oilville, then perhaps the number would be in service again by the time I arrived.

"Question," I said to my hosts. "How far is Oilville?"

"Oilville?" Dave echoed, and consulted the ceiling. "Uh…twenty-five, thirty minutes away, I guess. Why?"

"Has Annie mentioned the portals?"

They nodded. "She did," said Maggie, "but they're able to get us in and out without trying to sneak us through the portal system."

"And that's the Hunt for you," I muttered. "Anyway, the closest portal is in Oilville. I don't want to tax your hospitality, but if you'd let me stay here until nightfall, I'll walk—"

"You are not *walking* to Oilville," Maggie interrupted. "That's not safe! You can't just go for a hike down I-64."

"There's a secondary road, is there not?"

"Yeah, but that's, what, fifteen miles? In the dark? *Barefoot?*"

"It's doable," I protested.

"But risky, I think," Dave chimed in. "Tell you what, we'll drive you out there a little bit later today."

"Uh…not to be rude, but *how?* I, um…I don't fit well in human-scaled cars, and the sun's going to rise soon…"

"Leave that to me," he replied, and tapped his temple. "Got a plan. Now, I have a little more work to do this morning, but if you could wait a few hours…"

"Of course," I said. "Thank you. Whatever you need from me—"

"*You* just take it easy," Maggie interrupted. "Sweetie, better tank up before your call with Dublin."

Groaning, Dave pushed himself from his chair. "Yes, dear."

"And start a new pot, will you?"

"*Yes*, dear," he repeated, heading for the kitchen.

As Dave dealt with the coffee, Maggie lowered her voice and said, "I certainly don't know fashion in your neck of the woods, but am I correct in assuming that you're in pajamas?"

I pulled the quilt more tightly around my shoulders with my free hand. "Pretty obvious, huh?"

"Mm-hmm. I can tell you right now that I don't have a darn thing in my closet that'll fit you, so let me get your measurements, and I'll see what I can find."

"Oh, no, you don't have to—"

"It's no trouble. Wait right there."

Once Dave had retreated to the basement, Maggie brought in a well-stocked sewing kit and pulled out a tape measure and a small notepad. "All right, now that it's just us girls, let me see what we're working with."

I stood and squatted as needed, letting her collect data. "The nice thing here," she said, cinching the tape around my hips, "is that you don't have a significant bustline or backside."

"We tend to be fairly flat all over," I explained.

She pointedly glanced down at her more generously proportioned chest and grunted. "Lucky. But what this means is that I can look in the men's department. Their clothes will be larger, and since men's sizing actually makes *sense*, I might be able to find something that works the first time. Here, step on the little end piece and pull the tape up to your crown...let's see, straighten up...oh, goodness, eight foot two," she said as I handed it back to her. "My word."

"I'm actually not the tallest in my family," I told her.

Maggie whistled low. "Well, I'm just glad it's not the dead of winter—I may not be able to find pants long enough."

"I'd be grateful for anything longer than the ones I'm currently wearing."

As she knelt with the tape measure to inspect my feet, she said, "I know that feeling, hon. Back in college, I was sleeping over in Dave's room one weekend—his room-mate had gone home for a few days, and the RA looked the other way—but around two in the morning, one of the guys on the floor got drunk and tried to make popcorn, and he started a kitchen fire. We all evacuated, right, but I'd gone to sleep in my *underwear*, and I was too disoriented to hunt for my clothes in the dark, so Dave wrapped me in his towel and hustled me outside. Barefoot. In *February*," she muttered. "So, there I was, hopping from foot to foot on the sidewalk next to a pile of refrozen snow, clinging to that gross, threadbare towel for dear life..." She shook her head, chuckling. "I bought him new towels the next day and made him throw the old ones out. Bet you a million bucks that thing hadn't seen the inside of a washing machine all semester."

Having walked past my share of odiferous agent lockers, I could well imagine.

Maggie consulted her notes, then searched on her phone for a moment, frowning. "Slight problem."

"Oh?" I asked, settling back on the couch.

"Unfortunately, I'm not going to be able to find you shoes off the rack. You'd take a *special* order, and I don't know of anywhere around here that would have something workable…"

"Really, it's fine," I assured her. "I don't need them, but thank you. As you said, it's not winter yet."

Though she seemed troubled by this development, Maggie stood and packed her tape measure away. "We'll see. Okay, I'm going to run to the store and do my best."

"*Now?*"

She shrugged. "Walmart often works in a pinch. When I get back, I'll make a proper breakfast—I don't think I made enough bacon, for starters."

Before I could fib, my stomach growled, and heat rose up the back of my neck.

"Don't you worry," she said, "I've cooked for Wylan, and that man's got the metabolism of a teenage boy. We'll make do. In the meantime, come upstairs with me, and let me show you the guest room."

I followed after her, clutching my security quilt. "Guest room?"

"We weren't expecting you to hide in the den all day," said Maggie. "Thought you might like a little privacy, and if you need to sleep off whatever sedative they gave you, you're more than welcome to stretch out."

She climbed the staircase, then turned right down the corridor and opened a white wooden door near the end. "Here you go. Bathroom's next door. The master suite's at the other end of the hall, so don't worry about bothering us."

I ducked through the doorway and quickly took in the space. Shades covered the pair of windows flanking the headboard of a four-poster bed—mahogany, perhaps, or else stained to match the appearance of such. The bed was made up with a pale green comforter and decorative floral-print accent pillows, and for a human visitor or two, it would have been decently large. On one wall was a matching dresser with a mirror, and I suspected that the door beside it led to a closet. Along the other wall was a plush armchair and a folding luggage rack, and Maggie opened the door to show me the adjoining bathroom. Overall, it was a comfortable space, though I'd need to take precautions around the ceiling fan.

"Again, make yourself at home," said Maggie. "The coffee should be finishing up downstairs if you want a refill, and help yourself to the TV—Dave won't hear you down in his hole. I'll be back as soon as I can," she said, then gave me a little pat on the arm and departed.

Alone, I carefully sat on the edge of the bed, listening for the warning groan of overstressed supports, and released a long, slow sigh.

I wasn't dead yet, so...progress, I supposed. Annie's parents were being surprisingly hospitable. I just had no idea what to do with myself. More coffee sounded like a wise choice, though I was still deeply desirous of a toothbrush. A shower might be a good idea, as I was going on twenty-four hours since my last one, and while I suspected my hosts couldn't pick up on my stench yet, *I* could.

Having tested the structural integrity of the bed, I stood, dropped my wrappings on the comforter, and turned on the lamps atop the dresser to give myself a better inspection. My headache was fading, and nothing else seemed to hurt, which came as a small relief that day. No cuts or bruises that I could see, but...

Wait.

I poked my left thigh, just below the hem of my shorts, and felt a slight twinge. Frowning, I went next door to the bathroom, flipped on the much brighter lights, and inspected my leg.

Yes, that was absolutely an injection site, tender and slightly raised.

Befuddled, I grabbed my blankets again and retreated to the warm kitchen. Coffee might not fix my problems, but it wouldn't hurt.

CHAPTER 3

When Maggie bustled in through the mudroom about an hour later, the sun was up, Dave was still in his basement lair, and I was well and truly caffeinated. Having consumed the second pot, I'd put on a third and hoped Maggie wouldn't notice.

"Okay," she said, depositing two armfuls of plastic shopping bags on the kitchen table. "Let's see if any of this works."

As she pulled a few breakfast supplies from the bags, she said, "I'm sorry, but most of this came from the Big and Tall section in the men's department. Probably not going to be the most flattering clothes you ever try on…"

"Believe me," I said, "I'm less concerned about fashion than about having clothes, period. Thank you again for trying."

"Sure thing, hon. Why don't you take those upstairs and see if anything fits?" she suggested. "I'm going to get started on round two of breakfast…and I see that Dave ate the early bacon," she added, opening the microwave. "Fine, more for us."

I carried everything to the guest room and unpacked it on the bed. Maggie was right—the clothes were absolutely not my style, and I suspected they'd fit oddly—but anything was better than my current skimpy ensemble. Better still, I found a bag full of toiletries: a toothbrush and paste, floss, a stick of deodorant, coconut-scented shampoo and conditioner—not terrible—a hairbrush, and even a bottle of lotion. Whatever else could be said for Maggie, she'd done her best, and I was beyond grateful for her kindness.

The men's underwear she'd bought was...*interesting*... but the fit wasn't terrible, and it was clean. Full-length trousers being out of the question, she'd found a couple pair of brown cargo shorts that were probably designed to be a bit loose and long but hit me mid-thigh—not a fantastic look, but the shorts buttoned, so I called it a success. The black polo shirt I dug from one bag actually wasn't terrible; tight as it was on me, it showed off my toned arms and pecs. I topped it with a black hoodie that was also rather form-fitting on my frame, and after I'd ripped the neck hole slightly, it was comfortable. Taking a look at myself in the dresser mirror, I couldn't say it was the nicest outfit I'd ever thrown together—and it was a far cry from my favorite pink blouse—but I was warmer and much more covered, and all things considered, that'd do.

I brushed my teeth and hair, then returned to the kitchen to find Maggie cracking eggs in a ceramic bowl. "Better than I'd thought," she decreed as I did a twirl. "You know, I probably should have asked, but any food allergies? Dietary restrictions?"

"If it's not moving, it's fair game," I replied. "Eggs?"

"Scrambled okay?"

"Perfect. Do you want a hand?"

"Nah, but I wouldn't mind company."

I fixed a cup of coffee for her and poured another for myself, and eschewing the questionable bar stools along the kitchen island, I leaned against the granite counter while Maggie worked. "I hope you know that as soon as I get home, I'm reimbursing you for all of this."

"Nonsense," said Maggie.

"No, I mean it. I'll send it with Annie."

"And I'll send it right back with her." She paused in her egg cracking just long enough to give me a look. "I know what DPP did for my kid."

"Your kid has done more for the agency than DPP has ever done for her. Seriously," I said when Maggie cut her eyes to me, "she's a little badass. Did she and Wylan ever tell you how many agents they helped save from the previous Hunter?"

She paused, frowning. "When Wylan, um…"

"Stabbed his father? I was there. Annie drew the Hunter's attention to give the rest of us a fighting chance, and that was *after* she fell off her horse and hurt her leg."

"She didn't mention falling…"

"I accidentally shot her horse, and the poor thing reacted. We were all in the air at the time, and Annie should have been okay, but her safety tether snapped."

Maggie stopped again, eggshells in her hands, and stared up at me. "Say *what*, now?"

"We were using old equipment. The good gear was blown up by a bomb, but that's another matter. Anyway," I said before Maggie could ask more questions, "the Hunter kidnapped ten agents, and we saved nine of them, and a lot of that is due to Annie." I paused to sip my coffee, then said, "Did she ever tell you about Georgia?"

"Some. What about it?"

"So, there's this baby sorcerer who was raised in a little town in northern Georgia—"

"Jane Fortune?"

I stiffened, briefly surprised, then recalled what Maya had said. "That's right, you've met her, haven't you?"

"Oh, yes, we had her over. Her and a young man…" She pursed her lips as she tossed the last of the eggshells into the garbage. "Connor Willow, that's it. Knew it was a tree. Nice kids. She was in some trouble, and he was trying to take care of her, and Annie asked us if we could hide them for a bit. They weren't here long, but Annie said they're all right now. You know them?"

"Uh…well, Jane's at DOI these days. I've met her and Connor—and one of my agents is married to Jane's cousin, so the gossip gets around. Has Annie mentioned Pars Mera?"

Maggie nodded. "Thinks the world of him. She says

he's a massive teddy bear until the shooting starts."

"She's not wrong," I replied. "And it was Pars who told me what happened in Georgia. There was this group of illegal producers hiding in the mountains, and they'd kidnapped a bunch of people, and Annie was brought in to help because she knows humans, right?"

"I should hope so," said Maggie, chuckling.

"That, and she's not skittish around them, which is rare for a young agent."

She gave me a quizzical look. "Y'all are scared of *us*?"

Shrugging, I said, "We abandoned this world for a reason."

"Granted," she allowed, "but on a more practical level, there's no way I could hold my own against you. And that's not factoring magic in."

"I don't have any talent for magic—"

"Okay, but some of y'all over there do. I mean, Annie said Jane's a sorcerer who's especially good with *fire*. Why the heck would someone like that be scared of me?"

"One on one might not be much of a contest," I replied, "but ten on one? A hundred? How many of you are there now, eight billion? We can't compete. And aside from Wylan, we're not bulletproof. But as I was saying, Annie went to Georgia to help Jane, and Pars said she was fantastic. Kid's a full agent, and she's still underage. That should tell you how much we appreciate having her aboard."

"You're not just buttering me up, are you?" Maggie asked, but she smiled.

"Not in the slightest. Kid got into a shootout with some growers on accident when she was a trainee—and this is pre-Hunt, mind you, so we're talking a human with a gun—and she ended up shooting two of them while riding bareback on a centaur. That *does not* happen."

Maggie began whisking the eggs with a splash of milk. "She did mention a centaur…"

"Tylla Zom?"

"That's it."

I nodded. "So, Interdiction is about a third of the agency, and I've subdivided it into three groups to make it manageable. My second is a guy named Emarae, and Tylla is *his* unofficial second. Annie's in their group with Pars. Solid team. Emarae and Pars are both good teachers, and that's why I put Annie there at the start—that, and that group had worked with a Virginian before."

"Who, Rose?"

"Exactly. You know her?"

"I know *of* her," said Maggie. "Your kids grow up and move out, and they stop bringing their friends home for playdates, but Annie still talks to us." She considered the eggs, added salt and pepper, then set them aside. "Do you have any kids?"

"Me? No," I replied. "Never married, no kids yet. Someday, perhaps, but the way things are going, I kind of doubt it."

"Gotcha. I love mine, but they're not for everyone."

"Oh, I wouldn't be opposed to children," I said, "not in the future, I mean. It's just, uh…" I hesitated, wondering precisely how much Maggie knew of the Hunt, then asked, "Has Annie mentioned that I'm seeing one of Wylan's brothers?"

"Sure. He's mentioned it, too. They're happy for you both. You're what, the second long-term relationship anyone in that brood has ever maintained?"

"Something like that. We've been together a little over two years."

"Sounds serious to me," said Maggie, turning her attention to a large package of bacon.

"Feels serious," I murmured. "And if it continues…"

"Kids are unlikely?" she finished.

"I'd say impossible. We can't crossbreed. There've been a few trolls who've tried—and frankly, I'd rather not consider the details—but it never works."

That, and the Hunter had created all of his sons infertile. I'd heard plenty about that already, and my boyfriend kept offering it as an out if I changed my mind, but I wasn't overly bothered. With Wylan's promotion to head of the Hunt, I didn't know whether kids were in his and Annie's future, and that wasn't a matter I wanted to bring up with Maggie if her daughter hadn't already broached the topic.

Before we could go further down that road, Dave returned from the basement and glanced hopefully around the kitchen. "More breakfast?"

"Patience," Maggie chided. "You had the early helping."

"And I've been working since four," he countered, skirting the island to kiss his wife's cheek. "I'm a growing boy."

"Uh-huh," she said with all due skepticism. "How's Dublin?"

"Oh, just peachy." Having brought his coffee mug up with him, he set about refilling it, and I made room at the counter. "They say they're considering the proposal, and I'm *pretty* sure they're on board."

"What's in Dublin?" I asked.

Dave looked up, grinning. "The Guinness factory."

Maggie rolled her eyes. "Dave is a senior member of a sales team for, uh…"

"We fabricate bits and pieces needed in various types of manufacturing," he said, coming to her rescue. "Especially pieces for older machinery that may no longer be supported—you know, functional equipment that the makers try to deem obsolete so you'll buy the next shiny thing off their assembly lines. And because we're willing to help keep machinery running at a decent price, we've got international customers—hence my unfortunate morning schedule when we need to chat with our folks in Europe." Stirring sugar into his drink, he said, "I've been at this for years. Got to work partly remotely when Annie was a kid, which was rare at the time, but all I really need is a computer and a phone for much of what I do."

"And he's going to retire soon, *right?*" Maggie hinted.

It was Dave's turn to roll his eyes. "I'm sixty-three—I'm not done just yet. And aside from the odd call, there's no reason that we can't travel and enjoy ourselves. I mean, emergencies aside, I'm finished for today. Got underlings to do the paperwork."

That, I could appreciate.

Soon, breakfast was up: eggs, bacon, quick grits flavored with bacon grease, and half a loaf of toast. At Maggie's insistence, I squished around the table with them, trying not to drool. I was starving, and judging by the smell of the meal, everything Annie had said about her mother's cooking was true. Maggie brought glasses of orange juice to the table—little cups for them, a pint glass for me—then gestured to the platters and bowls. "Y'all dig in."

While I could have inhaled the spread, I forced myself to remember my manners and take small portions, gauging my plate by Dave's. But Maggie caught on in short order, and she pushed the egg bowl back toward me. "I know you're hungry," she murmured. "Go ahead, I made plenty. Wylan's a bottomless pit, so you're not going to offend anyone if you go for seconds."

"And if this isn't enough, we've got leftover chicken in the fridge, don't we?" Dave asked Maggie.

Her mouth tightened. "I hate to put out leftovers for company…"

"I'm sure this will be more than plenty," I fibbed, helping myself. "Smells amazing." As I went for the bacon, I asked, "Did Annie, uh…"

Following my thought, Maggie replied, "She said you had a healthy appetite—you and Pars both. Enjoy. I'm just glad to see people eat."

With as much decorum as I could muster, I downed anything the two of them didn't claim, and while it didn't leave me full, I felt much better. I started to help with the cleanup, but Maggie shooed me off. "Why don't you get a nice shower?" she suggested. "Try to relax. You've already had a day, hon."

She *was* a tad mothering, I decided as I headed upstairs, but I wasn't complaining.

The guest bathroom was amply sized for the average human, meaning I had to move carefully and duck through the shower door. But the shower was larger than I'd anticipated, and while the head was too low to be comfortable, it was detachable, a welcome mercy that morning. I washed quickly, trying not to waste water, then towel-dried my hair, dressed, and came downstairs to check in, only to find the house abandoned. There was, however, a handwritten note left on the kitchen island: *Gone out to get transportation. Back soon!*

About forty-five minutes later, just as my paranoia was starting to ramp up, I heard the rumble of approaching vehicles and peeked from around the curtains at the front of the house in time to see a car and a large RV approaching. The car pulled into the driveway, but the RV bypassed it, then reversed at a crawl, narrowly dodging the mailbox. As I watched, the mudroom door opened, and I heard Maggie call, "Gentle Breeze? We're back!"

"And how," I replied, heading to the kitchen to join her. "Heavens, that thing is unwieldy."

Maggie smirked as she put her purse on the table. "Never been RVing?"

"It's not really done at home. Can Dave, uh…safely…"

"Not his first rodeo," she said, patting my arm. "We used to go camping in those things when Annie was young. By the time she was a teenager, I think she'd rather have died than be caught with her parents at an RV park," she added, "but that's kids for you. Anyway, don't worry— we can handle that big boy."

A moment later, Dave walked in, brushing off his hands. "Ah, madam," he said, spotting me with Maggie, "your chariot awaits. Ready to hit the road?"

I hastily packed my few belongings in one of the

Walmart bags, then followed the Humphrieses out to the driveway. Dave went first, announced the coast was clear, and opened the side door of the RV. "Come on," he said, beckoning to me. "No one's watching."

After making my own brief check, I hustled up into the vehicle, then hunched over and paused to get my bearings as Dave and Maggie climbed into the front seats. The floor inside the long vehicle was some sort of artificial wood, a detail echoed in the furnishings. Directly across from the door was the tiniest kitchen I'd ever seen outside a gnome-scaled model house, which gave way to a pair of booths flanking a faux-wooden table. To my right was a couch covered in the sort of institutional black fabric that would be easy to clean and would hide stains. To my left, at the rear of the RV, was a bedroom that I calculated would comfortably sleep two human adults or one cramped troll, along with some storage space. Between the bedroom and the living quarters were a tiny shower and toilet, situated across the aisle from each other, neither of which I suspected I'd be able to comfortably use—but then we weren't going far, fortunately. The final interior area was a lofted space that hung above the cab—extra headroom, I thought on first glance, then saw the pair of thick mats stacked at the rear of the loft and realized it was an extra sleeping platform, complete with small, curtained windows. The rest of the windows in the RV were covered with curtains as well, and I saw the wisdom in Dave and Maggie's choice. I'd be able to fit in the back, and if I kept the curtains closed, passing motorists wouldn't see me.

Adding to my running tally of how many marks I'd need to have converted to dollars and sent home with Annie, I made myself comfortable on the couch and waited while Dave adjusted the mirrors.

"Gentle Breeze has never been RVing," Maggie informed him as he started forward.

"No?" Dave glanced over his shoulder, and I shook my head. "Oh, these things are great. Gas-guzzlers, to be sure, but they're fun. I wanted to buy our own—"

"And I reminded him that a hundred grand is an awful lot to fork out for a vehicle you're going to use maybe twice a year and then pay to store," Maggie interjected. "So, we rent."

"But they *are* nice," said Dave. "There's plenty of room underneath to bring a grill or bikes or whatever you like for a long weekend."

"I'll keep that in mind," I said, "but it's frowned upon when we go outside for unauthorized reasons."

"They don't let you go *outside*?" he asked, aghast.

"I think she means here, dear," Maggie suggested.

"*Oh.* Gotcha." He cleared his throat. "So, Oilville. I can get us there if you can guide me to this portal of yours."

"I normally approach from I-64…"

"No problem. We'll be there in a jiffy," Dave promised, and off we went.

I watched through the windshield as he navigated, trying to orient myself, but the neighborhood was unfamiliar. Not until we turned onto the Interstate did I recognize my surroundings—we were northwest of Richmond, and I took note of the signs as we chugged along. Oilville was only a few miles to the west, and as Dave eased us up the off-ramp, he called back, "Where to?"

Having made dozens, if not hundreds, of trips through the Oilville portal, I could have guided him blindfolded. I navigated us along a couple of turns and onto a secondary road, then told Dave to slow and pull onto the shoulder. "Do you see that gravel path through the trees?" I asked.

"Yeah…"

"It's down there."

"Huh." Dave considered the road for a moment, hazard lights blinking, then said, "I'm not sure we're going to *fit*. That's pretty narrow. Is there a turnaround at the end?"

"There's a small clearing, but…yeah, I think you're right," I muttered. "I guess I'm walking from here."

"Not alone," said Maggie. "Unless you're hiding a

phone…"

I'd forgotten. "Oh, uh…well, crap. Do you mind? It's not terribly far—maybe fifty yards from here."

"That's fine, I wore my tennis shoes. Dave, watch the RV. I'll be back," she said in a tone that would tolerate no argument, then slid down and opened my door. "Okay, we've got two cars and a truck coming, so hold on…"

Once the road was clear, I darted for the break in the trees, then waited in the shadows until Maggie joined me. "I cannot *believe* you're walking barefoot on gravel," she said as we started off.

"It's really not that bad," I said, though I moved slowly and stepped carefully. The path was deeply rutted, and the debris that had blown in complicated our walk. "Once we get past that fallen oak, the road will turn to dirt, and that's where the portal opens."

"Mm." Keeping pace with me, Maggie said, "Guess we wouldn't have gotten far with that tree across the road."

"Oh, no, it's just a deterrent. Ensorcelled. If you drive into it at sufficient speed, you pass right through. As for us, however…"

"We climb?"

"Unfortunately."

The tree that the Portal Authority had long ago left as a barrier to non-Pact traffic was ancient, far thicker around than I could reach, and rather than wade through the underbrush, I helped Maggie over the top. She slid down the far side, a little winded but resolute, and brushed off the seat of her leggings before we carried on.

Finally, the gravel gave way to dirt and scraggly grass, which ended in a clearing. It really would have given the RV trouble, I mused, and waited while Maggie pulled out her phone. "Okay," she said with a nervous smile, handing it to me, "fingers crossed."

I tapped out the familiar number and paused with a claw over the button. "Here goes nothing…"

And just as before, the call failed to connect.

"Oh, no," Maggie murmured as my face fell. "Still no luck?"

"Let me try again," I said, but the sick lump in my gut already knew it would be for naught. Three failed calls later, plus another round of calls to Annie, Syvin, and my boyfriend, I admitted defeat and returned Maggie's phone. "So…I guess I could stay here," I told her. "It's hidden, and the next time someone comes through Oilville, I'll catch a ride."

Planting her hands on her hips, Maggie said, "We are *not* leaving you in the woods. Don't be silly."

"I've inconvenienced you enough—"

"Look at me," she ordered. "You're *fine*, Gentle Breeze. You can stay with us until we figure this mess out—and since I can't reach my daughter, I'm in this, too. Yes?"

Annie really had come by it honestly. "Yes, ma'am."

"All right. Now, let's get back to the RV before Dave leaves us to hitchhike home, eh?"

Throughout the afternoon, we kept trying to reach the Pactlands. I dredged my memory for phone numbers, calling everyone from my cousins to a couple counselors at the Division of Laws, but the result was the same each time. Maggie then turned to email, sending messages to Annie's old address and waiting, but each time, the email bounced.

By midafternoon, I was dragging, a side effect of the previous night's sedative and the emotional rollercoaster of the morning, and Maggie encouraged me to nap. The guest bed creaked when I stretched out, but it held my weight, and the white noise of the ceiling fan lulled me unconscious almost as soon as I burrowed beneath the sheet and comforter. True, the bed wasn't quite long enough, but I slept at a diagonal and didn't stir until Maggie sent Dave up to knock and announce that dinner was served.

I apologized as I came to the table, lured by the aroma

of garlic, onions, and tomato, but Maggie waved it off. "It's spaghetti," she said, "nothing fancy. Fair warning, the meatballs are a venison mix."

They were incredible, and I fought the urge to dump the entire bowl onto my plate. "Annie mentioned that you hunt," I said to Dave. "Is this, uh…"

"Some," he replied, chuckling as he twirled his fork in his pasta. "There are legal limits to how much you can shoot, but Wylan really seems to like Maggie's meatloaf, so he keeps bringing venison, and I don't ask questions. Saves me on processing fees, anyway."

Though the meal was great, the sauce flavored to perfection, and I ate more than my hosts combined, dinner sat heavily with me, and I stuck around to help Maggie with the cleanup after she sent Dave to make a quick shopping run. Not bothering with the cars in the garage, he simply drove off in the RV, and his wife shook her head as we heard him depart. "He does like his toys," she said, packing away the little that remained of the spaghetti, "and I'd tell him to buy an RV of his own if we had the space for it, but our neighbors would kill us if we tried to park one of those here long-term."

"He's a good man," I said.

"A dear. I wouldn't trade him," she replied, smiling. "Put this in the fridge, will you?"

I did as she asked and turned back to find her soaping up the saucepot. "So, uh…"

She glanced up from her work expectantly.

I hesitated for the space of a long breath, then said, "I…I just wanted to apologize for what you and Dave must have gone through when Annie disappeared."

"Y'all did the right thing—"

"That doesn't mean it was fair to you."

She scrubbed at the tomato residue for a moment, then softly said, "I'm not going to stand here and tell you it was easy. I thought my baby had seen someone get murdered and there was a killer after her. Guess Wylan's father was actually worse," she allowed, "but no, it wasn't great. Has Annie ever mentioned her brother?"

"She has."

Maggie nodded and continued washing. "Alan was such a good little boy. *So* smart, and he loved his baby sister. But then he developed leukemia. Poor little fellow fought as hard as he could, and he was brave—*oh*, he was my brave boy," she said, her voice barely above a whisper. "We lost him a couple months before his ninth birthday. After that…I don't think we *smothered* Annie, but we were always close, see, the three of us remaining. Then Annie was gone, and…"

I waited until Maggie's jaw ceased trembling, the only indication that she was on the cusp of losing her composure. "We should have allowed her to contact you again, at least let you know where she was and that she was safe…ish."

"I do understand," said Maggie. "Sometimes, the needs of the many take precedence, and if it came down to letting Dave and me worry for a while or leaving Annie in Richmond with antlers, then there's no choice. I'm not upset," she said, glancing at me again.

"You two seem to have adjusted well to…you know, us," I said lamely.

She chuckled and turned on the sprayer. "Didn't happen overnight."

"No?"

"*No.* Annie walked in with Wylan and told us they'd gotten married, and then he dropped his mask."

"Oof."

"I know, right? 'Surprise!' But they came clean with us, and we got to know him, and since he makes Annie happy, he's family."

"And the converse?" I asked.

She grinned. "We have a standing invitation to the lodge, and Annie said that's basically 'honorary Hunt' status, so I'll take it. Plus, between us girls, he almost cried when I knitted him a cardigan last year, so I think we're all still in each other's good graces."

As I'd grown up with a healthy fear of the Wild Hunt, my brain simply refused to consider the notion of the Hunter getting weepy over a sweater, even if the Hunter was my former trainee.

"He's a nice boy," Maggie continued, "and I don't care if he's old enough to be my father—he's my son-in-law, so in my mind, he's Annie's age. Certainly looks the part," she added, then dumped the water, considered the pot, and scrubbed at a stubborn patch of sauce. "Mind if I ask you something?"

"Go ahead," I said, readying the dish towel.

"Well, I was taught to never ask a lady her age, but I assume you're nowhere close to Annie, right?"

"Two hundred seventy-eight."

She winced. "Not even in the neighborhood." Giving me a quick inspection, she said, "*Dang*, woman. I'd have never guessed. Tell me the secrets of your skincare routine."

"Shooting for a greener complexion?" I joked.

"If that would remove the wrinkles…"

"I'm not there yet. Roughly old enough for my quarter-life crisis," I explained.

"Huh." Passing me the dripping pot, she asked, "Does this qualify?"

I chuckled as I wiped it dry. "My parents still insist that my agency career is just a phase, so who knows? I might give it all up and run home to the farm."

"Your parents are farmers?" asked Maggie.

"You sound surprised."

"Well…I guess I never really gave much thought to career options for trolls."

"Just about anything that doesn't involve magic," I replied. "We can't cast, and we can't brew potions, but if you've got an unknown solution and want the components sniffed out, you call a troll. Quite a few of us work as healers—I've actually got three cousins who work in emergency medicine. If someone comes in as a suspected overdose, they can figure out what he's taken. It's faster than doing bloodwork much of the time. But my immediate family and a good portion of my extended kin—most of the older folks in the clan, really—are farmers. They're all out in Vengoti, which is the sort of town where you try new drugs just to relieve the boredom."

"Where's that?"

"So, you know that the Pactlands is sort of built atop this world? Like, if it were to collapse, our capital would land in Richmond."

"Yeah," Maggie replied, washing a serving spoon, "that's what Annie said…"

"Thinking of it that way, Vengoti is in Kansas, and not an exciting portion of Kansas. It's a farming district, so the land has additional magical support to allow it to produce crops, and no one wants to waste that on things like, you know, *civilization*." Taking the wet spoon from her, I said, "My kin have done well for themselves, but I wanted something more, and I thought I could make a difference at DPP."

Maggie began to wash down the sheet pan that had held the garlic bread. "I'd say you've done so."

"Oh?"

She nodded. "Annie described you as the sort of boss who makes sure her people come home alive. Makes a difference to me." As I tried to think of a response to that, she said, "I know I can't control what my daughter does, and I've never liked the idea of her doing anything remotely dangerous—I mean, when she told me she was learning to be a PI, I tried to change her mind. But if she's set on doing something risky, then I'm glad to know there's someone keeping an eye on her."

"Never mind me," I said. "Wylan's made it clear that he'll destroy the world if it means saving Annie, so as long as he's around, I wouldn't lose too much sleep." I paused, then said, "Humor me. Just how many times have you been to the lodge, anyway?"

"Oh…half a dozen, maybe? We don't sleep over or anything, but the kids like to have us visit for dinner." Cutting her eyes up at me, she faintly smirked. "Does that make *you* lose sleep?"

"Honestly?" I squeaked.

"It's all right, and I understand why you're not overly fond of my species," said Maggie, "but I hope you know that Dave and I wouldn't do anything to hurt Annie or the folks she cares about."

"You've made that rather clear," I said, and frowned at the pan. "That goop is baked on. Want me to scrub for a while?"

"Would you mind?"

I switched places with her, taking note of her pale pink manicure. "Claws are occasionally useful. You should see my mother cleaning up after a family feast."

Despite the stupefying effects of a carb-heavy meal, I lay awake in my borrowed bed that night, gingerly tossing and turning as I wondered what to do.

Our after-dinner calls had been as ineffective as all the others, which meant the Pactlands was nearing a full day of unreachability…well, at least from the Richmond area. I hadn't known a telecommunications outage of that extent in a century, not since the early, experimental days. Had something more serious occurred?

And surely my absence had been noticed. Emarae, if no one else, would have started asking questions of the rest of Interdiction, as my vacation days were clearly marked on the office calendar. Perhaps someone had tried to call me…but if the phones were down, then would they have bothered to drive out to Old Farm and check my house? Maybe Pars, another Old Farm resident, would have been dispatched. But if they'd realized I was missing, then wouldn't word have gotten around to Annie? Wouldn't she have told Wylan and Moonless Night? Surely one of them would have come searching for me...

Except they had no idea where I was...

Or did they? I wasn't significant enough to warrant DOI's attention, but Rose was *our* in-house farseer. If I didn't come to work, if I didn't answer my phone and wasn't at home, wouldn't someone have asked Rose to look in on me? Pateme was protected from farsight—well, not Rose's, since she was blood kin—but I was wide open. Okay, so my absence would have been detected, and eventually, someone would think to ask Rose, and once she found me, all it would take would be a word to Annie or any of the Hunt, and boom, I'd be home.

Why, then, was I curled up in a too-small bed with humans down the hall?

As I began to drift off, a sickening thought pulled me back from sleep.

Maybe my colleagues knew I was missing.

And maybe I wasn't the only one.

CHAPTER 4

The rumbling noise of a car slowing in front of the Humphries house almost made me bolt from the breakfast table Friday morning. As I prepared to flee—which was safer, the guest room or the unexplored basement?—Dave motioned for me to wait, then peeked out through the mudroom. "It's just Maya," he called back. "Stand down."

"Maya?" asked Maggie, frowning, and rose from the table.

It didn't take a genius to deduce the direction of her thoughts: they still couldn't reach their daughter, and perhaps Maya had received the sort of news that should be delivered in person.

Leaving Maggie, I followed Dave into the mudroom and spotted Maya's red Beetle in the predawn gloom behind the RV. Judging by the engine smell, the restoration hadn't been *quite* as successful as she might have imagined, but that news could wait.

"Hey, there, Maya," said Dave, inviting her inside as she walked up the driveway. "How's it going?"

"Hi, Dave." She gave him a brief, one-armed hug and nodded to me in greeting. "Just came by to check in. Any word from Annie?"

"No, but let's take this into the kitchen. Come on, hon. Coffee?"

Maggie hugged Maya as well, and though she relaxed slightly once she knew that Maya was still in the dark, her worry peeked through in the stiffness of her carriage.

"No luck, huh?" Maya asked me.

I shook my head. "Dave and Maggie drove me out to Oilville yesterday, but the portal number doesn't work."

She cut her eyes to our hosts. "Hence the RV?"

"It's big enough, isn't it?" said Dave, spreading his hands.

"No judgment here," she assured him. "And that's probably a hell of a lot better than my van." Accepting a mug from Maggie with her thanks, she took a sip, then said, "I tried to call Annie several times yesterday, but the phones are still down. So," she said, turning to me, "do we have a plan?"

"Not exactly," I admitted. "The only thought I've had this morning—and it's unlikely—is that the problem could be localized around Richmond. Maybe there's an issue in Beukal that's somehow blocking calls. Again, *highly* unlike-ly—"

"But if we got out far enough and tried, maybe we'd be able to reach Annie," said Maya.

"*If* that scenario were possible. Technical magic isn't my strength," I said. "Could something have happened in the capital, maybe some novel spell or construct?" Shrug-ging, I said, "I wish I could tell you, but this isn't my area of expertise."

Maya considered that as she drank. "Wonder why Rose hasn't told Annie what's going on."

"Perhaps she's unaware."

"Could be," she allowed. "But wouldn't *someone* have realized you're missing by now?"

"If they haven't, then my boyfriend will sound the alarm tonight. That's some comfort," I said, cradling my oversized mug. When he came by my house to pick me up for our dinner date and I wasn't there, then surely he'd tell Wylan and Annie. Annie would then call Rose, and Rose would find me. With any luck, I'd be home before morn-ing.

Unless, of course, I wasn't a priority.

"What's the nearest portal beyond Oilville?" Maggie

asked.

I squinted at the ceiling, thinking of the geography. "Well…there's at least one in every state east of the Mississippi but for Maine. Surrency's down in southern Georgia, Crossville's about midway into Tennessee, Maysville is in North Carolina, but it's close to the coast…"

"What about Central?" Dave suggested.

I eyed him across the table. "Annie tells you our portal locations, does she?"

"Just that one. She mentioned that when she went to north Georgia, the nearest portal was in South Carolina. Probably a good thing she doesn't need it, eh?"

"Sure, but I don't think she's had much reason to be sent there of late…"

Dave and Maggie traded a look, and then Maggie said, "Brunch."

"Come again?"

"Girls' brunch," she clarified. "Annie and some of her friends hop down to the mountains on occasion. Jane knows the area, and they go brunching."

"Sometimes at wineries," Maya quickly mumbled. When I stared at her, she said, "What? Everyone's of legal age."

"You're part of this brunch bonanza as well?" I asked, hoping she'd clarify in the negative. That Annie sneaked out was understood, but cross-pollinating her social circles was flirting with disaster.

Unfortunately for my breakfast digestion, Maya nodded. "Not every time, but Annie picks me up on occasion when I've got full coverage at Mangia. Come on," she added when my expression didn't shift, "I'm Rose's friend, too, and Jane's part of the expat club. It's all copacetic."

Technically not, but I let it slide, as the mention of Jane had given me a sudden burst of inspiration. "Do you know Connor Willow? About six feet tall, brown hair, brown eyes, distinctive mole near his left temple—"

"Jane's fiancé? We met once," she replied. "If that's

who you're thinking of…"

"Exactly."

Maya flashed a thumbs-up. "Backwoods elves brigade. Check."

"They might dispute that characterization," I said, wincing, "but yes—"

"Oh, did they get engaged?" Maggie interrupted. "Annie didn't tell us!"

I ran the quick calculation. "Uh…about two months ago. Fairly fresh. Anyway, I know that Laws has been trying to woo him, but last I heard, he was still the chief of police in his hometown…what was it…"

"Whitford," Maya supplied. "Jane's from Ragged Gap, and Whitford's the next town over. Not a lot of brunching opportunities in either location, so we usually end up around Blue Ridge."

"Do any of you have his phone number?" I asked the others. "If he's outside and can reach Jane, then we'll know the problem is localized."

Maya pulled out her phone and opened the contacts list, then scowled. "Sorry, no. Just Jane."

Maggie shrugged helplessly. "We never asked for it when they were here. But why don't we call the police department? Surely someone there would know how to get ahold of him."

After a moment's search, Maya located the non-emergency number in Whitford, then dialed and flipped the phone on speaker mode. She put it in the middle of the table as it rang, and I leaned closer, willing the call to connect.

I was almost shocked when it did. "Whitford Police Department," said a male voice with a distinctive drawl, pitched lower with the early hour. "Can I help you?"

"Hi," I replied. "I'm trying to reach Chief Willow."

"Speaking."

At that, I switched to Pactish. "Lord ti'Catama, this is Gentle Breeze from DPP. Uh, Interdiction. I don't know if you remember me, but—"

"Holy *shit*," he swore, failing to make the linguistic shift with me, "hang on, let me call you on another line. Is this a good number?"

"It is," I said, returning to English. "I'll be here."

"Two seconds," he promised, and the call ended.

As we waited, Dave regarded me, perplexed. "What did you call him?"

"Officially," I said, "he's the head of one of the elven Halls. Also its only current member, if I have the facts straight, but their politics are murky from the outside, and I'd rather not chance causing offense…"

Maya's ringing phone cut short my explanation, and I tapped the screen. "Hello?"

"Hey, Chief, it's Willow," he said in accented Pactish. "*So* glad you called—I can't get through to anyone in the Pactlands, and Jane didn't come home last night. Is something wrong over there?"

Damn it.

"That's what I'm trying to figure out," I told him. "I woke up in an alley in Richmond yesterday—"

"Oh, hell."

"*Without* my masking pendant."

The line went quiet for a beat, and then he said in a rush, "Are you okay? Safe? I've got a contact or two in the city—"

"Hey, Connor, this is Maya Mackay," she interjected. "I'm here with Annie's folks."

"And I see you found them," he said, sounding relieved, then switched tongues once more. "Morning, y'all. How's it going?"

"Could be better," said Maggie. "We can't reach Annie, Gentle Breeze can't reach any of her people, and the portal phone number didn't work at Oilville."

"Fuck," he muttered, followed by a quick, "'Scuse me, ma'am."

"Oh, no, that's the common sentiment," Maggie replied, smirking slightly at the phone on the table. "We were hoping you might be able to call across, but if you're having the same issues we are…"

"I am, but it sounds like y'all've got bigger problems than I do. Sorry, Chief, *how* did you get to Richmond?"

"Not entirely certain," I said, reaching for my coffee. "I know someone broke into my house and drugged me, but the who and why are still unknown."

"And you're unmasked?" he pressed.

"Yeah. They took my necklace off."

"But they left her next to my restaurant," Maya added, "and she's staying with the Humphrieses for now, so she hasn't incited a mass panic just yet."

"Oh, good," he said dryly. "But that ain't sustainable, especially if this blackout or whatever it is goes on much longer. Chief?"

"I'm here," I said between sips.

"Is there any way you can get to me? Janie has a stash of masking jewelry at her place."

That took me aback. "Sorry, *what?* Why does she need—"

"She doesn't need it—she's just good at making it. Yacovi taught her, and she's got a knack for it. Her pieces work," he stressed. "They're just not as polished as she'd like, so she fiddles with them sometimes while we're watching TV. Got a whole box in the closet."

Sorcerers, I mused, were an odd bunch.

"I'd come to you," he continued, "but one of my guys is in Atlanta today—his brother's having an outpatient procedure, and he's the ride home—and we're short-staffed. I'm pulling a double shift as it stands. If you can wait a couple days until we get things back on track here, then I can drive up, but if you've got a way to head down now…"

"We're on it," said Dave before I could answer. "Got the RV gassed up and everything. Can you send us the address?"

"Yes, sir. Is this your number?"

Dave gave him his phone number and Maggie's, and both phones beeped with an incoming message. "That's my address," said Connor. "I've got space to park an RV, and Janie's house is halfway up a mountain, anyway. Now, I don't know what sort of hookup you need for those things, and there's an RV campground outside of Ragged Gap if you just want to sleep in there, but y'all are welcome to stay at my place. Plenty of beds."

"We don't want to put you to any trouble..." Maggie began.

"After Annie and Wylan dumped us on your doorstep without warning? *Please*. Janie and I owe y'all," he insisted. "Get here when you can—I'll leave a spare key under the flowerpot with the, uh...well, they *were* strawberries once," he muttered. "The terracotta one. Can't miss it. Should I plan to see y'all tonight?"

"Depends on how long the drive is," said Dave, but Maggie quickly made the calculation on her phone.

"About seven hours," she announced. "Sure, we can make that in one day. We should be on the road by mid-morning, I'd think. Pack a bag, buy some snacks, lock up..."

"I'll bring my computer, but I'll tell the team I'm taking leave," Dave added. "One of the kids can cover Monday's call with Toronto if we aren't home by then."

"Great," said Connor. "And I'm not even going to try to cook, so if y'all could text me with what you want on your pizza, I'll swing by on the way home."

Maggie's mouth tightened in faint disapproval. "I could throw something together..."

"No, ma'am, not with what I've got in the fridge. I'm not even sure about the milk, so I should put that on the list—"

"You do what you need to do, hon," she said, cutting him off. "Don't worry about us. We'll shoot you a message if something comes up along the way."

"And thank you," I added. "*Seriously.*"

"Hey, no problem. My family and I still owe quite a few favors," he replied with a weary chuckle. "But what could be going on in Beukal to mess up the phones, anyway?"

"I don't know," I admitted, "but should you hear from Jane—"

"I'll call," he promised. "And y'all do the same, okay?"

Once Maya hung up, I looked at Maggie and Dave and said, "I can't ask this of you—"

Maggie shook her head. "You're not asking, we're offering. And believe me, we've done better than a seven-hour drive." Cutting her eyes to her husband, she added, "Might be closer to six with his lead foot."

"I'm a good driver!" Dave protested.

"Never said you weren't, dear." She glanced at the microwave clock. "Let's plan to be out of here by nine-thirty. That'll give us time for breaks without needing to push it, and we'll be in well before sunset. Dave, I'll start packing. Gentle Breeze, do you want to go ahead and shower?"

"Any room for one more?" Maya asked.

The Humphrieses shared a brief look, and then Maggie smiled. "Sure, hon. Ever driven an RV?"

"No, ma'am, but I'm a decent navigator...DJ...purveyor of snacks..."

"What about Mangia?" I protested.

Maya shrugged. "What about it? My staff's fantastic, and after a few days of entertaining my cousin's family, I could use a trip out of town. Now, does that thing have a fridge?" she asked.

"Oh, sure," said Dave. "Smaller than a standard model but bigger than a cube. There's a freezer, too."

"*Perfect.* Tell you what, I'll handle the groceries," she offered, and grabbed her purse. "See y'all in a bit."

"I'll extend the RV reservation once the rental place opens," Dave told Maggie. "Sounds like we've got ourselves a road trip, eh?"

"You truly don't have to do this," I tried again, but

Maggie squeezed my arm to silence me.

"Unless Annie calls soon, we're doing it. Something's wrong, and it's not just the phones," she said, staring up at me. "That's what my gut's saying, anyway. What about yours?"

"Agreed," I murmured.

"Then it's settled." Nudging me toward the staircase, she said, "Go on while the hot water tank's full."

Leaving the chef in charge of snacks meant that the RV's fridge was stocked with an assortment of standard road fare, goodies from Mangia's day-old stash, and a few basics to help Connor host, including a gallon of milk, two six-packs of Budweiser, and a bottle each of red and white wine. "I don't know what his bar's like," Maya explained as she unloaded her grocery bags, "and I don't know about y'all, but after a day on the road, I can always use a drink."

When we set off, right on schedule, I still couldn't quite believe the lengths to which the Humphrieses and Maya were going to help me. While the silence from Annie surely urged them on, the fact remained that they were putting out time and money to keep me safe, and "thank you" didn't seem quite sufficient to cover my gratitude.

Despite our continued inability to contact the Pactlands, I felt better than I had since Thursday morning. We had a destination, at least, and the promise of masking jewelry—and if Connor had oversold Jane's abilities, then perhaps her father would be able to make the necessary adjustments. I'd known Yacovi Hewt before his retirement, when he was the chief of the DPP greenhouse, and we'd parted on good terms. Surely enough agency camaraderie remained that he'd give me a hand in a crisis.

The more I thought about it, the more that Georgia seemed like a good idea. While I'd never frequented the area, I knew the northeastern corner of the state was mountainous and populated with little towns—great for tourists in need of trees and relaxation, and even better for someone hoping to lie low. To be sure, there were growers who lived closer to Richmond than Yacovi did—Liliol ti'Cren, Rose's great-aunt over in the Blue Ridge portion of Virginia, came to mind—but all of my notes on growers' addresses and phone numbers were in my phone, which was presumably on its charger in Beukal. Plus, while Liliol's father was a jeweler of great repute—well, when he wasn't acting as the murderous crime boss known as Silver—I didn't know whether Liliol had any talent for making masking jewelry. Raiding Jane's stores seemed like a safer bet than turning up on Liliol's doorstep and hoping.

And besides, once I could show my face in public, I'd be able to go wherever I needed to figure out this mess. The drive to Georgia would be a long haul, but it was for the best.

We kept the shades pulled in the back of the RV, but the daylight streaming in through the windshield and cab windows allowed Maya and me sufficient illumination to move around and read. A conscientious passenger, she'd brought along with her snack stash a selection of magazines, and I entertained myself with the sudoku pages while she worked on her computer at the dining booth, checking orders for Mangia and corresponding with a few prospective catering customers. Unable to comfortably fit in the booth, I hung out on the couch across the aisle, occasionally getting up and crouching my way to the kitchen. Maggie and Dave were good company, chatting from the front as we wound our way to the southwest on I-85.

Dave made a western turn onto I-40 once we reached Durham, and around noon, we were on our way to Winston-Salem in light traffic when I heard a faint siren behind us. Dave glanced in the rearview mirror and swore, then pulled his admittedly heavy foot off the gas.

"It's okay," said Maggie in a placating tone. "This happens. Don't panic."

Maya tensed and closed her computer. "Cops?"

"Looks like a state trooper," Dave muttered, guiding the RV onto the right shoulder. "Uh…Gentle Breeze…"

The cab windows were high, but not so high that the officer couldn't look in and spot me lurking in the rear. "Going to the shower," I said, and squeezed myself into the tight cubicle. The faux wooden door went all the way to the vehicle's interior ceiling, fortunately, but I was still crammed in, hunched over and listening in the darkness as I tried not to scratch any of my claws over the smooth shower walls.

Holding my breath, I heard the engine cut off, then the muffled sound of an unfamiliar male voice coming from the front. "Afternoon, sir," he said, his accent slightly nasal and drawled. "Going somewhere in a hurry?"

"I'm sorry, Officer," said Dave. "This is a rental, and I'm still getting used to it. Did my speed get away from me?"

"Oh, about twelve miles over the limit. Can I see your license and rental contract?"

I heard shuffling in the cab, and then the officer said, "Thank you. Where are y'all heading?"

"Down to Blue Ridge," Dave fibbed. "Going to do a little hiking and camping before the fall crowds hit."

"Georgia?"

"Yes, sir. Our daughter's in Asheville, so we'll pick her up along the way."

"Huh. Plenty of good hiking around Asheville," said the cop. "What's in Georgia?"

Maggie smoothly intervened. "We've got some old friends who moved to Atlanta years ago, and they found this place in Blue Ridge, so we used to meet up when the kids were little. It's tradition by now. Ever been?"

"Can't say that I have." He cleared his throat. "Y'all mind if I take a look in the back?"

Dave paused for the briefest of moments, then said, "Uh…no problem, Officer. Maya, hon, would you mind getting the door for him?"

Oh, this was bad. What cause did he have to search the RV? Fine, Dave had been speeding, but didn't the cop need more than that to come aboard?

Could he smell Maya's vape pen? Surely not. *I* could, and I knew damn well that wasn't tobacco in the cartridge, but could a human pick up on the scent of marijuana? Maya hadn't vaped in the RV—she hadn't even taken the pen out of her bag, which she'd stowed in the bedroom at the rear—so unless the officer had a superhuman sense of smell, he couldn't know. Then why was he poking around?

The side door opened, and heavy footsteps mounted the little staircase. "Miss," said the officer, his voice far closer and suddenly suspicious. "Who are you?"

"Maya Mackay, sir," she replied, all sweetness and minding her manners. "Do you want to see my license, too?"

"That won't be necessary. You, uh...you're going to Georgia?"

"I'm friends with Annie—their daughter in Asheville," she explained. "We went through high school together. I've never been camping with the Humphries family, but Annie asked if I wanted to come along, since we haven't seen each other in a while, and Dave and Maggie were nice enough to let me carpool."

Trafficking. That had to be it. I didn't think Maya fit the profile of a woman being held against her will, and she sounded calm to me, but I could smell her perspiration. She was nervous as she lied to the cop—not unusual, but not great for us.

And now that he was only a few feet and one flimsy door away, I could smell the cop all too well: a little sweat, a hint of coffee, gunpowder—clearly, he was armed—and atop it all, the most godawful cologne I'd ever had the misfortune of inhaling. It clung to him like a chemical fug of musk, spice, and citrus—all artificial scents, almost metallic in quality—and I cringed at the stench.

Then, as if the smell weren't bad enough, my nose began to itch.

Oh, heavens, I could *not* afford to sneeze.

I bore down, tightening whatever muscles I could to stop the imminent expulsion. If he heard me, he would demand to look in the shower, and I suspected the flimsy lock wouldn't hold him indefinitely. So, what was my best plan? I could throw open the door and jump out, which would end with him pinned against the door to the toilet. With surprise and bulk on my side, I could probably disarm him. I trained alongside my agents for a reason, and I was no one's favorite sparring partner. But even if I got his weapons off of him, he'd still *see* me, and I was fresh out of memory potions. Maybe I could hit him in the head, knock him out...but what if his car had a dashboard camera? That would have captured him climbing into the RV, and it would likewise record the moment if I tossed him out, conscious or not. And once he came to, he would call in the RV's license plate, wouldn't he? Though Dave drove hard, the RV couldn't outrun the police.

What could I do, then? Kill him? Send one of the others to drive the cop's car until we could dispose of it and the body?

Deep in the recesses of my mind, as I begged my nose to cooperate, I heard my father's voice: *It's just a human.*

Maybe so, but humans were saving my ass just then, and I had no desire to kill a man for doing his job, even if he *was* a nosy bastard.

Finally, and to my great relief, I heard the officer say, "Okay, Mr. Humphries, I'm going to let you off with a warning, but *slow down*, got it?"

Dave promised, and shortly after the side door opened and closed again, I released the sneeze I'd been struggling to hold back with every drop of my willpower.

"Gesundheit," muttered Maya, but a moment later, the engine started again, and we were moving.

I unlocked the shower door and staggered back to the couch. Only once I had settled in did I realize my hands were shaking.

"Hey," said Maya, "you okay?"

"Just…anxious."

"Want a hit off my vape?"

As the third in the DPP chain of command, I kept clean of all but alcohol…but I wasn't born an agent, and I'd tried far worse things than a little pot.

"If you don't mind sharing," I mumbled.

"Dave, Maggie," she called toward the front, "can y'all be 420-friendly for just a minute?"

"If you can cover the smell," Maggie called back.

Maya ducked into the bedroom, returning with the vape pen, a lemon-scented candle, and a bottle of air strong freshener. "All right, Chief," she said, handing me the vape. "Let's get this party started."

CHAPTER 5

We made decent time, even with Dave taking pains to keep to the speed limit, and rolled into the mountain hamlet of Whitford around five-thirty that evening. The address Connor had given us led to a two-story brick house set back from the narrow road at the end of a cracked asphalt driveway. While the place wasn't exactly massive, it had privacy on its side; the property had to be at least an acre, with a row of tall holly bushes on one side and a few crape myrtles on the other to delineate the boundary line. The best I could say for the landscaping was that the grass and weeds were mowed—the few bushes flanking the front door seemed to be more brown than green, and there wasn't a flower in sight. I suspected that Connor's job left him little time to play in the yard, and in any case, mid-September was the downward slope, horticulturally speaking.

Or so I assumed. While my neighborhood had once been an agricultural district, the magical supports were long gone, leaving me with a healthy lawn and one stunted oak of considerable age that rose only to my knee. Sure, I knew a fair amount about a particular subset of plants after nearly two and a half centuries at DPP, but I didn't *grow* them.

We pulled up behind a Ford Explorer marked with police insignia and outfitted with blue lights, which was parked behind a black SUV—Connor's personal vehicle, I assumed. Dave cut the engine, but before anyone could get out to explore, the garage door rose, revealing a space stacked with boxes on one side and barely open enough for a car on the other. Out stepped Connor, who still wore his dark blue uniform but for his gun holster. By human metrics, he was nothing extraordinary on first glance: about six feet tall, with wavy, dark brown hair, brown eyes, and a five o'clock shadow. Thanks to Pars, who didn't mind sharing the odd bit of gossip, I knew that Connor had been born with pointed, flopped-over ears, but the surgery he'd had as an infant had resulted in an unremarkable human-passing pair. His cousins, all of them of mixed human and elven extraction, had worked with a brilliant research healer and a novel potion to enhance their elven genes, leaving them with heightened magical abilities and incredible longevity. Connor, who by all accounts was deeply in love with a sorcerer, had opted for a lifespan closer to hers, and while a mere three centuries seemed like a ludicrous choice beside the possibility of immortality, my inner romantic understood.

As my boyfriend was also functionally immortal, I sometimes wondered what decision he'd make if given the option of a troll's lifetime.

"Hey, y'all," said Connor as Maggie and Dave opened the cab doors. "Come on in—my neighbors aren't home yet. Pizza's on the table and beer's in the fridge, so help yourselves. Want a hand with your bags? And hey, you," he added as Maya pushed her way out through the side door. "How's it going?"

"Better now that we've stopped," she said, and gave him a quick hug.

Maggie's hug was longer, while Dave opted for a handshake and murmured thanks. "Beer, you said?" he asked.

Connor grinned. "Yuengling okay?"

"I've got Bud in the RV if it isn't," said Maya, and thumbed her hand toward the vehicle. "And some other pantry essentials. *Men.*"

"I'll get the groceries," Connor offered, waving her into the garage, then climbed into the RV and nodded at me.

"Evening, Chief," he said, switching to his oddly accented Pactish.

I stood from the couch, hunching so as not to crack my head against the ceiling. "Thank you for having me, Lord ti'Catama—"

"Oh, *please* don't start with that," he muttered. "It's Connor."

"Gentle Breeze."

We shook, his hand smaller than mine but his grip firm.

"I did a drive-by on my way—there's no one home on either side. Go on in and get situated, and I'll, uh…" He opened the fridge. "Damn, Maya wasn't kidding."

"Here are the shopping bags," I said, opening the cupboard under the tiny sink. "You pack that, and I'll carry in the luggage."

"You sure? I don't mind helping…"

"I need to stretch, anyway. Step aside, will you? There's gear in the bedroom."

Soon, I followed Connor into the house, where I found five large pizza boxes spread on the kitchen counter and my other three companions seated at the wooden table. They'd barely made a dent in the food, but someone had found the beer and a bottle opener. Connor did the quick math and realized we were a chair short at the four-seater table. "I'll just grab a chair from the dining room," he began, but I blocked his way with my arm.

"I've been sitting all day. This is fine," I said, disinclined to test my luck against his furniture's strength. "So, what's the plan?"

"Dinner, I thought, and I want to change clothes, and then you and I can head over to Jane's to go through her jewelry once it's decently dark. Oh, and Yacovi is expecting us later tonight—he's on his way back from Atlanta right now. Does that work?"

"Fine by me," I replied. "Go ahead and get comfortable. I'll save you a slice or two."

He headed upstairs, and after I'd shoved the few perishables into his largely empty refrigerator, I laid claim to a pepperoni pie and ate over the box. It wasn't bad, and as my hunger abated, I took in the rest of the kitchen. Oak cabinets, serviceable but dated. A dusty red-checked valance hung over the window at the sink. The countertops were of some sort of composite, a little scuffed but nothing a potholder couldn't cover. Of all the appliances, the microwave seemed to be of the most recent vintage, but considering the state of Connor's fridge, I doubted that anything in that room saw heavy use.

On the counter beside the garage door were an insulated green water bottle, a canvas tote bag, and a collapsable umbrella—Jane's, I thought, if I recalled her scent correctly. But while it was unsurprising to find her belongings in her fiancé's house, what made me drop my pizza and hastily grab a paper towel was the logo I spotted on the silver laptop plugged in beside her things by the old wall phone.

Maggie looked up curiously as I marched across the room. "Need something, Gentle Breeze?"

I didn't answer her until I'd verified that the logo on the lid was indeed an eight-pointed star with a recessed green circle around it. "Jane left her work computer here." Opening it, I watched as the screen lit up with the DOI insignia and a password blank. "Why would she leave *this* outside?"

The others had no answers for me, and so I confronted Connor once he returned to the kitchen in jeans and a tan polo shirt. "That's a DOI machine," I said, pointing to the computer. "What's it doing here?"

He didn't flinch. "Downloading a patch. Well, it's finished by now."

"A *patch*?"

His brow wrinkled as he looked up at me. "You seem upset."

"That's a major security risk! We don't leave Pact equipment sitting out here unattended, especially not computers! I can't imagine that DOI would condone this—"

"Whoa, *whoa*," he interrupted, motioning me down. "It hasn't left my house, I lock up when I leave, and I'm the only person around who knows how to get in."

"*You* have her password?" I yelped.

"It wasn't hard to guess. But this isn't normal," he continued, pointing to the laptop. "DOI's tech division warned everyone that a major security patch was coming down on Wednesday, and they needed to keep their computers stationary until the download was complete because an interrupted partial would screw up the system. Jane brought her laptop with her when she came home Tuesday afternoon—she was going to take the rest of the week off to go camping with me after my schedule eases up," Connor explained. "Then she got slammed with some last-minute meetings on Wednesday, so she agreed to go back for those, but when she was ready to leave here Wednesday morning, the patch was just beginning. I told her my Wi-Fi was strong and that it'd be finished when she got back." Shrugging, he added, "I checked when I got home Wednesday and used her credentials to reboot, just making sure everything was working. Her startup software came online, and I put the system to sleep—I didn't go looking for agency secrets, if that's what you're afraid of," he told me.

"But she didn't drive back Wednesday," I said.

Connor shook his head. "Nope. Meetings went long, and I suggested she stay at DOI and get some rest. She said she'd call me Thursday when she left, but she never did, and I haven't been able to get through."

A thought suddenly occurred to me. "You said her startup software was working?"

"Yeah…"

"What launched at startup?"

"Uh…antivirus, calendar, and her case management software. I don't know what it's called."

"Can you log me in?"

He hesitated, then said, "Guess so," and opened the lid. He was slow to input Jane's password, but I suspected I knew the cause, as I'd had the same difficulty the first time I used an English keyboard. The language potion was nearly miraculous in its effect, bestowing the linguistic donor's fluency after only a few days, but it did nothing to help along the drinker's accent or typing ability.

Finally, the lock screen cleared, and Connor stepped aside. "Be my guest."

Pausing only long enough to make sure there was no marinara sauce or grease on my fingers, I slid into position beside him and considered the computer. As would be expected, it was scaled for a sorcerer, but I knew how to get by with claw-tip precision. I'd never been on a DOI computer, but if their case management software was anything like DPP's, then it was connected to the servers back in Beukal—and for DPP, at least, those connections were *protected*. Yes, the phones were still down, and no one had answered the emails I'd sent from Maya's phone that day, but maybe...*maybe*...

I clicked the icon for the program, and the window popped open to fill the screen. It looked vaguely familiar, I thought, a collection of internal icons that would surely lead to menus. If I could just dig through them, perhaps I would find—

A *very* familiar feature suddenly appeared in the top-right corner of the window, a color-changing ball with a pair of googly eyes. "Hi!" it chirped in Pactish, flashing green. "It's me, Sprik! What can I help you with today?"

"The hell is that thing?" Connor muttered beside me. "'Buddy'?"

"That's the assistant," I explained. "We've got the same feature on our program—"

"If you want me to go to sleep, just let me know!" said Sprik, cycling to purple.

Okay, so DOI's version of the annoying help menu

was better than ours. Figured. Still, I could work with this.

"Sprik," I said, "open the last case file."

"You've got it!" the assistant replied, and a report appeared on the screen.

I didn't bother reading the details beyond noting that the matter was assigned to Jane. "Sprik, flag this case for IT."

The ball turned a silvery blue. "Is there a problem? I can help!"

"No. Flag for IT."

"Are you sure? I bet we can find a solution—"

"Sprik, *flag this case for IT*," I ground out, dearly wishing, as I had so many times before, that I could throttle the assistant.

"Okay!" Sprik said with its eternal pep. A new window appeared atop the report, a large text box. "Please leave a message for IT detailing your problem and your contact information."

"Let's hope someone's checking," I said under my breath, then typed out a message:

This is Gentle Breeze, DPP. EMERGENCY. I was abducted and left outside without masking jewelry. Safe for the moment, writing this from Jane Fortune's computer in Georgia. Phone calls to Pactlands will not go through from outside phones. Requesting assistance and contact.

I added everyone's cell phone numbers to the end of the message, then sent it. "Leave the computer up and running," I told Connor, heading back to the pizza. "If anyone responds, I want to hear it as soon as it comes in."

Connor helped himself to the pizzas I hadn't claimed and pulled up a seat at the table. "How was the drive?" he asked.

"Not too bad," said Dave. "This is improving the situation," he added, lifting his beer bottle.

Maggie rolled her eyes, then turned to Connor. "How

are you, hon? I hear congratulations are in order."

He beamed. "Yes, ma'am. Turns out Janie is crazy enough to marry me."

"Aww. When's the wedding?"

Instantly, his smile faltered, and he took a long pull of his beer. "That's still up in the air."

"Work in the way?" she asked.

"No, it's…" Briefly, he paused, collecting his thoughts, then said, "Janie's grown up with the idea of a white wedding, right? Nothing *huge*, but the standard bits—the gown, the flowers, the big cake, you know? And I'm cool with that, sure. There's actually a nice little vineyard around here that does events, and a spring wedding would work."

Maya flashed a knowing smirk. "But?"

"But," drawled Connor, "my East Branch kin want us to have a celebration like they always did in the community, which is quite a bit simpler, while Janie's aunt wants her to throw a blowout event."

Maggie cocked her head. "Jane has an aunt?"

"It's complicated. Xila Aniap—her half aunt, technically, and about ten years younger. She's a nice kid, but she's been through the wringer with her father, and she thinks Jane should have a big society wedding to get some good press for the Aniap name. Xila's mother is pushing that, too."

"Except Jane doesn't go by Aniap," Maya pointed out.

Connor nodded. "Bingo. She doesn't want an Aniap pageant, *I* don't want some huge, 'Hey, look, ti'Catama exists!' event, and I don't think either of us wants an East Branch affair, but we also don't want to hurt everyone's feelings. Honestly," he said, lifting his beer, "I'd be fine with going to a judge and being done with it."

"Oh, don't do that," said Maggie. "Dave and I would have so loved to see Annie get married…"

"My parents are dead, Jane's got Yacovi—that's her adopted dad," he added for the Humphrieses' benefit—"and he's already made it clear that he won't be heartbroken if she doesn't make him dance in front of a crowd. But that's a problem for another day," he muttered, "assuming I ever see my fiancée again."

"Don't be dramatic," I chided, shoving down my anxiety. "Of course you will. This may be nothing more than a telecommunications outage."

The look he shot me told me we both knew I was lying around my tusks.

"Anyway," said Connor to the others, "Gentle Breeze and I will drive over to Jane's tonight. Her neighbors aren't too close, and if they're there, they should recognize me, especially if I take the Whitford SUV. I go by pretty frequently to check on things while she's in Beukal," he explained. "So, take your time with dinner. The two of us will head out once it's dark enough, and as for everyone else, if y'all want to figure out the sleeping situation, I've got two guest rooms upstairs and a halfway decent couch in the den."

"Or there's the bed in the RV," Dave pointed out.

"Sure, wherever you're comfortable. Not going to hurt my feelings. And there *is* an RV park not too far away if you want to hook that thing up and dump the toilet."

"Oh, it'll keep," Maggie assured him. "Thanks for having us, hon."

"Of course. Make yourselves at home, let me know if you need anything. It ain't fancy, but—"

"No one was expecting the Ritz, dear," Maggie interrupted, patting his hand. "I'm just glad to stop moving for a minute."

"Ditto," said Dave. He sipped his beer and studied Connor briefly, then said, "Uh…this might be a rude question…"

Connor waved it off. "I had to deal with a woman from Atlanta doing ninety in a Maserati SUV with her Pomeranian in her lap today, so I'm pretty much immune to rudeness. Hit me."

"Yikes," he muttered, then cleared his throat. "So…can

you do, like, *magic* now?"

"Eh." Connor grunted and wiggled one hand. "More than I could two years ago, but they tell me I'm still behind for my age. Whatever. Useful on occasion, but I'm not exactly changing the world with it." He paused, considering Dave's expression, then grinned. "You want to see?"

"*Yeah.*"

"Really? I mean, Wylan's power is *insane.* I'm not even close." When Dave continued to watch Connor with an expression not unlike that of an excited child, Connor said, "Okay, underwhelming magic coming right up," and made a quick gesture at the refrigerator. The door opened, and the second six-pack he'd squirreled away to chill flew across the kitchen and landed gently on the table. Another gesture closed the fridge, while a third brought the bottle opener sailing over from the counter. "Ta-dah."

"That's *awesome,*" Dave whispered.

Maggie looked embarrassed, while Maya, who'd spent long enough in Beukal to see a bit of everything, bit her lip and locked eyes with me as I continued to eat.

"Come on," Connor said to Dave, "I *know* you've seen better from Wylan. Anyway, Yacovi's the best around here—full-fledged sorcerer," he told Dave and Maggie. "If Jane's masking jewelry doesn't cut it for some reason, then I bet he'll be able to figure out the problem. The plan is for me to take Gentle Breeze over to his house when he gets home to loop him in, anyway…"

He fell silent when Jane's computer beeped, and then I heard Sprik's obnoxiously happy voice: "Message received from IT support. Marked urgent. Would you like me to open it?"

Dropping my pizza, I raced across the room and opened the message:

Received and escalated. DO NOT CLOSE THIS PRO-GRAM. This may be the only working conduit to the outside world. Please stand by.

Progress, yes, but maddeningly vague. I wiped my hands and quickly typed a message in the reply box:

WHAT IS GOING ON?!? Why are the phones down? Can DOI clear me through the Central portal? I can't call for access!

With that sent, I stood over the laptop, swigging beer and silently begging the person on the other end to respond. It took the rest of my beer and part of a second—and really, for a troll, Yuengling went down like hoppy water—before the computer beeped again with the incoming message alert.

Certain information is still embargoed. We understand your concern. Please stand by.

While I'd have described the sound that emerged from me at that moment as a growl of frustration, I glanced toward the table and realized that Maggie and Dave had tensed and were watching me with wide eyes. "Oh...sorry, just annoyed," I mumbled. "DOI's giving me the runaround." They relaxed fractionally, but I chided myself to be more mindful of my all-too-human company. Resisting the urge to unload on my new pen pal, I turned back to the reply box and typed:

I'm a credentialed agent, damn it. Interdiction chief at DPP. I've been outside UNMASKED for nearly two days. Tell me what's happened. If you don't believe I am who I say I am, then call Pateme ti'Tam—he'll vouch for me. Or call Rose ti'Dana at DPP and ask her to check with farsight. I'm not on blinding potion.

That time, the response was far quicker in coming:

Chief, we believe you. Your absence was noticed, and there's

an alert out. Please bear with us—we're working within pro-
tocol. We've requested authorization for you, but this may
take time. Just leave the program running, please.

I groaned as I stepped away from the computer and
stalked back to my pizza box.

"Any luck?" Maya asked.

"Not exactly, and if I don't get some answers soon, I'm
going to find my way back to Beukal and shove Director
ti'Dana's head up his own ass. I *swear*, DOI..."

Connor snickered. "Farseers can be useful, I'll grant
you that, but sometimes, you just want to *slap* them."

"You're telling me," I muttered. "The future-oriented
bunch are the most infuriating. Fortunately," I added,
smirking at him between bites, "you'll be working with the
past-oriented group, if any, at DOL. Maybe Rose, too, if
we loan her out."

He gave me a tired stare in response.

"Come on," I said, "anyone in agency management
who's had contact with East Branch knows that Director
Erenani is gunning hard for you. She wants you aboard,
and between us, you could have far worse bosses. I
wouldn't *cross* her, now. Got a healthy respect for that
woman, but she's very reasonable. That said, if you were
more interested in DPP, I *might* have a slot..."

"Y'all do remember the part where I'm employed,
right?" Connor said. "Company car's parked outside."

"You could do better than Whitford."

"I made a commitment to Whitford," he countered.

"Uh-huh," I replied. "Well, do yourself a favor and talk
to Annie before you turn us all down. We have fun in Interdiction."

One eyebrow arched. "That's not what Yven says."

I rolled my eyes. "Ti'Ansha is hopeless, and he's very
much a Regulatory boy."

"Be nice to Yven," Maya protested. "He's a sweetheart."

"And very good behind a desk. I'm not criticizing him for that," I said. "He just lacks the mettle for Interdiction. Now, I realize you're underage," I told Connor, "but allowances can be made…"

"I appreciate that, I do," he insisted, "but I'm not ready to move just yet. It's…inevitable, I guess," he mumbled, "but not today. And I'm not making any career decisions coming off a double shift," he added, then pushed back from the table. "Y'all enjoy. I'm going to nap so I don't fall asleep behind the wheel tonight."

As Connor's footsteps rose up the staircase, Dave looked at Maggie and said, "That's not a bad idea."

"Dibs on the couch," said Maya, heading to the dishwasher with her plate. "Y'all go pick a bed upstairs. Gentle Breeze?"

"Still working through this pie," I said, and slumped over the counter to eat, willing Jane's computer to beep again, as the others shuffled off to rest.

CHAPTER 6

Just after eight that evening, with the sun down, Connor climbed into his Whitford vehicle and waited as I crammed myself into the back seat. "I'm sorry it's so tight," he said from the other side of the clear plastic barrier. "Hang in there, and I'll be as quick as I can."

"As long as you don't wreck," I said, angling myself across the bench to give my legs a place to go. The last thing I wanted was for Connor's SUV to break down, leaving me at the mercy of whatever helpful soul stopped to assist.

"Haven't yet," he replied, then backed out, avoiding the RV by reversing across his lawn.

The police vehicle had tinted windows, an added layer of protection that wasn't particularly needed. The road out of Whitford was winding and largely empty, and Connor tried to orient me as he navigated by his headlights. "We've got two little valleys here," he explained, "running along a southwest–northeast line. Whitford's the town in the more northerly valley, with East Branch having been built all the way at the far northern end—the property's scrunched up against the mountains. Most of Whitford used to be the Cavanaugh farm, but that's all been sold off over the years. The town's nothing to write home about, but we've got our fair share of tourist cabins and such. Now, once we're through the pass, we'll come out in the more southerly valley, and that's where Ragged Gap grew up. It's larger, cuter—they jumped on the tourist bandwagon earlier, so Ragged Gap's more of a destination than

Whitford will ever be—but it's smaller than, say, Blue Ridge."

"Out of the way?" I asked.

"That's part of it. The railroad never came through, and the roads are narrow, but the tourists still find us—a lot of folks from the flatter part of the state looking to see some mountains and fall color. Anyway, Ragged Gap proper is in the flat part of the valley, and a lot of neighborhoods are built into the mountains ringing it. Jane's halfway up one of the mountains, about fifteen minutes from downtown. Quiet area, so we should be able to sneak in."

Connor was right about the character of the neighborhood. I didn't see a single neighbor as he wound his way up the hillside, and Jane's nearest neighbors were hidden due to the woods. Her home was more modest than Connor's, a single-story cabin set back from the road at the end of a gravel driveway. Only the portion nearest the street had been paved at one point, and it was badly cracked. A bright security light glowed on a pole in the front, illuminating the overgrown grass and the modest, unadorned wooden porch fronting the house.

We pulled up close to the porch, and Connor released me from the rear. As I stretched my legs, he jogged to the door and tapped a code on a key panel, and the door clicked open. "Come on," he said, motioning me closer, and I climbed the porch steps and ducked through the door after him.

Though Jane's home was small, the ceilings were amply high, perhaps ten feet, which gave me much-desired breathing room after the ride over. I stood in the foyer by a droopy Christmas cactus while Connor bustled around, turning on lights. The place was relatively tidy, if a bit dusty, and the scent profile was interesting: Jane, certainly, with plenty of notes of Connor, all topped with overtones of lavender, sage, mint, citrus, honeysuckle, and various other florals. I'd heard that Jane had made bath products in her former life, and the bouquet endured, though it had faded, perhaps, for which I was grateful. Sneezing fits are miserable.

The foyer opened to a den on the left and a kitchen straight ahead, at the rear of the house, hardly a showplace but serviceable. Much of the back wall by the kitchen table was a sliding glass door, and I opened it and peeked out into the night to see the yard beyond the porch: a wooded, sloping stretch that, by the sound and smell of it, bottomed out into a creek. The porch was set with a pair of wooden chairs, a matching table, and several citronella candles, and I coughed as I closed the door.

A moment later, Connor joined me with a plastic box in his arms and set it on the table. "Okay," he said, popping the lid, "here are the goods. Let's see what works."

The box was full of jewelry supplies, neatly separated by tiny dividers: glass beads, bits of polished stone, tiny pieces of metal, and even a few compartments containing small, faceted gems. I lifted the top tray to find a selection of tools stored below, mostly miniature pliers, plus a tape measure, a couple spools of a cord that resembled fishing wire, and a little tube of superglue. Nestled in the middle was a purple velvet Crown Royal bag, and I pulled the drawstring and dumped the contents into my palm. Several necklaces had been inside, pieces with various focal pendants and strung with accent beads, and I could feel the power strumming through them.

"Something wrong?" asked Connor as I sorted through the selection.

"These feel...I don't know, supercharged," I said, examining the necklaces. "The masking pendant I use feels like any other necklace, but *these*..."

"Yeah, Janie's working on that. She can make masking jewelry, but she says it's not the most subtle. Then again, she's largely self-taught, so..."

"Oh, I'm not complaining," I insisted, and selected a necklace from the pile. The focal bead was a simple oval of rutilated quartz about the size of the pad of my thumb, and the cord was covered with onyx chips. It wasn't my favorite of the bunch, but it was the longest, and functionality trumped form that night. "This might work."

"Want to go try it on?" said Connor, and pointed to the short hallway off the kitchen. "Bathroom's straight through there. I'll wait. Also," he said before I could depart, "there's a hitch with those necklaces. Jane *can*, uh…program them, or whatever you call it, to hold a default mask, but these aren't programmed, and I wouldn't know where to begin. But I've been the guinea pig on all of those, so just hold the pendant and think about what you want to look like."

I took the necklace and headed for the bathroom, but I paused in shock on the threshold when I turned on the light. The space was *massive*, far larger than the cabin could have accommodated, and as luxurious as any spa. "Um…Connor?"

"Hmm?" he asked, leaning back in the kitchen chair he'd claimed.

"What's up with this bathroom?"

"*Ah.* Janie went a little overboard."

"A *little*?" I echoed, looking from the marble counters to the generous bathtub to the huge shower—a shower tall enough that I could have stood beneath the rainfall head. "This is a security risk. There's no way this space could exist without magic!"

"Then it's a good thing Janie doesn't have many visitors, right?"

That attitude was far too cavalier for my taste, but the question of the bathroom's condition could wait. I closed the door, stood in front of one of the mirrors, and clasped the pendant around my neck.

Building my mask from scratch was a pain, but I'd certainly done it before. I had a decent sense of my chosen mask, and I could recreate it from memory. That said, I wasn't deeply fond of it. Masking was a necessary evil, not something I sought out.

Human beauty standards—which were close to those for sorcerers, elves, gnomes, and even centaurs, in part—did little for me. While I knew what they found attractive, I didn't share the sentiment. My female beauty ideal was tall and muscular, with a strong brow and well-proportioned tusks. "Petite and thin" did nothing for me. But when I began needing to mask, I'd worked with another troll at DPP who'd had a firm grounding in human aesthetics. "You're beautiful," she'd told me, "and you should have a mask that reflects that. If nothing else, it'll make fieldwork simpler. Men will do anything for a pretty face, and nice breasts don't hurt out there."

I'd employed the mask we designed ever since, adjusting the hairstyle and makeup as needed, and it had served me well. My boyfriend certainly approved…

A flicker of doubt flared in my gut, and I tamped it down. That was hardly the time to be worried about his preferences…though I couldn't quite manage to silence the soft voice that whispered my fears back to me.

Moonless Night told me I was gorgeous. If I ever hesitated around him, he was quick to reassure me that I was stunning, strong, the kind of woman he'd never imagined finding. I didn't always believe *that*—looking past his role as the lead sportscaster at Channel 1, he had a pleasant gray complexion, a short strip of orange hair that I loved to run my fingers through, and soft brown eyes. He was slightly shorter than me but sturdily built, and his voice…well, used properly, it gave me shivers.

And it was all an illusion. *Moonless Night* was a long-running fabrication. The man I loved was a Huntsman under the mask, over eleven hundred years old, and his asshole of a father had dubbed him Morial.

Wylan, the baby of the lot but now their leader, hadn't tried to force his exiled brother home to the lodge. Once cast out of the Hunt, Morial had lived as a troll for some eight centuries, masking, learning our language, and eventually being adopted into a clan. They'd named him The

Sound of Deer Running Through the Forest on a Moon-less Night, and he'd worn that name ever since, even after his first and second clans had passed on to the ancestors.

I hadn't been looking for a serious relationship when I met him, but admittedly, I'd harbored a crush—among trolls, he was a *very* eligible bachelor, and I'd watched him on TV for decades. I'd barely had a chance to get to know him when he outed himself—in front of a Forum commit-tee, no less—but…well, I was intrigued. I'd pursued him at first, and once he realized I was serious, he'd pursued me in turn.

He'd spent two-thirds of his life posing as a troll, so I was confident that he knew what we generally found at-tractive…but what did *he* like? Yes, he swore up and down that he thought I was beautiful whether I was masked or not, but knowing what he looked like in truth, I couldn't help but wonder if he preferred my false face. Annie had assured me that it was pretty, and Huntsmen were far clos-er to human in their appearance than they were to us. Moonless Night had never asked me to mask when we were intimate, but what did Morial think?

I shook my head to dispel those thoughts. If I kept worrying about my boyfriend, I'd end up looking like him as I designed my mask, and *that* would be no help.

The first step was the simplest. I lightly gripped the pendant, feeling the energy running through it, then imag-ined myself shorter. My usual mask put me around six feet in height—tall for a woman but not grotesquely so. With that accomplished, I focused on my body and the complex process of flattening, poofing, and tucking. Trolls exhibit minimal sexual dimorphism—through exposure and expe-rience, *we* can tell female from male with a glance, but oth-ers have difficulty. Humans, however, have more external differences, and I tried to remember them all as I envi-sioned my mask. My shoulders narrowed, my chest swelled, and my waist curved inward on either side of my abs. With the rough cuts made, I began the finer alterations. Easiest was my skin tone, which I shifted from green to what a human would consider a pale olive complexion. I whittled down my claws to short nails and added an extra digit per hand and foot, bringing the total from sixteen to twenty. My limbs thinned, losing some of their muscular bulk but not their tone, and I concentrated on my feet until they shifted into a daintier form.

Which left the matter of my face, never my favorite part. Having already messed with my coloring, I lightened my hair from sandy blonde to a shade closer to platinum and lengthened it until it fell past my shoulders. My eyes were fine—brown was an acceptable human shade—but I trained my eyebrows into narrower arches and darkened them, then recessed my browbone into what was considered a more feminine form. Last to be altered was my mouth, as that was inevitably a pain. I switched my tongue from gray to pinkish red, then removed my tusks and shifted my jaw until my underbite had become a slight overbite. Pausing in my work, I wiggled my jaw and flexed my facial muscles, acclimating once more to the changed structure. With my luck, my tongue and the insides of my cheeks would be sore for days from my accidental bites. I parted my pink lips in a grimace, examining my teeth for oddities, but the mask was as I remembered it.

With a sigh, I stepped back from the mirror, at which point my cargo shorts fell from my curvy hips and pooled at my feet. My usual masking pendant had been set up so that my clothing shrank and grew with me, but Jane's had not, and swimming in my new clothes, I was sorely in need of a belt.

And a bra, I thought, turning in profile and giving my new breasts a test bounce. They were firm enough, but I'd work better with something to strap the fleshy annoyances in place.

But for all the headache of masking, I was relieved to have my false face back. The mask was strange, a look I'd never quite acclimated to seeing in the mirror, but outside, it promised safety. Nothing to see here, just a reasonably attractive woman in oversized clothing, on the hunt for suitable undergarments and perhaps shoes.

Satisfied, I pulled up my shorts—my underwear was barely staying on—and returned to the kitchen to find Connor. "Question," I said, "does Jane have some rope around the house? I don't want to walk off with one of her belts without asking her."

Connor, who'd been playing on his phone, started to look up? "Rope? Uh—holy *shit*," he yelped, jerking away from me.

I patted my face, feeling for abnormalities. "Sorry, did I forget something?"

"Uh…" He stammered for a moment, then paused and collected himself. "No, um…no. That looks…great. Really great. Like, uh, ten of ten."

I smirked at him. "Easy, boy."

"Do you even buy your own drinks out here?"

"There's no point in drinking human booze unless I down the bottle, and that draws attention," I replied. "So…rope?"

"Probably some in her workshop," he said, and let himself out the sliding door. I watched as he unlocked the shed in the back yard—Jane's former workshop, I surmised, judging by the smell—and in short order, he returned with a ball of twine. "Will this do? I've got rope at my place, and bungee cords, too."

"This should get me back," I told him, then cut off a piece and knotted it through the belt loops. "Okay, decency maintained. Any chance that you can adjust my clothes to fit?"

Connor made a face. "That's a solid *maybe*, and I think it'd be in our best interest if I didn't risk it."

My limited dignity appreciated his honesty.

"Do you want to borrow something from Jane's closet?" he offered. "I don't think she'd mind…"

"In case of accidental unmasking, I'd better not," I replied. "I'd hate to shred her things."

After Connor had locked up, we climbed back into the SUV—me in the front passenger seat that time. "We've got to get you some shoes," he said as the interior lights faded.

"My soles are tough—"

"You *cannot* go around without shoes," he insisted. "Even down south. Put that on the list for tomorrow morning unless Yacovi can whip up some tonight. Speaking of whom…"

I waited while he placed the call. "Hey," he said, "I'm at Janie's. Got Gentle Breeze, and she's masked up. Are you close?" He listened for a moment, grunted, then said, "Okay, let me know when you get in. Be careful, eh?"

"Problem?" I asked as Connor put his phone away.

"Bad wreck on 400," he replied, starting the SUV. "What else is new? The trip's two hours unless someone forgets how to drive, and then God only knows when you'll get out of that mess. Freaking Atlanta," he muttered as he backed onto the road. "I almost went for a job down there a few years ago."

"Glad you didn't?"

"Grateful. Janie's the best thing that ever happened to me."

I smiled to myself as we started down the mountain. "Even with the ti'Catama stuff?"

"Yup. She's got a murderous grandfather, I've got a whole passel of murderous kin—it works."

"Makes sense to me." Adjusting my hoodie, which had become far less form-fitting in the last few minutes, I said, "Wherever we go for shoes tomorrow, I'm going to need a few other things as well."

"Oh? Like what?"

I hesitated, then said, "You know, that's probably a conversation you'd prefer I have with Maya and Maggie."

"Uh-huh. Say no more," he mumbled, and flipped on the radio for the trip home.

Maya, who'd never seen me masked, laughed aloud as we walked in the front door around nine. "*Nice*," she declared, pausing the TV. "Dang, you don't do things by halves, do you?"

Dave, who was sitting on the overstuffed floral couch with his wife, gawked at me, while Maggie, ignoring her husband's stare, cleared her throat. "That's, uh…that's your mask, hon?"

I spread my arms and let them flop at my sides. "Apparently, this is a fair approximation of my actual appearance mapped with human preferences."

"I mean, it's very pretty…"

Looking from her to silent Dave, I said, "I can, uh…I can change the mask if this doesn't work—"

"You're *fine*," Maya interrupted, pushing herself from her chair. "But those clothes are way too big. Let's see if there's anything in my bag that fits you…"

Her voice faded as Jane's computer beeped, and she fell in behind me as I hastened to the kitchen.

When I reached the laptop, Sprik was flashing gold in the corner of the screen. "Request for video conference from IT," it reported cheerily. "Accept or decline?"

"Accept, *accept!*" I shouted, and hunched at the counter to be on eye level with the camera.

The screen switched to a conference setup very much like the ones DPP's software produced, but when the video started, to my surprise, I saw Kabno Erenani in the window. Laws' director was usually put together, a tiny, white-haired woman with pale blue eyes and expensive taste in formal robes, but that evening, she looked exhausted, and unbelievably, she'd donned a gray hoodie bearing the DOL logo.

"Director Erenani," I began, almost babbling in my rush to get out the words, "I'm Gentle Breeze with DPP. I, um, I can drop the mask, but my clothes won't change size, and I've tied the shorts on—"

"Whoa," she interrupted in her high voice, raising her

palms to stop the verbal flow. "I believe you, it's all right. Nice to see you safe, Chief. Breathe."

I released a long breath, letting my hammering heart slow. "Dare I ask what you're doing answering IT questions for DOI?"

She smirked, barely chuckling. "We've got ourselves an all-hands situation. IT sent word up immediately, and their superiors passed the message along. One of Diriem's assistants called Pateme and me, since the farseers are currently in crisis mode. They sent a copy of the DOI software to my account, and so here I am, overnighting in my office."

"Doing my director's dirty work?"

"I don't mind. Pateme's looking in on Rose. I don't think he fully trusts Diriem to monitor her in a situation like this, and DPP would hate to lose their lone farseer…" Her brows drew together, then quickly relaxed. "Ah, Connor. I'd assumed you were lurking."

I glanced back in time to catch him waving at the screen. "Evening, ma'am," he replied in Pactish. "And if there's any question, I can vouch for Gentle Breeze. She's wearing one of Jane's pieces."

"No need, youngling. I know her voice, and that's *quite* a low one for a female human."

I shrugged. "Never bothered masking it, and no one here seems to mind…but forget my voice," I said. "What the hell is going on? I woke up in an alley in Richmond yesterday, *without* my masking pendant, and I'd been drugged. Smelled it and found the injection site."

Kabno winced. "That's a very poor sign for the other missing, but it's more information than we had."

"*What* other missing?" I demanded.

"There's a list," she muttered. "Been growing since yesterday."

"Other people were dumped out here? How many? *Where?*"

"At least six, including you, and we don't know. Rose is working on it."

Connor leaned closer, regarding the director over my shoulder. "Who would do this? And how?"

Her lips tightened. "Ever heard of the Unity Plan?"

He looked bemused, but I snorted. "Sure."

"Uh, what's…" Connor began.

"The Unity Plan?" said Kabno. "A fringe group. Annoying but largely harmless to this point, though that designation *will* be changing. It's mostly a sorcerer thing. They're convinced that it would be not only possible but a *great* idea to abandon the Pactlands and just move outside."

I watched his face twist in the window showing my camera's view. "What, all of you? How would that work?"

"It wouldn't, and they're dumbasses," I said.

Kabno nodded. "But they've built themselves a little echo chamber online, so they're convinced of their own brilliance. You don't see agents in the Unity Plan because those of us who do go outside know better, but these idiots have 'done their research,'" she said, her voice heavy with sarcasm, "and they've accessed enough external websites and such that they imagine they know how the other world works."

"They keep making proposals to the Forum," I added, "which go nowhere because they're fucking crazy."

"*Correct*," said Kabno. "The gist is that we could walk outside unmasked, announce ourselves, and lay claim to territory."

Connor's brows rose. "What would possibly make them think that's a viable plan?"

"Are you familiar with the concept of…let me be sure I'm pronouncing this correctly, *cosplay*? The Unity Plan sees this as a sign that we wouldn't be attacked—"

"Wait, *wait*," interrupted Maya, who'd been standing out of the camera's range until then, "you're telling me these folks found, like, videos of some LARPers and Comic-Con and think that means you're safe out here? Look, I totally put on pointy ears and glitter wings for Halloween as a kid, and that did *nothing* to prepare me for landing in

Beukal."

By then, Kabno's eyes had gone saucer-round with shock. "What...how..." she stuttered.

"Sorry. Hey, Director. How's it going?"

"*Maya?*" she finally managed to squeak. "But...but your memory was altered..."

"Didn't work. Roulette's one hell of a potion. I mean, I know the official cover story," she said, patting my shoulder, "but it didn't quite *take*. Probably a good thing, seeing as Gentle Breeze woke up beside my building on Thursday."

Spotting the Humphrieses peeking in behind Connor, I took the plunge. "And she's not the only one involved," I told Kabno before the director could recover her composure. "Maggie and Dave here are Annie Humphries's parents," I said, thumbing one hand toward them. "Or the Hunter's in-laws, if you prefer. They're the ones who got me to Georgia."

"Um...hello," said Maggie, giving the computer a little wave. "Sorry to butt in."

Kabno's mouth opened and closed twice before she found her words again. "I'm sorry, Gentle Breeze, but am I correct in assuming that you've informed *multiple* humans about—"

"Oh, we already knew," Maggie cut in. "It's not her fault. The head of DOI is aware, or so we've been told."

"Aware?" Kabno echoed.

Dave and Maggie traded looks, and Maggie said, "Annie and Wylan filled us in, but that Diriem fellow apparently told them to do it, so..."

"We can help," Dave piped up. "Got an RV parked outside, and I'm overdue for vacation, so if you've got people needing to be picked up, we're game. Right, honey?"

Maggie nodded emphatically. "Absolutely. Doesn't take a genius to see that it's a terrible idea to have unmasked trolls wandering around. Tell us where to go."

Though still stunned, Kabno composed herself as they spoke. "This is, uh…*unexpected*…but thank you. I am going to have a long, possibly even civil conversation with Diri-em when we all come up for air," she muttered, "but for now…wait, how do you two speak this language?"

"Wylan," said Maggie.

"Makes it easier to chat with his family," Dave volunteered.

For a moment, Kabno just blinked at them, and I knew exactly where her thoughts lay: without the slightest bit of oversight, humans had been made privy to our secrets and almost certainly granted access to the Pactlands.

On the other hand, I could think of far more concerning threats than that particular middle-aged couple.

"We can talk about that later," I said to Kabno. "What does the Unity Plan have to do with this mess?"

"Everything," she replied. "They're behind it." She paused, clearing her thoughts, then said, "Mr. Humphries, Mrs. Humphries, tell me if I'm mistaken, but I believe Maya has the right of it when it comes to how well the Unity Plan's grand scheme would play out."

"Oh, absolutely," said Dave. "One hundred percent. We've got enough crazies out here shooting other people over shit like skin color. You want to add elves and trolls and whatnot to the mix? A bunch of sentient non-humans with language and culture and *magic*? No way."

"That's a recipe for disaster," Maggie concurred. "And I'm sorry to say that, but there's no need to sugarcoat it. And the religious implications…*oof*."

Maya and Connor grimaced in agreement.

"Which is why we fled in the first place," said Kabno. "But since the Unity Plan hasn't been able to convince the Forum to see matters their way, they've resorted to terrorism."

"What do you mean?" I asked.

She smiled bitterly. "They've attacked the foundations of the Pactlands."

"*What?*" I cried. "How?"

"We've been piecing that together for the last two days." Sitting back in her chair, she absently rubbed one temple. "In brief, they caught one of the sorcerers on the maintenance team on Tuesday night and threatened her husband and children if she didn't give them access. She let them in on Wednesday, and they just released her this morning, now that it's too late. They put a hex in the system."

Maya frowned. "A hex?"

"Think of it as a computer virus," I explained. "It's a malignant spell, and unless the conditions are met to break it…"

"It remains active," Kabno finished. "Fortunately, the poor sorcerer they kidnapped didn't give them *full* access. The hex hasn't spread as far as it might have, and so the Pactlands remains intact for now. But the system is in self-preservation mode…or that's the way the maintenance team explained it, anyway. I'm no expert."

"I'm sorry," Maggie cut in, "but you've lost me. Maintenance team?"

"Our world is held together by complicated spellcraft," Kabno told her. "Sorcerers built it, and only they can maintain it. There's a dedicated team constantly monitoring the structure, making little tweaks and patching old bits, and this is the biggest emergency they've *ever* had. So now, every member of the maintenance team is either racing to neutralize the hex or passed out." With a sigh, she said, "Apparently, DOI saw this coming, but the details kept *shifting*, so they sat on it. Diriem claims that had they foiled this plot, the alternative would have been worse, but I'm not sure I believe that."

He could be inscrutable at the best of times. "Shit," I muttered. "All right, how do I get back inside? Which portal is working?"

Kabno shook her head. "I'm afraid you can't come in right now."

"Huh?"

"Open portals tax the system, or so say the sorcerers," Kabno replied. "Even the phones are locked down because those create a strain when they connect outside. DOI's on its own system, but the fact that Jane's computer is still connected is a fortunate fluke. You *cannot* close the program," she stressed. "IT suspects we won't be able to reestablish access if you do. Keep it running, charged, and close to a signal."

"Uh...all right, yeah," I mumbled, trying to process everything at once. The phones weren't just down—the Pactlands was virtually *sealed*, and I was stuck outside, at the mercy of acquaintances, until the maintenance team was convinced that our world wasn't at risk of collapsing.

Unless...

"Could you please tell Annie or Wylan where I am?" I asked the director. "Annie knows how to get to this part of Georgia, and I trust that Wylan does as well." Even if Moonless Night didn't know the way, surely one of those two would give me a lift out.

"I assume this is to avoid a call to Channel 1?"

Precious few others knew of my boyfriend's unmasked identity, but Kabno was among their number. "Partly. I suspect that my agent would want to know where her parents are."

Her expression quashed my hopes. "We'll inform them of the situation there, but the Hunt's not coming. The maintenance team made it clear this morning that their little jaunts in and out stress the system—they've got a long history of spikes that synch up to the times the Hunt's gone riding."

"That's dozens of them at once," I protested. "If just one or two came through—"

"This hex is *nasty*, Gentle Breeze. We can't risk it. Wylan's already agreed to keep the boys in here, and that goes for Annie as well. But you're not in immediate danger, are you? That mask is holding?"

"Yes, ma'am, the pendant works…"

"She can stay here with me, no problem," said Connor. "I've got spare bedrooms and Netflix, so she can hang out until things stabilize."

"Thanks, kid," I muttered.

He smirked. "Of course. Not going to make you wander the woods…"

"And that's most appreciated," said Kabno, "but if the lot of you are able, we could use some help."

I saw the Humphrieses exchange glances behind me, and I asked, "What sort of help?"

Kabno's mouth thinned to a tight line. "Last night, the Unity Project posted a video on their usual channels explaining what they've done and why."

"A fucking manifesto?" said Maya.

"More or less. They stated that to speed along the…*discovery* process, shall we say, they've dumped people outside without masking jewelry."

I grunted.

"Precisely. So, they've given us a difficult choice: either the portals will have to be opened in order to find and rescue the abducted, or else humans are about to learn in dramatic fashion that they're not alone."

My horror at the news was tinged with annoyance—how had the little bastards gotten past my security system? Assuming I made it home again, my security company would have some groveling to do.

But that could wait. "I'm guessing the people they tossed out here aren't sorcerers or elves, huh?"

Kabno's mouth twitched. "How did you know? Turns out that none of the identified missing are able to pass for human."

"You said Rose is working on the list?"

"If we sent it to you, could you help on the search-and-rescue end?"

I turned from the laptop to question the others, but Maggie beat me to it. "Absolutely," she said, and Dave nodded. "Tell us where to go."

"For what it's worth, I'm in," said Maya, lifting a finger.

"As am I," said Connor. "Let me call my team and make the arrangements…"

He left the room, phone in hand, and, touched, I turned back to Kabno. "That's us, then. When should we expect the list?"

CHAPTER 7

About ten minutes later, as Maya was making tea with the supplies she'd wisely thought to bring, Sprik reported an incoming message from IT.

"What *is* that thing, anyway?" Maya asked, watching over my shoulder as I opened the message.

"What, Sprik? It's the assistant for the program. Annoying if you know what you're doing, but it's helpful for the trainees—"

"*Oh*," she said, chuckling. "Annie named hers Asshole."

"I'm very much aware, and while I cannot officially condone it…I mean, she's not wrong. Now, let's see what we're dealing with…"

By the time I'd read the message, Connor had returned. "All right, the guys aren't happy, but I'm at your disposal…ooh, thank you," he said, accepting a mug from Maya. "What is this?"

"Black tea with artificial vanilla and chai seasonings," I said, scanning the screen again.

"You like it?"

"Haven't tried it yet, but the scent profile is promising…*ah*," I said, glancing up to smile at Maya as she brought me tea. "Have I mentioned yet that Mangia Due's not the same without you?"

"This is literally a teabag, hot water, and two percent," she replied, but seemed pleased. "So, what did Kabno say?"

I waited while Maggie and Dave doctored their tea,

then carefully carried the laptop to the table and sat in one of the wooden chairs I hadn't dared to try unmasked. Masking not only shrank my proportions but also shaved off weight—precisely how, I couldn't say—which was convenient for trying to pass as human. "Okay," I said, opening the word processor on Jane's computer and beginning to type a few notes. "There's no indication of where everyone was dropped, but Laws assumes they're all within an hour of a portal."

"Why's that?" asked Connor.

"Portal Authority is cooperating. Laws and DOI went over the list of everyone who went out or came in from noon Wednesday until the portals were closed around four Thursday morning. Of those who returned, no one was gone for more than two hours."

"So...not everyone came back?"

"Yeah, and not a damn one of the travelers who stayed outside used agency credentials. I don't know these names, and I can almost guarantee they have no business being out here."

"Don't you have to log where you're going when you use the external portals?" Maya asked.

I shook my head. "*Technically*, the attendants are supposed to log your odometer readings going and coming, but that only regularly happens with agency vehicles. It's an extra step, and the Portal Authority doesn't hire many high achievers."

"But you have to tell the attendant where to send you, right?" she pressed. "I thought there's only one external portal."

"You're correct, and that would be useful data, had the hex not scrambled it."

She grunted and sipped her tea.

"In that case, where do we begin?" asked Maggie, cradling her steaming mug. "There's the portal in Oilville and the one in Central..."

"And you mentioned Surrency, yeah?" said Dave.

"That's one," I replied. "Crossville, Maysville, close to Miami, Tampa, Andalusia, Mansura…Midland…"

"Midland, *Texas*?" said Dave. "That's a hell of a drive."

"Oh, it gets worse," I muttered. "Several in New England, up around the Great Lakes, the Pacific Northwest, a few in Canada and Mexico…"

"Hawaii?"

"No, fortunately, but we do have one outside of Anchorage."

The room quieted as we digested *that* sobering thought. The States was close to three thousand miles across, and Canada was even larger.

"Well," said Connor after a moment, "nothing we can do about that tonight. Who all is missing?"

"It's an interesting assortment," I said, "and I'm not sure of the rationale, but if these cretins planned well enough to get past my home security system, then they had to want *me* for a purpose. They could have kidnapped some drunk kid coming out of a bar and saved themselves the trouble, so we need to figure out the connections in this list."

"Gotcha." He sank into the chair beside me and drummed two fingers on the table. "Start with the easy one. You're high up at DPP, so they'll miss you and want you back. You're a troll, so no masking—"

"And you're dating a celebrity," Maya cut in. "Maybe they couldn't get to Moonless Night, so they grabbed you instead."

"Consolation prize—just what every woman wants to be," I said, but the idea had merit. "Moving on, the next name on the list is Taug Berek. I know *of* him—he's a DOL agent, and I went to a training he did some years ago. Good speaker."

"Species?" asked Connor.

"Centaur."

He winced. "Let's hope he was dumped somewhere rural. That's two agents…"

"Number three is Hoska Shilg."

Maya perked at that. "Shilg? You think he's any relation to Korek Shilg? Or, uh, *she's* any relation?"

"Who's Korek Shilg?" Connor asked.

"*He*," I said, beginning with Maya. "Hoska is a masculine name. Korek works at Mangia Due," I told Connor. "And I'd be surprised if there's a relation. Shilg is a fairly common surname. Hell, one of the Forum reps is a Shilg."

Dave leaned closer. "And, uh…*what* is our Mr. Shilg?"

"A faun," I told him. "Continuing, we have Galibe Yentera. I don't know anything about him, but his surname is Gnomish."

Counting off on his fingers, Connor said, "Troll, centaur, faun, gnome…who else?"

"Ermonir venTala," I replied. "Another mystery, but she has to be a female naga."

"Sorry," Maggie cut in, "a what?"

"They're kind of like centaurs or fauns, but they're snakes below the waist," Maya offered, and quickly said to me, "Which is not how I would describe them in other company. Save the lecture."

Seeing the Humphrieses' confusion, I said, "It's *highly* insulting to describe, say, a centaur as half horse. They're not half *anything*, and they take comments like that extremely personally. But here, tonight, just among us…imagine someone close to human from the waist up and close to an anaconda below that."

"Huh," said Maggie, though her expression betrayed her unease.

"And finally," I said, returning to the list, "we have Keppa Amarr. Juvenile nymph."

"You know him?" asked Dave.

"No," I said, "but nymphs don't publicly choose their gender until adulthood, and they give their children gender-neutral names, and not just the personal names. Nymphic surnames take different suffixes depending on the gender. Here, the stem is Amarr, so you'd have Am-

arru for males, Amarrae for females, and Amarrid for neither. Nymphs have a third gender that's neither female nor
male," I said before Dave could ask. "Doesn't matter right
now. Keppa's a child, whatever gender they ultimately
choose."

"Naga and nymph," Connor murmured. "That's six.
No sorcerers taken, no elves…"

"Presumably none of the Hunt," said Maggie. "They all
live at the lodge except for Moonless Night, so how would
your kidnappers have reached them?"

I cocked my tea mug toward her. "Good point. And
there's no siren, either."

Dave frowned bemusedly. "Siren, like…a mermaid?"

"Not in the slightest. They're amphibious, and they
hunt with the help of a hypnotic song. They're not picky
eaters, either, which made them less than popular at the
time of the Pact. But there aren't many left, so maybe it
was too much trouble to try to grab one." I considered the
message and my largely empty notes document, then
tapped on the reply box. "I need a better dossier. Let's see
if Kabno can give me anything."

I put in the request and waited, assuming it would be
hours before I heard back from her. Instead, a little after
ten, I got a reply, and I settled in with a second cup of tea
to review Laws' findings. A few moments later, as Connor
wandered into the kitchen in search of more TV snacks for
his company, I snapped my fingers and slapped the table.
"Got it."

"Yeah?" He paused, giant bag of potato chips in hand,
and waited as I downed the dregs of my drink.

"The Forum," I said, pushing my mug aside. "All of us
have Forum connections. Taug's cousin is a representative,
Puln Berek. Hoska is a member of the Mountain Patrol,
and his sister is the Shilg on the Forum. Ermonir is a Forum aide. And the other two are younglings—"

"Both of them?"

I nodded. "Unfortunately. Keppa's mother is the sister

of Tennel Peolid, one of the nymph reps, and they're just six."

He grimaced.

"Galibe's little better," I continued. "He's ten, and his grandfather is a representative. But it makes sense, doesn't it? Hit the Forum where it hurts, make it personal, and they're more likely to do something rash and desperate to save the people they care about."

"It makes sense," Connor allowed, "but what about you? Are you kin to one of the troll reps or something?"

"No, but I have a suspicion. What do you want to bet that I was chosen because of my boyfriend? If these sorcerers are smart enough to build a catastrophic hex, then surely they understand that they can't kidnap a Huntsman and expect anything good to come of it. The only non-Huntsmen close to that group are Annie and me...and she's technically one of them," I amended, "which leaves me as the weak link."

"Maybe you're a twofer," he said. "A troll with a connection to the Hunt—that's two groups with an interest in getting you home safely."

"But if that's the case, then someone involved in this knows the truth about Moonless Night," I murmured. "Only a few of us in the agencies know, and the Tribunal Committee and a couple of researchers. Fucking Gerem Aniap. And Hakk Frondan, but there's no way he's caught up in the Unity Plan."

Connor's head tilted. "Who's Hakk Frondan?"

"Horsemaster to the Pact. He taught Annie to ride. Nice fellow, almost got blown up a couple years ago. He's older than Yacovi, though, and I trust he has sense enough to avoid the Unity Plan idiots."

As Connor left to tell the others and deliver the snacks, I requested another call with IT, and Kabno answered in short order. "Everyone has a tie to the Forum," I said without preamble. "That's why we were taken."

"That was my thought," she replied, "but I didn't want

to color your impressions."

"Glad we're in agreement. So, what about an abducted siren? Has anyone been reported?"

Kabno's face tightened like she'd just licked a lemon. "There was, shall we say, an *attempt*. Three men broke into the home of one of the siren reps and tried to grab their daughter. She woke before they could subdue her."

I had a terrible idea where the story was going. "Let me guess: no ear protection?"

"Exactly. The youngling started singing, and it seems that youth does little to affect the potency of the effect."

I paused briefly, taking that in. "Have the men's families been notified?"

"They've been told there's little left of their loved ones, and the attack was in self-defense. But on the bright side, those idiots probably never knew what hit them before their throats were ripped out."

Having been under a siren's hypnosis before, I concurred. The feeling had been lovely at the time, like my brain was floating in a warm bath, but knowing how close I'd come to death had soured me on the experience.

"Still no idea where everyone was dumped?" I asked Kabno.

"Not yet."

"In that case, can Rose work with us? She's our best bet—"

"Arrangements are already being made," the director interjected. "She's busy trying to bring in one of the suspects right now, but she'll be at your disposal in the morning. The girl's under orders to take sleep breaks."

"Can't fault her for that—she's a baby."

"And you should rest as well," said Kabno. "What time is it there?"

I glanced up at the microwave clock. "Ten-thirty-ish. We're on Beukal time."

"Great." With a shooing motion, she said, "Go sleep until daylight. I'll have Rose on standby as soon as she's available."

"All I've done today is ride," I protested. "I'm fine for a few hours more…"

Before Kabno could chastise me, Connor popped his head into the kitchen and announced, "Yacovi's finally back. Want to head over?"

"Absolutely." After signing off the call, I left the computer open and stood to unkink my back. "So…are we all squishing into your SUV, or what?"

On paper, both of Connor's SUVs seated five, but no one was in the mood to cram together for the ride. Instead, he loaned Dave and Maggie his Hyundai, while I climbed into the front of the Whitford Explorer and Maya gamely slid into the back seat. "Just promise to let me out," she teased as Connor waited for Dave to join him on the street.

"Come on, don't you trust me by now?" he replied.

She sucked her teeth. "No offense, man, but…*cop.*"

"Uh-huh. And I'm going to pretend that you're just vaping nicotine."

"I have *some* nicotine cartridges," she protested. "Don't be a narc."

"Technically, *I'm* the narc," I said, looking back at her through the divider. "He's more of a generalist, right, Connor?"

"Oh, my God, y'all," Maya muttered.

Beside me, Connor snorted. "Look, my soon-to-be father-in-law is a freaking moonshiner. If you've got pot on you, I don't give a damn."

"Yacovi's in good company. I've never known a brewer who didn't go a little rogue," I told him. "If it's a real problem, we can crack down—"

His incredulous laughter silenced me. "I'd be one of the most hated men in the county if it got out that I shut down Coby Hewt's still. Absolutely not. Besides," he added, "his hooch is pretty smooth."

"*Right.* And do you get the family discount or the law enforcement discount?" I asked.

"Both," he confessed, coughing into his fist.

As late as it was, we made good time through the pass and into Ragged Gap, and Connor led our tiny convoy up another of the surrounding hills. Once he was about half-way, he braked, then turned onto a long driveway. Through the trees, I could make out a two-story farmhouse further up the hill, its windows glowing with yellow light.

Before reaching the house, Connor slowed to a rumbling idle, then picked up his phone. "Hey, we're here," he said when the call was answered. "Wards off?"

A bright flash around the house answered *that,* and Connor said, "Thanks," before driving up to park behind a pair of old pickup trucks and a gray sedan. He jumped out, opened Maya's door, then motioned for the Humphrieses to come closer. "The wards are down," he said once Maggie poked her head out of the SUV. "If you walk on the grass, it's not going to trigger anything."

She froze with her hand on the open door. "I didn't know that was a possibility."

"Oh...sorry," he muttered. "Probably should have mentioned that."

As the five of us trooped toward the house, the porch light flicked on, and the door opened to reveal a figure I knew well: a middle-aged man of average size for a sorcerer with short brown—well, graying—hair, sporting a summer tan, a pair of faded jeans, and a long-sleeved T-shirt that might once have been white but now was streaked with colorful stains and a few small holes.

Brewing could be risky, after all.

"Hey, y'all," called Yacovi, raising a can of beer in salute. "Come on in, nothing's cooking in here. Hi, Connor," he said, patting the boy on the back. "Maya, right? Good to see you again. And y'all must be Annie's folks," he said as the couple climbed the stairs.

"Maggie," she said, shaking his hand, "and this is Dave."

"Yacovi," he replied, shaking Dave's hand, "or Coby, if it's easier. I'll answer to anything. I'm so glad to finally meet y'all—haven't had a chance to thank you for taking care of my Janie."

"Oh, no problem," Maggie told him as Dave wrapped his arm around her shoulders. "She and Connor were only there for the night. We hardly had a chance to host."

"Still, I *appreciate* y'all sticking your necks out for my kid," Yacovi insisted. "Means the world, you know?"

"Absolutely. And your daughter was just lovely," said Maggie. "I'm glad everything worked out for y'all."

Yacovi chuckled softly and drank. "As well as it could have, I suppose. Annie's something else. *Good* kid," he said. "Goes without saying, but y'all should be proud of her."

"Preaching to the choir," said Dave. "Heard you got stuck in traffic…"

He groaned. "*Shit*. Tell y'all about it once we're situated. Go on inside, help yourselves to the beer—it really is beer, promise." As they slipped past him into the house, Yacovi turned to me and grinned. "Hey, stranger," he said in Pactish. "*Now* you come visit me?"

"You've never given me reason," I replied, meeting his hug.

"You needed a reason?"

"This part of the state has been pretty quiet—"

"Until recently, but we've managed." Releasing me, he said, "A social visit won't kill you, Gentle Breeze, and we both know Teme will look the other way."

Yacovi and Pateme had been friends even before Yacovi was tapped to head the greenhouse, and from what I'd witnessed, Pateme's rise to the corner office hadn't chilled their relationship. Both were workaholics with a deep knowledge of obscure plants, perpetual bachelors married to their jobs, but Yacovi had pivoted into the private sector some thirty years prior to protect a young couple, only to end up raising their baby—Jane—in secret. Pateme, on the other hand, showed no signs of tiring of agency life—and honestly, knowing my boss, I couldn't imagine him settling on a little homestead in the mountains to run a greenhouse and brew potions. Ti'Tam was only a middling Hall, and Pateme was his parents' fourth child, but something told me there'd be hell to pay if Lady ti'Tam's boy decided he wanted to move out of the Pactlands…even though he'd helped send his eldest sister to a penal farm.

"Better late than never, right?" I said, and cocked my head toward the door. "Let's bring you up to speed."

He armed the wards again with a mutter, then followed me inside and locked the door. "First things first. Is Janie okay?"

"As far as I know. I assume she's at DOI, but I haven't spoken to her. We've got a line open through her laptop and dumb luck, and I talked to Kabno a bit tonight through DOI's case management program—"

"Kabno?" he echoed, his face crinkling. "She's moonlighting at DOI, eh?"

"I get the feeling that they're all pitching in. It's *bad*, Yacovi," I said, lowering my voice.

"How bad? Connor's been vague…"

"There's a hex in play so destructive that they've closed the portals to keep the Pactlands intact."

He paused, staring at me, then took a long swig of his beer and grunted. "All right, give me the rundown. Where's everyone else?"

We found the others in the kitchen. "By the way," said Connor as Yacovi leaned against the counter, "what were you doing in Atlanta?"

"Brewers' convention," he replied.

"You're going to start brewing beer, too?"

"Nah. Met up with a distillers' group. A little session off the agenda, you know? Anyway," he said, eyeing us, "I tried to check on my greenhouse when I got home, and I can't access it."

"Makes sense," I said, and opened the fridge in search of a beer.

"Sorry," said Dave, "you've lost me…"

"Let me back up, then," Yacovi replied. "I've got a hidden, highly regulated greenhouse on this property. My license allows me to grow, process, brew with, and sell any number of restricted plants. We build greenhouses out here because the soil is infinitely better—that, and with the growers scattered as we are, it'd be difficult to cut off the supply of any one potion or plant, see? But our greenhouses are partially tethered to the Pactlands so that they can be hidden. I mean, mine looks like a standard garden shed until I unlock it, and then it's *massive* inside. Those locks are designed by DPP to control access, and while I *can* give permission to others to open the greenhouse without me, it's discouraged for obvious reasons."

Maggie nodded along. "Sure…"

"So, if I'm not working in the greenhouse, I hide it," Yacovi continued. "And I damn sure lock up when I leave the property. Now it won't open, but since Gentle Breeze told me the Pactlands is on lockdown…"

"What about the brew room?" Connor asked.

"*That*, I can open. It's not connected like the greenhouse. But someone fill me in—what the hell is going on?"

I quickly gave Yacovi the news from Kabno, then explained what I was doing in his house with three people who, by rights, shouldn't have had any clue of the Pactlands' existence. He listened, finishing his beer as we spoke, then put the bottle on the counter, nodded to Maya and the Humphrieses, and said, "Damn strange times we're living in if Laws has dragged y'all into this mess."

"We volunteered," said Maya.

"Still…" Turning to me, he said, "And you're waiting on Rose for directions?"

"Pointless to leave here until we have a destination in

mind," I replied. "But we'll be off once she gets a hit."

"Mm." He considered that briefly, then asked, "Room for one more in the RV?"

Maggie smiled. "Sure! *Sleeping* might be a little tough, now, but we've got seats. You want in?"

"Ma'am, I'm a former agent of the Division of Plants and Potions, and right now, that's about the best backup y'all're going to get."

I thumped him on the shoulder. "Hoping you would say that."

"Shit, woman," he muttered in Pactish, "you know I'm in." Glancing at the others, he asked, "Do they understand this?"

"Oh, yeah," said Maya in kind. "Don't go telling secrets, now."

"Just checking." Reverting to English—the politer option, I surmised—Yacovi said, "If I understand you, there are members of the Unity Plan unaccounted for out here, sorcerers almost certainly. What's your ammo situation like?"

Dave and Maggie shared a look. "Uh," said Dave, "we didn't exactly come *armed…*"

"Neither did I," said Maya.

"I know you've got a few firearms to your name," Yacovi told Connor, "and Gentle Breeze, am I right in assuming you don't have a field kit?"

"I got dropped off in my pajamas," I reminded him. "I don't even have *shoes* right now—and not for lack of trying," I added, nodding to Maggie. "But no, I'm fresh out of potions."

"Well, then," he said, cracking his knuckles, "let's see what I've got in stock."

We followed Yacovi out of the kitchen and into a hallway at the rear of the house. He approached an empty section of plaster, then faced the wall and began making a series of complex hand motions.

"I thought sorcerers used words when they cast," I said

once an ordinary-looking door appeared.

"Generally," said Yacovi. "But that lock's more challenging, and most wouldn't suspect it at a sorcerer's residence, right?"

Ceding the point, I waited as he turned the knob and flipped a light switch, illuminating his brew room: a space with a concrete floor, a long lab bench outfitted with wooden stools, and shelving and racks loaded with glassware and potion bottles. A cleared space on one end held a trio of self-heating cauldrons, each large enough to contain a small child or two, but nothing was simmering. Another door at the rear led into what I took to be a supply room. Along one wall were stacks of reinforced cardboard cartons, each labeled in black marker in a neat hand—potions ready for delivery.

"All right," Yacovi muttered, heading for the boxes, "what do we have...a few healing potions, that's something," he said, crouching to read the labels. "Knockout, useful. Dampening, *that's* a good one. Happy Juice." Peering over his shoulder at us, he said, "Looks like y'all could use a sip of that tonight."

"What's Happy Juice?" asked Dave.

"Nothing you want," Maya quickly told him, shooting Yacovi a look of disapproval.

"It's got a crash, but it *works*," Yacovi protested, then returned to his perusal. "Invisibility...couple of memory potions...spell detector...scent neutralizer...a few painkillers, but I know this box is mostly empty. Oh, and here's one for motion sickness, if anyone needs it."

"Not a full kit," I said.

"No, but a better start than you currently have," he countered.

"Could there be anything in the closet?" ventured Maggie.

Yacovi straightened with a wince and shook his head. "Not unless you're thirsty. That's where I keep the 'shine." Considering the boxes again, he said, "I can decant some of these into useable bottles tonight, and I'll pack them for travel. Got plenty of padding." Turning back to us, he gave our group a long look, then said, "So."

I arched a brow. "So?"

"Well, taking stock, we've got the Interdiction chief, a retired agent who can reliably cast, *three* humans, and a quasi-elf with LEO credentials and limited magic training."

Connor spread his hands. "I'm doing my best…"

"That wasn't condemnation, son, just stating a fact. But any way you slice it, that's a motley crew."

"A thought," said Maggie. "Does anyone here have first aid training? We don't know what condition these folks we're trying to find are going to be in, especially if they've been on the run for a few days. I know CPR, but I'm not certified in anything else."

"I mean, I've got a few healing potions," said Yacovi. "That should help—"

"Got a better idea," Connor interrupted, pulling out his phone. "Tabitha."

Yacovi's eyes widened. "Ooh. *Tabitha.* I don't hate that notion."

"Who's Tabitha?" I asked.

When Connor hesitated, Yacovi took the lead. "She's a pharmacist here in town. Very bright, capable—"

"Human?"

"Yes," he admitted, then hastily added, "but hear me out: she *knows.*"

"Dare I ask?"

"When Gerem Aniap's assassin squad was camping at Yacovi's house, Tabitha helped us put eyes on the place," Connor volunteered. "And helped with logistics the night we raided. She kind of got roped in when some rogue sorcerers came to town and started trying to kidnap some idiots at the woo-woo shop in Ragged Gap—"

"The *what?*" I interrupted.

He rolled his eyes. "Crystals, incense, all that jazz. They were shitty to Janie for a long time, but they've struck a truce now. Anyway, Janie said Tabitha helped her back then, and things sort of snowballed."

"And go easy on the woo-woo snark, eh?" said Maya. "She's a Wiccan."

"I know, I *know*," Connor replied, lifting his palms in surrender, "and I'll behave myself. But that store leaves a bad taste in my mouth."

"So…*what* does this woman know?" I asked.

Connor hesitated, then said, "Well…a fair bit."

"She's part of the brunch club," Maya volunteered.

Which sounded like a bigger security headache every time it was mentioned—we were going to need a *roster*—but I pushed that aside for later. "Did no one think to alter her memory?" I asked Yacovi.

He cleared his throat. "Apparently, Janie told Lord ti'Dana in no uncertain terms that that wouldn't be happening, and he blinked first."

"Oh, no *apparently* about it," said Connor. "I was there. He backed off. Ganti wasn't happy, but Diriem said they wouldn't touch her." Barely frowning, he added, "Wonder if he saw *this* coming."

"I wouldn't put it past him," I said, and sighed. "All right, unless you've got a healer stashed away, she sounds like a decent option. You trust her?"

"Absolutely," said Connor, and Yacovi nodded as Connor found her contact information. "Now, let's hope she's up late."

Tabitha had been spending a quiet Friday evening at home with ice cream, wine, and a long playlist of cooking competitions, but she agreed to make herself a big cup of coffee and come to Yacovi's.

She arrived around eleven-thirty, and I gave her a once-over as Yacovi welcomed her at the door. Tabitha was a dark-skinned woman of average height, probably on the younger end of middle-aged—still relatively youthful and rather pretty, but there were flashes of silver threads in her black hair, which she wore in a thick ponytail composed of tiny braids. Her attire, a ratty T-shirt over a pair of black stretch pants and scuffed tennis shoes, suggested she hadn't been lying about her evening activities.

Yacovi closed the door and chuckled. "Good thing Janie isn't here."

"What, this?" she asked, tugging at her shirt. "I can't help it that she chose the wrong school."

On closer inspection, I saw that Tabitha's shirt bore a drawing of a black and yellow insect—a collegiate mascot, I assumed. That humans could be passionate about their school sports was common knowledge among those of us who went outside, but I couldn't keep the teams or the rivalries straight.

"I'm sorry about this," said Connor, heading for the door. "Thanks for coming—"

"Not my first Pactlands emergency. What's the deal…*hey*, you!" she said, spotting Maya. "They've dragged you into this, too, huh?"

"Volunteered," said Maya. "Tabitha, this is Dave, and that's Maggie," she said, pointing to the couple. "Annie's parents."

Tabitha's smile widened. "Hey, there. Tabitha Bradley," she said, shaking their hands. "Nice to meet y'all."

"Nice to put a face with the name," Maggie replied. "Annie tells us about her friends, but it's not like she brings people *home* with her these days."

"The perils of adult children, right?" she replied, then spotted me. "Hi. And you are?"

"Part of the problem, you might say," I told her, and shook her hand in turn. "Do you speak Pactish?"

"Aside from a little profanity, nope."

"*Ah.* In that case, I'm Gentle Breeze," I said, offering the English rendering. "You're the pharmacist?"

"Bingo." She gave me a quick inspection, then said, "You, uh…I don't mean to be rude, but do you need clothes?"

"These fit much better when I'm not masked," I explained, and lifted the sweatshirt I was swimming in to show her the twine holding my shorts up. "Been a weird couple of days."

"Yeah?" She folded her arms and glanced around the knot of people in the foyer. "All right, y'all, start talking."

Yacovi coaxed Tabitha into the den at the rear of the house, and while she sipped her coffee from a massive tumbler, she listened as we gave her the details of the situation. Once we'd finished, she turned to Yacovi and said, "So...you want me along for medical assistance?"

"Exactly."

"For the tenth time, you know I'm not a doctor."

"I know you've got more medical training than anyone in this room," he replied, "and since we don't know what we're going to find out there, we'd appreciate having you on board."

"I hear you, I do," said Tabitha, "but, uh...you know my training is *very* much human-specific?"

"The basics translate," he assured her. "Now, I've got a small stash of healing potions, and that *may* be enough for us to get by, but—"

"No, I'm in," she interrupted, "but I want y'all to be aware of my limitations. Like, I know how to do stitches, but they ain't going to be pretty. And if you come to me with questions about, you know, drug–potion interactions, I'm not going to have a freaking clue. If the FDA doesn't schedule it, it's not in my wheelhouse."

"Understood," I said, "but Yacovi's right—you're the closest thing we have to a healer at the moment, and we are...uh..."

"Making do," said Yacovi. "So, assuming Rose gets her act together, we'll be pulling out sometime tomorrow morning. Will that work?"

Tabitha squinted into space, clutching her tumbler. "I think so, yes," she said slowly. "Packing's not a problem, but I've got a couple prescriptions coming due for re-fills…I can say it's an emergency and send them to Blue Ridge. Not ideal, but oh well. I'll head to the shop and check my files—"

"*Alone?*" Dave interrupted. "At this time of night?"

"Ragged Gap's a pretty safe place," she told him with a little smile. "Most of the time. I'll be fine."

"I'd really feel better if you'd let me go with you," he replied, and Maggie nodded. "Please. Just in case."

Tabitha seemed poised to protest, but she paused, considering the offer, then shrugged. "Okay, sure, if you want. And I'll take you back to Connor's, yeah?"

"Works for me." He pushed himself from the couch and stooped to kiss his wife. "Get some sleep, honey. I'll be along."

The rest of us followed them out, and while Maya rode back with Maggie, Connor and I had the vehicle to ourselves. "Question," I said as we headed down the hill toward the lights of Ragged Gap.

"Shoot."

"Tabitha's a local here, yes?"

"No, she's from Savannah," said Connor, slowing as a deer bounded across the road. "Came here ten or fifteen years ago. Why?"

"Just checking, but there's no chance that she's a stealth sorcerer, is there?"

"Nope. Janie said she actually tried to cast after one brunch when they all got a little tipsy, but Tabitha doesn't have the touch. Standard human."

"And you trust her."

He glanced my way ever so briefly. "*Yeah.* Tabitha's good people. You trust Maya and Maggie and Dave, right?"

"Maya used to work at DPP, and Maggie and Dave have a kid they want to protect. Tabitha has no connection to us, so what's keeping her from telling the world about the Pactlands?"

"Aside from the fact that no one without a tinfoil hat would believe her?" he countered. "I'm telling you, she's all right. Helped Janie with the Golden Children, with Sage Voln, with Gerem's crew...she even kept an eye on Yacovi's house after East Branch was burned down to make sure there weren't any more elves lurking." He slowed again as a grazing deer raised its head on the side of the road, then said, "It's really okay to trust the occasional human. Been doing it all my life."

"You understand my hesitation, don't you?"

"Yeah, I guess," said Connor, "but we're in 'any port in a storm' territory right now. And if you don't trust my judgment or Maya's, you trust Yacovi's, right?"

He had a point there. "Yacovi knows her well?"

"Oh, yeah. She's on the good hooch list."

And that, I suspected, was the best guarantee I'd get that night.

CHAPTER 8

By one-thirty that morning, my body was begging for sleep, but I silenced its complaints with a slow infusion of Maya's vanilla chai and stared at Jane's laptop, waiting for an update.

The house had quieted shortly after our return from Yacovi's, with the only disturbance being Dave's arrival about half an hour prior. He'd whispered a greeting and tiptoed upstairs to sleep with Maggie, who, having initially announced her intent to wait up for her husband, had let Maya persuade her to get some shuteye. Maya had crashed in the other guest room, and Connor, sleep-deprived as he was, hadn't stirred from the master bedroom. I'd insisted on taking the couch, and Maya had helped me find a sheet and blanket before retiring, but the linens sat undisturbed in a pile on the coffee table. Anxiety and restlessness kept my mind churning, and so I kept vigil alone in the kitchen, trying to parse the logistics of an operation with little data and suboptimal resources.

Sure, we trained for emergencies in Interdiction, but not like *this*. And with so many of the missing being civilians...*child* civilians...

I'd gotten up to refresh my tea and was pouring hot water from the kettle when, out of nowhere, Sprik cheerfully announced a request for video chat. The surprise made me jump, almost scalding myself, and I abandoned my drink to hastily slide into my chair and accept the call.

Once again, Kabno was seated on the other side, and she looked about as haggard as I felt. "Director," I murmured. "Please tell me the hex has been fixed."

She smirked at me. "I wish. And Rose hasn't emerged yet, so I don't have that information for you. But I do have messages I promised to relay."

"I'm listening."

"So, we've been passing word to the appropriate parties of your situation…" Consulting a gnome-sized notepad, she said, "Jane wants all of you to be careful. She says that if you need additional passwords or such for her computer, just say the word. Also, you're welcome to use her masking jewelry—take the stash, do whatever is required." Glancing back at the camera, Kabno added, "Regarding the computer, I should inform you that DOI has taken steps to limit your access to cases outside of this one. Nothing personal, apparently, but you know how these things go."

"I suspect we'd do the same."

"No one likes a security breach," she concurred. "Now, let's see…Annie sends her love to her parents and Maya. Please tell them she's okay. She asks you to look out for her folks, and I quote, 'They're not decrepit by any means, but that doesn't mean I'm not worried. Remind Dad that the speed limit exists for a reason.'"

I chuckled. "Dave's been officially warned, but sure, I'll pass that along once they're awake."

"They're sleeping?"

"*Everyone's* sleeping—which is good, since someone's going to have to drive. I'm sure I could manage the RV, but I'm not on the rental agreement."

She grunted. "How are they holding up, truthfully? Second thoughts?"

"Not that I can tell. They're being team players," I insisted. "Maggie and Dave jumped in immediately, and Maya…I mean, she understands the stakes. So does Connor. And we've got two more aboard now—"

"*Two?*"

"The first is Yacovi Hewt."

Kabno's face relaxed immediately. "Oh, *good.* Does he

have any potions he can hand out?"

"A fair number, and he's preparing them for travel."

She nodded, making a note of that on her pad. "Well, if you were going to pull an agent out of retirement, you could do worse than him."

"Absolutely. He doesn't have full Interdiction training, but the greenhouse side goes through weapons basics— and more than that, he's been living out here full-time for the last thirty years."

"Useful," she concurred. "There's nothing like taking younglings into the field who get an arm's length from the portal and start jumping at their own shadows."

"Oh, believe me, I've broken in my share of trainees," I replied, shuddering.

"And I thank the heavens that upper management gen- erally isn't called upon to do that these days," said Kabno with a little grin. "You said there were two—another agent?"

I hesitated, then said, "No, she's human, but she has some medical training. Yacovi and Connor thought it wise to bring her in. She's called Tabitha."

The tightness of Kabno's mouth told me how much she disliked the idea. "Friend of theirs, I trust?"

"One who knows quite a bit about the Pactlands for someone never having been across the border."

She muttered under her breath. "Who's got the big mouth?"

"It may have been a group effort, but my guess would be Jane," I replied. "Connor said Tabitha has pitched in of late to help her."

"Mm." Jotting that down, Kabno said, "I wouldn't be surprised if Jane told her. You weren't at the Forum for Yacovi's trial, were you?"

"No, ma'am…"

"Jane had…quite a bit to say."

"Oh?"

"Basically told the Forum to go fuck themselves, and

she was going home. Considering the circumstances, I can't say I entirely blame her. But back to this Tabitha—have you vetted her?"

"I met her tonight," I said, "but from what I was told, she's already made contact with DOI. I'll let you guess."

Kabno stared back at me for a moment, then released the sort of long sigh that only years of frustration can produce.

"I suspect he had a reason…" I ventured.

"We're just going to add this to my ever-growing list of things to *discuss* with Diriem," she grumbled. "But not tonight." She paused, thinking, then said, "That's seven of you, then? And majority human. I've heard of odd groups…"

"It's an odd situation."

"Tell me about it. But considering that we've been taught for so long to fear them…" With a weak laugh, she said, "Maybe the Unity Plan is on to something, eh? Maybe they're not so bad."

"Individually, no," I replied, "but collectively—"

"I'm joking, I assure you," Kabno hastily clarified. "Which, considering the hour, is probably unwise. But in all seriousness, we need allies right now, and I'm not going to be overly picky. If you and Yacovi trust them…"

"They've given me no reason not to," I told her. "Director, if I may?"

She motioned toward her screen. "Please."

"You look like shit, ma'am. Get some rest."

"Likewise. Put down the Happy Juice."

I lifted my mug. "It's just tea. Caffeinated, allegedly, but I'm barely feeling this."

"Then take it as a sign and go to bed, Gentle Breeze. We'll call back when we've got intel for—" A sharp rapping interrupted her, and she glanced off-screen with annoyance. "Excuse me. Good night."

The feed ended, and I rubbed my eyes. Kabno was right—I needed to sleep—but though my body was weary, my mind refused to stop circling.

Perhaps, I mused, a sedative would do the trick...but since Yacovi's potions were in the next town over, I'd need to get creative.

Connor's liquor cabinet left much to be desired—the boy had three bottles, two of which were Jack Daniel's and Jim Beam—but the third was an unlabeled gallon-sized glass jug three-quarters full of golden liquid. I uncapped it and took a test sniff. Yes, as I'd suspected, that was aged, high-proof liquor, and I'd have bet my right arm it had come from Yacovi's still. I found a juice glass in a kitchen cabinet and poured myself a healthy drink, then shot it back, letting the burn trickle down my throat like liquid sunshine.

Smooth, though I'd have expected nothing less from Yacovi.

Unfortunately, while the mask could temporarily change my size and form, it did nothing to alter my tolerance level, and I estimated that it'd take most of the 'shine jug to build up a pleasant buzz. The rules of hospitality only extended so far, however, and it would be rude for me to drain Connor's best bottle. Instead, I filled the juice glass almost all the way and headed for the den, hoping that I could find something sufficiently dull on television to take me over the finish line to sleep.

Instead, Sprik alerted me to another call, and so I ran back to the table, slid into my still-warm chair, and took a quick sip off the top of my hooch as the video started.

Kabno was back, but she seemed more peeved than exhausted. "Ah, good, I caught you," she said. "Busy?"

"I was just going to stretch out," I replied. "Update from Rose?"

"No, not yet. I left in a hurry because one of my aides interrupted to alert me to a call from the lobby. Seems there was a *commotion* down there that required executive oversight," she said, rolling her eyes, then looked to her left. "All right, she's here. Talk to her," she said, then slid her rolling chair out of the way.

The burgundy fabric of a formal robe filled the screen as someone moved into her place, and then the newcomer took a knee, the better to be on eye level with the director's computer.

I smirked and shook my head. "Making trouble?" I asked in Trollish.

"Wylan's been keeping me apprised," said Moonless Night in kind, his dark eyes searching me as if checking that all my major parts were accounted for.

He'd seen me masked, so my appearance didn't confuse him, but I resisted the urge to switch back because my clothes' structural integrity was highly questionable. Reminding myself that he was masked, too—even if he wore his far more comfortably than I did—I settled for leaning closer and swigging my drink. "Sorry I missed dinner tonight."

"You're alive," he said in his rumbling baritone—also a product of his mask and necessary for him to fully produce the tones of my mother tongue. "Are you hurt?"

"No. I've been treated kindly," I replied. "What are you doing at Laws?"

"I got an update once the late show was finished, and then Annie called to say that Director Erenani had spoken with you, and so I, uh…"

My brows rose. "You what? Made a spectacle of yourself in the lobby?"

"I've been worried sick," he protested.

"The Sound of Deer Running Through the Forest on a Moonless Night, do you not trust that I can take care of myself?" He had the grace to look a little embarrassed, and I grinned even as I shook my head. "I'm *fine*, sweetest. I've connected with one of my former colleagues and a few others, and I'm safe."

He didn't seem entirely convinced. "Wylan said Dave and Maggie were with you…"

"You've met them?"

"Once. I went to the lodge one night for dinner when they were visiting…which you're probably not supposed to know about," he added with a faint smile.

"Oh, I've been learning *so* much of late," I replied. "But yes, they've been helpful."

"And the others?"

"Yacovi Hewt, for starters. He was the greenhouse chief for fifty years, and he knows how to get by out here, so really, you needn't worry."

A grunt answered that. "The rest?"

"Maya Mackay—you know, the other Roulette victim with Annie?"

"Of course. What about the memory potion you gave her?"

"Failure, fortunately enough. We've camped for the night at the home of Connor Willow—he's the last of the East Branchers left out here."

Moonless Night nodded. "The cop, yes? I remember him from the coverage of the ti'Ammaas trial."

"Exactly. Seems like a decent kid, but he gets twitchy if you use his title. And there's a human who's allegedly known to DOI."

"You trust him? Her?"

"Her, and Yacovi, Connor, and Maya do," I said after a moment's thought, "and I…have no specific reason not to. Yet," I allowed. "She's had medical training. We've been asked to try to find the other people dumped out here, and heavens know what state they'll be in, so she might prove useful."

"I hope she's unneeded," he replied, then held my stare through the screen. "Say the word, dearest, and I'll come get you," he murmured. "I can see enough of that room to lock on."

"I thought the Hunt had specifically been asked *not* to teleport in and out. It stresses the system, doesn't it?"

"You think I give a damn?"

I chuckled softy. "And *there's* the family resemblance.

I'd wondered."

"Huh?"

"I seem to recall Wylan killing your father without any thought as to what it might do to magic as we know it."

"That was different—"

"Yes, it was," I said, nodding vigorously. "Annie was in mortal peril, and I'm just sitting here, having a drink in the mountains." Taking a sip, I added, "Weak, but not bad."

"Dare I ask?"

"Yacovi distilled it. Connor's liquor selection isn't great, but this is quite palatable. I don't know how *effective* it will be, now…"

"If he had troll-strength liquor on hand, I'd be concerned," he replied, then sighed through his tusks and shook his head.

"Don't worry, sweetest," I said, pushing the glass down. "I'm fine, truly. My mask is convincing, isn't it?"

"Flawless, but…" He hesitated, his face shifting as he chose his words, then said, "I know you're strong, and I know you're capable, and I wouldn't dream of insulting you by suggesting otherwise…"

One corner of my mouth rose in a slight smile. "But?"

"But damn it, I love you, The Joy in the Spirit at the Scent of Rain on a Gentle Breeze, and I can't help but worry."

Even if I hadn't been able to see him, I could hear the anxiety in his voice.

"I appreciate your concern," I said, "and you know I love you, too. But don't destroy the Pactlands on my account, eh? I can handle myself."

"I know," he mumbled, "I just…"

"If our places were reversed, I'd worry about you as well. But I've got a team here, and shelter, masking jewelry…alcohol of questionable efficacy," I said, lifting my drink toward the camera. "I'm fine. Now, let Director Erenani have her office back and go home before she has you arrested for interfering in a Pact operation, okay?"

Though he seemed poised to protest, Moonless Night surrendered. "Be safe," he told me. "And know that I'm one photo away. If you need me, I'll come."

"I know you would. Sleep, sweetest."

Reluctantly, he ceded the computer to Kabno, who signed off with an admonition to get some rest. Taking her advice to heart, I knocked back the rest of my drink, then left the computer on the kitchen table and headed into the den to bed down.

I stretched out on the couch, still surprised that I fit between the armrests, and pulled the borrowed blanket to my chin. As I burrowed down and listened to the house settling and the white noise of the ceiling fan, I thought of my worried boyfriend, who'd surely received a tongue-lashing from the diminutive DOL director on his way out of the building.

As far as the single troll population of Beukal was concerned, I'd snagged a true catch. Moonless Night was handsome, famous, and commanded an impressive salary. He could have had just about any female troll in the city, but he'd never dated. Had luck not been with me, I might have been just another rebuffed admirer, but I didn't begin my pursuit until I saw what lay beneath his mask—and that, I believe, was the difference for him. Plenty of women wanted Moonless Night, but I was willing to try my luck with Morial, and two years on, he had eyes only for me.

Moonless Night was just *likeable*, an enthusiastic sports reporter with an encyclopedic knowledge of games and players. He could pull a comment from almost anyone, and he had a way of putting people at ease on camera. One of his great joys was making school visits, as the student athletes were always so excited to see him, and he legitimately loved covering youth games—particularly melee, the stats for which he could rattle off like he was reading them from an invisible book. Aside from the occasional jealous glare or catty comment from his other admirers, it was *easy* being with Moonless Night, and when we went out in public together, he treated me like a queen.

But early in our relationship—a few weeks after he took me up on my offer of a drink, once we'd begun seeing each other in earnest and we were alone on my couch—I asked him what he wanted to be called. Did he prefer Moonless Night or Morial? He hesitated to answer me, and only after I poured refills—by then, I kept a bottle of whisky in the house that wouldn't leave him blackout drunk—did he finally try to give voice to his thoughts. He'd been Moonless Night for so very long, he told me, and it was such a comfortable mask to wear that he almost forgot he was masked much of the time. But we both knew that wasn't truly him. I told him then that I liked Moonless Night and greatly enjoyed his company, but I wanted to know Morial as well.

Morial was harder. Older, certainly—Moonless Night never gave his fake age on air, but it was far younger than Morial's true millennium and change. He wasn't even entirely certain of his birthdate. Moonless Night loved younglings, while Morial had never been one. He'd come into existence fully grown, with a pack of brothers and a tyrannical father, and he'd known only the Hunt until his father expelled Morial for daring to defy him. Having lost his family, he'd ground down the stumps of what was left of his broken antlers and lived with a group of sorcerers for a few years. They'd given him the masking ring he still wore, and when he'd moved on, he'd accidentally settled near a troll clan. In time, they'd welcomed him as a neighbor, then a friend. He'd learned Trollish the hard way, masking his voice to make the proper sounds. Eventually, he'd moved in, masked as one of them, and was named and adopted into the clan. He'd loved them as family until sickness and humans killed them all, and when he found another clan to take him in, he'd kept the truth of his identity a secret. By the time I met him, he was the lone survivor of two clans and an elder by our metrics, awkwardly trying to help the little brother he'd only recently met adapt to life outside the Hunt. Morial had scars that Moonless Night could never have fathomed, and when the cameras were off and the two of us were alone, he allowed me to see glimpses of the pain behind the mask.

I was careful to always call him Moonless Night in public—far be it from me to destroy the persona he'd built over centuries—but in private, I used both names.

I understood that after so many lonely years, he was desperate to be what I wanted. He insisted that he was happy to be Moonless Night for me, that I didn't have to acknowledge...*that*. But I told him I loved all of him, and I meant it—and for that, he knew he was damn lucky.

Part of the problem for him was, having been Moonless Night for most of his life, he'd almost forgotten how to be Morial. Two years prior, when Wylan had killed their father and become the Hunter in turn, he'd welcomed his banished brother back into the fold. Morial had his antlers once more, and he'd learned the way to the Hunt's hidden lodge. From what he'd told me, his brothers had received him warmly—Wylan certainly had. I'd encouraged him to sneak off to the lodge and take the time he needed to reconnect with them, to meet the ones born in his absence and rediscover his place in the Hunt. The last time they'd gone on their big ride, he'd ridden along, and he'd been so *happy* when he showed up on my doorstep the next day, a little windblown and smelling of sweat and horse and blood but content in a way I'd seldom seen him.

Morial was strong—*so* strong—but he'd been broken and was still trying to heal, which was why I didn't take offense that he worried about me. He cared, and I appreciated the novelty of having someone in my life who supported my endeavors.

Imagining him spooned behind me instead of the couch cushions pressed against my back, I allowed sleep to come.

It was shortly before six a.m. that I decided the programmer responsible for Sprik was a sadist.

"Hi! It's me again, Sprik! Request for video conference from IT," it shouted from the kitchen, yanking me from sleep. "Accept or decline?"

Sprik wasn't sentient, I reminded myself, as I untangled my legs from the blankets and hurried to the laptop. It was just a feature of the software. And yet, its perpetually happy voice was so eminently *punchable*.

Wiping the sleep from my eyes, I sank into the chair I'd left halfway pulled out the night before and accepted the call. The video started a few seconds later, and there sat Rose, who looked about as shitty and under-slept as I felt. Her red hair fell limply around her face, desperate for a wash, while her puffy eyes—gray ti'Dana eyes, somewhat unsettling once you knew about the farsight in that family—squinted blearily back at me. And though she had the ti'Dana look, I could still see Fradin ti'Cren, her grandfather, in her expression. He and I had pulled many an overnight shift together in the early days of our careers, and catching Rose so exhausted as she evidently was, I could trace the transposition of his features down the family line.

"Hey, Chief," she croaked in a voice trending toward trollish in its pitch, and stifled a yawn. "Sorry. How's it going?"

I grunted, which seemed as appropriate an answer as any. "Found something?"

She nodded. "Been working all night. I've got some notes, and Annie's been helping me check potential locations."

That woke me in a hurry. "Annie's been going outside?"

"No, *no*," Rose hastily clarified, "Annie's been sitting here with her computer, seeing if she can match photos to my sketches. And we think we have some hits."

"Hang on." I pushed back from the table and searched the kitchen until I found a magnetized grocery list hanging on the fridge. Ripping off a piece of paper and snagging a pen from the cup on the counter, I returned to the table and clicked the pen open. "Start talking."

"So," said Rose, "from what I've seen, everyone who was dropped outside the Pactlands was in the same condition you were—no masking jewelry, nothing but the clothes on their backs. Everyone is *alive*, I know that much, but—"

"Time is of the essence," I finished. "Because if they're unmasked and the wrong humans see them…"

"Shitstorm," Rose concurred.

"Who's closest? We're in, uh…"

"Whitford? You're at Connor's, right?"

"Yeah. Trying to wake up," I muttered, rubbing one temple. "Anyway, who's closest to us?"

"Taug Berek," she replied without hesitation. "He's with—"

"Laws, yes. He's an agent, but I don't know the details. Doesn't matter," I mumbled to myself. "Where?"

"He was dumped near the Central portal," said Rose. "I'm sure of it. I haven't *seen* the portal, but I recognized one of the roads running nearby—I've been to Ragged Gap the long way."

"As opposed to via Annie?"

She smirked. "No idea what you're talking about, Chief. But the area does look familiar, and with the number of South Carolina plates I've seen, I'm pretty sure I'm right. Annie concurs."

"Good. And Taug is…where?"

"Hiding somewhere close to the portal. The area is wooded and swampy, and he's probably been in the forest for a couple of days, considering his state. He's limping," she said. "Looks like there's dried blood on one of his back legs—he's managed to get it somewhat clean, but his hair is stained. Tabitha's with you, right?"

"Yes…well, she'll be joining us when we leave here. I think she went home to Ragged Gap, but—"

"Close enough. Tell her she might want to read up on

equine anatomy on the way, eh?"

"Noted." I paused, replaying that, then said, "Perhaps I should mention to her that we don't make equine comparisons to centaurs, yes?"

Rose grimaced in agreement. "That…might be *really* wise, yeah."

CHAPTER 9

"You know," said Tabitha as Dave backed us out of Connor's driveway, "this is actually not my first centaur rodeo."

"Ooh," Yacovi muttered, wincing as he clutched his travel mug, "I get what you're saying, hon, but that is *not* a great choice of words."

"Sorry," she mumbled. "But I was there with Sage, remember?"

"Sage is only half centaur. This Taug's the full deal."

"Then *you* might be better suited to treat him," said Tabitha, cocking her bottle of Coke toward Yacovi across the aisle. "You deal with horses—"

"I shoe them and trim hooves," he protested. "Someone else vets them. Now, if he does have an open wound, are you comfortable suturing it?"

She considered the question as she drank her breakfast. "Skin, sure," she replied after a moment. "If we're talking about a flesh wound, I know how to do stitches, but they ain't going to be neat. This is, like, field medic stuff. If we're talking torn tendons or ligaments, now, I'm not going to be of any use."

"I'm just impressed that you can do stitches," said Connor, who'd squeezed onto the couch between Yacovi and me.

"Eh." With a shrug, Tabitha said, "I thought about going to med school before I decided on pharm—blood doesn't bother me. And I've always figured that it didn't hurt to be prepared for emergencies, so I took all the first aid courses I could find back in college. Choking, seizures, frostbite, hyperthermia…you know, if you're on a hike or something, you're probably not going to have a doctor around."

"Didn't know you were a big hiker," Connor remarked.

"I'm not anymore. Did plenty in college, but then my knees started to go. No sense in exacerbating the problem," she replied. Noticing my bemusement, she explained, "Couple of injuries when I was younger and some unfortunate genes mean my cartilage isn't what it could be. Middle age *sucks*."

"Doesn't get any better!" Maggie called from the front of the RV.

While I was no great judge of human age, I guessed that Tabitha was somewhere in her forties or fifties, older than Maya but younger than Dave and Maggie. I had *trainees* her age, kids barely out of school whom I didn't fully trust to point their guns in the right direction. Given their heightened fecundity, it was probably a good thing that humans' lives were so brief—they'd have overpopulated themselves into extinction otherwise—but that calculation seemed awfully cold when applied to actual *people*.

And they'd been willing to jump into action as soon as I woke them that morning. Tired but rapidly caffeinating, they'd piled into the RV about an hour after I got off the chat with Rose. Dave drove, with Maggie sitting in the navigator's chair, guiding him toward South Carolina; one of us with actual knowledge of the portal would take over for the final approach. Everyone else crammed together, Connor, Yacovi, and me on the couch, Tabitha at the little dining table. The only person missing was Maya, who'd reluctantly agreed to stay in Whitford and babysit the laptop. While Dave volunteered the use of his Wi-Fi block, we couldn't risk losing the tenuous connection we had to Beukal, and so the computer remained at Connor's house, safe against everything but power outages. Granted, Maya wasn't at all authorized to access Pact software, but I trusted that she could follow Sprik's prompts.

As for the rest of us, Tabitha had brought her full medical kit with her, Yacovi had packed a cabinet with potion vials, and Connor had brought along not only Jane's masking necklaces but also a stuffed duffel bag. "Clothes," he'd explained. "Assuming we find this guy, he's not going to be carrying pants, is he?"

There was no time to make another Walmart run to better clothe me, so I made the best of my oversized wardrobe and my trusty piece of twine. The one thing I'd been able to snag was a pair of old hiking boots from Connor's closet. Masked, my foot was about a size eleven in women's shoes, so his size ten boots were only a little too big. Thick socks helped, though I paid attention to the movement in the boots, on guard against blistering.

I sincerely hoped that Taug had learned to walk bipedally at some point along the way.

The sun was rising, and we'd just reached the state line when Maya called Maggie with an update. "Rose has eyes on him," she said, her voice rendered tinny by Maggie's phone's speaker. "He's still in the woods."

"How deep?" I asked.

"Not overly, she thinks. He's been hiding out near the tree line. Still limping—she doesn't think he can doctor himself well because of the injury location."

"Where is he in relation to the portal?"

"It's visible from where he is," said Maya. "Uh, Rose said it's a house or something?"

"That's right." I'd had occasion to come through Central over the years. Like most portals, it was hidden away from population centers—or as close as could be managed, given the constraints of human sprawl. Central was a town of about five thousand located in the northwestern tip of South Carolina. While the portal had once been closer to Central proper, it had since been moved to an undeveloped area near a lake west of town, north of Clemson. An unmarked dirt road off one of the paved routes led into the pines and dead-ended in a clearing. At the center of the clearing sat a gray, abandoned house—or rather, the shell of a house, as the back of the rotting building was missing, and the rest seemed one storm away from crumbling into the dirt. It might have attracted explorers, had it been more structurally sound and less overgrown with weeds. But in truth, the house had been magically shored up, and a call to the Portal Authority would open a portal where a living room might once have been. The clearing around the house wasn't large, only about twenty yards in any direction, but that offered room for convoy staging and the rare backup at the portal.

"Well," said Maya, "according to Rose, he's not straying far. He seems to be alone, but he's going to have to move soon to find food."

"We're almost there," I assured her.

"Great. If Rose calls while you're hunting for him, who should I contact?"

I thought briefly, considering my ragtag team. "Let's have Maggie and Dave stay with the RV. Call Maggie, and if they don't see us, one can relay. Connor, Yacovi, Tabitha, you'll go with me."

"We can go, too," Dave protested from the front.

"Sure, but someone needs to guard the getaway vehicle," I explained, "and should a cop come snooping, better for you to try to talk your way out of it than me."

Though Dave grunted, he didn't protest further, and Maggie raised no objection to hanging out in the comfortable RV.

Once Maya hung up, I traded seats with Maggie and guided Dave toward the portal, directing him north around the lake, then off the main road. "I'd have never thought to come down here," he said, slowly bumping over the rutted track. "Wouldn't have expected to find more than, like, an old cemetery or someone's hunting camp."

"That's the idea," I said, bracing myself with the door handle. The road to the portal was clear, but it wasn't exactly *smooth*.

Finally, the trees parted, and the decoy house came into view. "That's the place," I said, pointing to it through the windshield. "Park alongside, okay? The ground should be firm."

Dave did as I asked, then joined us in the back of the RV, cracking his back after his drive. "Y'all going to be okay? Really, we can come…"

"We'll be fine," said Yacovi, loading potions into a padded backpack, "and if not, we'll call. Hang out, stretch your legs."

"And call me if there's a problem," said Connor, patting his pocket. "Do you have my number?"

They quickly traded information, and then, with an admonition from Maggie to look out for ticks, we descended into the calf-high grass.

I walked a few paces away from the RV, then paused, closed my eyes, and sniffed deeply.

Water, yes. We were close to the lake. Moist soil, the funk of wet decay. Grass, plenty of grass, and *pine*, the resin almost like a punch in the face with its sheer power. Exhaust from the roads nearby, gasoline and diesel and oil and warm rubber.

Again.

My new clothes, incompletely adulterated by my own scent. Several varieties of shampoo and soap and deodorant, none of it fresh. Shea butter—Tabitha. Coffee breath. Gunpowder…Connor was packing, then. Traces of a dozen potions from the load Yacovi was carrying, their ingredients subtle but present in the bouquet.

Again.

Sorcerer—that was Yacovi, of course. Faintly different was Tabitha's human scent, the species undercurrent beneath the other smells she produced and carried. Connor's was interesting, a blend of human and elf—heavy on the elf, though the human notes carried through. Rose's scent was similar, I recalled, a mélange—odd but not unpleasant.

And…

There.

"He's that way," I said, opening my eyes and pointing toward the north. "And there's blood on him."

"That trick never ceases to impress me," said Yacovi, shifting his pack. "How do we want to play this?"

"Let's just try not to spook him," I muttered, then walked a few yards closer to our hiding target and called in Pactish, "Taug Berek! My name is Gentle Breeze, and I'm from DPP. We're here to help."

I listened for a moment, but there came no sound but the wind through the grasses and pines.

"Agent Berek," I tried again, "we're the search party. Director Erenani told us you'd been abducted." When there was no response, I said, "I'd offer to show you my badge, but they abducted me, too. We have masking jewelry, food, water. You're hurt, aren't you?"

Though he didn't speak, his scent didn't move.

"I think we're going to have to go in after him," I said to the others. "No sudden movements, yeah? Last thing I want to do is try to run down a fleeing centaur, even one with a bum leg."

My companions nodded, and I called toward the woods in Pactish, "We're coming in to find you. Just stay where you are."

The others fell in behind me as I cut across the clearing, following my nose into the woods. The edge was a mess of low bushes and vines, but once I pushed past it and acclimated to the altered scent profile, I could pick Taug out of the jumble. He seemed to be staying still, a small mercy, and I pressed forward, trying to find a path through the close trees and dense undergrowth.

Finally, after about a ten-minute search, I spotted a suspicious lump of leaves and branches that smelled tellingly of centaur and blood. "Agent Berek," I said, dropping to a crouch, "it's all right. If you want me to unmask, I'll do it, but I can't guarantee that my pants will remain intact."

The leaves began to shift, then fell away as Taug, who'd curled up on himself, poked his head out of the pile. He squinted at me, and then, in a cracking voice, said, "You…"

"I'm The Joy in the Spirit at the Scent of Rain on a Gentle Breeze," I said. "I head DPP Interdiction. Seriously, if you need to see the tusks, I'll unmask."

"No…no, that's all right, that…thank you." His dark eyes began to water, and even with the camouflaging dirt smeared all over his skin, I could tell that his jaw was trembling. "*Thank you*," he repeated. "Can you get us through the portal? I don't have my phone, I don't know what happened—"

"It's all right," I soothed as he sat up in a shower of debris. "The portals are closed, and I'll explain everything, but first, let's see that leg."

"How'd you know about—"

"Baby ti'Dana told us. The kid's watching remotely."

He chuckled weakly. "How did I warrant a farseer?"

"Again, I'll debrief you, but we need to see the leg."

Carefully, pulling himself to his hooves with the aid of a young tree, he stood and brushed at some of the junk clinging to his brown hair. "Left rear," he said, swishing his tail toward the injured limb. "It's in an awkward spot, and I haven't been able to do much with it but let it clot."

"Are you hurting?" asked Yacovi, unzipping the potion bag. "I've got a few painkillers to take the edge off."

"That would be fantastic," said Taug. "You're DPP, too?"

"*Was.* I retired from the greenhouse. Yacovi Hewt," he said, giving Taug a nod before he began rummaging in his bag. "I brewed everything in here, so I'll vouch for it."

Taug's expression shifted. "Oh, I've heard about *you*."

Yacovi's mouth twitched. "Yeah?"

"It's an honor."

He glanced up and grinned, then produced a vial of

pale green liquid. "Let's start with this, and here's a chaser," he said, handing Taug the potion and a plastic bottle of water from the RV fridge.

Taug mumbled his gratitude as he uncapped the vial, then slugged it back and downed the water in three long gulps. "There's water around here," he said as he wiped his mouth on his filthy arm, "but it's mostly stagnant, and I *really* don't want a parasitic infection."

"Here," said Connor, pulling a thermos from his backpack. "It's just water. Go ahead, you can have it."

He didn't have to be told twice, though he eyed Connor curiously as he stifled a belch. "DPP? Sorry, I'm trying to place your accent…"

"No, and you're hearing Georgia," I interjected. "He's one of the East Branch group—"

"*Oh*," said Taug, his eyes widening. "*That's* why he sounds so weird."

Connor shrugged. "Doing my best, man. And we haven't heard your English yet…"

"I've been told my accent needs work," he replied, "so no judgment here. There's not much need for it in Internal Affairs, anyway."

"But you do speak English?" Connor asked.

Taug nodded. "Took a potion for it when I was still doing fieldwork. Why?"

"Well," he said, switching languages and slinging an arm around Tabitha's shoulders, "that's what our one-woman med team speaks, so now's your chance to practice. Meet Tabitha."

He stiffened and briefly studied her, then looked to me for an explanation.

"Human," I murmured in Pactish, "but vetted by DOI. She's the best we can do right now."

"Vetted *how*?"

"All I know is that they agreed not to alter her memory, and Yacovi here trusts her. How about letting her work on that leg, hmm?"

Taug hesitated, then cleared his throat and looked back at Tabitha. "So...I'm guessing you've never treated a centaur before," he said in awfully accented English.

"First time for everything," Tabitha replied. "And full disclosure, I'm a pharmacist, not a doctor. I'm up on my first aid, but this isn't my specialty."

He nodded. "And you'd probably be more comfortable with a torso wound, right?"

Her lips quirked in a little smile. "No comment."

With a grunt, he beckoned her closer. She gently peeled away the poultice of forest litter that had adhered to his wound, then hissed through her teeth. "Oof. Let me get this clean," she told Taug, "and then I'm pretty sure you're going to need stitches. When did this happen?"

"Last night. Three coyotes sneaked up on me," he said. "I gave them a few good kicks to drive them off, but not before one got a chunk."

"Mm. Do me a favor and lie on your side."

He lowered himself into position, tucking one arm beneath his head. Tabitha took a bottle of water from her bag, wet a sponge, and began wiping away the dried blood. "It's still seeping," she said after a few minutes' work, "and I can't tell if it's infected, but I want to start you on an antibiotic, just in case. Any drug allergies? Can you handle penicillin?"

"Uh..." he mumbled, and looked at Yacovi and me for help.

"Probably," said Yacovi. "I've never heard of a centaur with a 'cillin allergy."

"Well, once we get back to the RV, let's send word to Maya to make Rose ask someone over there for help. I can procure the drugs, but I'm going to need guidance as to dosing. You're a big fella," she said to Taug. "But I'm thinking a broad-spectrum antibiotic and a topical to be safe. And then the issue of rabies..."

"I don't think the coyotes were rabid," said Taug, "and in any case, we're immune."

"Really? Convenient," she muttered, and went back to work.

Once Tabitha had the wound clean-ish, she sat back on her heels and studied it. "Two questions."

"Yes?" said Taug.

"Are you going to be mad at me if I shave the hair around the area, and what's your pain tolerance?"

He made a face. "Um…shave away, I guess. Whatever you need. And as for pain—"

"I can handle that," Yacovi interrupted.

While Tabitha pulled a disposable razor from her kit and began baring Taug's skin, Yacovi drew up the contents of another vial of green potion into a syringe. "Here," he said, passing it to Tabitha. "If you inject it into the muscle, the effect is much more localized and concentrated. He won't feel more than a little discomfort once that goes to work."

She did as he instructed, and within minutes, Taug murmured, "I can barely sense your fingers back there. It's almost numb."

"Great," said Tabitha, who by then had finished Taug's shave and was wiping the wound with alcohol swabs. She rubbed disinfecting gel on her hands, then slipped on a pair of disposable gloves and pulled a long, curved needle from her kit. "Taug, how squeamish are you?"

He hesitated. "Honestly?"

"Okay. *Do not* look back here. Y'all, why don't you distract the patient for me, eh?" she said to the rest of us. "Give him the skinny."

As Tabitha stitched and Taug steadfastly stared anywhere but behind him, Yacovi brought Taug up to date, and Connor showed him the cache of masking pendants. "They work, but they're not fancy enough to change your clothing size," I heard Connor explain as I sat apart, keeping watch.

Taug snorted. "Well, since I obviously slept in the buff Wednesday night, that won't be a problem."

"*Right.* I brought some extra clothes—no clue if they'll fit, but—"

"It's a start. Thank you..." He hissed sharply—the potion was great but imperfect—and Tabitha muttered an apology. "No, no, keep going, you're fine," he told her.

"This is probably a stupid question," said Yacovi, "but you *have* learned to get around bipedally, haven't you?"

"Yes," said Taug, drawing out the word, "but it's been a few years. Like twenty. Internal Affairs is largely a desk job, you know? But I've had field training, and I've done it before, so if you can give me a little time to find my balance, I should be salvageable."

"Of course. There's no rush—I'm just thinking about how we're getting you into the RV and back to Georgia."

"I still can't believe the *Unity Plan* is behind this," said Taug. "They've never been a real threat! Bunch of misguided idiots, sure, but to pull off something on this scale, with a hex like you're describing...and why me, anyway? There are plenty of better targets at Laws."

"They snatched people with Forum connections," I explained. "You're Puln Berek's cousin, right?"

He groaned, then hastily added, "Sorry, not you, Tabitha. Carry on."

"Something wrong with Puln?" I asked.

"No, we've been close since we were younglings. He's only about four years older than me—more like a brother than a cousin. Our kids are close, too. They were sleeping over at his house on Wednesday..." He fell quiet, possibly contemplating a scenario in which his children had ended up fighting off coyotes instead of him. "Heavens," he mumbled.

"I don't mean to be rude, but is their mother in the picture?" asked Connor.

"Hm? Oh, certainly. She's a counselor, works in family law. Her hours can be strange, and there was a situation that came up on Wednesday with an emergency removal, and...well, I had an early morning planned for Thursday, so Puln agreed to take the kids for the night. We trade off babysitting sometimes, you know? She's safe, thought, right?" he asked anxiously. "She's not out here?"

"She's not on the list," Yacovi soothed. "You're the only centaur who's come up missing."

He sighed with relief, but I missed whatever he said next, as I'd picked up on the sound of an approaching engine. I couldn't see the RV through the trees, hidden as we were within the woods and undergrowth, but the sound was different than the large vehicle's rumble. This was more like a car, I thought. It crescendoed, then stopped somewhere in the clearing…and since I couldn't smell the usual engine scents, it was either electric or a Pactlands model. But I could *listen*, and I quickly silenced the others as I heard the echo of a door slam.

"What's that?" Connor whispered.

"Another car. Shh." Looking at Tabitha, I asked, "How much longer?"

She eyed the wound. "Ten minutes? I'm going as fast as I can, but this is amateur hour."

"That's fine. Everyone, just be quiet and stay down."

Sniffing the air, I picked up on a new person—human or sorcerer, though I was too far away to make a positive identification. The overwhelming pine scent around me only complicated matters. I heard the dull sound of knocking—probably on the door of the RV, I surmised—and then low voices.

I held my breath. This would be fine. If someone had come to chide Maggie and Dave for trespassing, surely they'd apologize and drive on down the road. We could catch up, no problem…

A man shouted, but the sound was quickly muffled following the slamming of another door. Though I listened, I could hear nothing further of their confrontation.

Connor stared at me, wide-eyed and waiting for a cue, then twitched as his pocket began to buzz. He pulled out his phone—thankfully, he'd left it vibrating—and scanned the screen before wordlessly passing it to me.

The message came from Maya. *Rose says someone's taken D&M hostage. Thinks he's UP. Sorcerer. They're in the RV.*

Weapon? I texted back.

After a pause, she wrote, *No.*

Is he alone? I replied.

The response was quicker that time: *Yes.*

I handed Connor his phone, then beckoned him and Yacovi into a huddle around Taug. "We've got a rogue sorcerer in the RV with Dave and Maggie," I murmured. "Unarmed, but…"

"Sorcerer," Yacovi finished, nodding. "He may not need one."

"Rose thinks he's Unity Plan."

Yacovi muttered under his breath. "I'm a little slower than I was in my prime, but I'm pretty confident that I can take him."

"Do you have knockout on you?" Taug asked.

"No, I figured we wouldn't need to use it on you," he replied. "Lesson learned…"

"In any case, they're in the RV," said Connor. "How effective is that stuff if they're inside?"

"That thing ain't a closed container, especially if the air conditioner's running," Yacovi answered, "but yeah, knockout would be less effective. Slower to work, anyway. So," he said, looking between Taug and me, "what's the plan? I don't want to do anything that's going to get those two hurt."

We looked at each other for a moment, silently running the variables, and then Connor said, "I've got an idea."

"*You?*" said Taug.

"You know, they didn't hand me a badge for my rugged good looks and charm," he retorted, folding his arms. "I'm going to leave my gear here. Y'all approach on foot from this direction. Give me time to get around, and I'll approach from the road. Can you lure him out?"

"Pincer maneuver?" said Yacovi.

"Something like that. Subterfuge. Let me have a head start. When you hear an engine, head for the RV."

"An engine?" I echoed.

"If this works like I think it will. Fingers crossed," he said, flashing his, and set off through the woods, heading toward the exit route under the cover of the trees.

Tabitha, who was knotting off her latest stitch, muttered, "What the hell is that boy up to?"

"I'm not sure," I replied, "but if this goes sideways, *he* can explain it to Annie. Need a hand?"

"Under control."

We waited for a few long minutes, listening for the signal. Tabitha finished her work, but before she could bandage the wound, Yacovi stopped her. "Let's get him masked first. The band-aid will bunch up if you put it on now."

Taug sat up, wincing, but the stitches in his flank held. He thanked Tabitha and accepted a pendant from the plastic baggie in Connor's pack, then glanced at Tabitha and me and cleared his throat. "I don't mean to be crass, but unless you want an eyeful…"

"*Nope*," said Tabitha, turning her back, and with a snort, I joined her, leaving Yacovi to supervise the detail work.

Though he'd been on a desk for a time, Taug had a good memory for his mask, and he pulled it together with barely any adjustments from our resident expert. The two men dug in Connor's bag until they came up with a pair of gray sweatpants and a black T-shirt, and Taug gave us the all-clear once he was decent.

At least Connor's clothing fit. Masked, Taug was only a couple inches taller, and since Connor was of a more muscular build than the standard-issue elf, the two were roughly of a size. There were socks but no shoes in the bag, not a great help in the woods, but Taug was too busy finding his balance with the aid of a tree to worry about his soles. "Stand on your toes, if you need to," Yacovi suggested. "I had a centaur in the greenhouse who swore by that to acclimate."

"And I still need to get you bandaged up," said Tabitha. "Um…how do we want to go about this?"

Yacovi got creative with some spare clothing, and Taug bared his hind end to the poor pharmacist, who ignored his rump and bent to look at the wound. "The stitches are much closer together with the mask on," she reported, carefully applying bandages to the site. "You're still seeping a little, but we'll change the dressing this afternoon and see how you're doing. Assuming we survive our new buddy, of course. Uh, you can put those back on now," she muttered, retreating.

Taug pulled up his borrowed pants. "You're skittish around nudity."

"I'm unaccustomed to dealing with asses in my face. Aside from the odd customer."

He frowned. "They disrobe to buy medicine?"

"She's talking about assholes," Yacovi clarified, then repeated the term in Pactish. "See?"

Before Taug could answer that, I heard a mechanical revving on the other side of the clearing. "Save it," I said to the men, "that's our signal. Let's go. Taug, can you carry Connor's bag?"

And so we set off, me in the lead, Yacovi hanging back to help limping Taug, and Tabitha, armed with a folding knife, bringing up the rear. As we broke through the tree line, I kept my eyes on the RV, looking for motion within. I couldn't smell blood from that direction, which I took as a positive sign, but I didn't want the sorcerer to get jumpy and lash out. A steady pace seemed like the best bet. But how did we want to make our final approach? Stand outside the RV and try to coax the sorcerer into facing us in the grass? Bust through the door? Good luck with that if he'd bothered to lock it…

At least that portion of the plan was decided for me. We were perhaps two-thirds of our way to the vehicle when the side door opened, and then Maggie, her face drawn, slowly descended the steps. Behind her was a youthful blond with a complexion that suggested he hadn't seen much sunlight in the last decade. He wore jeans and a long-sleeved shirt, nothing unusual, but when he hailed us, it was in perfect Beukal Pactish. "Well, well," he said, smirking. "What do we have here?"

"That depends," I replied in kind. "You tell me, are we about to have trouble?"

"Hmm…you're the troll, aren't you?" he said, cocking his head. "Now, how'd you get all the way down here, huh? This is a friend of yours?"

I followed his finger to Maggie, who stood silently beside him. "Who's asking?"

"Is she with you, yes or no?"

"Why does it matter?"

He shrugged, then whispered, and suddenly, Maggie was clawing at her neck, gasping for air. "I mean, if she's not with you, then you won't mind if I dispose of her, right?"

"*Stop it*," I snapped, and his smirk deepened.

Another whisper released his chokehold on Maggie, who gasped and fell to her knees. "Thought so. You tripped my perimeter alarm," he said as she coughed. "Figured something was up, and when I spoke to them in Pactish…well, let's just say they need to work on their poker faces. Isn't that right, sweetheart?" he said, nudging Maggie with the toe of his boot.

"They're civilians, they're no part of this. Let them go."

"On the contrary," he said. "You've got *humans* working with you. That's proof that the Unity Plan is viable—"

"Those two are a special case," I said, cutting him short, "and you're out of your mind! Can't you see she's scared to death?"

In truth, I was trying not to look at Maggie. She'd been good to me, and the fear on her face made me want to try something violent and unwise with the sorcerer.

"Where's the man?" I asked.

He tossed his head behind him. "A little tied up. He's alive, if that's what you were wondering. But this won't do," he continued, and tsked. "Not at all. The point is for you to be *unmasked*—you and him both," he said, pointing to Taug. "Don't think I didn't recognize you, buddy. So, first things first, you're going to give me whatever masking jewelry you've found. If you don't...well, I'm sure the locals will have just as much fun with a dead troll and centaur as they would with the live models. Now, be a good girl and—"

The rest of his instructions were drowned out by the roar of a large motorcycle as it raced across the clearing. The sorcerer stiffened—clearly, this wasn't one of his friends—and he took a step back toward the RV's side door as the bike pulled around and came to a stop. Sitting atop it was a heavyset man with a full black mustache and beard, sporting a brown uniform, tall black boots, and a pair of mirrored sunglasses.

"Morning, y'all," he said with a pronounced drawl, dismounting the motorcycle, then straightened the holster at his hip and tapped the side of the RV. "Got a flat?"

Maggie, still kneeling in the grass, looked up and yelled, "Get out of here! That man's dangerous—"

Before she'd finished, the officer had his gun drawn and aimed on the sorcerer. "That so, ma'am?" he asked calmly. "Why don't you let me be the judge of that? Sir, step away from the vehicle, nice and slow." Glancing at the rest of us, he said, "Y'all step back, give us some room."

We heeded, and the unnerved sorcerer walked away from the door, showing the officer his empty hands. "I'm not here to harm anyone," he said, his English almost too accented to be intelligible. There were damn good reasons why we worked on pronunciation with those agents sent outside. "I've got *amazing* news for you—"

"I've already found Jesus," the officer interrupted, "and I ain't interested in whatever cult you're selling. Let's have some ID."

"No, listen, you don't understand," he said in a fumbled rush. "Magic is real. Those creatures in your stories? They're real, too. That woman's a troll," he said, jabbing his finger toward me, "and—"

"That woman's a goddamn *dime*," he said with an appreciative glance in my direction. "Shit, why would you call her a troll? Who're *you* dating, fucking supermodels?"

"No, she's masked, see? She's hiding her appearance, but if you take her jewelry off—"

"What're you on, meth or crack?"

"Uh…um…neither?" he said bemusedly. "I'm not sure what you're—"

"*Right.*" Not lowering his gun, he cut his eyes to the grass and picked up a long stick. "Okay, buddy, see this?" The sorcerer nodded, and the officer dropped it. "You're going to walk along that, real easy-like. Show me how we're doing."

At that, the sorcerer seemed to understand the problem. "I'm not crazy," he insisted, "and I'm not on anything mind-altering. If you'll let me prove it to you—"

"Just come over here, sir. Stand next to me."

Huffing an impatient sigh, the sorcerer did as he was told, then started to walk a straight line beside the stick. "Do whatever you need to do," he said as he moved away from the officer. "I'll pass any test. But humanity needs to know that magic exists, and it's time you learned to share—"

The officer made a quick gesture, and a blast of power hit the unwitting sorcerer in the back of the head. He grunted and fell face-first to the ground, and the officer said, "Yacovi, tranq him."

While Yacovi dug in the bag, I sat on the sorcerer's back, just in case. "Nice mask, kid."

"Thanks." With another gesture, Connor appeared where the officer had been, and then he flicked two fingers at the motorcycle, which vanished.

"How'd you do that?" I asked as he put his gun away.

"Heavy masking," he said, slumping like he'd just dead-lifted a car, then pulled a silver ring off his finger and showed me. "Experimental piece. One of my tutors at DOI wanted me to play around with it out here."

"What does it *do*?"

"Levitation and a short burst of speed—it's good for maybe a minute before it has to recharge. I just cooked up the bike to go with it." Pulling Maggie to her feet, he asked, "Are you okay? Did he hurt you?"

"I'll be fine," she said, rubbing her throat. "He tied Dave up and put him in the bathroom…"

"Let me," said Connor, and headed into the RV.

By the time he and Dave emerged, Yacovi was jabbing a needle into the sorcerer's shoulder. "What's that you're giving him?" asked Tabitha.

"This," said Yacovi, finishing the injection, "is a damp-ening potion. It'll prevent him from casting for a while…about a week, I'd wager." He carefully packed the syringe away and got to his feet. "Long enough for us to get out of here without any more trouble from him."

Connor looked at me and folded his arms. "How do you want to play this, Chief?"

Climbing off of the unconscious sorcerer, I replied, "I believe this one was *your* collar…Chief. Think I'll defer to local law enforcement."

"Oh, I'm *way* outside my jurisdiction," he replied, "but in that case…Dave, y'all got any duct tape?"

While Tabitha tended to Maggie and Taug introduced himself to the Humphrieses, Yacovi, Connor, and I bound the sorcerer's arms and legs, then carried him into the de-coy house and taped him to a support beam. Connor wrapped one of the sorcerer's hands in duct tape, and then, perhaps with a flash of conscience, grabbed a bottle of water from the RV fridge and taped it into the sorcer-er's other hand. He cracked the seal, loosening the bottle-cap sufficiently for the captive to remove it, and left enough of the man's arm unbound to allow him to drink.

He then gave the sorcerer's pockets a thorough pat-down and found a small knife and a phone, which he handed to me.

Yacovi had just slipped out with our prizes when the unlucky man began to come around. He groaned, then tried to move, and finally opened his eyes to find himself secured to a post and held off the ground by layers of duct tape. "What the hell..." he began, struggling to break loose, and then noticed us standing nearby.

"Hey, there," said Connor in his accented Pactish. "Looks like you're in a bit of a pickle, buddy."

The idiom didn't translate, but the sorcerer was too busy fighting for his freedom to worry over linguistics. He thrashed, trying to loosen the unforgiving tape, then started muttering...which increased in volume and urgency as the spells he was casting failed.

"Dampening potion," Connor told him, and the sorcerer stared at him in wide-eyed horror. "Don't fight too hard, now. Make that water last. You're going to be here for a while."

"You—"

"I'm going easy on you," he said, his voice dropping toward a growl. "But if I were you, I'd pray to whatever higher power you believe in that the portals open sooner rather than later, know what I mean?"

"You...you can't leave me here!"

"Watch us," I said, and started off with Connor right behind me.

As the sorcerer frantically begged us to come back, Connor muttered, "Sorry about the 'troll' comment back there."

"No offense taken." I gave him a sly glance, then said, "So, you think I'm a dime, eh?"

"Objectively speaking, that's one hell of a mask."

I chuckled. "Best not to say that too loudly around Jane."

"Eh, pretty sure she'd agree with me."

I slowed to let him catch up, then nudged him in the shoulder. "Interesting work with the bike. Got to admit, it's odd to see the elf come out of nowhere. Same goes for Rose," I added. "You don't have the look, but you've got the talent, kid."

He snorted. "Hey, what's the point of having magical power if you don't get creative with it from time to time?"

"Fair." Eyeing him, I said, "I heard all the East Branchers were getting, uh...makeovers, but not you?"

He tucked his short hair behind his ear, uncovering the rounded top. "Had the rest surgically removed as a new-born. Even if I'd wanted it back, it'd have been a pain to manage. But at least this way, I don't have to worry about masking."

"See, this is the kind of practicality that Laws is looking for...not today," I said as he shot me an exasperated glare. "But Kabno's persistent, just bear that in mind."

When we returned to the RV, we found the others huddled inside: Taug drinking water like he'd marched across a desert, Tabitha keeping wary watch over the patient, Dave rubbing his wrists, and Maggie sipping a pain potion under Yacovi's supervision. "Is everyone okay?" I asked.

"Getting there," Maggie muttered, and finished the vial. "You're right, that doesn't taste terrible."

"Vanilla and honey, yeah?" said Yacovi. "Better tasting than most liquid meds."

"Maggie, are you hurt?" I pressed.

She paused before answering that. "Shaken, I think. I'll be fine. I wasn't, uh...I wasn't expecting..."

"Magic?" Yacovi murmured.

"You're allowed to be weirded out," said Tabitha, leaning against the kitchen counter as Taug guzzled. "I've had a chance to come to terms with it."

"So have we," she protested. "Wylan certainly has abilities. But, um..."

"But you've never been attacked by spell," said Yacovi,

"you couldn't begin to defend yourself, and it was painful and terrifying." Maggie looked at him strangely, and he shrugged. "Hon, I've been out here for decades. I like to think I know a *teensy* bit about humans by now."

"Can you do that, too? What he did to me?"

Yacovi released a long breath. "Technically? Yes. That's not how we train in the agencies, mind you. If I wanted you unconscious and subdued, there are far quicker and easier ways to get you there. *That* was a kid who's watched too damn much *Star Wars* and thought it was a cool move, or whatever."

"But you *could* do it," she insisted.

He nodded. "Yeah," he said softly. "There's a lot that I can do. Quite a bit that I wouldn't do outside of an emergency, you know, but...I mean, cards on the table, I have significant talent. It's just who and what I am," he said, looking between Maggie and Dave. "I can sit here and tell y'all I'm not going to hurt you until I'm blue in the face, but somewhere deep down, you're not going to believe me. And *that*, in part, is why we need the Pactlands: you fear me. Now, maybe I can reason with the two of y'all, maybe you can get to the point where Tabitha is, where the twitchiness is mostly gone, but I can't reason with a *mob*. And here come these Unity Plan idiots, risking everything we've built because they think we can all just get along. Morons," he grumbled.

I cleared my throat. "Maggie, Dave, you've been wonderful to help us. If this is too much, if you want to go home, no hard feelings—"

"What? No," said Maggie, "*no*. We're in, right, Dave?"

He nodded. "Might not hurt to get a gun, though."

"I'll hook you up," said Connor. "Got a few back at the house."

"Not like you need them," said Maggie, faintly smiling. "I saw what you did to that guy..."

He cracked his knuckles. "This is all pretty new."

"Did you kill him?" Dave blurted.

Connor shook his head. "No, sir. Immobilized and up shit creek, but he's alive. And we took his toys," he added, producing the sorcerer's knife and phone.

"He mentioned a perimeter alarm, didn't he?" said Taug, and wiped his mouth on the back of his arm. "Do we want to find and disable it? Who else might be monitoring this portal?"

"Problem," said Yacovi. "If you take it down, it'll quite probably send out an alarm in the process. Better for whatever wards he's laid to stay intact. Still, there's no rule saying we can't throw his little friends off his trail..."

He and I traded looks, and I said to Connor, "Give me the phone."

It was locked, unfortunately, and so the sorcerer's contacts were hidden from us, but the phone was a Pactlands model, and I knew how to access the emergency contact. "All I've got is a first name," I reported. "Faran."

"And a number?" asked Tabitha.

"Yeah. That's one of ours..."

"Let me."

Frowning, I handed over the phone, then showed her what button to press to dial the emergency number. She made a quick search on her own phone, then called Faran on the sorcerer's phone and held it to her ear. When I heard a muffled greeting in Pactish on the other end, Tabitha's voice *changed*. The accent, the cadence—I barely recognized it, and I was staring straight at her.

"Hey, there," she began, her tone more nasal and her words more rapid and clipped. "Who is this?" She paused, listening, then said, "Well, Freddie, I've got some bad news about a friend of yours. I'm calling from Oconee Memorial in Seneca...Seneca, South Carolina, that's right. This phone came in with a John Doe. He was hit by a car, and they're stabilizing him, but he hasn't regained consciousness. The phone's messed up, looks like it's in Malaysian or something, I don't know. Guess I got lucky with you, huh? So, do you know this number?" Again, she listened, then made a face. "Jim Jones? You kidding me? His mama and daddy named him Jim freaking *Jones*?"

Connor snickered on the couch. "Looks like he *was* a cult leader."

Motioning for silence, Tabitha continued. "Okay, well, that's unfortunate, but at least we've got a name. Do you have any way to get in contact with his next of kin? In case he winds up in a coma…oh, *great*. Thank you so much. Look, tell them to come to the Oconee Memorial ER and ask for Trixie Donovan. That's me, I'm the charge nurse. Redhead, can't miss me. Want me to spell it?"

As she hung up, Connor pointed finger guns at her. "That was freaky."

"I have no idea what you're talking about," she replied, then returned to her normal voice. "What, you don't like Trixie?"

"I'm just impressed. That sounds, uh…"

"White?" she finished as he faltered. Smirking, Tabitha said, "I've dealt with my share of assholes who second-guess a black woman trying to keep them alive and healthy, so Trixie comes in handy on occasion. She works *deep* in the back of the pharmacy."

I glanced awkwardly at Maggie, unsure of my footing, then said, "When I first started masking, I was cautioned to go pale for my own safety. That was two hundred years ago, but…"

"It's somewhat better now than it was then, but it's not perfect by a long shot," said Tabitha. "You want to go blonde, I'm not going to hold it against you." She paused, then asked, "That's not your natural complexion?"

"Hell, no. I'm green."

"*Green*? Huh," she said, and gave me a longer look, as if she could see through the mask. "Like, um…"

"Somewhere between mature leaves and pond scum, if that's what you're after."

"Fascinating. I'm just wondering, but what's the cosmetics scene like in there? I mean, can you match foundation?"

"If the line is troll-made, yes, and *occasionally* you'll find something workable from nymph-owned companies—"

"*Whoa*, now," Yacovi interrupted, "before y'all go down that path, what're we doing with Jimmy boy's phone? And his car?"

Adrenaline and lack of sleep was a potent cocktail for disaster, I mused. "Right. The phone's coming back with us—surely someone at Laws knows how to hack it."

"Can confirm," muttered Taug, opening another water bottle.

"And as for the car...what about the university? We could hide it in a parking lot."

"On it," said Connor, heading for the door. "Assuming he left his keys in there. Y'all follow me, okay?" he said, looking back at Dave and Maggie. "I'd really rather not walk home."

CHAPTER 10

I'd never felt so warmly about a human as I did that morning when we shuffled back into Connor's house to the smell of blueberry muffins, eggs, bacon, and strong coffee.

"Figured y'all might be hungry," said Maya, scraping the last of the eggs into a bowl. "Any takers?"

"Where…where did all of this come from?" Connor mumbled, staring around his almost clean and highly fragrant kitchen as if he'd never seen the room before.

"I did some shopping before we left Richmond, remember?" said Maya, then pointed to his keyring. "And I drove over to Ragged Gap to pick up a few things I'd forgotten. Hope you don't mind."

"No, no…I think I love you."

She snorted. "Grab a plate. And hey, Maggie, I made you this," she said, pulling a tall mug from the microwave. "Thought it might help your throat."

"Oh, aren't you sweet," Maggie replied, taking the mug, and peered down into it. "Um, what is…"

"Lemon-flavored tea, honey, a little sugar…and a healthy splash of 'shine."

Maggie glanced at the clock, then said, "You know, that's okay," and took a bracing sip.

"Come on in," Maya called to the back of our pack. "Breakfast is ready. And hey, you must be Taug," she added in Pactish as he wobbled into the kitchen on his unsteady legs.

"Yes, I…" He paused, then frowned at her bemusedly. "Have we met? You look so familiar…"

"Ever been to the café in the DPP tower?"

"Sure...*oh!*" he cried, recognition dawning. "You had wings the last time I saw you."

"Got better, didn't I? And I also got a mind wipe that didn't really take as a parting gift, so what're you drinking?"

Though I could have devoured most of what Maya had put on the counter, I tried to be polite and limit myself, letting Taug eat his fill. Considering that he'd been in the woods for two days, it seemed only fair. But when the serving platters began to empty, Maya took stock of our plates, then pulled more eggs and bacon from the fridge, as well as a whole loaf of bread, which she toasted and buttered. In the end, I stuffed myself, and I wasn't the only one groaning in the den after our unexpected brunch.

"Has Rose called lately?" I asked, reconsidering my dietary choices.

"Nah," said Maya. "She's back at work, I think. Cut out after warning me about the sorcerer."

"So...she didn't leave our next coordinates, then?"

"Nope."

"Which means we rest while we can," said Yacovi, grunting as he pushed himself out of an armchair. "Taug, I'm not going to tell you how to live your life, but might I suggest a shower and bed?"

"That sounds *amazing*," he replied. "Um..."

"You stay here," Yacovi continued, and Connor nodded. "Gentle Breeze, I assume you'll want to camp near the computer."

I nodded.

"Okay. Since space is going to be a concern, can I offer y'all beds?" he asked Maya and the Humphrieses. "I've got two guest rooms. Or, uh..."—he hesitated, suddenly uncertain—"if y'all aren't comfortable with that, I'm sure Janie wouldn't mind if you crashed at her place. I've got the door code, and there's two bedrooms there as well."

"One hell of a bath," I muttered from the couch.

Dave and Maggie looked at each other briefly, and then Maggie, who seemed almost relaxed after her spiked tea, patted Yacovi's arm. "If you wouldn't mind having us, I think that'd be lovely."

"Are you sure? You're not going to hurt my feelings," said Yacovi.

She smiled. "Last time I checked, we're on the same team."

"That, we are."

"Besides," she said as Dave helped her up, "if you were to try anything, my son-in-law would have your hide."

Yacovi stiffened, then chuckled low. "Ma'am, there are few people in this world I'd like to cross less than the freaking Hunter. Y'all will be perfectly safe." Turning to Tabitha, he asked, "Are you okay to drive home, hon?"

"Actually, if Connor's okay with it, I'd like to stay here," she replied. "Keep an eye on the patient."

"Oh, you don't have to—" Taug began.

"I don't mind," said Tabitha, cutting him short. "And once I hear back from someone who knows the first thing about centaur biology and pharmacokinetics, I'll get you on an antibiotic. But for now, go upstairs and shower, and then let me check the wound site, okay?"

We shooed him along, and after Yacovi left a selection of pain potions on the kitchen table, he departed with his houseguests. Tabitha and Connor both offered to take a turn on the couch, but I insisted it was fine and sent them upstairs after Taug. "I'll be listening for the computer," I told them, then stretched out on the couch, pulled up the blankets, and promptly blacked out.

My respite was far too short. Around two-thirty, I woke with a cry when Sprik announced an incoming call, and I took a moment to untangle myself and remember where I was before I went to the kitchen to answer the summons.

Uncharacteristically for the well-dressed director, Kabno was still sporting her gray DOL hoodie when our cameras clicked on. She seemed better rested than she'd been the night before, but she hadn't taken pains to hide her weariness. "Morning, Director," I mumbled.

She arched a white eyebrow. "Afternoon, actually. Did I wake you?"

I groaned in the affirmative. "We had an early morning. Taug's asleep upstairs."

"I'd heard you'd found him. Is he all right?"

"Coyote bite to the flank, but our pharmacist sewed him up. She wants to talk to a healer about medicine dosing—"

"Yes, I saw the note in the system from Rose," said Kabno. "Just sent it to Canna Nerin. I know it's Saturday, but she's usually fairly prompt with these matters."

My lips twitched toward a smile. "And she can keep her mouth shut."

"*Precisely.* I'll send a message once I hear from her—no need to go to video."

"Anything from Rose?"

She sighed. "The kid's working, trancing, whatever it is they do. I'm waiting for updates," she said, flashing her phone at the camera, "but there's been nothing since she sent word about Berek. Anything I need to know?"

"Actually, yes. One moment," I replied, then slipped away from the table and returned with the sorcerer's phone. "Pulled this off of a Unity Plan member this morning. I can only get as far as his emergency contact, but I assume you can do more with it."

Her eyes lit. "Oh, *delightful.* That's one of our phones?"

"It is, but Connor's power cord fits. I can plug it into this laptop if that would help..."

"Yes. Connect it, let the computer access its data, and then you're going to run a backup scan on *everything.* Once that's finished—and it may take a few hours—upload it through this program and let me know. We'll take it from there." Smirking, she asked, "And did you just relieve him of his phone? Do I want to know?"

"He's alive," I told her, and plugged in the phone.

"Well, that's a start. Get me the scan as soon as you have it, and I'll be in touch." She paused, then said, "And go back to bed, Gentle Breeze. You look awful."

I ran one hand through my overly long blonde mop. "Can't be *that* bad. The mask hides the grease."

"I've seen enough masks to learn to see through them," Kabno replied. "Off with you, now."

I had the phone's contents to Kabno by four, and in the interim, she'd sent dosing directions from Canna. As I'd dozed while the phone was uploaded, I was rested enough to be antsy. When Tabitha came downstairs half an hour later, she found me in the den, watching television with the sound low. "Thought I heard movement," she said, her voice froggy. "Tea?"

"If you're making it, sure. Did I wake you?"

"Nah." Heading into the kitchen, she said, "Got a few hours of sleep and played on my phone. Are we going somewhere tonight?"

"Not to my knowledge," I replied, following her. "No word from Rose yet, but I did hear from one of Laws' healers."

"Who, Canna?"

I sighed. "Don't tell me she's part of the brunch crew."

Tabitha glanced at me and winced. "How much trouble would she be in, hypothetically?"

"I don't know whether she's authorized to be out here, but...*hypothetically*, you're acquainted?"

"She's a delight."

"She speaks English?"

"Well, *now* she does."

Assuming I made it home intact, I really would need to have a long talk with the quasi-human expats. "Anyway," I said, "she sent you notes. Come see."

Canna read over my shoulder as I pulled up the message, then grunted. "Yeah, okay, that's doable. I'll get the drugs tonight. In the meantime, should we think about dinner?"

We started rummaging around Connor's kitchen, but even with the groceries we'd brought, the pantry and fridge were sad. "I don't know how he lives on these," said Tabitha, pulling a boxed dinner from the stack in the freezer. "*Men*, I swear. Do you cook?"

"Passably."

"I'm decent in the kitchen. Any opposition to spaghetti?"

"Not at all."

"Great. I'm going to run to the store and pick up what we need…and maybe some more beer," she added, checking the selection in the fridge. "Bottle of wine. We'll see."

"Do you want, uh…company?" I asked. "I don't have *funds*, but—"

"Don't worry about it," she replied. "Why don't you get a shower, eh? You'll probably feel better."

I grinned. "The funk's strong enough for you to notice?"

"Barely, but it's not getting any fresher. I'll make tea when I get back."

Connor's guest bathroom paled in comparison to his fiancée's magical wonderland of marble and glass, but if I stayed masked while I showered, I could stand under the water without crouching. My masked form was about Connor's height, and he'd positioned the fixtures appropriately. Jane's presence in his life had extended into the shower, I noted, looking from the value-sized bottle of two-in-one shampoo and conditioner to the array of lavender-scented bottles with "Fortune's Fancies" labels, and I helped myself to the offerings. As long as I was dealing with the mask's hair, I figured it should get a good lather and smell nice.

Taug and Connor were up by the time I emerged, both

slumped in kitchen chairs like they'd been hit between the eyes. They grunted their hellos, and I explained where Tabitha had gone. "She doesn't have to cook," Connor protested. "I can order pizza again…and what about the others?"

A quick call to Maya revealed that they'd had a pleasant afternoon nap, she and Maggie were tearing up Yacovi's kitchen, and Dave was out in the barn with Yacovi, assisting. "Guy drove up with a couple of horses in a trailer," said Maya over the sound of sizzling. "Both of them threw shoes today. Yacovi's getting them shod, and Dave is, uh…"

"Staying out of our way," Maggie called.

"Exactly."

"He kills it, I cook it," Maggie added. "And things don't work well when we swap places."

I reported that there was no news from Rose, and with an admonition to keep them informed, they let me go to attend to dinner.

Tabitha returned in short order, her arms laden with bags of pasta, produce, and packs of hamburger. But though we offered to help, she declined, instead ordering Connor to take Taug and me out in search of clothing. "Walmart's open," she noted. "Or the clothes closet at First United Methodist stays open late on Saturdays—I think the youth get talked into running it or something."

Connor grunted. "Walmart's closer. And I still don't get why they're *First* United Methodist—they're the only Methodist church in either valley."

"I don't know, aspirational?"

Taug and I tried to protest that we didn't need much, which both Tabitha and Connor knew to be a polite fiction, seeing as my pants were literally hanging on to my shrunken hips by a string and Taug was barefoot and in need of underwear. And so, we piled into Connor's personal SUV and headed off to the supercenter in search of passing apparel, me with my hoodie pulled low over my waist and Taug sporting a too-big pair of Connor's sandals.

We made quick work of the shopping trip, and while Connor helped Taug find shoes that wouldn't throw off his balance, I tallied up the haul: jeans and athletic pants for both of us, T-shirts, a hoodie that actually fit me, undergarments, and pajamas. I felt guilty for the waste, considering what Maggie had bought me on Thursday, but it was so nice to put on clothes that were roughly my size.

The guys met up with me in the toiletries section as I assembled a kit for Taug. "A thought," said Connor. "Do we have any idea how big or small the other missing people are? Maybe we should pick up a few things now to save time down the road."

"Uh…" I made a face as I went over the list in my mind. "We've got a female naga, but I don't know her. Male faun, so he'll probably be on the short side masked—they don't often make themselves enormous. The other two are children."

Taug swore under his breath. "Who would dump fucking *younglings* out here?"

"Someone stupid, cruel, or desperate," I replied. "Probably best to wait, Connor. We'll make do, yeah?"

With the two of us clothed and Taug armed with a toothbrush, we headed back to the house, where Tabitha was just pulling garlic bread from the oven. "The sauce is nothing fancy," she cautioned. "My go-to recipe needs to simmer for hours, so this is mostly Prego."

I didn't care. Tabitha's spaghetti wasn't as complex as Maggie's meatball-topped delight, but dinner was more than passably good, and with our stomachs satiated—even my bottomless pit—Connor pulled out his good moonshine and offered a selection of games to pass the evening. I didn't recognize many, but I was an old hand at Uno, and I tried to keep the gloating to a minimum as I took the others down, one by one. After a couple rounds, Connor announced he was going to keep working on paying down his sleep deficit, while Tabitha took Taug upstairs to check on his wound before slipping back to Ragged Gap to pick up his antibiotics and a few more medical supplies. Alone, I kept vigil on the couch with a bottle of beer and the TV turned down low, waiting for the call to come.

It was nearly ten before Sprik yelled for attention once more. I jumped awake, having dozed off with a home renovation show, and ran to the kitchen to find Kabno waiting on the screen. "Sorry," I said, smoothing my couch-mussed hair. "What's up?"

"And I apologize for the late call, but…" She rolled her eyes. "We work with what's available, don't we? First, the phone."

"Any luck?"

"Oh," she said, smiling evilly, "*absolutely*. We broke in, and I had my people cross-check the contacts against our list of Unity Plan suspects. So very many matches."

"Now to find them…"

"Easier than you might think. DOI has been involved in this mess since Thursday," said Kabno, "and they've got locations for many of our new friends. With the phone records and an assist from the Tribunal building, we've brought in six already."

I grinned. "Who's the judge?"

"Smoke. He and Diriem have been chummy for ages, and Diriem called in a favor to pull him to the office on the weekend."

I knew the judge—The Scent of the Smoke of the Home Fire, who was still working deep into his seventh century. He'd been on the Tribunal longer than I'd been alive, and while we weren't more than professional acquaintances, he'd always been polite…well, as judges went.

"Has anyone flipped?" I asked.

Kabno shook her head. "Not yet, though the night is young. Someone will talk soon, I guarantee it. The evidence is stacked against them, and at least one of them will wise up after a couple days in the cells. But that's not the best part of the phone cache."

"Oh?"

"Mm-hmm. Turns out your boy had a *number* of portal agents in his recent calls."

I winced. "*Ooh.* You don't say."

"I do! And DOI says they're dirty, every one of them. They've also been arrested—we've kept Smoke busy in the last hours." Shaking her head, she said, "I don't know why DOI doesn't clamp down harder on the Portal Authority. They've got oversight, right? If I were Diriem, I'd move to bring the Portal Authority fully into DOI and put one of my people in charge, but…"

"More of a headache than it's worth?" I guessed.

"Possibly," she allowed, "and while I didn't tell you this, there have been *large* campaign donations made to several Forum reps from the executive end of the Portal Authority. Something tells me they wouldn't relinquish their autonomy without a brawl…but that's not my problem today. Now, here's the good news: the portal agents caught up with the Unity Plan were lazy."

"How so?"

She chuckled. "If they'd been smart, they'd have sent you all over the continent. But they didn't bother looking beyond the southeastern cluster of portals."

My heart lifted. "So—"

"Everyone is relatively close to Beukal," Kabno finished. "You won't be driving to Alaska. But I swear, if those agents had been halfway competent, this could have been catastrophic."

"It still could be," I reminded her. "We have four in the wind. Far too soon for congratulations."

"Perhaps, but I'll sleep better, anyway." She paused to rub at her eyes. "So, how's Berek?"

"On the mend. We fed him—well, *Tabitha* fed us," I amended. "She's a good cook. Connor got clothing for Taug and me, and the boys have gone to bed…hold that thought." I rose and glanced out the front door, then returned to the computer. "Tabitha's back, so she's probably sleeping as well. She left to get meds for him, and I must have been dozing when she returned."

"Glad you're getting some rest. Now," she said, and pointedly cleared her throat, "Rose *might* have told me what became of the sorcerer whose phone you retrieved."

I shrugged. "He's alive, isn't he?"

"For now, yes…"

"And he's in a situation of his own making. What else were we meant to do with him?" I protested. "The portals aren't open, we couldn't let him go, and we certainly couldn't drag him back here."

"Correct me if I'm mistaken, but you're currently staying with the local chief of police, yes? Does he not have access to a secure facility?"

"I'm sure he does," I replied, "but one, Central's an hour away, and we'd have had to drive him back here— and that's with Annie's parents having been attacked and left spooked. I wouldn't do that to them. Two, even neutralized, that's a sorcerer we're talking about, and I doubt that Connor would leave him with his team here. Unnecessary risk, especially since he speaks English."

Kabno flinched as the ramifications hit: the Whitford officers might think he was a lunatic, but then again, they might not. "So, you just left him to his fate?"

"He's got shade and water, and that's more than Taug and I had," I retorted. "Yes?"

"Fair point," she muttered, "and frankly, I'm too tired to argue with you. Did he hurt them? The humans?"

"He tied Dave up, but he strangled Maggie. She seems to be made of sturdy stuff," I said, "but she's shaken. The first time you're attacked by magic is seldom fun."

"No, certainly not."

"And while we're on the subject of sorcerers, how many more are out here?"

The director hesitated before answering. "We're unsure of an exact number. Probably not more than ten, but between bringing in the ones here and looking for the missing out there—"

"It's not a priority," I finished. "Understood. One more question."

"Of course."

"Is anyone involved in this connected with Gerem Aniap?"

She frowned. "We haven't made a connection yet. What's roused your suspicion? Is Connor concerned for Jane's safety? I assure you, Aniap's secure out at Cavimet."

I didn't doubt it—DOL's penal farms were notoriously difficult to escape. "He hasn't mentioned Aniap if he's worried," I replied. "I've been trying to figure out why I was targeted. The other five have Forum connections, and the only explanation I can come up with is that I'm as close to the Hunt as they can get. Every member of that office's staff is a Huntsman, and Annie's one of them now. I'm the only weak link, but considering how few know of my boyfriend's *other* identity…"

"Aniap knows," she murmured, nodding.

"Exactly. Moonless Night unmasked in front of the Tribunal Committee a couple years ago…uh, let me see, that was Kug venDar, Mirrik Voln—"

"Those two are clean," said Kabno.

"Right. Then there was Sunlight Breaking Across a Foggy Lake—he was actually respectful to Moonless Night as an elder, so I can't imagine him being involved. Um…two elves," I said, squinting at the ceiling, "ti'Ansha and ti'Pon, if I remember correctly. And Puln Berek. Who else was there?" I muttered to myself, counting on my fingers—and since my masked form had five instead of four, I skipped the thumb. "Me, Wylan, Moonless Night, Annie, the committee…there were two researchers in the room," I recalled, "experts in theoretical magic. A sorcerer and a nymph. I remember that they were female and Aniap was being an ass to them, but that's all."

"Easy enough to investigate. I'll call Kug—she'll know where the minutes are."

But I wasn't finished. "Hakk Frondan knows—Moonless Night had to unmask because his horses weren't strong enough."

Her mouth twitched into a little smile. "Hakk would tell the Unity Plan that they're idiots. I sincerely doubt that our horsemaster is involved."

"As do I. But I don't recall exactly who was training in that rescue group. Moonless Night and Wylan, me, Annie, Emarae ti'Mal…Kov Venanu and Fell ti'Mal from Laws…"

"I've got that list."

"And then there's Director ti'Dana, naturally. I don't know how many in his household are aware, but I doubt that he or Rose have joined the Unity Plan. Or ti'Ansha," I added. Rose's fiancé lived in the mansion with her, but the kid was one of our Regulatory agents—and as long as Rose wasn't in danger, he tended to play things straight. "And since I don't see any of the Hunt trying to piss off Wylan, that leaves Aniap as my best source for the leak. Given his history, I don't trust anyone in his old office."

"You're probably not wrong," said Kabno. "I'll pass this to DOI—pretty sure they'll concur."

"Thanks. So," I said, wearily chuckling, "any idea where we're headed next?"

She shook her head. "Rose was pulled to assist with the arrests. The youngling's working hard, and she needs to sleep. I assure you, as soon as I have word, I'll be in touch. Go back to bed."

Kabno could be bossy, I thought, snuggling in on the couch, but she made a convincing argument.

Sunday morning dawned cool and drizzly, and when I peeked over the back of the couch to look out the windows, I discovered that the fog had stolen our vehicles. As there was no need to get up yet, I buried my face against the cushions, feigning sleep while Connor, trying and failing to be quiet, made coffee. When the computer blared to life and Sprik announced an incoming call request with *far* too much enthusiasm for the hour, Connor yelped, then swore as something hit the tile. He'd dropped a full scoop of coffee grounds, I saw as I walked in to silence the damned thing, and with an impatient gesture, he gathered them off the floor and floated them across the kitchen to the trash can.

The boy wasn't fully elven, sure, but he was making progress.

I slid into my chair, swiped my hair from my face, and was grateful that the person on the other side of the screen couldn't smell my morning breath, as I was still tasting the garlicy ghost of dinner. But when I accepted the call, it wasn't Kabno on the other end.

"*Rose?*" I said, taking quick stock of her. Charitably, she looked like she hadn't slept well in a week, a slumping mess with dark circles beneath her weary gray eyes and long, snarled red hair in dire need of shampoo. Fradin had rarely reached that point during our shared cases, and when he had, I'd usually coaxed him off to bed with the threat of bodily harm.

"Hey, Chief," she mumbled, and paused to drain the dregs of a large mug that I sincerely hoped had been full of espresso. "How's it going?"

The fact that she was speaking English was testament to her exhaustion. "Hey, kid," I said in kind. "Tell me you're not running on Happy Juice."

She smiled faintly. "Nah. I hate that stuff. Just good, old-fashioned java…oh, thank you, sweetie," she said as a hand holding a steaming mug appeared on the side of the screen. Rose took it and drank, squeezing her eyes closed as the hot drink went down.

"Is that ti'Ansha with you?" I asked.

Yven popped into the frame behind Rose and waved. "Morning, Chief," he said in Pactish.

"Ah, good. Yven, I assume you've been excused from

work for the duration, yes?"

The pair nodded. "Syvin said it's okay," mumbled Rose.

"And speaking of whom," said Yven, "she, Emarae, Pars, and a handful of others I'm forgetting because it's far too early—"

"Five-twelve!" Connor called from across the room.

"Right. They say hello and ask that you take care of yourself out there."

It was nice to be remembered, both by my Regulatory counterpart and by some of my agents. "Thank them for me," I replied, then joked, "but what, no word from the director?"

At that, Rose smirked before sipping. When she came up for air, she said, "Pateme's downstairs right now, strategizing with Kabno and Pop. Yven's babysitting me—"

"Poorly," he quipped.

"Because I've got too much to do to sleep," said Rose, though she shot him a fond smile. "And I'm working from home because the furniture is *infinitely* more comfortable here than at the office."

I could believe it. The guest mattresses in the ti'Dana mansion were theft-worthy.

"And the office is working with a reduced crew right now, anyway," added Yven. "All available personnel have been put at the other agencies' disposal to find the culprits and get the Pactlands stabilized."

"I see you've avoided being drafted by Laws, then," I said.

Yven rolled his eyes. "You and I both know that arrests aren't my specialty."

"Only teasing, ti'Ansha," I replied. "You're where you need to be."

Suddenly, Connor leaned over the back of my chair and waved. "Hey, y'all. How're we doing?"

They made nearly identical faces, and I bit my lip to

stop from chuckling.

"Not so great," said Rose. "Plenty more Unity Plan members still in hiding, and since Laws needs current information, that's all on me. And I'm trying to keep an eye on the missing as well…"

"It's all right," I said gently. "Do you have the next pick-up for us?"

"Yeah, who's most at risk?" asked Connor.

She groaned into her coffee. "Look, I'm worried about all of them, but the one in most immediate danger is Ermonir venTala."

I'd expected her to name one of the children, but Ermonir also made sense. Nagas could hide in thick enough woods, but there was no telling where she'd been dumped—and to human eyes, a woman who seemed to be half snake might well incite a panic.

Connor pulled his phone from his sweatpants' pocket. "Where is she?"

"She was dumped near the Crossville portal," said Rose.

"Crossville…"

"Tennessee."

He grunted, then tapped at his phone. "Okay, we're looking at a four-hour drive. Can you give us any landmarks as to where she is?"

"Some. The area south of Crossville is forested, and there's a state park, so you've got a fair number of hiding places. She's in an isolated house in a wooded area."

His eyebrows rose. "Convenient hiding spot."

"Not exactly. She was discovered."

My gut clenched. "What do you mean, *discovered*?" I demanded. "Like Maya found me, or…"

I left that unfinished, hoping Rose would confirm the first option, but she shook her head. "She was dropped along a backroad, and she could have hidden in the woods had she come to in time."

"She was captured?"

The girl nodded. "Ganti and I pieced it together."

I hadn't had much cause to work with Ganti ti'Van, perhaps the best of DOI's past-oriented farseers, but I knew the name. "And?"

"Some men in a pickup truck were driving through and spotted her—she was lying halfway in a ditch, and they stopped. Once they saw what she was, one of the group wanted to leave her or shoot her on the spot, but the other two had a better idea," she said sourly. "They loaded her in the bed, tied her up, and took her home with them."

"To what end?"

Rose's disgust deepened. "The guys who found her make porn—"

"*Porn?*"

"Yeah, and not the consensual kind. They've got a house back in the woods that they use for filming—sets, equipment, too many hard drives. There's a whole dungeon in the basement, and Ganti says these guys are traffickers on top of everything else. He, uh…he found some filming sessions."

"Well, that's awkward," said Connor.

"I've mentioned the concept of brain bleach," Rose replied, "and he dearly wishes it existed."

"But what's their plan with Ermonir?" I asked.

"From what we've gathered, it looks like they want to film some freaky fantasy stuff with her," she explained. "They've got her locked up in the basement."

"She's…cooperating?"

"Not exactly. She can't speak English, so she probably doesn't have a clear idea of what's going on, but she tried to escape once, and they shot her."

"Fuck," Connor muttered. "Is she…"

"Two bullets in the tail. They're small, and she's in pain, but she's not bleeding out," said Rose. "Assholes have her manacled to the wall."

"But she doesn't understand them?" I pressed.

Rose shook her head. "Nope. We cross-checked with

the Forum—she's never had training for going outside. She's an aide, you know? Never had a need for a human language."

I could only imagine the woman's terror. As panicked as I'd been on awakening, at least I spoke the local tongue and had some firsthand experience with humans, and thank the heavens, I'd been treated kindly. Ermonir was injured and chained, and even if she couldn't understand her captors, surely she had some sense of her predicament.

"And we don't have an address?" asked Connor. "Co-ordinates?"

"I'm working on it," she said. "Get to Crossville, and I'll guide you in as well as I can."

He started to respond, but I interrupted. "Get some rest," I told Rose, "and contact us when you can. We'll leave someone here with the computer as before." Turning to Connor, I said, "Call Yacovi. I'll wake Tabitha and Taug. We need to move."

By six-thirty, everyone had rendezvoused at Connor's house. Dave and Maggie seemed almost refreshed—I suspected Yacovi had supplied a little potion to take the edge off—and while Taug grimaced when he moved too quickly, he insisted he was fit for duty.

I left Maya in charge of the computer, and she didn't fight me. While the other seven of us *could* have crammed into the RV, Connor suggested that he take an SUV, a vehicle certainly easier to maneuver in tight spaces. Dave climbed behind the wheel of the RV again, and I designated Maggie the point person for communications while I slipped into the shotgun seat of Connor's Hyundai. Yacovi and Tabitha joined the Humphrieses—welcome passengers, as Yacovi magically handled the RV's waste situation before they set off.

Though I wasn't altogether surprised when Taug opted to ride with us, I tried to dissuade him. "It's a decently long drive," I warned, "and there's room to stand in the RV."

"My leg prefers sitting," he countered, and sprawled across the back. "And if I'm in there, Tabitha will keep checking on me. She needs a break."

"She's been hovering?" Connor asked, watching as Dave began backing down the driveway.

"Not badly, she's just attentive, and I'm fine."

I grunted. "How many pain potions are we on, again?"

"No comment." Settling in, Taug asked, "So…four hours, was it?"

"At least," said Connor, "depending on how quickly Rose can narrow the search area."

"And when you tire—"

He laughed low, then slipped into English. "You ain't from around here, are you?"

"Huh?"

"Four hours isn't bad at all," he said in Pactish. "You're just spoiled by the internal portals. And this shouldn't be a rough trip—we won't be on the Interstate, but at least it should be somewhat scenic," he added, consulting the map on his SUV's screen. "Sit back, try to relax. If we need to stop or you want to switch to the ride with an actual bed, just let me know."

Taug muttered his thanks as we pulled in behind the RV, letting the slower vehicle set the pace. We were approaching the town line when he spoke again: "Does no one think this is a massive security risk? Four humans caught up in this, and one of them left alone with a *DOI* computer?"

I glanced back over my shoulder at him. "Maya worked in the DPP tower, remember."

"Yeah, but in your café. That's a sensitive piece of equipment—"

"Which we can't bring along," Connor interrupted. "Personally, I'd rather have you, Gentle Breeze, and Yacovi in the field, Tabitha doesn't speak Pactish, and it's generally a safer bet to leave an unfamiliar computer with a Millennial over a pair of Boomers, no offense to Maggie and Dave."

"Come again?" said Taug.

"Trust the younger person to handle the tech," I clarified.

"But do you *trust* her? Really, with everyone's safety on the line, *can* you trust her?" he pressed. "I mean, she's human…"

That hung for a moment, and then Connor cleared his throat. "Have you ever lived out here in this world?"

Taug shook his head. "No, of course not. I'm no grower."

"You don't, like, predate the Pact—"

"Uh, *no*," he replied with a snort. "I would be ridiculously ancient."

"So, what you're saying then is you don't have much experience with humans."

Taug hesitated before answering. "I've been trained…"

"That doesn't count. Look," said Connor, "I come from a community that had to isolate itself for safety, but I live with the general public. And folks had *all* kinds of questions about East Branch. Made jokes—I could do at least a solid ten-minute routine from that material. But in the end, they tried to do right by my family. When East Branch burned"—he paused and swallowed hard—"multiple agencies came out to help. Volunteers, too. The case is still open, and though I'm pretty damn sure they're never going to solve it, they've still got a reward on offer for information. And the county's worked with me to deal with the cleanup and, you know, the general lack of documents." After a long sip of coffee, he said, "Humans aren't inherently evil. They're not inherently *good*, but most folks aren't fucking monsters."

"Individually…" I murmured.

"Sure, you get a mob together, and shit goes down, but people out here aren't all bloodthirsty maniacs, which is what I sense most of you seem to believe."

"Perhaps not *bloodthirsty*," Taug mumbled from the back. "Just…you understand why we fled this world, don't you?"

"Yeah, I've heard. And I'm not judging—hell, East Branch kept outsiders at bay with guns. But considering the hundred-percent-human half of this group…come on, man, Maya's fine, Dave and Maggie are decent people, and Tabitha's played nice with freaking DOI." When Taug didn't immediately respond, Connor said, "I get it. My cousins at East Branch were taught to fear outsiders, too. But speaking as someone who grew up human, living and working with humans, they're not all out to kill you."

"Okay, so if I unmasked right now and went for a stroll through the nearest town—"

"Either panic or people wondering how the *obvious* illusion was being done," Connor replied. "Not a great plan. *But*." He chuckled and adjusted the air conditioning.

"But what?" asked Taug.

"Don't get offended."

"Very well…" he muttered warily.

"So, there are centaurs in human mythology, right? All those Greek and Roman stories. You're supposed to be either, like, really good at medicine or prone to running off with women."

"I've heard as much. Just so we're all clear, human women do *nothing* for me."

"Noted. Anyway, there was this girl in my year all through school, Jill Cowper. She was freaking obsessed with horses when we were little, and then she discovered Greek mythology."

Taug groaned.

"Used to draw centaurs all over her notebooks," Connor continued. "She grew out of it eventually. Jill's a large-animal vet now, and she breeds horses on the side. She's done some rescues with Yacovi, actually—rehabs abused horses, finds good homes for them."

"Sounds decent," I said.

"Oh, I've got no quarrel with Jill. But here's the thing: I know in my *soul* that if Taug were to walk up to her unmasked, that'd be the happiest day of her life. She'd lose her ever-loving mind."

Taug laughed quietly behind him. "I'm really not that exciting."

"You've never met Jill." Sobering, Connor said, "In all seriousness, I understand the fear. Coming at it from the other side, I freaked out a little once I got to know Jane and everything going on in her orbit. You think you've got life figured out, right, and suddenly, there's a nymph detective and a half-centaur kid and so many damn *elves*—"

"Wait, half-centaur...the abandoned Voln girl?" he interrupted. "You were mixed up in that?"

"Tangentially. Jane and Tabitha took the lead with her, and I came snooping around because my lovely fiancée has a bad habit of vigilante arson. So, all of that was weird, and it got exponentially worse once I figured out I was a part of the weirdness...but if I can work with DOI when they'd stalked us clear across the continent, then surely you can give the other half of our group a chance, yeah? They're not running and screaming yet."

"And they're expending resources on this mission," I added. "Money, time...they don't owe us anything, but they're here."

"I...suppose that counts for something," said Taug, and turned to stare out the window in contemplative silence.

CHAPTER 11

Several hours and one most welcome pit stop later—a necessity for the gas-guzzling RV—we were about twenty miles outside of Crossville when Connor's phone began to ring. He answered with a touch of a steering wheel button. "Yes, ma'am?"

"Connor? Hi," came Maggie's voice. "Can y'all pull off and come join us for a minute?"

"Yeah, sure, I'll follow you. Everything okay?"

"Maya just called. Tell you once we're stationary."

After a few minutes, the RV pulled into the cracked parking lot of an old strip mall, and we followed suit. We disembarked, and Tabitha opened the side door as we walked over. "Got an update," she said. "Huddle time."

Once the seven of us were clustered in the seating area, Maggie took the lead. "So," she said, "Rose called, and Maya passed the message along. The farseers have more information."

I arched an eyebrow.

"The people who have Ermonir—the *filmmakers*," she said with pursed-lip distaste—"have a contact with a Pactlands accent."

"What sort of accent?" Taug asked. "Are we talking standard Beukal, old elf, what?"

"They didn't specify, but they're pretty confident that he's a sorcerer. He's been instrumental in bringing his partners some of their, uh…talent."

I grimaced. "How so?"

"Apparently, he's been around here enough to know

how to find girls in bad situations, and he's got the toolkit to subdue them and bring them to the house for filming. When the men are finished, he knocks the girls out again and dumps them elsewhere. That way, they don't know where the house is."

"Oh, lovely," Connor muttered.

"And they bring in a steady stream of new talent," Maggie continued. "High viewer numbers, and since they specialize in…um…"

"Fetish," Tabitha supplied. "BDSM. Kinky stuff."

"Thank you, dear," Maggie mumbled, reddening. "They need a lot of fresh faces because they're not exactly gentle. Anyway," she said, "Rose's colleague who sees things in the past, uh…"

"Ganti," I said.

"Yes, that's right. Rose said that he watched some of the more recent events and saw the sorcerer promise the guys a *really* interesting delivery in a few days' time."

Connor grunted. "Lines up with when they found Ermonir, huh?"

"That's Ganti's thought," said Maggie.

The plan was evident: the sorcerer wanted them to make Ermonir notorious. If they had a sufficiently large audience and people shared the videos…

Taug seemed to have reached the same conclusion, as he said, "They get her online, humans see her, they start talking…shit."

But Connor and Tabitha shared a look, both clearly unimpressed. "I'm not super-concerned about that," said Connor. "If this sorcerer thinks some online porn is going to lead to a mass revelation, he's way too optimistic."

"If people see her—" Taug began.

"They'll think it's special effects," Tabitha interrupted. "Look, the Internet is full of amateur porn, even freaky porn. Folks will think she's in a costume, or maybe there's CGI involved…"

"Or maybe the whole thing's AI," Connor suggested.

"*Right.* No one's going to believe she's an actual naga unless they're also in the market for a tinfoil hat."

"Exactly," he said, and turned to Taug. "Man, you could film Bigfoot out for a stroll in the woods, and most people wouldn't believe the video was real."

His brow furrowed. "Bigfoot?"

"Sasquatch? Giant apelike creature that leaves footprints yet somehow manages to go almost undetected?"

"Bigfoot doesn't exist," said Tabitha.

Connor wiggled one hand. "I wouldn't be so sure. Swear to God I heard a 'squatch call back in the mountains when I was in high school."

At that, she glanced at Yacovi, who shrugged. "Never seen anything myself," he said, "but…maybe?"

"Whatever," Tabitha replied. "The point, Taug, is that the tech is good enough now that it's far more likely that people would see Ermonir and assume she's either fully virtual or heavily edited."

"Really?" He turned to me, doubt in his eyes, then looked to Yacovi. "You think?"

"Oh, she's right on the money," Yacovi said without hesitation. "And I see the grand agency tradition of not keeping up with the tech out here continues."

"We do a decent job of it," Taug protested.

"Dude," said Connor, "I have *seen* your decoy human operating system. It's decades out of date."

Sliding in before Taug could argue, I said, "Which means that maybe this sorcerer doesn't understand the flaws in his plan. But that's not important. We've got to get Ermonir out of there."

"Of course," said Maggie, "and that's the other thing I was going to pass along. Rose is watching the house right now. She's going to give us a call once she has a good idea of who's there so we don't go in blind."

"*You* two aren't going in," I said, pointing to her and Dave, "and Tabitha—"

"Our victim's been shot. Save it," she ordered.

"You go at the rear, then," I told her. "We need you intact, eh?"

With the update delivered, we returned to Connor's vehicle and continued toward Crossville, eventually stopping about five miles outside of town at another gas station. As Dave headed for the convenience store, Maggie's phone rang, and she put it on speaker. "Maya?"

"Hey, there," she replied. "Good news: there's no trace of the sorcerer at the house. Just two of the guys and a handful of women."

"These women are…"

"Probably not going to get in your way," said Maya. "From what Rose was saying, they're restrained."

I gritted my teeth.

"And Ermonir is still in the basement," she continued. "As are the guys. They seem to be editing right now. All yours."

"Do we have an address?" Maggie asked.

"Oh! Yes, sorry. They actually sent me a pin on a map…hang on, I'll text it…"

While Maggie waited for the directions and Dave settled in with his Sprite, I considered our numbers and vehicles. "Right," I said once the promised map had arrived. "Here's how we're doing this. Yacovi, you're with Taug, Connor, and me in the SUV. Dave, Maggie, Tabitha, you *follow* and keep your distance. At least a hundred yards, let's say."

"I can help…" Tabitha protested.

"I know," I said, not wanting to insult her, "but let us hit them hard before you come in to save the day, all right?"

The look she shot me told me she knew *exactly* what I thought of her usefulness in a raid, but she didn't argue.

Once Maggie and Connor were clear on the directions, we loaded up again, with Connor taking the lead that time. Slowly, being mindful of the trailing RV, he drove into the wooded mountains southeast of the city, then pulled onto the side of a road that was barely two lanes and in dire need of repaving as we neared the target.

"Why are we stopping?" asked Taug.

"Because," said Connor, unbuckling as the RV rumbled into place behind us, "engine noise is a giveaway. Have you noticed the lack of traffic around here? If we drive up, they might hear us."

"The basement could be soundproof," I suggested.

"Maybe, maybe not. Personally, I'd like to give these assholes as little warning as possible." Turning in his seat to Taug and Yacovi in the rear, he asked, "Is walking going to be a problem?"

They shook their heads, and with a curt nod, he climbed out and raised the trunk. As we joined him, he opened a bag and began passing out armored vests. "Thought these might come in handy," he said, adjusting his. "Better for Tabitha to not have to practice on a chest wound, right?"

As our medic and the Humphrieses watched, we passed around Connor's selection of pistols, and he slung a rifle across his back. Yacovi returned to the RV long enough to grab makeshift potion kits for himself, Taug, and me, bandoliers of tiny bottles held in place with elastic. With final assurances to Maggie that we'd be careful and would call once the coast was clear, we started up the road single file.

Our destination came into view around a bend, a decently sized cabin that had seen better days. The porch sagged, one shutter seemed to be hanging on through sheer inertia, and the small front yard, which contained little actual grass, appeared to have been mowed with a weed whacker. Connor, who'd taken point, lifted a hand to stop us and studied the house, then beckoned Yacovi closer. "I see a camera by the door," he murmured. "Any wards?"

"Nothing obvious," Yacovi replied, "and I won't be able to sense them until I'm right up on them if anything's there. Honestly, that camera may be their only warning—

hard to reset wards if you can't cast, you know?"

Too well. My security company charged a fee every time my alarms were tripped, as I couldn't manage the wards on my own.

"Okay. Do we want to split up and look for a back door," Connor asked the group, "or do we want to go in the front?"

I sized up the cabin briefly, then said, "Front. If the basement is where they keep captives, then there's probably no door on that level. Let them get away if they can—we're here for retrieval first, yeah?"

Taug and Yacovi concurred, and Connor made a final check of his weapons. "Ready?"

"Ready," I said. "And kid?"

"Yeah?"

"Leave the door to me."

We jogged toward the house, Taug muttering curses under his breath at the abuse to his injured leg, and the others clustered on either side of the door as I took the central position. While masking changed my size and shape, it did nothing to my constitution—nor did it affect my strength, merely compressing it into a smaller package. With the men armed and prepared, I gave the door a quick inspection, then delivered a firm kick near the knob. To my surprise, it splintered—the door was as old and decaying as the rest of the house, not a reinforced piece as I'd feared, and with a second kick, what was left of it swung open.

We swarmed into the cabin, and I scanned for threats. Standing in the main room, a combination den and dining space, I could smell multiple humans, a fug of unwashed bodies, sweat, waste, alcohol, and greasy food—a mixture of male and female, if my nose was working properly. And *yes*, half hidden in the scent profile was a distinctive sorcerer note. I saw nothing of concern...but then I caught movement from the corner of my eye and wheeled to my right to look down a shadowed hallway. A disheveled woman was peeking out of a door—a girl, more like, perhaps twenty—and she stared at us with round, frightened eyes.

"Where are they?" I whispered.

A hand emerged from her hiding spot, and she pointed to the floor.

"Where's the door leading down?"

Before she could answer me, I spotted an unassuming beige interior door by the kitchen garbage can. Connor caught it as well, then swept his empty hand toward the door and whispered, "Ladies first."

I opened it with a swift kick, but before I could charge, Yacovi tugged me back. "Allow me," he said, then muttered until a pair of fireballs appeared in his hands.

"Learning from your daughter?"

"Please. This goes back to my school days," he said. "Connor, shield."

To the kid's credit, he managed to pull together a decently solid shield in about three seconds, and he took point again on the way down, with Yacovi lighting the way behind him. Taug and I hurried after, clutching our borrowed guns, which we trained on the pair of pasty men who'd jumped from their swiveling computer chairs and been herded against the back wall by the advance party.

Sure, trolls were inherently strong, but there were *reasons* for having sorcerers or elves along on a raid.

The first room in the basement wasn't well lit, mostly illuminated by the quartet of monitors sitting on the long folding table pressed against the wall near the stairs. I picked a pair of towers out of the jumble of components, plus several dozen labeled hard drives. Considering the images on the screens, the men had been in the middle of an editing session when we came in—well, or so I dearly hoped. I could smell evidence of sex in the basement, but it wasn't so fresh as to suggest that we'd caught them in the act. Much more concerning was the scent of blood...and *yes*, there it was.

"She's here," I said, training my gun on the duo. "I can smell her."

"Excellent," said Yacovi. "Would you two mind holding our little friends here for a moment?"

As Taug and I kept the frightened, and now babbling, humans pinned to the wall, Yacovi extinguished his fireballs and pulled a pair of potion vials from his bandolier. A syringe came from an interior pocket, and he quickly drew up the peach sedative from one vial and jabbed it into the nearer man's shoulder. The human fell to the floor with barely time to yelp, and as his companion began hyperventilating, Yacovi injected him as well, knocking him out.

"The grab-and-stab. Classic," I said. "Didn't get to do that much in the greenhouse, did you?"

"Never hurts to keep your skills sharp," he replied, putting the used syringe and empty vials away. "All right, let's find her."

The search wasn't long. A door across from the stairway opened into what had to be a filming set, a dimly lit dungeon outfitted with equipment whose purpose I could only guess at. The room smelled of leather and plastic, of blood and vomit and other fluids, of cheap floor cleaner. And there, attached to the wall by manacles, was a naga.

She was naked—no great surprise there—and her black and brown tail coiled protectively around her tanned torso. Unusually for a naga, she hadn't shaved her head, and her black hair fell in dirty tangles past her shoulders. Her eyes were blue, I saw, once Connor flipped on the overhead lights, and she shook, stinking of fear. As her tail shifted, I spotted the bullet wounds, which had partially scabbed but continued to ooze over her scales. The poor woman had to be in pain.

"Hi," I said in Pactish, dropping to a crouch. "Ermonir venTala? It's all right. We're here to rescue you."

Ermonir stared at me for a few seconds more, processing that, and then her lip trembled and she burst into tears.

"One of you find a blanket," I told the men, then glanced around the room until I spotted a ring of keys on a hook on the wall. After a few false starts, I unlocked Ermonir's wrists, and Connor, who'd run upstairs, returned with a slightly soiled comforter. I wrapped it around her shoulders and shushed her, waiting as she pulled herself together with the others standing awkwardly by. Once she began to calm, I said, "I'm Gentle Breeze with DPP. That's Taug Berek from Laws," I continued, nodding to him. "We were tossed out here, too. We've got masking jewelry and clothes for you, okay? And there's, uh…well, she's the closest we can come to a healer right now—"

"She can get the bullets out," Taug interrupted. "Stitched me up yesterday. We've got healing potions, pain potions—"

"Water?" Ermonir rasped.

"Absolutely," I said. "Can you move on your own, or do we need to carry you upstairs?"

"I, um…" Rubbing her chafed wrists, she pushed herself upright and started to slither across the concrete floor, then winced and cried out.

"Hey, hey, it's all right, don't force it," said Connor, catching her by the arm. "We'll get you out of here."

She stiffened briefly at his accent and studied his face, and then recognition dawned. "You're one of the ones from outside, aren't you? That place…"

"East Branch?"

"Yes, that," she said, nodding. "I saw the reports, the citizenship documents…but I thought all of you were moving into the Pactlands."

"Almost all," he replied with a slight smile. "I've got responsibilities out here. Connor. Now, hold still for a moment. Let me make sure I can do this…"

"Do what?"

"Take your time, son," Yacovi murmured. "You need me, I can help."

Connor shot Yacovi a grateful glance. "You're on

standby, yeah?"

"Roger that."

He took a deep breath, then slowly, precisely, began gesturing. Ermonir rose from the floor with a surprised cry, then drifted toward the staircase and floated up. We'd left the door open, fortunately, and we followed behind her as she hovered in the den. "Couch or floor?" Connor asked. "We'll take you outside in just a minute, but we've got some cleanup to do first."

"Floor, please," she said, and grunted as her injured tail touched down.

Once he'd released his hold, he grabbed his phone and called Maggie. "Hey, we're clearing the place. Drive on up if y'all can," he said, switching languages. "The bag of clothes and masking jewelry should be back in the bedroom, and we're going to need Tabitha."

"Connor," I muttered as he ended the call, and pointed down the hallway.

Three women had crept out of the rooms while we were downstairs, and from the smell of them, they hadn't bathed in at least a couple of days. They were barely dressed, all three sporting lingerie that made my pajamas look modest, and none held a weapon. I saw why they hadn't bolted for the door: two wore metal ankle cuffs connected by a short length of chain, while the third's cuffs were locked to a metal bar, leaving her able to walk only by pivoting her hips.

And from the looks on their faces, they'd seen Ermonir's levitation.

"Fucking hell," Connor whispered, then took a cautious step toward the women, empty palms upraised. "It's all right," he said slowly, "I'm police. We're going to get y'all out of here."

The woman with the bar at her ankles—the one who'd pointed out their captors' location—quietly asked, "How'd y'all do that? *What* is that thing? They didn't tell us nothing about—"

"Chief," said Yacovi, clapping Connor on the shoulder, "why don't you let me handle this, huh? Go get those keys in the basement. Ladies, I know everything's confusing," he said to the women, deepening his fake drawl, "but y'all just bear with us, and we're going to get you some help."

When Connor returned with the key ring, I headed down to the basement with Taug. "So," I said, surveying the unconscious humans and their equipment, "thoughts?"

"How many sets of manacles were in the dungeon?" he replied.

I peeked into the adjoining room. "Four sets attached to the wall."

"*Perfect.* Give me a hand, will you?"

As Taug dragged the smaller of the men into the dungeon, I hoisted the other over my shoulder and slipped his wrists into the manacles that had held Ermonir. Taug picked another set down the wall, and we stepped back to examine our handiwork. "That's a rough awakening," I said. "Lights on or off, do you think?"

He flipped the switch, leaving only a dim lamp illuminated. "Mood lighting?"

"Works for me. Now, what do you say we take their gear?"

"Of course. We need to seize the evidence," he said with faux solemnity.

"Naturally."

He snorted. "I love interagency cooperation, don't you?"

By the time we'd carried the first load upstairs, the RV had arrived, and Dave and Maggie helped us while Tabitha attended to the patient. There was, however, an immediate problem.

"Uh, y'all?" said Tabitha. "We can't understand each other."

Leaving Taug with the Humphrieses and Connor and Yacovi with the other women—who, I could smell, were drinking memory potions in the bottles of water the guys had given them—I sat beside Ermonir and murmured, "This is Tabitha. She doesn't speak Pactish, so I'll translate."

Ermonir eyed her dubiously. "Is she..."

"Human," I confirmed, "but DOI has worked with her, and she's helping us." To Tabitha, I said, "No chance you've got a herpetology hobby, is there?"

"Nope, but I should be able to dig out the bullets once I get some of this blood cleaned off. Yacovi," she called, "pain potions? Something to numb her?"

Leaving Connor to babysit the women, who were by then nodding off on the floor, Yacovi carried over several vials and a clean syringe. "Need some help?"

"I think we'll be fine," she replied, and quickly injected the potions into Ermonir's injured tail. To me, she said, "Tell her I'm going to give that a minute to kick in while I get my gear ready, and then I'm going to fish the bullets out."

Tabitha worked quickly but methodically, and I held her phone's flashlight on the wounds while she dug around with a penknife and a pair of tweezers. "Small caliber," she said, dropping the second bullet onto the floor, "and it doesn't look like they fragmented. At least nothing hit her spine." With that, she began opening sterile packages of gauze and tape, then frowned. "Gentle Breeze, ask her if there's a preferred way to bandage this area. I don't want to mess up her scales with adhesive—"

"Wait," I said, "let's get her masked first."

She swore and smacked her forehead. "Sorry, got too focused..."

"You're doing fine." I asked Ermonir, "Have you ever masked before?"

"No," she replied. "Do I have to?"

"Uh...well, yeah. It's not safe otherwise," I told her, thinking of Dave's speeding. "But it doesn't hurt at all, and I'll walk you through it..." My voice faded as I thought of one hitch in the plan. "You...do you have any idea what a sorcerer looks like below the waist?"

"I mean, I've seen legs, certainly, but…um…"

"Not the private bits?" She shook her head, and I said, "Right, then. Boys!" I called. "Out of the house. We need girl time."

Connor and Yacovi hastily wrapped up their work with the other women and carried them into the bedrooms, and as they and Taug left, Maggie appeared with the bag of clothing and pendants. "Anything I can do to help?" she asked in Pactish.

Ermonir peered up at her. "You're from East Branch, too?"

"Not exactly." Before Ermonir's fear could ramp up, Maggie said, "You work at the Forum, right? Do you know Wylan?"

"The *Hunter*? I know him on sight, but we don't work together…"

"Well, he's my son-in-law, which means I'm here to help," she said firmly. "Okay? Now, what's up?" she asked me.

As delicately as possible, I explained the problem to the others. "I see," said Maggie. "Kind of like a mermaid situation, huh? We'll fix this," she told Ermonir, then asked Tabitha in English, "Could you pull up some pictures or diagrams on your phone, hon? Something *anatomical*, not—"

"Porn," Tabitha finished. "Gotcha."

Maggie handed Ermonir a necklace, and with a fair degree of trepidation, she put it on. Once Tabitha had located the appropriate resources and Ermonir had made a series of enquiries about the illustrations that I'd honestly never imagined answering, we were ready to begin. Step by step, I coaxed her through her mask's creation: switching scales for skin, splitting her tail into legs, adjusting her feet to approximate Tabitha's, and then working through the more delicate parts. When we'd finished, she didn't look *quite* right in my estimation, but she was close enough to go unnoticed once she'd dressed, and Maggie and Tabitha were satisfied. We helped her pull on one of Connor's T-shirts, but before tackling his sweatpants, Tabitha set about re-cleaning and bandaging Ermonir's wounds on her new right leg.

As she worked, Ermonir hugged her flat chest and looked at me. "I should have tried to lure them in, I know, I was just—"

"You were hurt and scared," I said. "None of that, now."

"I thought about it, but if they just got excited and didn't unlock me…"

Under ordinary circumstances, nagas could be powerful hunters, and they preferred to ambush prey. Lying in wait, a naga would secret pheromones capable of inciting lust in *several* species, including humans. As the besotted prey approached, the naga would strike, using their powerful tail to squeeze the prey to death before unhinging their jaws to…well, frankly, a *disturbing* degree and swallowing it whole. While Ermonir probably would have been able to draw her captors closer and get them hot and bothered, and might have been able to fatally constrict them even with her wounded tail, she'd still have been chained to the wall—less hungry, surely, but trapped all the same.

"You did nothing wrong," I soothed.

"How are you feeling?" Maggie asked her.

Tentatively, Ermonir moved her left leg, which had come through unscathed. "I'm not in pain right now—those were good potions. Hungry and thirsty, I guess."

"We'll take care of that in a minute. Let's get on the road, and we'll get you fed."

"We're going back to Beukal?" Ermonir asked, brightening.

I grimaced. "Not exactly. The portals are closed right now—there's been an emergency," I explained, glossing over the details for later. "But Connor lives a few hours away, and his house is safe. We can stay there until the portals are open again."

While she didn't seem thrilled by this news, she cooperated as we wrangled her into the borrowed pants. "How did you find me, anyway?" she asked once she was decent.

"Farseers. We'll explain everything," I promised, "but let's move. Uh...sorry, this is going to be awkward," I mumbled, then hoisted her over my shoulder like a sack of grass clippings and started for the door.

I carried Ermonir up into the RV, where the guys were waiting, and plopped her onto the couch. "Stay right there," said Maggie, who'd followed us. "I'll get you some water."

As she bustled in the kitchenette and Tabitha stowed her gear, I asked Yacovi, "What's the plan with the other women?"

"Memory wipe," he replied. "I told them that a hunter found them and freed them, but he didn't want to stick around. They should come to in forty minutes or so, and Connor found the keys to the truck," he said, pointing to the oversized Ford parked in the weeds, "so they can make their escape."

"Think they'll bother calling the police if they find the two locked up in the basement?"

His smile wasn't kind. "You know, I can't rightly say..."

He fell quiet as the rumble of an engine intensified. "I'll go check," I said. "Lock up once I'm out."

"Gentle Breeze—"

"*Do it*," I snapped, and slammed the side door.

A moment later, another pickup truck slowed and parked behind us. The driver, a blond man in a white T-shirt and jeans, hopped down and spotted me. "Hey, baby," he said, walking up with a smirk. "You lost? Just got here? Where are Sam and Joe?"

His Beukal accent was unmistakable, and I didn't waste time with subterfuge. Instead, I grabbed my pendant to disengage it, and as my clothes ripped, I threw myself onto the sorcerer, pinning him to the dirt, and smashed his nose. He screamed in pain, but before I could hit him again, Yacovi called, "Here!"

I rolled off just enough to give him access to the sorcerer's arm, and he injected a strong sedative, followed by a dose of dampening potion. As the sorcerer passed out underneath me, I stood and brushed myself off, then realized that my clothing had far surpassed the limit of structural integrity. "Uh…"

"Come here," said Tabitha, hurrying down the steps with Connor's bag of clothes. "Yacovi—"

He turned around, and I hastily masked and dressed. Once I was covered, Connor emerged and pointed to the unconscious sorcerer. "Basement?" he asked.

"Please."

I followed him downstairs, and we chained him to the wall between the humans. Task accomplished, I returned to the den, then frowned at the hallway where we'd found the women. "Worried about them?" Connor asked.

"A little. I'm sure Yacovi did a fine job, but I'd feel better if I knew they'd left."

"Then let's wait. We'll send the RV on, and you and I can hang out and make sure they're all right."

The plan seemed workable, and the others were amenable to it. With Ermonir eating and Taug on hand to fill her in, Dave set off toward civilization, and Connor and I staked out a position behind the remains of a shed.

About half an hour later, the front door opened, and the women, wearing ill-fitting clothing and no shoes, ran out onto the porch. The one I'd thought of as the leader clutched the truck keys, and all three climbed in. Within seconds, they were shooting down the road, briefly fishtailing before they rounded the bend and disappeared.

"And that answers that," said Connor. "Ready to go?"

"Almost. Want to pull your car up here? I'm going to check the basement one more time."

He walked off, and I returned to the house, noting how

faint some of the smells had become with the recent departures. I walked downstairs and flipped on the lights in the dungeon, only to find that the larger human had come to and was struggling. Seeing me, he froze, then tried to free himself with renewed vigor.

"You're a real piece of shit, you know that?" I said, watching him with my arms folded.

He tried to kick at me, but I was standing just outside of his range.

"We freed those girls you had upstairs," I continued. "They took your truck. If I were you, I'd write that off. Now, word of advice: if you get free, you should *really* look into a new line of work. One that doesn't involve trafficking, for starters."

He glared up at me. "You won't get away with this. We've got a friend who's an actual fucking *wizard*, see, and—"

"Who, that guy?"

The man looked to his left, and his jaw dropped when he recognized the bloodied face of the sorcerer chained next to him.

"Listen to me closely, kid," I murmured as he blanched. "You're playing a dangerous game, and you don't even know the rules or the other players. Best to forget you ever saw anything even *remotely* connected to magic. Understood? Because the only thing stopping me from beating the three of you to a pulp is my own conscience. These are borrowed clothes, and I'd hate to return them bloody."

He swallowed hard but nodded.

"Now, you should know that we've taken the liberty of removing all of your hard drives, but in case we overlooked something and you were to post video of that naga you had down here…well, that would be a terrible mistake. Not that anyone would *believe* you had a genuine naga, but I would be peeved, and I'd have to hunt you down." Crouching in front of him, I gripped my pendant and removed just enough of my mask to let my tusks come forth. "And you do *not* want that."

I could smell the sharp scent of urine as I stood and fixed my face. "Think it over," I said, and turned off the overhead lights. "If I'm feeling generous, I'll call the sheriff in a day or two. That should give you plenty of time to reconsider your life choices."

The man started whining that I couldn't just leave them like that, but I ignored him and closed the door behind me.

In all honesty, I was leaning toward leaving them there to rot, but Connor was persuasive. At least the sorcerer we'd restrained by the Central portal had people looking for him—we had no clue who the Crossville sorcerer was or where his backup might be, and if we left the three there until his dampening potion wore off in a week's time, they'd be dead of dehydration. Reluctantly, I listened while he called 911, pretending to be the mysterious hunter who'd released the women, and relayed word of the captives he'd left prepared for retrieval.

We drove hard for Whitford and made it home shortly before five. Walking inside to the scent of baked chicken and warm rosemary-infused bread was an unexpected twist, and I could have kissed Maya when she put a large bottle of beer in my hand. "Local high-gravity ale," she said. "Best I can do—"

"*Thank* you," I said, and downed a long swig.

With no vegetarians in the group, and factoring in my considerable appetite, we emptied the serving dishes and raided Connor's stash of frozen novelties for dessert. As Dave and I washed up, Connor tapped his knife against his beer bottle for quiet, then said, "We should figure out the sleeping arrangements before the food coma hits."

"What's your thought?" asked Maya.

"Well…this house isn't big enough for everyone unless

we get out sleeping bags, and there's no need for that."

Taug muttered a translation for Ermonir, who was still sucking chocolate off the stick of her ice cream bar.

Turning to Yacovi, Connor asked, "Can you take Maggie, Dave, and Maya again?"

He nodded. "Sure."

"Great. Taug, why don't you and I go to my fiancée's house? She's got two beds, and that'd free up some room here."

Taug agreed, and I saw what Connor had done: assuming Tabitha stayed with the newest patient, that would leave the two of them and me in his house—an all-female group.

Yacovi sent Taug off with more healing and pain potions, and Tabitha told him to call if he needed medical attention overnight, but soon, the three of us were alone in the suddenly quieter space. I offered to carry Ermonir upstairs to a bedroom, but she insisted that the couch would be fine, and so I fixed it up for her while Tabitha made the drive to Walmart. "Y'all both need clothes," she insisted, and though I protested that Connor's castoffs were suitable, she wouldn't hear of it.

With Tabitha out of the house, I carried Ermonir to the couch and showed her how the TV worked. "I'm sorry about the language issue," I told her. "Do you know how the language potion hits you? If it's not bad, we might be able to get one from Yacovi…"

"I've never taken it," she confessed. "Never had a need." She adjusted her position, then asked, "Can I unmask for the night? Tabitha's seen me, so surely it wouldn't bother her."

"Safer not to," I replied. "In case of an emergency."

"But I can't walk."

"I know, so let's see…" I hunted around the house for a moment, then spotted a decorative pewter bell in the dusty china hutch and brought it to her. "Ring that, and one of us should wake. I'll sleep with my door open." I hesitated, then asked, "Do you want to bathe? I can wrap your leg in plastic to keep it dry."

Ermonir couldn't stand to shower, but Connor had a bathtub in the master suite. She groaned when I lowered her into the warm water, and I left her with bottles of Jane's lavender-scented products and a washcloth. By the time Tabitha returned, Ermonir was asleep on the couch, her wet hair splayed across a towel and the blankets tucked to her chin.

"This was totally unnecessary," I whispered as Tabitha pressed a shopping bag into my hands, "but thank you."

"Sure. I always feel gross after wearing the same thing for a few days," she whispered back. "Next time someone calls from the Pactlands, tell them I need antibiotic dosing for a naga, okay?" I promised, and with that, Tabitha left Ermonir's clothing on the coffee table and headed upstairs to rest.

Though it was barely eight that night, I changed the sheets on one of Connor's guest beds and slept deeply. If anyone wanted to video chat, I told myself, they could damn well wait until morning.

CHAPTER 12

But Monday started sooner than I'd hoped.

The bedside alarm clock showed it was nearly three when I awoke to the ringing of Ermonir's bell, and I stumbled downstairs to check on her, assuming she needed the bathroom. Instead, she pointed to the kitchen and the open laptop. "It started talking," she explained. "Something about a video conference?"

I thanked her and plopped into the chair nearest the computer, then turned the screen on to find Rose waiting. If I'd thought the girl looked rough on Sunday, she seemed dead on her feet as she raised a shaky hand in greeting.

"Kid, I don't make a point of recommending Happy Juice, but under these circumstances…"

Rose shook her head. "I'm okay."

"No, you absolutely are not."

"That's what I've been saying," protested Yven, who slid into view behind her. "She hasn't slept."

I scowled back at the screen, a tactic akin to the one that had worked well on Fradin. "*Rose…*"

"I can manage," she mumbled. "Pulled some all-nighters in college. This is fine…" Glancing back at Yven, she said, "Is there any more coffee?"

"I can make a fresh pot," he said, kissing the top of her head, "but wouldn't a nap be better?"

Her lips tightened in annoyance, and he backed off to handle the caffeine deficiency.

"He's right, you know," I said. "You're exhausted."

"Can't trance in my sleep," Rose replied, and rubbed

her eyes. "So."

"Any chance that the portals have reopened?"

"*Ha*. No. That's still a work in progress—the hex hit *hard*. But that's not why I called. You've got to get to Louisiana as soon as possible."

"Louisiana?" I echoed, trying to work through the geography with my sleep-muddled brain.

"Someone said Louisiana?" asked Tabitha in English, and I turned to see her on the edge of the kitchen in an old T-shirt and plaid boxers.

"Sorry, did I wake you?" I mumbled.

"No, that was the bell. What's up?"

Rose certainly didn't protest the linguistic shift. "Your next pickup's in Louisiana," she explained. "Near the Mansura portal."

I grunted at the news. "That portal is *awful*."

"What's wrong with it?" asked Tabitha.

"Deep in the bayou, at the end of a dirt road that barely exists. I came through once to find four alligators just sitting there, blocking the path. You've got to have an all-terrain vehicle to go through Mansura, especially if it's been raining."

"The good news is that you don't need to get to the portal," said Rose. "Just Pierreville—it's a little town nearby," she told Tabitha. "A wide patch in the road with a Family Dollar, a bar, and a bait shop."

I'd been through the hamlet several times on my way to and from the portal, and I'd never given it much thought. "Who's there, and where are they hiding?"

Rose grimaced. "It's Galibe, the gnome. He's alone."

And only ten. Assuming he was dropped on Thursday morning with the rest of us, he'd been on his own for four days. "Do you have coordinates? A landmark or something?"

"Oh, I know *precisely* where he is."

"Well, that's good—"

"And so does the entire town, a good chunk of the parish, and several media outlets. Mostly small websites, but there's been at least one live truck from a station in Baton Rouge. Went up to cover the festivities. Slow news day, I guess."

My guts knotted. "I'm sorry, *what?*"

She smiled mirthlessly. "Per Ganti, the sorcerer who dumped him left him by a tree while he was still unconscious, then took pictures and ran to the bar. Since it was about two a.m., the crowd was sparse and drunk, but they eventually paid attention when the sorcerer started passing his phone around, claiming he'd found a fairy."

"Oh, shit," Tabitha muttered. "And people *believed* that?"

Rose shrugged. "Gnomes are small, gnome children are tiny, and people are stupid. Plus, before the kidnapper left Galibe, he stole the kid's shirt, and he started showing that around. Proof, right?"

"Son of a *bitch.*"

"Yep. Some of the locals got a hunting dog and took him down to the tree to sniff around. Galibe had woken and climbed to safety by then, but the dog he alerted on *something*...so now folks claim they've treed a wingless fairy, and they're waiting him out. It's almost like a party— people are keeping watch, there are food vendors, the whole nine yards. Plenty of beer," she added.

"Lovely," I said. "Okay, so we go in with knockout potion and rescue Galibe while the humans are sleeping it off."

"Not a bad plan," Rose replied, "but for the live feeds."

Tabitha groaned.

"Exactly. I believe there are three cameras—two are YouTubers, one's for a TikTok account. I know that one of the YouTubers is a folklorist, but the other two may just be going for views. Doesn't matter—bottom line, if you use knockout, it's going to be caught on camera and broadcast."

That put us in a more difficult position. Gnomes are

innate masters of camouflage, and so I had no doubt that Galibe was nearly invisible in his hiding place—but any hunting dogs would surely smell him. Had Galibe eaten since Thursday? Had it rained on him?

"While we've got you," Tabitha said to Rose, "Ermonir was shot, and—"

"I know, and I put in a request for dosing overnight. Got what you need right here," she said, lifting a scrap of paper. "You ready?"

I waited while Rose passed along the medical information, then asked, "Any suggestions for retrieving Galibe?"

"Nothing concrete," she replied, "but whatever you do, you need to move quickly. The kid's getting weak, and he's tired. If he falls…"

"On it. *Sleep*, girl," I said, and cut the feed. Turning to Tabitha, I asked, "How long is the drive from here?"

She returned to her room for her phone, then gave me the bad news from the top of the staircase. "Ten hours if we drive hard."

I swore and pushed back from the table. "We need to go *now*. Can you call the others and get them here?"

"Yup."

As Tabitha set about waking the rest of our crew, Ermonir asked, "What's happened?"

I joined her in the den and switched on a lamp. "Another kidnapping victim"—I *hated* that word in relation to myself, but it was easiest at that hour—"turned up about half a day's drive away. He's a child, so we need to retrieve him next."

"Heavens," she murmured. "Is he injured?"

"Sounds like he's been up a tree all this time. He's got an audience, so we'll need to work around that, too." I massaged my temples, trying to wake up. "No offense intended, but I think it'd be best if you stayed here. I mean, unless you've learned to walk overnight…"

Ermonir laughed incredulously. "No offense taken.

But, um…if all of you go, I'm not sure that I can manage by myself if I need to stay masked."

"Which is why we're splitting up," I told her, and began making my cuts.

About half an hour later, the others arrived almost simultaneously, bed-mussed but with packed bags. "Here's the plan," I said before matters got out of control. "We're leaving the RV—Ermonir won't travel well, and we'll make better time in smaller vehicles. Connor, Tabitha, and Maya, you're with me for the road trip. Everyone else, stay here and babysit the computer."

"Whoa, now," said Yacovi, frowning, "let's think about this—"

"You know agency protocol, and in case of emergency, you can defend the others," I said, cutting him short. "Taug knows the software, yes?"

"Ours is fairly similar," he said. "I've dealt with fucking Sprik…"

"That'll do. And Taug, I know you're willing to help, but it wouldn't kill you to stay off that leg for a day and let the healing potions work. Maggie, Dave…" I turned to them and shrugged. "Again, I know you're willing, but I'd feel much better if you stuck around. I'm sure Ermonir wouldn't mind having another woman in the house," I added, looking pointedly at Maggie.

She got the hint. "Sure, we can man the fort."

"Thank you. Tabitha, what are you doing?" I asked, seeing her frowning at her phone.

"Looking for footage. Want to see?" she replied, and turned the screen around.

There was almost a carnival atmosphere in Pierreville—or there had been on Saturday, when the story aired in Baton Rouge. Yes, the presenters at the desk in their suits chuckled at the rubes out in the country, but that didn't make our job any easier. People in denim and camo clustered around a big oak tree, cooking on portable grills, drinking beer, and letting their dogs sniff at the base, and to a one of them, the dogs were excited. A few of the locals agreed to be interviewed and gave their theories as to what was up in the branches—a fairy, perhaps, but definitely something supernatural. Some suggested that whoever caught the creature would be granted riches or a wish. Another put out a call to voodoo practitioners in New Orleans to come up and see for themselves.

"What a mess," I muttered, and shouldered my bag. "Let's take two vehicles in case of breakdown. I don't want to delay retrieval."

"Fine by me," said Connor. "Tabitha, do you mind driving?"

"No problem, I just need to get gas."

"Shotgun," chirped Maya.

"Speaking of which," I said, "we should pack weapons. Connor, are the pistols still in your trunk?"

"Yeah, and the rifle. Just a minute, I need to get some stuff upstairs," he said, and jogged to the second floor.

By the time Connor returned, Yacovi had outfitted us with plenty of potions, which we'd divided—along with snacks—between Connor's SUV and Tabitha's Camry. Tabitha turned over her bottle of antibiotics to Taug with instructions for sharing them with Ermonir, and Yacovi quietly promised her that he'd see that the two took their medication. Connor tossed a duffel bag into the rear of his vehicle, then showed me an oval-shaped wooden piece with holes drilled in the top. "What's that?" I asked.

"This," he said, turning it over in his hands, "is an instrument that used to be made at East Branch. It's basically an ocarina," he explained. "My mom made this one, and I've kept it."

I stared bemusedly at him. "Dare I ask?"

"Got a plan. I'll tell you on the way," he said, and tucked the ocarina into his bag for safekeeping.

Admittedly, the portal system at home had spoiled me.

The trip to Crossville had been tedious but tolerable. *This*, however…

"Humans have been to the fucking moon," I groused from behind the wheel as Connor took a well-earned break, "and the best they can do is seventy miles an hour on I-20?"

"There's been talk of high-speed rail," said Connor, leaning against the door with his eyes closed, "but that's mostly in New England and out west. Folks down here aren't in love with public transportation."

"Forget public transportation, would it kill someone to develop, I don't know, a tiny wormhole or something? Surely there's a way to mimic the portals without magic—"

"A *wormhole*? How much sci-fi do you watch, woman?"

"A reasonable amount," I said stiffly. "All I'm saying is that humans are creative, and if they put their minds to it, they could do better than this."

"I'm still waiting for my flying car," he replied. "Speaking of which, we could have flown."

"What *we*? I don't have identification on me, let alone the funds to buy a plane ticket."

"Ever flown?"

"No," I admitted. "Unless you count a winged horse. That might have been fun had we not been squaring off against the damn Hunt…" I glanced at Connor and asked, "You?"

"Mm-hmm. Few times, vacations and a couple of training conferences out of state. Sheriff got me up in a helicopter once, and that was cool. *Loud*, but fun. The problem is that everything goes through Atlanta, and I'm not convinced that Hartsfield-Jackson isn't actually a level of Hell." Shifting in his seat, he said, "Guess we probably could have gotten tickets to Baton Rouge—those of us with actual IDs—but we'd still have had to rent a car there, and assuming we can find Galibe, we'd have to drive him back. That, or stuff him into a carry-on bag, and that's frowned upon for some reason."

"Gnomes are excellent at hiding themselves…"

"I'm not putting a kid through an X-ray scanner. Plus, if TSA wanted to take a closer look, what would we do? Open the bag, and *surprise*! What then? Toss a knock-out potion at a crowded security checkpoint, with cameras all around?" He shook his head. "If we made it onto the plane, someone with cuffs would be there to meet us in Atlanta."

"So, what I'm hearing is that we have no good options," I said.

"I'm just glad we're not driving to California. Did that with Janie," said Connor. "Cross-country trips are probably better when you take time to enjoy them."

We drove along in silence for a time, but Connor's mention of his fiancée had stirred up a nagging doubt in me. "Question," I murmured.

"Shoot."

"If you hadn't been able to, uh…limit your lifespan…would you still marry Jane?"

"Absolutely," he replied without hesitation, then straightened and turned to me. "I love her, there's no one like her. If she aged faster than I did, so be it." He paused, then said, "The shoe was on the other foot for a while, right? I couldn't bring myself to propose to her because she'd have been stuck with an old man in another fifty years, and I didn't want to do that to her. Jane kept insisting that she didn't care, and…I think I get that now," he said quietly. "There's really no guarantee how long I'm going to be around or what I'll look like when I get to the end—the research healer who worked on all of us did her best, but she'd tell you it's all still experimental. I just don't want to keep going indefinitely without Janie."

"That's…sweet," I allowed.

He chuckled. "Crazy, you mean? Short-sighted? I don't care, you're not going to hurt my feelings."

Silence fell on the SUV once more, but then Connor cleared his throat. "This wouldn't have anything to do with

Moonless Night, would it?"

I considered denying it but decided there was no point. "Am I that transparent?"

"Eh, educated guess."

He let me stew for a time, and though I knew damn well what he was doing, I cracked first. "I'm aging. He's not. Two centuries from now, I'll be middle-aged, and he won't look a day older."

"Yeah?"

"My clock is ticking," I continued. "I have an expiration date. Someday, I'll be an elder, and I'll look it, feel it...perhaps my mind will slip..."

"He loves you."

"He loves me *now*, maybe, but in years to come..."

Connor let that hang, then slid in his seat to better face me as I drove. "Wylan and I hang out sometimes, you know?"

"I...did not."

"Yup. Brunch is usually just for the girls. Sometimes, while they're off getting eggs benedict or mimosas or Waffle House or whatever, he'll pop by the house."

"Male bonding?" I asked. "I'd think he'd have enough of that."

"Oh, absolutely, but he can come to my place, crack open a breakfast beer, and not be bothered, see? Up at the lodge, there's always someone who needs something. Me, I'm just a dude with Netflix and bacon, and since the ladies in our lives get along, we do likewise. Anyway, on occasion, he mentions Moonless Night."

"And?"

"He's thrilled for his brother. That guy's head over heels in love, and for reasons Moonless Night can't quite fathom, you haven't run for the hills yet."

"Why would I run?" I pressed.

"To hear Wylan tell it, because you're young and gorgeous and a respected agent, and Moonless Night's older than dirt with a career in sportscasting. Your boy thinks you could do better."

I laughed at the superficial ridiculousness of that notion. "He's the famous one. I'm just a government em-
ployee—"

"This may come as a surprise," Connor deadpanned,
"but Wylan says he's something of an old-fashioned guy.
He remembers how things went back in the clan days, and
he doesn't think he measures up. You're the one getting
into fights."

"*Rarely*. We try to avoid brawls," I protested.

"Fine, but the most he does is get out of the way of
melee sideline incidents."

"Well," I said after a moment's contemplation, "when
you see Wylan next, should the subject arise, tell him that
Moonless Night doesn't need to worry about me seeking
out someone stabbier."

Connor laughed low in his throat. "Is that so?"

"It is. Because I know damn well what he is, and I'm
almost positive that he could qualify on every weapon in
our arsenal and wipe the floor with at least half of my
agents. Maybe not Pars," I allowed, "and Emarae would
put up a good fight."

"Annie would win."

"Absolutely not."

"Oh, yes, she would. Because if he beat the crap out of
her, what do you think Wylan would do?"

"Ooh...a fair point," I said, and tapped the brake as
the navigation system warned me of a cop lying in wait.

Though we drove hard, stopped infrequently, and gained
an hour during the trip, it was still nearly four that afternoon before we rolled into Pierreville—or more properly,
to an abandoned gas station a few miles outside of town, a
dilapidated structure in danger of being swallowed by kud-
zu. Parking behind the crumbling convenience store, safe
from the view of any passing motorists, we stretched our

legs and prepared.

I watched Connor mask himself, using the SUV's tinted window as a mirror: his face grew more weathered, his eyes lightened to hazel and his hair to graying blond, and he gave himself a thin scar through one eyebrow, inoffensive but memorable. Once that was accomplished, he dug in his duffel and produced a black long-sleeved shirt and pants, and awkwardly changed inside the vehicle.

Nearby, Tabitha shook her head. "Think this'll work?" she muttered.

"It'd better," said Maya.

When Connor emerged, he pulled a long black cloak from his bag and clasped it around his neck. "Well?" he asked us.

"Happy Halloween," said Tabitha dryly.

He shrugged, making the cloak flap. "This is the best I could do in a pinch."

"Ah, yes, your finest rayon."

"Excuse me for not making a habit of buying freaking *cloaks*," he retorted. "Seriously, is this passable?"

"I mean, you look a little deranged," Tabitha replied, "but that's de rigueur for a significant chunk of the Mystic Mountains crowd, so…hmm. Let's see." Reaching behind her neck, she unhooked the silver chain she'd been sporting since Friday, revealing a pentacle she'd kept hidden beneath her shirt. "Here, put this on," she told Connor. "It'll help."

He hesitated. "I don't want to take a risk with your jewelry—"

"It's fine. You need to sell the act," she insisted, and helped him fasten the chain. She stepped back to take him in, and then, satisfied with his appearance, she asked, "You ever had an acting class? Been in a play?"

"Not since our first-grade Thanksgiving pageant…"

"Mm. Pilgrim, right?"

"I'll have you know I was a *very* convincing brave in a paper feather headdress," he retorted. "Why do you ask?"

"Because this character you're playing—what do you know about him? His background, his motivations, his knowledge base?"

Connor frowned. "I think I did a convincing job winging it the last time I masked up..."

"Yeah, seeing as you were playing a *cop*."

"Touché," he muttered. "All right, what do you suggest?"

"Give me a minute." Tabitha consulted her phone briefly, then looked back at Connor. "Your name is Lucian LeBlanc."

Maya snorted. "Seems a little much..."

"Not in some of the circles I've come across," said Tabitha. "Guarantee that ain't your government name, but it's the one you use. You're a Wiccan out of Orleans Parish, a solitary practitioner, but you meet up with a more ecumenical pagan group every so often for socialization, lectures, workshops, and such. Druids, Heathens, et cetera."

"So...we talk spells and stuff?" asked Connor.

"And get drinks and watch the Saints play. Look, we're not 'all magic, all the time,'" Tabitha told him. "You know how churches hold fellowship activities that aren't entirely religious? It's nice to get together with likeminded people and just hang out every so often." Squinting at him, she said, "Be honest with me: how much do you actually know about Wicca?"

"Um...I know there's crystals involved."

She closed her eyes and rested her forehead on her fingertips, muttering under her breath. "Okay. Uh...short version, there's a lot of wiggle room for personal belief, but most of us worship the Goddess and the God. You've heard of the Maiden, the Mother, and the Crone?"

"Actually, yes."

"Great. That's the Goddess in her three forms. The Horned God is her consort, see?"

Connor's expression shifted. "So...Wylan?"

She folded her arms and gave him a scorching look. "Boy, did you really just ask me if I worship freaking *Wylan*?"

He held up his hands in placation. "You said—"

"I said the Horned God is a *deity*. And yes," she grudgingly allowed, "the imagery can be similar, but leave Wylan out of this."

"Sorry," he mumbled. "No crystals, then?"

"Getting there. Many of us practice spellcraft—healing, hexing, banishing, whatever you like. Some craft involves crystals. They're considered to have particular energies, and they can be used to amplify your intentions. You work with the crystals, you benefit from their energy, and they help you achieve your ends."

"And there's jewelry," said Maya.

"*Oh*, yeah. An easy way to use crystals is to wear them," Tabitha told Connor. "Make them into amulets, put them in wands, mark the boundaries of sacred circles. And that's why places like Mystic Mountains have so many polished rocks on offer. But look, you don't need to understand crystal magic right now—just know that it exists. Lucian would be familiar with it and *appreciate* it," she added with a pointed stare.

Tabitha spent a few minutes more with Connor, giving him information he would need in case another practitioner was on the premises, then nodded to Maya. "We'll be waiting here," she said. "Call if you need backup, but I think y'all are right that we should limit the size of our group. And where are *you* going?" she asked as Connor headed toward his SUV.

He paused. "Uh…I was going to start the car…"

"Lucian doesn't drive—fake a bad limp. Give Gentle Breeze the wheel." When he arched a brow, she said, "Don't be difficult, elf boy. Go on, git."

He rolled his eyes but climbed into the passenger's side.

I pulled a potion vial from the trunk and went to work on the license plate, making the numbers impossible to

remember. Once I was satisfied that we'd taken all available precautions, I lowered my voice and asked Tabitha,
"This spellcraft you do…"

"Yes?"

"I don't mean to be rude, but does it, um…"

"Does it work?" she finished with a little smile. "I like
to think so. Not as…*dramatically* as the shit that Yacovi and
Jane and Connor pull off, but…I think so, yeah. And if
nothing else," she added, "speaking from personal experience, it's a hell of a lot less freaky to see their kind of magic when you come to the table already believing that magic
exists. Good luck," she said, and thumbed one hand toward her Camry. "We'll be on standby."

By the time we reached the tree where Galibe was hiding—and the circus all around it—I'd altered my mask,
making my hair darker and shorter, my eyes a watery gray,
and my face rosy with a sprawling rash. Neither of us was
a beauty, which I hoped would work in our favor; if nothing else, the masks might throw any lurking sorcerer off
our trail. I parked behind a boxy van marked with a television station's logo and cut the engine. "Ready?" I asked.

"As I'm going to be," said Connor, then tucked his ocarina into his pocket and climbed out of the SUV.

I allowed him to lead the way, limping around the clus-
ters of the curious with their beer and grills, the smirking
reporters, and two bored-looking deputies—all human,
according to my nose. Faintly, I could smell the sorcerer
who'd made the drop, but his scent was fading, buried under the fresher notes of the locals, booze, engine exhaust,
tobacco, and some sausages that I was almost positive contained alligator. The tree had been marked off with yellow
caution tape, and a bloodhound circled it madly, whining. I
didn't have to get close to pick out the scent of the child
hidden up in the branches, particularly the acrid smell of
his fear.

A fat, balding man in an off-white sleeveless shirt approached us, beer in hand. "Afternoon, y'all," he said, eyeing us curiously. "Where'd you come from?"

"Merry meet," said Connor, drawling like his life depended on it. "I heard y'all have some trouble with the Fair Folk."

The man grunted. "Not *trouble*, no. Might be it's got some trouble with us," he added with a yellowed smile.

"You don't think it's dangerous?" I asked.

He gave me a quick once-over. "Don't rightly know, cher. Got it treed, know that much, but it's a sneaky little thing. Hanging on up there," he said, pointing to the canopy with his can.

"That so?" said Connor. "Well, I've come to offer y'all my services. Lucian LeBlanc," he continued, extending his hand, and the man shook it. "Not my first tussle with the Fair Folk. I believe I can coax him down before he gets up to no good."

The man studied him more carefully. "You ain't from 'round here."

"Nawlins. Heard tell and came up to see for myself."

"And…you're some kind of, uh…"

"Wiccan," Connor lied. "And I follow the right-hand path, so y'all don't need to worry none, see? Just wanted to help." Cocking his head toward me, he said, "My driver. Leg don't work for shit these days."

The local's gaze traveled down Connor's cloaked side toward the foot he'd left dragging. "That so?"

"Hit by a streetcar a few years back. Damn thing near ran me over," he groused. "But this ain't getting it done. Mind if I try something?"

He swept his beer can toward the tree in invitation. "Help yourself, friend. Mind where you're walking, now. Them dogs have been all over the place."

Duly cautioned, we approached the tree, and our one-man greeting party was soon joined by a few of his less-than-sober friends, who muttered and sniggered to each other—if I'd had to guess, I'd have said they thought Connor was nuts. Pulling the ocarina from his pocket, Connor showed them the instrument, then said, "This came to me from my great-granddaddy, and he was Irish— he *knew* the Fair Folk. It'll summon whatever's up there to come on down and see."

"And then you grab it?" one of the more inebriated men asked. "Poke it with a magic wand?"

Connor remained solemn. "Only a fool would try to grab it. You got to be *respectful*," he said, and produced a tiny, ornate glass vial full of bright green liquid. "I'll tell it this ain't its place, and I'll give it this. You want something from the Fair Folk, you've got to trade."

"What *is* that?" another man enquired.

Connor leaned toward him and lowered his voice to a whisper. "Water and food coloring, but it's shiny, and it'll do the trick. Now, here's how this'll work," he told the group. "I'll summon it down, and I'll show it this," he said, shaking the vial. "Then I'll leave the bottle in the tree. If the Fair Folk takes it, it'll go on its way, and y'all won't be subject to its mischief no more."

"And if it don't?" the first man asked.

"If it don't, then I'll be back with reinforcements," Connor assured him, then lifted the ocarina into position. "All right, let me see how this goes…"

He played a melodic line with surprising facility—I hadn't taken Connor for a musician—but when he paused to sing, his voice was close to the pitch but mediocre. The singing followed the same melody as the one he'd played, a tune unknown to me, but I had to bite the inside of my mouth to keep from laughing when I heard the lyrics. Whatever words ordinarily went with the song had been cast aside, and Connor ad-libbed in Pactish.

"*Galibe, we know you're up there,*" he sang, concentrating on the tree. "*We're here to help. Some Pact agents told us where to find you.*"

On he went for a few minutes, alternating played and

sung stanzas as the locals conversed around us. The television station's cameraman walked over and began filming, and I stepped between him and Connor before he could record more than a few seconds. "Please," I whispered, "don't break his concentration. He's terribly shy when he's on camera." The man relented, and I relaxed a degree. While I assumed there were few, if any, Pactish speakers around Baton Rouge, I didn't want to take a chance on any Unity Plan members seeing the footage.

"*Come down at full dark,*" Connor concluded. "*I'm leaving you a scent neutralizer. Drink it, then leave the tree and run to the south, where the vines are taking over a low building. See our black vehicle? We'll be waiting for you.*"

With that, he nodded at the tree, put his ocarina away, then beckoned me over. "Uh…Mary Francine, would you do the honors?"

Of course he couldn't climb with a bad leg. Gamely, I hauled myself up the trunk, then left the potion vial in a hollow beside a steady limb. As I descended, Connor told the others, "No charge, and I hope that works. If it doesn't, reach out to the Orleans Circle, and I'll be back. Come on, Mary Francine," he said, and made a show of leaning on my arm as we walked away to a chorus of guffaws.

The sun had set about twenty minutes past, and the four of us huddled up in Connor's SUV to wait. Tabitha and Maya had passed an uneventful afternoon while Connor and I play-acted at mysticism, napping in the Camry with the windows down to catch whatever passed for a breeze in the bayou. Connor had shed the ridiculous cape, returned Tabitha's necklace, and packed his ocarina away, but he and I remained masked in the front seat so as not to spook the boy. We'd left the windows open and the car off, conserving fuel while we watched the road from around the back of the abandoned gas station.

Around seven-thirty, I heard soft, rapid footsteps approaching in the darkness and sat up straighter. I couldn't smell anything—a good sign that the neutralizer was working. "Turn on the headlights," I ordered, then climbed out and walked around the front of the vehicle.

From out of the shadows raced a shirtless, barefoot gnome, a little boy who froze in the sudden glare of the headlights before spotting me and sprinting closer. Even with my mask on, he barely reached my knees, and I crouched to intercept him as he ran at me like wolves were chasing him. When he slammed into my chest, I scooped him into my arms and stood, rubbing his thin back as he sobbed with terror and exhaustion and relief.

"It's all right, sweetheart," I murmured, stroking his filthy white hair, which hung to his shaking shoulders. "You're safe now. Try to breathe, youngling."

I turned when Maya approached with a red fleece blanket. "Thought we might need this," she explained, switching to Pactish, and wrapped it around the crying child. "Hey, big guy," she said as he turned his face toward hers, "it's okay. You did such a good job, and we're going to tell everyone how brave you've been."

He sniffled hard, and with a couple of false starts, he managed to squeak, "Where...I don't know...where are..."

"You're outside," she replied. "Place called Pierreville."

"*Outside?*" His breathing grew more rapid. "I...I don't know how, I didn't mean to—"

"Galibe, honey," Maya soothed, patting his back to calm him, "you're not in trouble. You were kidnapped. We're going to get you home."

"Not quite yet," I said before his hopes could rise. "The portals are closed right now. But we've got a safe place to stay and masking jewelry for you, so don't worry."

"I don't know what happened," he mumbled.

"You were probably drugged and taken from your bed. I was, too," I told him. "And under this mask, my name is

Gentle Breeze, and I'm from DPP."

He took a long, ragged breath but held himself togeth-er. "Why me?"

"We think it's because of your grandfather. I'm sure your family is worried," I said. "There are some people with, uh...*foolish* ideas who are frustrated because they're not getting their way. So, they kidnapped some of us and tossed us outside in hopes that we'd been seen."

"That's *awful*."

"I know," I said, holding him more tightly. "But a far-seer back in Beukal told us where to find you, so at least you're out of that tree. Now, how about dinner?"

I climbed into the back seat so that I could hold Galibe while Connor drove. He and I removed our masks—well, my second mask—and once the boy was convinced that we weren't going to hurt him, we set off, following Tabitha and Maya back toward civilization.

After a few miles, as we approached a crossroads, I saw familiar golden arches in the distance. "Galibe, are you a vegetarian?"

"No…"

"Perfect. Connor, call the girls. Take us to the drive-thru, eh?"

As the youngling gorged himself on chicken nuggets and fries, Maya knocked on the front passenger-side window, and Connor unlocked the door for her.

"Much better," she said, large soda in hand. "But Tabi-tha and I have been talking, and we don't think it's safe to drive back tonight."

I frowned. Our group was strange, yes, but there was safety in numbers. "What did you have in mind?"

"Google says there's a motel about twenty miles ahead. We vote for overnighting and getting an early start in the morning."

Connor nodded as she spoke. "Not a bad idea. I'm

coasting on fumes. Gentle Breeze, you okay with getting some sleep?"

"Um...sure," I replied. Anxious though I was to get back to Georgia, if I were honest with myself, I was weary after the long day. "How do we want to do this?"

"I'll get the keys. Follow us, and leave everything to me," said Maya, then left our vehicle with a last slurp of her drink.

Galibe didn't seem to mind when we pulled into the parking lot of the motel. Full of meat and potatoes and grease, and having slaked his thirst, he snuggled against me with his eyes closed, almost lulled to sleep by the rocking of the SUV. When Maya returned, she said, "I got two rooms, so let's do girls and boys. Connor, will you be okay with Galibe overnight?"

"Yeah, we'll be fine," he said, then climbed out, slung his duffel bag over his shoulder, and took Galibe from me, still wrapped in his borrowed blanket. Our rooms adjoined, and we quietly said our goodnights as we separated to crash.

Tabitha and Maya offered to share, which suited me *just* fine. As I kicked off my shoes and made a brief inspection of the room, Maya called Maggie to update her. "We've stopped for the night," she said. "If anyone calls on the laptop, tell them Galibe is safe."

I burrowed under the musty blankets, musing that since Rose was barely sleeping, word of our progress would probably make it around Beukal before we returned to Whitford. Tabitha slipped next door to check on Galibe, but she soon returned, medical kit unopened. "Poor little fellow's out like a light," she reported. "Connor's got him in a nest of pillows and blankets, so hopefully, he won't fall off the bed."

I was, I realized, more exhausted than I'd thought after the day. While the others flipped through the few available TV channels, I closed my eyes, and I'd passed out before they'd settled on a program.

CHAPTER 13

There was nowhere to eat at the motel, especially not in the dark of five that morning, and so Tabitha and I slipped back to McDonald's to secure provisions while Maya groggily bathed. As roommates went, I'd had far worse than the two women, neither of whom snored. A shower had helped wake me, and while I wasn't thrilled to climb back into to the previous day's clothes, years of field work made the experience little more than an annoyance.

We returned with heaping sacks of mostly warm food and a four-pack of drinks I'd kept balanced on my knees during the drive. Maya had made herself closer to present-able by then, though the room's hair dryer was dead, and as we spread the repast on the little table by the curtained window, she went next door to rouse the boys.

I wasn't entirely surprised to find Connor already awake and dressed, but Galibe shocked me. In the hours since we'd split up, Connor had tended to him, coaxing him back to sleep when he woke in the throes of a night-mare, then helping him through the masking process. The little gnome was suddenly only a bit shorter than Tabitha and Maya, a skinny, long-legged kid with dark brown hair, and while Connor's extra clothes swamped him, he was able to make do by rolling his cuffs and shoving back his sleeves.

"We went darker," Connor explained as Galibe eyed the wrapped breakfast sandwiches, "since I thought white hair would be too noticeable."

Forget the hair—it always unnerved me slightly when

gnomes masked for the field, as agents I knew to be a certain size were suddenly unnaturally large. I supposed the same could be said for my kind, albeit in reverse, but if it bothered my team, they had the wisdom not to mention it.

"Come on in," said Maya, beckoning Galibe closer. "Help yourself. We've got bacon, egg, and cheese...sausage and egg...bacon and egg...it's pretty egg-centric, really, so I hope that's okay."

"Don't forget the hashbrowns," I added, unable to ignore their salty, greasy, nearly ambrosial scent. "And there's an orange juice in the cupholder for you, youngling."

Watching him rummage through the offerings, Tabitha asked, "Something he can eat?"

"Oh, I'd say so," I replied, slipping into English for her. "He's probably still hungry after last night."

Galibe paused, two sandwiches in one hand and a hashbrown in the other, and cocked his head. "What'd you say?"

"Just that you're probably hungry," I told him, trying not to twitch at his artificially lowered voice. "Tabitha doesn't speak Pactish."

He glanced at Connor, then back at her. "She's...human, right?"

"Yup," said Maya, clapping him on the shoulder. "So am I. He's...I don't know, what, thirty percent?" she asked, nodding to Connor.

"Fifteen, but who's counting?" Connor retorted. "It's all right, Galibe, no one's going to hurt you."

The boy plopped onto the carpet—the dark colors and heavy patterning told me all I needed to know about its cleanliness—and regarded the rest of us warily between rapid bites. We divided up the rest of the food and drinks and ate quickly, eager to be off. As I downed my fourth biscuit, Tabitha threw her garbage away and washed her hands, then opened her bag of tricks on one of the unmade beds.

"What's up?" asked Maya, licking the hashbrown leavings off her fingers.

"Thought I'd give Galibe a quick check before we hit the road," she explained, and dug a penlight and thermometer from her kit. "I'm going to need an interpreter, y'all."

Galibe wasn't entirely keen on the idea, but he relented and let Tabitha look him over, following the light with his eyes and gamely holding the thermometer under his tongue until it beeped. She asked him about aches and pains—well, *I* asked him on her behalf—and aside from a few scratches and a selection of insect bites, the boy seemed intact. Finally, Tabitha announced, "You need to keep water going down today, yes? You're probably dehydrated. If that means we make more bathroom breaks, so be it."

He listened while I translated, then said, "I'm not *really* thirsty…"

I told Tabitha, who replied, "Better safe than sorry. Also, you've had a lot of salt in the last twelve hours, so don't fight me on this."

As Galibe refilled his cup at the bathroom tap, Connor asked, "Are we not going to stick around and look for the sorcerer involved? He might be lurking, right?"

"I didn't smell him yesterday," I said, "or at least not a recent scent. A pity, but since he doesn't seem to be close, we should return to the others."

He smirked. "You just don't like leaving Maggie in charge of the computer."

"I prefer hearing updates personally," I said, and tossed my wadded trash into the squat can by the dresser. "So, how are we dividing up?"

I have the utmost respect for adults who are able to cheerfully entertain children while traveling. After making the long drive back to Whitford with Galibe in the back seat, I felt like I needed a stiff drink, or possibly a medal.

Oh, the boy was well behaved. With a full stomach and reassurances of safety, he began to open up once we were on the road, and he kept his nose to the window as the sun rose, watching the strange land pass. He *also* kept up a steady stream of chatter, for which I couldn't entirely fault him—he'd been hiding up a tree for days, after all—but the commentary from behind me didn't cease except during brief periods of snacking and napping.

I had no right to be annoyed. Galibe was but ten, he'd been through hell, and he was seeing the outside for the first time...but a pair of earplugs would have been appreciated, all the same.

We made the trip more slowly heading east, giving ourselves breaks to refuel and stretch and run to the bathroom, and with the hour lost as we crossed into Georgia, we didn't pull into Whitford until around eight Tuesday night. Galibe, who'd dozed off during a long, boring stretch of I-20, had awakened in time to begin our drive into the mountains, and he loudly and frequently admired the scenery, asking endless questions about...well, *everything*.

There was, I supposed, a reason why parents seemed so frazzled around their young.

Tabitha parked behind us, and we shepherded Galibe into the illuminated house, where we were greeted by the mouth-watering scents of beef and rosemary. "Hello!" called Maggie from the sink, where she was scrubbing a heavy blue baking dish. "Y'all made it! Come on in, we saved you dinner."

Connor frowned at the scene. "Where'd you get the Dutch oven?"

"Walmart, dear," she replied with a hint of reproach. "You didn't seem to have one."

"It broke a few years ago," he mumbled. "Sorry..."

"Oh, don't worry about it. Grab you a plate, hon. Everything's in the oven. I made a pot roast, and there's potatoes, carrots, some broccoli…rolls are on the counter," she added, nodding to a towel-covered green ceramic basket sitting by the cannisters.

"I…didn't have one of those, either," said Connor.

"Well, now you do," Maggie said cheerily. "Put your things down and eat. Beer's in the fridge. Oh," she said, glancing past me, "and is this Galibe?"

The boy hung back, and as I watched, he nearly vanished into the shadows by the door.

"It's all right, sweetie," said Maggie, switching to Pactish. "Come in. Are you hungry?"

Galibe might have had reservations about humans—and after his time in Louisiana, that was understandable—but Maggie was warm, middle-aged, and non-threatening, and she had mothering down to a science. To my surprise, he ate his dinner standing at the counter, chatting with her as she washed up, while the rest of us gratefully sank into the kitchen chairs and devoured the food.

As much as I missed having Maya's culinary delights in the DPP tower, I was going to miss Maggie's home cooking nearly as badly.

While we ate, Dave, Yacovi, and Taug came in to get the latest, abandoning Ermonir on the couch in the den. Noticing the problem, I carried her into the kitchen and plopped her at the table, then finished my meal standing in the corner—which, after a day on the road, wasn't terrible. We did the best we could to keep Tabitha in the conversation, but she seemed content to sit back, sip a beer, and quietly decompress.

"So," I said once I'd sopped up every drop of gravy on my plate, "what's the latest from Beukal?"

Taug shook his head. "Not a peep all day. The director checked in last night—"

"Which one?"

"Mine. Erenani," he clarified for the others. "We told her that Galibe had been recovered, and she said she'd get word to his family, but that's the last we've heard from them."

"No chance that the portals have reopened, huh?"

He smirked. "Surely they wouldn't forget us if *that* had come to pass."

"In that case, then," I said, "I think I'll rest while I have the chance. How are we bunking tonight?"

Maggie pointed to the staircase. "The bedrooms are open. Tabitha, honey," she said, switching back to English, "you look like you're about to fall asleep over your plate. Why don't you stay here tonight? I'd feel so much better."

Tabitha didn't take much convincing, and she and Maya agreed to share again. I dearly wanted to crash in the bed I'd left Monday morning, but manners dictated that I not be hasty. "Uh...where are the rest of you sleeping?" I asked.

Dave and Taug shared a look, and Taug cracked his knuckles. "So, while you were gone, we looked in the closet for a board game or something—"

"Oh, no," Connor muttered.

His smile turned wicked. "Oh, *yes*. And since you have the manuals, am I correct in assuming that you were the DM?"

The boy's cheeks flared scarlet. "It was a *phase*. There's nothing to do around here when you're a teenager except go for hikes, get drunk, and smoke shit, and *that* was an alternative my parents wouldn't give me crap about."

I looked queryingly at Yacovi, who said, "Dungeons & Dragons."

"Fourth edition," added Taug. "Personally, I prefer the fifth, but I can work with the fourth."

Connor's brows rose. "You..."

"Also DM. I've got a group from Internal Affairs that meets once a fortnight."

"I'm sorry, but how the hell did you get into D&D?"

"Eh, one of my friends heard about it and brought back some books in the eighties, and I've been keeping up with it. It's fun. And if you play with sorcerers or elves, it's *really* easy to get decent miniatures cobbled together." He nodded to Yacovi, who grinned. "Anyway, I started running a one-shot yesterday, and it went long. We stopped for dinner tonight, but we've still got a couple hours of gameplay to go, I'd wager. We could stay downstairs and keep it quiet."

Having napped, Galibe was curious about the game, and so Connor, Tabitha, Maya, and I laid claim to the beds. I didn't know where the others planned to crash once they found their dragon or whatever, but that was a problem for someone who couldn't still feel the road flying by beneath her.

Unfortunately for me, about three hours of sleep would be all I'd have in that bed that evening.

I snarled and swatted at the hand shaking me out of deep slumber, then woke just enough to comprehend that Taug was calling my name. "Come on, get up," he insisted, shaking me again. "We've got video."

I groaned and tried to tug the blankets over my head, but Taug was persistent. "Chief, it's our farseer," he insisted. "Don't make me rip the covers away. I'll do it."

"Fuck you," I muttered, but then, as the words he was saying took on meaning, I slid off the mattress and tugged down my T-shirt. "She on yet?"

"Just called," said Taug. "I thought you'd want to talk to her."

He was right, and so I grunted my thanks and hurried down the steep staircase to the kitchen.

Yacovi, Connor, Dave, and Maggie were already clustered around the laptop—Ermonir, I saw, was asleep on the couch, and Galibe had curled up in a chair—and I took the chair in front of the screen. "Sorry," I said through a yawn, "what's up...*shit*, girl," I hissed as my bleary eyes focused, "have you not slept yet?"

"Couple catnaps," said Rose, who looked like she

hadn't seen a bed in far too long. "I'm okay."

"You are?" I asked dubiously.

Yven, who seemed weary but better rested than his fi-ancée, popped into view behind her. "She's on Happy Juice."

"Narc," she mumbled.

In fairness, I couldn't chastise her too greatly over that—we all took a sip of the Juice from time to time in Interdiction, especially on long stakeouts, and I *had* rec-ommended it to her on Monday—but Yven's expression told me that Rose wasn't being safe with the potion. "It's not a long-term substitute for sleep," I told her. "And I thought you hated Happy Juice."

"Right now, it's doing the trick," she protested. "And it's taken me freaking forever to lock on to Hoska and Keppa, so sleep hasn't been in the cards."

I straightened in my chair. "You've found them?"

"Yep. They're together."

"*Together?*" I echoed. "Did the dump team get lazy?"

"Lazier, I'd say—they weren't great with any of you," she replied. "Both of them were taken through Oilville."

"Three of us, then. Whoever they were paying at the Portal Authority wasn't being bribed heavily enough…"

"Yeah, but they dropped you in Richmond. The others went west."

"Oh, dear," Maggie murmured. "You don't mean…"

"Into the mountains," Rose confirmed. "That's what's taken me so long—that, and they've been on the move. My saving grace is that they were dropped along Skyline Drive, about a quarter-mile apart. I think it was an acci-dent, frankly, but it works in our favor."

"Sorry," said Taug, leaning toward the screen, "where did you say they were?"

"Shenandoah National Park. There's a two-lane road through the Blue Ridge Mountains called Skyline Drive, a scenic route about a hundred miles long. Pretty in the fall. It runs near the Appalachian Trail," she explained. "So, based on what Ganti and I have been able to put together, Hoska was dropped further south and started walking north, and he found Keppa on the first night. Poor kid got scared of the dark and made a campfire—they're a fire nymph, see? Hoska's been looking out for them both, and they've been hiking along, hiding by day and searching for food at night."

"They're hiding on the *AT*?" asked Connor incredulously.

"No, not on it—way too many people right now. Hoska's a Mountain Patrol ranger, and he knows how to make shelters, so they've kept out of sight. Anyway, they've made it as far as the South River picnic area—it's got traffic, but there's no water available, and the only toilets are kind of primitive. They've got a little site back in the woods, and since Hoska can get into the bearproof cans, they've been able to eat."

"I don't know the park that well," said Dave. "I mean, I've been through Shenandoah, but where are they, relatively speaking?"

"Almost due east of Harrisonburg," said Rose. "You're going to want to stay off Skyline as long as possible, assuming you intend to get there with any speed. If I were you, I'd go in through the entrance at Swift Run Gap, then head north to the picnic area. Or so says Annie," she added, stifling a yawn. "She knows the park better than I do."

"Where *is* Annie?" Maggie asked.

Rose cracked a little smile. "She's fine, just sleeping it off in a guest room downstairs. I'll tell her you said hi, okay?"

"Please do." Sharing a look with Dave, Maggie said, "That's going to be a haul. How far, do you think?"

Before he could answer, Connor said, "Let me," and pulled out his phone. After a moment of tapping, he said, "About seven hours if we don't stop. Probably eight, practically speaking. But it's largely a straight shot up I-81, and then we'll hook east on 33 to the entrance and pick up

Skyline."

"Let me see that map, please," said Dave, and Connor passed him the phone. He contemplated the screen for a moment, then looked at Rose. "You think they're going to move between now and the time we can reach them?"

"I can't say," she admitted. "My knowledge of future events is barely more than a spider sense. You'd want Pop for that, and he's holed up elsewhere in the house...I think. He *was*," she mumbled. "I can try to find him—"

"No, hon, it's okay. Tell me, where's the next entrance south of Swift Run Gap?"

Rose frowned down at her desk—probably at a note-pad, I deduced. "That's Rockfish Gap near Afton. Closer to Charlottesville. It's about fifty miles south of Swift Run, and at Skyline speeds, that's going to take some time."

"Understood, but I've got two thoughts," Dave replied. "One, assuming we leave in the next hour or so, it's going to be broad daylight by the time we get to this picnic area, and people are going to be out and about."

"On a Wednesday?" asked Maggie.

He shrugged. "Kids are back in school, right? Nice time for a drive. Two, in case they move south, I don't want to overshoot the runway. Tell you what, Rose, we'll leave soon. *You* get some sleep and plan to get up around, oh, seven or eight. We'll head into the park once it's decently light, you do your spy thing, and if our targets have moved, you'll be able to tell us. Ta-dah."

"That...could work," she allowed, as Yven fervently nodded behind her. "But you're going to have a small window to find them."

Dave's brow knit. "Why's that?"

"Because," she said, rubbing her forehead, "someone on the future team saw that there's a Bigfoot expedition going into the park today, and I found them. Shenandoah's on the schedule, and I think they're heading for the area near Hoska and Keppa."

"Sorry...*what?*" asked Taug, folding his arms.

"Bigfoot," Rose repeated. "Plenty of folks think 'squatches are out there somewhere, and so they get their gear and go into the woods to listen and jump at cracking branches."

"Have they ever found anything?"

"Like, a carcass? No, not to my knowledge, but some people just really want to believe. The problem is that they're going to have microphones, and they'll be listening for *anything* weird. You've got to extract our two before the Bigfoot hunters stumble onto them."

"We're on it," said Maggie before Taug could press Rose for details. "Get some sleep, dear, okay?" she nagged, and I cut the feed.

Five minutes later, with the remaining sleepers roused, we clustered in the den to talk logistics. "We should all go together," said Dave. "It'll be cramped in the RV, but once we find them, we can take this party back to Richmond. Our house is plenty big enough, especially if we get some inflatable mattresses. Take some of the pressure off you, kid," he added to Connor.

"Hell, I'm fine," Connor protested. "And I'll follow in my car—make a little breathing room. But we can't all go, remember? The laptop can't be moved in case it loses its connection…"

I groaned. "Shit, you're right. In that case," I said, looking around at the group, "who stays back?"

Clearly not Ermonir or Galibe; neither could speak English, Ermonir couldn't walk, and Galibe, while bright, was a child. Not Tabitha, as she couldn't read the Pactish characters on Jane's computer. Dave and Maggie had rented the RV, and I was loath to split them up.

After a moment, Maya volunteered. "I can keep handling the computer," she said, "and I can take care of myself here for a few days, or whatever. Safest to let a local fly solo, right? Relatively speaking," she added as Connor quirked a brow. "Tell your cop buddies that I'm your distant cousin in for a visit, and we're set."

"They'd never buy that," he replied, shaking his head. "Everyone knows I'm from East Branch stock."

"Seriously?"

"This is a small community, and once word gets around that you're attached to the weird compound out in the county, folks have *questions*. I'll tell them you're Janie's college friend, hanging out here while you get over a bad breakup, okay?"

She shrugged. "Works for me. Go Dawgs."

"But you don't have a car," Maggie protested. "And I don't think Connor's going to give you the keys to the one with blue lights."

"You can borrow mine," said Yacovi. "Got an Altima that should do you—she's a tank."

With that settled, we hastily packed and loaded the RV with the drinks and snacks we could scrounge from Connor's kitchen, then raided his modest stash of outdoor equipment and weapons. But around one Wednesday morning, as we started to load up to leave, Yacovi took Connor's keys from him. "You've been on the road for two days, son," he said in a no-nonsense tone. "You're a liability until you sleep."

"I can do it," said Connor with less than full insistence.

"I'd feel better if you didn't. Get in the bus and get horizontal."

"Yes, sir," he mumbled, and slunk off into the RV.

Taug rode shotgun with Yacovi, and Ermonir, who'd had time to realize they weren't going to hurt her, curled up in the back seat. Maggie took the first shift behind the wheel of the RV, and Dave sat up front to keep her company, leaving Tabitha, Connor, Galibe, and me to bed down. The dining booth converted into a bed for the boy, and Connor volunteered to sleep on the couch, which meant that Tabitha and I had the option of sharing the bedroom or sending one of us to sleep in the loft over the cab. She and I eyed the loft space, and then she muttered, "You snore?"

"Not usually. You?"

"Nah."

Without another word, we retreated to the rear of the vehicle together, kicked off our shoes, and collapsed into the bed. It wasn't the best mattress I'd ever encountered, but my travel exhaustion was catching up with me, and I didn't give a damn.

The rain began around Asheville and dogged us all the way up I-81, or so I was told after we parked at a truck stop near Staunton around nine-thirty that morning. I could have kept sleeping, lulled as I was by the road, but Tabitha had stirred and noticed we'd stopped, and she'd awakened me. We'd shuffled out of the bedroom to find the Humphrieses and Connor preparing to disembark; the RV needed gas again—I'd slept right through our prior stop, apparently—and the breakfast offerings in the kitchenette were disappointing.

When Maggie and Dave returned with greasy breakfast biscuits from the restaurant attached to the convenience store, the SUV group joined us, and we clustered around to eat, mostly standing in the overcrowded room. As Connor ducked out in search of coffee, Tabitha consulted her phone and grimaced. "Rain's not letting up. We've got a *mess* coming through behind us."

"All day?" asked Maggie through a yawn.

"No…should be gone by late afternoon, but it's going to be gross for a while. Could be some flash flooding." She looked up from the screen and frowned at Maggie. "Hon, you look dead on your feet. What do y'all say we camp here for a bit, let the worst of the rain move through, and then take a stab at the park?"

"Maybe this will keep the Bigfoot hunters home, eh?" I said.

Tabitha shook her head. "Guilty pleasure, but I've watched some of those shows, and those folks operate in less than optimal conditions. Unless the park is impassable, I bet they'll film tonight…"

Her voice faded as Maggie's phone rang, and Maggie pulled it from her purse. "Maya," she said, and took the call. "Hello, dear, how are you?"

"Speaker," Tabitha reminded her.

Maggie did as asked, and we heard Maya say, "Rose checked in a few minutes ago. Got an update."

"Has she slept?" I interrupted.

"Uh…that's probably a negative, Chief. Certainly hasn't showered. Anyway, she said she got some more details on the Bigfoot crew. Had Annie go through their socials. They've been hyping this hunt in Shenandoah for the last *month*."

"Any chance of a rain check?" Tabitha asked.

"No, since they're planning to livestream it."

"*Shit*," she hissed. "We're about to get soaked here."

"Yeah, that's the other thing Rose called about. Got a warning from the future farseers: don't go into the park until lunchtime," said Maya.

"Why not?"

"Because a semi will merge into you if you leave now. Don't do it."

"No argument there," said Maggie, and though I was anxious to begin the search, I had to agree.

By ten, rain was sheeting down the sides of the RV, and thunder boomed in the distance. Maggie and Dave retreated to the bedroom to nap while they could, Yacovi claimed the RV loft, and Connor put Galibe into his vehicle to go for a drive around the nearby town. "I'm not crazy," he murmured when Tabitha asked what the hell he was thinking. "That kid's been sleeping, and now he's bored out of his mind." With the pair of them off to explore, Tabitha, Taug, Ermonir, and I sat around inside the RV, talking in low voices, playing cards, and in Taug's case, nodding off on the couch.

The storm hadn't broken when noon drew near, but

those of us keeping watch knew we couldn't wait much longer. Tabitha peeked out the window at the truck stop's restaurant, then called Connor. "Hey," she said when he answered, "where are y'all?…Uh-huh. Need you to do us a favor. Find a pizzeria, I don't care which. After breakfast, I'm not too keen on trying lunch here, know what I'm saying?…Great, thanks. Be careful." Hanging up, she looked at us and said, "I know we've been eating a lot of pizza lately, but—"

"You needn't apologize," said Taug. "No one's complaining, and it's not as if we could bring Ermonir in there without causing a scene." Hearing her name, Ermonir asked what he'd said, and Taug briefly filled her in.

"Beyond Ermonir," said Tabitha, "I checked that place out when I made a bathroom run, and I'm afraid the roaches are on the payroll." She sighed and unkinked her back. "Tell Ermonir I'm sorry her first trip outside has been such a dumpster fire."

Taug did as she asked, and Ermonir patted Tabitha's knee and smiled. "It's not your fault," she said. "You rescued me, remember? If I haven't thanked you properly, let me do so now."

Tabitha waited while Taug translated the other way, then took Ermonir's hand and squeezed it. "We're going to get you home. I'm not sure how just yet, but we will. And I think it's past time for your next pain potion, isn't it?" she asked, then looked at Taug. "You, too. Have you had your antibiotics this morning?"

They affirmed it, and Ermonir smiled gratefully when Tabitha brought her a pain potion from Yacovi's rapidly dwindling stash. After knocking it back, she said, "I'm sorry for all of the trouble. How many days have you been away from your family because of this mess?"

Taug repeated that, and Tabitha chuckled. "Don't worry about it. And it's just me and my plants, so they're not missing me too terribly."

That surprised Ermonir. "No partner, really? I apologize, I assumed…"

Tabitha lifted one of her tiny braids. "Because of the gray in here?"

She winced even before Taug finished the translation. "Yes, I…sorry," she mumbled.

"Hey, *hey*," said Tabitha, taking the other woman's hand. "It's all right. Most folks my age have partnered off at least once, so it's not a bad assumption. Is there someone special for you?"

Ermonir still seemed embarrassed when Taug passed along Tabitha's reassurance, but she squeezed Tabitha's hand. "I have a boyfriend, yes. We've been together for about three years."

Tabitha grinned. "Serious?"

She nodded. "He's a teacher. *Great* with children—and he wants some of his own, which is perfect…" Sobering, she murmured, "If he finds out what happened to me…"

After Taug passed that along, Tabitha frowned. "You're the one at Laws," she said. "Assuming y'all can bring these clowns to trial, would the details need to come out?"

"Some, yes," he reluctantly allowed. "I've known tribunals to close to protect sensitive testimony, but then that always leaves the question of *why* they were closed…"

She made a face, then said, "Tell Ermonir that if this boyfriend of hers is decent, he won't think any less of her. She's a survivor."

Taug did so, and Ermonir pulled her knees to her chest. "I'm damaged," she said. "Whenever I sleep, I dream of them. I…I keep thinking I see them in the shadows…"

"You need a therapist," I said firmly. "You're traumatized. Again, not your fault, and if he's worth a damn, he'll support you." She regarded me uncertainly, and I said, "I don't know a single agent in my area of work who hasn't had at least a session or two with a therapist. We…see a *lot*. So do a number of people at Laws," I added, and Taug nodded. "But we chose our professions, yes? You didn't choose any of this, and you're handling yourself well. I mean it."

Ermonir still looked miserable, curled in on herself as best as she could in her masked form, and Tabitha rose from her seat. "Hey," she said, joining Ermonir on the couch, and as Ermonir regarded her with filming eyes, Tabitha hugged her. Ermonir stiffened at the unexpected touch, then melted and, finally, with her head against Tabitha's shoulder, silently cried.

Sometimes, I supposed, trading awkward glances with Taug, words were unnecessary.

As Ermonir's tears slowed, Tabitha leaned back to see her face and smoothed the other woman's hair from her eyes. "You're going to be okay," she murmured. "Not today, but you're going to get through this."

Ermonir swiped at her eyes and waited as I offered a brief translation. "Thank you," she told Tabitha, and hugged her again before separating. "I, um…do you think I might visit the bathroom?"

Taug offered to carry her into the cubicle, leaving Tabitha and me to tidy the RV in preparation for lunch. "You know," I said quietly, wiping down the table, "Ermonir did make a good point. I'm surprised that you're single."

She snorted. "*I'm* not."

"You have a lot to offer," I protested. "I'm not going to pretend to be any judge of human aesthetics, now, but I'm sure you're not hideous…"

Chuckling, Tabitha said, "High praise, that."

"Sorry. In fairness, I'd be surprised if my actual looks did anything for you," I replied, trying not to dwell on my nagging fear of what my boyfriend truly thought. "Not that it's any of my business, but unlucky in love?"

She leaned against the window and folded her arms. "I'm the kind of pot that doesn't have an easy lid, especially in a place like Ragged Gap."

"Oh?" I asked, mentally running through a list of potential snags—race, religion, preferences…

"Yep. It's not that I'm not interested in being with someone, but…do you understand what I mean by 'ace'?"

"*Mm*. Don't like, uh, physicality?"

"That's one way of putting it. And since most people would prefer a partner who does…" She shrugged. "You know, there's worse things than being single." Eyeing me, she said, "You've got a guy, right? One of Wylan's—"

I motioned for her to stop talking, then bent to her ear and whispered, "Yes, he is, but that's not common knowledge."

"*Oh*, got it," she whispered back. "Sorry. Um…not to sound, uh, specist or anything," she continued, fumbling, "but how does that work out?"

"Masked," I replied in a tone that I hoped ended that line of interrogation.

It worked. "Uh-huh. Understood. No more need be said." Clearing her throat, Tabitha pointed to the loft and asked, "So, think we should wake Yacovi before the pizza arrives?"

"Yacovi is awake," he mumbled from above us. "Pretend I'm not, okay?"

CHAPTER 14

It was about one before we were roused, fed, and ready to head into the park. Though Dave looked like he could have used a solid night's sleep, he piloted the RV with Maggie grimly staring through the rain by his side. Connor followed in his Hyundai, ferrying Yacovi and Galibe, who'd taken a shine to the cop during their morning drive and pizza run. Maggie kept her phone close in case Maya called with an update, but there had been no calls all day—nothing but the occasional automated update as to the miserable weather.

The Rockfish Gap entrance was only about half an hour away, given the wet streets, and was a simple affair: we turned off the Interstate and quickly veered onto a two-lane road, then drove a little farther until we reached a tollbooth. The ranger who spoke with Dave didn't give our vehicle a second glance, though she did warn him to keep his speed down and be mindful of deer as she passed him a folded paper map.

"Okay," he said, rolling up his window, "how far is it to this picnic place?"

"Hold on," Maggie replied, arranging the map across her legs. She peered at the tiny markings, moving it closer and farther from her face to focus, then said, "Best guess, about forty miles."

"In this."

He didn't need to specify; the rain had momentarily intensified and was sheeting against the windows.

"Speed limit's thirty-five, honey. Just take it slow."

I sat on the couch with Ermonir while Tabitha and Taug shared the dining booth, all of us watching the woods for signs of life. The trees were beginning to turn, yet another layer of leaves to add to the litter carpeting the floor beneath them, and though I'd seen my share of full-sized trees, I couldn't bring myself to look away. At home, we had parks like Green Lake that were capable of supporting more than grass, and Annie swore that the Hunt's lodge was surrounded by a proper forest, but there remained something so *alien* about the easy proliferation of plants outside. Taug and Ermonir, I noticed, seemed similarly interested in the landscape, but our human companions were quiet until we reached the first scenic overlook, at which point they oohed over the mountainous vista…well, what we could see of it. I imagined that the view was probably lovely on a dry day, but the sky was leaden and low, and mist rose from the valley.

But the rain did give us one advantage: traffic was minimal, and few people seemed inclined to pull over and leave their vehicles to take in the scenery. We chugged steadily along for about an hour until we reached the Swift Run overlook, at which point I asked Dave to stop.

He obliged, though he gave me an odd glance in the rearview mirror. "Carsick?" he asked.

"No, I just want to take a good sniff."

I stepped outside, shielding myself beneath a flimsy umbrella purchased at the truck stop that morning, and closed my eyes as I inhaled.

Exhaust, yes. Petrichor and wet earth and old leaves and *green*, so much plant life. Animal life, too—I could smell their leavings, the odor made more pungent with the rain. There were deer nearby, hidden somewhere in the trees, and if I wasn't mistaken, a bear…maybe two. Mushrooms, ants, plenty of humans who'd stopped to gawk…

There. Faint, oh so faint, but there.

"Any luck?" asked Dave, who'd come out with his own umbrella.

I nodded. "Faun. Just a whiff, but I got it. I might hit on the nymph if I tried long enough, but the rain's not helping, and fauns just smell stronger."

"Like wet goat?"

"You know, I might not make that comparison in polite company, but…yeah, there's a definite goatish note. It's *not* a goat," I insisted before he could ask. "I know the difference. There was a faun here within the last days."

"But not now?"

"No, it's old. If they've doubled back, they haven't come this far."

Encouraged that we were on the right track, we started off again.

The picnic site was only a few miles further up the road, and we nearly missed the wooden sign with the rain. Dave navigated onto the access lane and steered us a short distance away to a grassy clearing ringed with spreading trees. A handful of picnic tables came into view, little more than spindly shadows in the mist, along with a bright yellow sign warning visitors of bears. I thought there was a small wooden cabin at the site until I took a second look and realized it was the toilets. The strip of parking spaces on the edge of the woods was empty, and Dave pulled the RV in with no regard for painted lines.

I disembarked, umbrella in hand, and walked into the clearing. There was an information placard with a map of hiking trails in the area—possibly useful—but I wanted to get another scent profile of my surroundings. The sickly sweet smell of garbage was prominent beneath the general scents of the woods and rain, as well as the unfortunate odors from the decoy cabin. While the smell of faun wasn't *strong*, it was fresher there. Obviously, Hoska wouldn't have made their camp on the edge of the picnic area, but perhaps he came through with some regularity. I lifted my head at a sudden whiff of deer and looked across the clearing to find a doe staring back at me, but as Connor slammed his door, she bounded off into the trees.

"Hey," he said, joining me with a tattered umbrella that might have been run over at some point. "Any idea where to look?"

"It'll be easier once the rain stops. I mean, we *could* go hiking in the deluge…"

"Rather not. Y'all got room for company on the bus?"

The rest of our party piled into the RV, and I asked Maggie to call Maya. "Has word come from Rose?" I enquired, leaning toward her outstretched phone.

"Negative," said Maya. "All's quiet here. Damp. Any luck on your end?"

"We reached the picnic spot," I told her, "but it's pouring. Unless Rose comes through with coordinates, I think we should wait out the worst of the storm before we go searching."

That suggestion met with approval, and between our playing cards and a handful of phones with decent data plans and streaming services, we whiled away the afternoon, sneaking the occasional peek at the sodden park but staying inside.

Shortly after four, as the rain finally began to slow, Maggie's phone rang. "It's Maya," she announced as she took it. "Hi, hon…*oh*, hang on, slow down." Quickly switching on the speaker, she brought the phone into the cabin and thrust it toward us. "Okay, start over. Rose called?"

"Yeah, and she said y'all've got to move *now*," said Maya, not bothering with Pactish. "The Bigfoot team is on their way."

I glanced out the window at the drizzly world. "How close are they?"

"She said they were coming up from Staunton…"

"Hour and a half, two hours, tops," said Dave.

I swore as Yacovi murmured a translation for Galibe and Ermonir. "Did she have a direction? Landmarks?"

"No, just that they've got a rough lean-to behind a deadfall. They didn't appear to be on a trail."

Of course not. "All right, we're on it." Once Maggie hung up, I said, "We can try to follow my nose, but there's a *lot* out there, and the rain is a problem. I suggest we split up."

Taug's eyebrows rose. "You don't trust your senses?"

"I'd rather not risk their safety for the sake of my pride."

We bundled ourselves into the little wet-weather gear we carried while Maggie bustled around the RV, checking packs. "Sunset's at seven-fifteen," she said, putting a pair of flashlights on the couch, "but with the clouds, you're going to lose daylight early. How many water bottles do we have left? Knives? I don't think there's an emergency whistle anywhere in here…"

"Or pepper spray," Dave muttered. "We've got guns, now…"

"Not in the park," said Maggie.

That was a sobering prospect. I knew there were bears in the area, and while I'd never fought one, I had a healthy respect for the creatures.

"Tell you what," said Yacovi, who was busy divvying his potions into bags. "I can give a bear a run for its money. Dave, why don't you come with me? You carry a phone. Maggie, hon, you stay put and look after those two," he added, nodding to Ermonir and Galibe.

The boy frowned once Yacovi repeated himself in Pactish. "I can help!"

"*You* can help by not getting hurt, youngling," said Yacovi in a voice I suspected Jane knew all too well. "Besides, if there's an emergency here, Maggie can't lift Ermonir by herself. You're on standby, understood?"

He huffed a sigh but nodded.

I turned to Taug. "Why don't you go with Yacovi and Dave? I'll take Connor and Tabitha."

"Why does this feel like PE kickball all over again?" Tabitha muttered, but she didn't argue with her assignment.

Soon, equipped with phones and Yacovi's potions, we set off in search of the missing. I stood in the middle of the clearing, trying to orient myself to their scents, but the traces of nymph were faint, and those of faun were all over the place. That made sense: Hoska had Keppa stashed somewhere and was foraging for them both. As I sniffed for subtle clues, Connor approached with the park map. "There's a trail heading east to a waterfall, which seems to be the big hike around here," he said, showing me the diagram. "But that trail crosses the AT, which heads either north or west…"

"Lovely," I grunted. "Which would be more trafficked?"

"Hell if I know—this ain't my neck of the woods. I'm guessing more day hikers out to the falls and more through-hikers on the AT, but I don't have any real data for you." Pulling out his phone, he ran a quick search, then groaned. "Looks like the route to the falls is about three miles."

"Not so bad…"

"Yeah, except for the twelve hundred feet of elevation change."

"Oh, *that's* delightful." Nothing promised fun like miles of rough, wet terrain. Beckoning Yacovi over, I showed him the map and said, "My best estimate is that they're to the north or east of this place. Your choice: the big trail or the waterfall trail?"

"Look," Yacovi murmured, "Dave isn't in his prime, and Taug's still not the steadiest on two feet. I'll take the AT."

He had a point. I made a quick search of the picnic grounds and found a downed limb of decent size, and then, armed with my makeshift walking stick, set off to search.

A miserable, damp hour later—including the crossing of

one swollen stream—we reached the observation point for the waterfall, a flat space with a low stone wall over which we could see the cascading water through the surrounding trees. We hadn't hiked more than a mile and a half, but the terrain wasn't friendly that day, and Tabitha, who said she'd been a recreational hiker twenty years prior, had long been sidelined due to knee pain. She gamely carried on without complaint, but she was the slowest of our trio, and I caught her rubbing her knees when we paused to call for Hoska and Keppa.

I yelled their names again at the top of the waterfall, then listened as my voice echoed and died without response.

"Smell anything?" Tabitha murmured.

"They've *been* here," I said, scowling at the trail. "But it's faint, layered…plenty of more recent human traffic. Deer, too."

She hesitated, then asked, "Bear?"

"Yeah." That, plus a peculiar funk I couldn't identify, one with strong notes of wet dog. I couldn't recall whether there were wolves in those woods, and as I didn't want to further unnerve my companions, I kept that possibility to myself. Of course, since we were near a drinking source, I wasn't surprised to pick up a muddled mix of scents— running water attracted all manner of wildlife.

"So," said Connor, checking his phone, "where would we rank this in terms of our worst hikes? Wet and muddy, but we've got the trail to ourselves, and no one's broken or sprained anything…"

Tabitha rapped her knuckles against the side of his head, and Connor pulled away, chuckling. "What?"

"Knocking on wood," she muttered. "Let's not jinx this, yeah? I ain't carrying your sorry ass back to the RV." Sitting on the barrier wall, she said, "I went on a hike junior year that was just *cursed*. We got lost, one guy sprained an ankle, another broke something in his foot, then a freaking bear wandered up, and we had to deploy the spray. I was fine, but this girl stood too close and down-wind, and she ended up getting some blowback."

Connor winced. "How bad?"

"We used every drop of water we were carrying to wash her eyes, and she could still barely open them on the way back. It's a wonder she didn't walk into trees." Nodding to me, she asked, "How about you? Any horror stories?"

"The hiking's been largely uneventful at home," I replied, joining her on the wall for a moment to rest my feet. "I haven't had the best of times in *these* woods."

"Oh?"

"Yeah. One of my colleagues went missing about four years ago. Turns out he was dirty, but I couldn't imagine that at the time, so I hauled a rescue group into the woods not too far from here. *December.* It was freezing, and we stayed out until the incoming snow made us leave. I couldn't find a trace of him, and I was desperate...but since he'd given us the wrong location, that made perfect sense in retrospect."

She whistled. "Kicked his ass when you found him?"

I paused, trying not to think of Kritsa as I'd last seen him: his arms ending in scarred stumps, his mouth firmly closed, his eyes wide and watchful, even in solitary custody. I'd visited him two years prior—he was still housed in a cell below the DOL tower instead of on the penal farms for his own safety—and though the man who'd ordered his mutilation was himself an inmate by then, Kritsa remained jumpy. He'd been given prosthetics that allowed him to feed himself and type, but he seldom wrote a word—and with his vocal cords severed, he never spoke. I didn't know whether the siren could still produce his hypnotic song in his condition, but the guards assured me that he'd never tried. Gray-skinned to begin with, he'd grown paler during his sunless incarceration, and he'd regarded me solemnly, curiously, as I laid a wrapped package of instant coffee and seasoning bags on his desk, precious commodities for one in custody. I hadn't yet brought myself to forgive him—he would have killed me, after all—but we'd been colleagues for years, and I'd counted him as a friend before he betrayed us. He'd be out in another few decades, and maybe with time to work with a therapist and reflect, he could start over.

I didn't know whether I'd be able to fully forgive him by then, but I figured that a visit every so often wouldn't hurt either of us.

"Yven shot him. Self-defense," I murmured. "I got a little rough with him during interrogation…and then his associates made sure he wouldn't tell us anything." I took another glance at the waterfall, then said, "I can smell them, but it's faint. I don't think they're nearby. So…what are your druthers?"

Connor pulled out the map again and gave it a quick perusal. "Bottom of the falls, maybe? Since there's no water at the picnic site, they might be camping down there."

Unlikely, I thought, given the scent profile, but I agreed and followed him as he picked his way forward.

It was less than a mile to the base of the waterfall, but the last leg was perilous, a narrow, natural staircase of wet rock. Tabitha almost went flying at one point, and even Connor nearly fell as we neared the bottom. The miserable trail ended in a pool, which might have been tempting in midsummer after the work we'd put in, but that evening, it stood as merely another reminder of how damp and clammy everything around us was.

And as I'd feared, there was no indication that Hoska and Keppa were hiding nearby.

"Well, this was a bust…" Connor began, then frowned and pulled his ringing phone from his pocket. "It's Maggie. Yes, ma'am?" he said, answering the call. His frown deepened as he listened, and then he swore under his breath. "Okay, thanks for the warning. Y'all be careful."

"Bigfoot team?" Tabitha asked as he put the phone away.

"Yep. They've parked near the RV. Maggie told them she's waiting for a bunch of hikers to return, and they bought it. But they're in the woods now, and they're going to have gear."

"Which way did they go?" I asked. "Did she know?"

Connor shook his head. "She couldn't see past the place where our trail crosses the AT, so she didn't see their direction, but they're likely heading for one of our groups."

I looked up at the gray sky, which was darkening too much for my taste—we were about forty-five minutes from sunset and still had a long way to go. "I'm calling it," I said. "Hoska's no novice. Hopefully, he can keep the youngling hidden until these idiots go on their way. We need to head back, and we can try again tomorrow."

"No argument here," said Tabitha. "Which way?"

After studying the map by her phone's flashlight, we decided that backtracking would be the shortest option. Unfortunately, that meant ascending to the top of the falls, and my legs burned by the time we limped to level ground. The climb had been faster than the descent, but it was seven by then, and the light was down to twilight conditions. "That way, yes?" I said, pointing to the trail.

"Yeah," Tabitha replied, just as her phone and Connor's chimed with an incoming message.

"What's that?" I asked.

Connor grinned as he read. "Yacovi. They found them."

"*What?* Really?"

"Yeah," he said, and chuckled wearily. "Few hundred yards off the trail. Hang on…" Sobering, he said, "Hoska's sick. He's got a fever, and Keppa's been caring for him for the last day or so. The kid was scared enough to show himself."

"Themself," Tabitha corrected.

"Sorry. Yacovi says they're about a mile from the picnic site, so they're heading back…" He paused as an eerie howling echoed through the trees, followed by a series of hollow thunking sounds.

"The hell is that?" I murmured.

"That'd be our Bigfoot hunters," said Tabitha. "Playing calls, knocking sticks together. They're trying to get a response." We stared at her, and she shrugged. "Or that's what they do on TV, anyway."

I could just smell them, unfamiliar humans at a distance…and something else. The wet dog scent had grown stronger. "They took the waterfall trail. How do we play this? Just hike back to the RV?"

"The other option is the fire road," said Connor, raising his voice over a rustling in some nearby trees that I *sincerely* hoped was a deer. "Follow that west to the AT, then hike south to the picnic…"

"Connor?" I said as his jaw went slack.

"Turn around," he whispered, not blinking. "*Slowly.*"

I did as he bade, and then my breath caught.

The source of the wet dog scent was…*something*, a hairy creature perhaps a little shorter than my true height but built like a wall. Its pelt was dark brown, and its—no, *his*, definitely—muscular arms were too long to belong to a human in disguise. In the fading light, I could just make out the sheen of his eyes beneath his heavy brow. He stared back at me and took a deep sniff.

"No sudden moves," said Tabitha. "Holy shit, that's a 'squatch."

And to my dismay, he was standing between us and the shorter trail. We held our ground, he and I, and then his upper lip lifted, revealing long eye teeth.

"Back away," I ordered. "Easy."

The three of us began a slow retreat, keeping our eyes on the apparent sasquatch. But before we could put more than a few feet between us, the recorded calls sounded through the woods again, and the sasquatch took notice. He straightened, then beat on his chest and *howled* back at the noise.

I'd hoped that might distract him, but then I stepped

on a twig, which snapped like a gunshot beneath my shoe.

The 'squatch wheeled on me, puffing himself up, and I made a quick decision. "Get ready to run," I said. "Fire road."

"What?" said Connor.

"Fire road," I repeated. "Get Tabitha out of here. I'll follow."

"Chief, wait—"

Ignoring him, I tossed my pack aside and gripped my borrowed pendant. My mask fell away in the blink of an eye, shredding most of my clothing in the process, including my shoes and pants. With my unnecessary bra now painfully tight and my underwear holding on by sheer luck, I squared off against the creature and growled, hoping he'd take the hint.

He did not. Though my transformation obviously surprised him, he recovered, pounded his chest again, then rushed me.

Connor might have been part elf, but having seen him in action, I knew damn well that I was the best weapon in our arsenal that night. While I seldom had occasion to get into a barehanded match, my agents and I trained regularly, and I knew how to use my natural advantages. I hit the creature head-on, ducking slightly and coming up to jab at him with my tusks, while my claws raked across his face. I bloodied him with the first blow—I could smell it—but as we wrestled for purchase in the shadows, I slipped on the wet leaf litter. While I caught myself before I could fall, I gave him the opening he needed, and the whore-get took a chunk out of my side. Screaming with the blinding pain, I managed to wrestle loose of his jaws, then went in with my own teeth, goring him through the shoulder. I spat hair and flesh, preparing to strike again, but the bleeding 'squatch had lost his taste for combat. He bellowed once, clutching his wounded shoulder, then ran off through the trees.

I waited until I was sure he'd fled, and then, groaning, I

turned to go…only to find Tabitha and Connor waiting behind me. "I thought I told you two to run," I muttered.

"We don't leave people behind," Tabitha snapped. "Sit down, woman. Where are you hurt?"

I touched my side, and my fingers came away wet and sticky. "Just one to worry about. I'm okay…"

"*Sit*," she ordered, and I plopped onto a rock while she rummaged through her bag by the light of Connor's phone.

"You know," he told me, "it's damn tricky to get off a shot when you're wrestling with the perp in the darkness."

"You're carrying a gun?" I asked.

"No, but I *have* learned a few offensive spells. I might have been able to stop him—"

"And you also might have been ripped in half." Turning to Tabitha as she hurried over with her first aid kit, I said, "So, this is me without the mask…"

"Uh-huh. Connor, light." He moved it into position for her, and she crouched to examine me. "All right, I'm going to field dress this, and I'll stitch you up once we're back in the RV. Also, you've got a little something on your tooth."

I felt around with my tongue, then realized she was referring to the small chunk of sasquatch speared on the end of a tusk. "Thanks," I said, flicking it away. "Well, let's look on the bright side. At least we don't have to worry about getting blood on my clothes."

"What clothes?" she retorted. "And unless you plan to walk back like that, you need to mask before I bandage you up."

"*Right.*" I engaged the pendant, taking the strain off my abused undergarments, and Tabitha quickly covered the hole in my side. "Let's hope we don't see anyone on the trail," I said. "Going to have an awkward conversation if we do."

"Not so bad as you think," said Tabitha, putting her kit aside. "Connor, turn around."

He didn't argue, and once his back was to us, Tabitha

shucked off her jeans, then the pair of mid-thigh black shorts she'd worn beneath them. "Little trick to cut down on chafing," she explained, handing the shorts to me. "They might be tight, but better than hiking in your skivvies, yeah?"

The shorts had plenty of give in the fabric, and Connor loaned me the rain jacket he'd worn to cover my bra and bandages before taking my pack. Barefoot and grateful for the pain potion Yacovi had added to my gear, I walked with them through the starless night, hoping their phones had enough power to light our way out of the woods.

A little after nine-thirty, we limped back into the picnic area, drawn to the glow of the RV. Tabitha had called ahead to see whether the coast was clear, and Maggie had given her the go-ahead; the stars of the Bigfoot show were still roaming the woods, and the only people left were a cameraman and an assistant managing their van.

The assistant poked her head out the open doors as we drew near. "Hey," she called. "Are you the last of the missing hikers?"

"Took a spill at the waterfall," Connor fibbed.

She made a face. "Lousy day to hike, anyway. See anything interesting in the woods? 'Squatches? We heard yelling…"

"No," said Tabitha, "but we *did* see a bear with a cub. They were at a distance, but, you know, be careful in there."

The assistant thanked us and turned back to monitoring the video feeds, and I shuffled up the steps behind Tabitha into the blessed warmth of our vehicle.

Yacovi was waiting to pull me inside. "What the hell happened to you?" he demanded.

"She fought off fucking Bigfoot," said Connor, bringing up the rear. "It's real! There was an honest-to-God *'squatch* in the woods tonight! I mean, I thought I heard one back home once, but to see it—"

Tabitha grunted. "For a damn *elf*, you sound really surprised that a supposedly mythical creature exists."

"And you're not shocked?" he countered.

She shrugged. "Dude, look around. There's a centaur making popcorn."

"Anyone want a bag?" Taug asked from the kitchenette. "We've got plenty."

"Wouldn't say no," Tabitha replied, and pointed me to the couch. "Gentle Breeze, sit there and try not to aggravate your wound. Where are our happy campers, and am I going to need a translator?"

The two had been put to bed in the back of the RV, and Keppa was bathing Hoska's forehead with a cold cloth as well as the child could when Tabitha came in. As it turned out, Hoska had done a brief stint at Laws before settling in with the Mountain Patrol, and he could speak English, albeit with a strong accent. Keppa couldn't understand a word, but Maggie went in to help keep them calm while Tabitha saw to the patient.

Both were filthy, having been in the woods for nearly a week. Keppa's brown skin was streaked with grime, and their long red hair was matted to their scalp. Even beneath a blanket, they shivered in their thin nightclothes. Hoska had slept in a shirt that might once have been white, and their brown curls were flat and dirty. Tabitha conducted a brief examination of the pair, then ordered Hoska into the shower while Maggie heated water in the microwave. "Is he all right?" I asked once the water was running.

"He's feverish—I have no clue what a normal temperature is for a faun, but he's flushed and warm to the touch. Had diarrhea for two days, and, uh…" She made a face. "That's an awful lot of hair to keep clean on his legs. It sounds like he drank bad water. Keppa seems fine, just scraped up and hungry. Scared, but Maggie's trying. There's hot chocolate mix somewhere in here, and the kid perked at the offer, so…"

"That's made it into the Pactlands," I replied, and held up an open bag of popcorn. "Taug left this for you. He's gone to the SUV with Connor and Yacovi to make some room."

Her mouth twitched. "And you got started, huh?"

"Woman, I'm *starving*."

"Fair. Scoot over, and if there's another pain potion handy, you might knock that back."

I did as she instructed, then braced myself as she peeled away my bandages and cleaned the wound again. "Yeah, this needs stitches, and you're getting an antibiotic as well. What's your dosage? Have you had penicillin before?"

"Something in the family. I got injured"—I hissed as my ragged skin stung—"sorry, injured in the field once, and my team leader was concerned. Found a phone, called it in, did as the healer said."

"How much, then?"

"I don't recall, but he told us to take the normal adult dose and double it."

"*Shit*." She shook out a few pills from the now communal bottle and passed them to me with a can of Coke. "Knock those back. Ain't no telling what that thing was carrying."

"You don't think he was venomous, do you?"

"No...doesn't look like a snakebite back here or anything," said Tabitha, "but better safe than sorry."

She worked quickly, and I tried not to tense up beneath the needle. Once she'd finished and redressed the wound, I slipped into a borrowed shirt and wrapped Connor's jacket back around me, sore and trying to warm up. Maggie pressed a mug of tea into my hands and gave me a look that forbade argument, then returned a moment later with a beach towel. "We didn't bring much in the way of linens," she said, "but your legs have to be cold. Cover up, hon."

By then, Hoska had staggered from the shower, dripping from horns to hooves. Tabitha wrapped him up, plopped him on the couch beside me, and gave him a handful of pills and a bottle of water. "For your fever," she explained, pointing to his loaded palm, "antibiotic, and that's for the diarrhea. Did anyone bring canned soup? Instant ramen?" she asked.

Maggie checked the cabinet. "There's a six-pack of noodles in here. Chicken flavor…"

"Are you a vegetarian?" she asked Hoska.

He shook his head. "I don't often eat meat, but I'm not opposed."

"Perfect. Stay there."

As she grabbed a bowl and the ramen, I said, "Hi. Gentle Breeze, DPP."

"Hoska Shilg," he replied, and sipped his water. "Thanks for coming after us. Taug and Yacovi told us what's happened…" He glanced around the RV, and Galibe, who'd claimed the booth, gave him a little wave. "Strange crew you have here."

"They've been great."

A few minutes later, Tabitha put a warm bowl in Hoska's hands. "Eat that *slowly*. I'm more concerned that you get the broth down you than the pasta—you need salt. Wish we had a damn Gatorade on this bus, but maybe we can make a grocery run after we get out of here." She dug through the stash of potions, which had been unpacked from our bags and consolidated, and pulled out a few tubes. "Looks like we have three healing potions unless I'm missing something. Gentle Breeze, Hoska, you're each getting one…and Maggie, could you get Keppa out here, please?"

"Hoska can have mine—" I began.

"There is a *hole* in your side," Tabitha snapped, thrusting a tube into my hands. "Take the damn potion."

Frankly, I didn't feel like fighting her, and so I downed mine as Keppa and Hoska did likewise. When Keppa showed interest in Hoska's ramen, Tabitha made them a bowl as well, and the kid sat at the table with Galibe, whose rapid chatter seemed to put the younger child at ease. With the shades drawn, we had a little time before we needed to worry about masking the newcomers...but that raised another question.

"So," said Dave, "where to? Looks like we can make it back to Richmond in a couple hours..."

Maggie phoned Connor to bring the others back aboard to discuss our options. "I wouldn't say no to your hospitality," Yacovi told the Humphrieses, "but we need healing potions. Taug's leg, Ermonir's tail, Gentle Breeze, now whatever's wrong with Hoska...you two stay healthy, you hear me?" he said to the younglings. "Pain potions would be good, too. I *think* I've got enough in my brew room to make a fresh batch."

"You *think*?" said Connor.

"Can't get into the greenhouse, remember? It's not going to be a huge batch, but it's the best I can do." He glanced around the RV at the wounded, then folded his arms and turned to Dave and Maggie. "You've been driving hard. I can take the first shift if we want to head back to Georgia."

"Wait," I said before they could answer that. "Yacovi, do you know Liliol ti'Cren?"

"Sure," he replied. "She's got a facility in...*oh*," he said, his eyes widening as he saw where I was going. "She brews. I wonder if she's got anything accessible."

"Where is she?" Connor asked, pulling out his phone.

"The town's called Briardale, if I recall," I told him. "She runs a garden nursery as a cover...Bounty, something Bounty..."

He tapped for a moment. "Eden's Bounty?"

"That's it."

"It's half an hour away." To Yacovi, I asked, "You wouldn't have her number, would you?"

He didn't, and so, despite the hour, we called the nursery's phone number and hoped. To my shock, the call was answered on the second ring: "Eden's Bounty, this is

Lily Thorn," said a female voice through the speaker—one that sounded rather aged and with nary a hint of a Pactlands accent. "Can I help you?"

"Ms. ti'Cren," I said in Pactish, "this is Gentle Breeze from DPP—"

"Oh, *heavens*," she interrupted, switching languages, "*finally*! I've been trying to get through for days, but I haven't been able to reach anyone! What's happened?"

As I stared wearily at the phone in my hand, suddenly exhausted and wondering where to begin, Yacovi gently took it from me. "Hi, Liliol? Yacovi Hewt. Gentle Breeze has had a rough night, so why don't I fill you in?"

"Yacovi!" she said, surprised. "Has your facility been affected, too?"

He chuckled low. "Absolutely. What's happened to yours?"

"Well," she said, "I'm not entirely sure. I was working late last Wednesday night, packing some big orders—or it might have been Thursday by then, I'm not positive—but suddenly, there was this...*current*, I guess you could say, that ripped through my greenhouse. Never felt anything like it. I jumped up to get out of there, and fortunately, my door was open."

He frowned. "You leave your greenhouse open when you work?"

"Sometimes," she admitted. "*I* close it, but my slither-trap likes to ambush whatever walks by in the dark."

"*Ah*. I'd heard you had a...rather large one."

"Sally's a big girl, and she snacks," said Liliol. "Anyway, she had a vine sticking out the door when the incident occurred, so I got out. But now the greenhouse is *stuck*—the door closes, but I can't hide it. I've been trying to reach DPP for days, but my phone calls haven't gone through, and since the mail stopped abruptly...what's the problem?"

I accepted a bowl of ramen from Tabitha while Yacovi brought Liliol up to speed, and I'd nearly downed it when he said, "Basically, I've got four injured people aboard, we're out of healing potions, our amateur healer is a human pharmacist, and I don't know that I have enough supplies to brew what we're going to need if they don't get the damn portals open soon. We're at the South River picnic area if you know Shenandoah."

"Not that well," said Liliol. "Are you close to me?"

"Half an hour, give or take."

"Well, then, less talking, more driving. I'll be expecting you."

"What, tonight?" he asked.

"Yes, tonight, silly. Unless you were planning to sleep in the park…"

Dave flashed a thumbs-up. "We can make it."

"In that case, we're on our way," Yacovi told her. "Just need to make a stop for supplies. Anything we can bring you?"

Liliol muttered, "Ooh. In case Gentle Breeze hasn't mentioned it, I only have two beds."

"Honestly, I'll take a floor as long as it's not moving," Yacovi replied, and nodded to Dave. "Let's roll. I'll drive the SUV. Connor, get Maya on the phone."

CHAPTER 15

Briardale was nothing special as mountain hamlets went, a wide patch of civilization that had grown up on a relatively flat piece of land, with encroachment into the surrounding hills. Its winding roads certainly had little to recommend them in the deer-haunted darkness. But after making a quick stop at a convenience store for electrolyte-heavy drinks and questionable packaged sandwiches, we'd driven hard to reach the place, and I was relieved to pass a sign welcoming us to town.

Liliol had built her garden nursery on a hillside, with her cottage a little further up the slope. Set off from her shop and racks of plants were a small shed for her maintenance tools, plus a half-buried storm shelter that she kept locked...well, most of the time.

She'd left the gate at the bottom of the hill open, and Dave took the lead, chugging up the driveway and parking in the gravel lot where the hill flattened out. "Uh...folks?" he called from the front as he turned off the engine. "What the hell is *that?*"

The storm shelter was a decoy, and if one stood in front of it and spoke with the proper credentials and authority, Liliol's greenhouse would appear, a liminal space partly in the Pactlands but anchored to the outside world. It was far too large for the tiny plot of land on which the storm shelter sat, and trying to come to terms with what my eyes were telling me made my head hurt.

"That's the greenhouse," I told Dave. "Stay out of there, okay? Those places are dangerous if you don't know what you're doing."

I gingerly climbed down from the vehicle, clutching my bag against my uninjured side, and watched as Connor strolled toward the open greenhouse door. "Hey, Sally," he called in the same syrupy tones one might use for a fluffy puppy. "Where're you hiding, girl?"

A green vine as thick as my forearm shot out of the building, rose like a snake, and bent at the top, forming a sort of head. It considered Connor for all of two seconds before it raced forward and wrapped around his arm.

"Need some help?" I asked, hurrying toward his side.

"Nah. She remembers me," he said, gently stroking the vine, which was visibly vibrating as it coiled around him. "Purring, see?"

Sentient plants had always left me uneasy, but I managed a polite, "Good evening, Sally," and patted the vine. Giving it another look, I said, "Do you think she understands this?"

"She's fluent in Pactish and English, and I'm pretty sure she knows a fair bit of Low Elvish," said Liliol, emerging from the greenhouse. "Whether she deigns to follow instructions in any language is another matter."

While DPP authorized a fair number of growers and brewers to operate outside the Pactlands, few were master growers, those given license to handle highly restricted plants because they'd proven themselves capable and trustworthy. Yacovi, naturally, was certified, but so was Liliol. When floramancy appeared in Hall ti'Cren, it ran strong, and she and her elder brother had inherited the family's wild talent. But while Lord ti'Cren remained in the Pactlands, working as an experimental botanist, Liliol had moved out of the mansion in the early twentieth century. She'd changed her address several times, an annoying necessity, but had stayed within the Appalachians, where she was seldom bothered. For a child of one of the most prominent of the Halls, Liliol was slightly feral.

By elven metrics, she was a tiny thing, barely more than

five feet tall and slight of build, albeit well toned from decades of nursery work. Her mask added nothing to her stat-
ure, but it did give wrinkles to her suntanned skin and
bleach her long blonde braid to white. That night, she
wore a black windbreaker over ratty jeans and canvas tennis shoes turned gray with ground-in dirt. "Hello, youngling," she said to Connor, then gave Sally a tap. "Let him
go, now. It's late."

Sally unwound herself and retreated to the greenhouse,
but the tip of one vine protruded through the open door
as if taking our measure.

"We really should stop meeting like this," I said.

Liliol grinned up at me. "I expect nothing less from
DPP. Come inside, I put coffee on."

We trudged up the hill to the cottage, and Liliol
watched from the porch as Connor floated Ermonir
through the door. "You're coming along, aren't you?" she
said approvingly. "Rosie said you were in private training."

"Yes, ma'am," he replied, and yawned as he deposited
Ermonir on the couch. "It's not there yet, but—"

"You've only just begun to learn," she chided. "Mastery
is a *process*, boy. Give it a few decades, eh? And *hello*," she
said, shaking Yacovi's hand. "You look exhausted."

"It's been a day," he muttered, then glanced around the
room. "Liliol, this is Taug Berek from Laws," he said, patting Taug's shoulder. "The lady on the couch is Ermonir
venTala—"

"That would explain why she got a lift," said Liliol, and
Ermonir shrugged helplessly.

"Hoska Shilg," Yacovi continued, nodding to the faun,
"Mountain Patrol, hasn't yet dealt with masking jewelry."

He raised a hand from his seat on the floor by the fireplace.

"Those little miscreants are Keppa Amarr and Galibe
Yentera," said Yacovi as the children, who'd perched be-
side Ermonir, watched with sleepy eyes. "And we've got
Maggie and Dave Humphries, our gracious chauffeurs, and

Tabitha Bradley, who's been patching us up for days," he said, nodding to the trio by the door.

Liliol beamed. "Humphries—Annie's parents?" she asked in English. They nodded, and her smile widened. "Lovely. My Rosie speaks so highly of her. And *Tabitha*, finally! I keep hearing of you, but Rosie seldom brings her friends over."

"You must be Aunt Lily," said Tabitha, smiling back at her.

"That's me."

"We keep telling Rose to invite you to brunch…"

"Oh, she has, but weekends are *slammed* around here, and you're looking at the entire staff of this operation. Now," she said, "I've got a dozen healing potions in the kitchen. Who needs them?"

We drained Liliol's coffeepot while she and Tabitha made the rounds with healing potions, then painkillers. "Are you hungry?" she asked in Pactish, then noticed Tabitha's blank look and translated. "Sorry, dear, monolingual?"

"A little Spanish and a smattering of Gullah."

"Neither of which is useful tonight, but I don't mind repeating myself. So, do we need food?"

The questionable sandwiches and the snacks in the RV were sufficient to tide us over until morning, and by then, the children were nodding off. "Come on, younglings," Liliol urged, shepherding the two into her guest bedroom. "Shoes off. Let me see those clothes…" With a quick gesture, both were clean, and she tucked them into bed. "I'll put the nightlight on in the bathroom for you," she said, and by the time she'd dug it from a drawer, Keppa was breathing deeply, with Galibe on the precipice of sleep right behind them. I finished inflating an air mattress pulled from Liliol's closet and put it at the foot of the bed, and we sent Hoska in to sleep with the kids. He protested that he was fine, but Tabitha pointed out the proximity to the toilet if he stayed in there, and so he relented and crashed.

We emerged to the sound of Connor's phone ringing, and he answered on speaker mode. "Maya?"

"Hey," she said. "I've got Rose."

"That was fast."

"They're checking for messages. Um…hang on, switch to video."

He did, then waved at Maya as her face appeared. "Don't you wish you were here?"

"Oh, no," she deadpanned, "I've had to hang out in a climate-controlled house with Netflix and Yacovi's hooch. Truly, this is a hardship."

"Don't drink all my good booze, now—"

"I'll get you a new bottle, son," said Yacovi, sliding into view. "Rose, can you hear me?"

"Yeah," she said after a few seconds' lag, her voice tinny with the setup. "You made it to Aunt Lily's?"

"They did," said Liliol, pulling the phone down. "Maya, yes? Would you please turn the phone around?" She waited, then hissed. "*Rosie*! When did you last *sleep*?"

"I'm fine," Rose mumbled.

"No, you most certainly are *not*. Girl—"

"We've been nagging her, too," Yacovi interrupted. "Rose, is Teme around? Or Director Erenani?"

"Hang on…uh, Pateme doesn't seem to be logged in, but Kabno is. You want to talk to her?"

"Please. And Liliol's right, honey—you need to rest."

"I'll get her," said Rose, and cut her feed.

Maya hung up as well, leaving us to wait in the den. "So," said Liliol, taking us in, "is there a reason that we're all masked? This place is private, I assure you," she added, and removed hers with a quick gesture in front of her face, shedding her aged guise in an instant and revealing her unmistakably elven features.

I was pleased to note that Dave and Maggie barely twitched.

"We three have stitches," Taug explained, pointing to

Ermonir and me. "I think mine are far enough apart to survive unmasking, but if the wounds open..."

"*Oh*, goodness," she muttered. "Sorry, I didn't even think of that..."

"Honestly, I'm more concerned about what Tabitha would do to us if we messed up her work."

Tabitha glanced up from her phone and cleared her throat. "Heard my name."

"Taug's telling Liliol why we're not going to unmask and rip open our stitches," I told her.

"Mm. Yeah, please don't."

"You'll want to remove them sooner than you might imagine, dear," Liliol said to Tabitha. "They won't dissolve, will they?"

She shook her head. "No, my stuff's not that fancy. This is first aid, not surgery. I'm doing my best—"

"I'm sure you are," she soothed, "but if you're unaccustomed to dealing with healing potions, you may be surprised by how quickly they work. I've had my share of mishaps over the years," she confessed. "Now, which of you has the oldest wounds?"

"Me," said Taug, lifting a finger. "Saturday."

"Four days, then. Want to remove the bandages and check?"

"Uh..." He glanced at Tabitha, then asked, "Got a private area we could borrow?"

The two headed off to the master bathroom, only for Tabitha to emerge alone a moment later, flabbergasted. "It's closed! That thing was *gnarly*, and it's already scarred over."

Yacovi looked pleased with himself. "I brew good stuff, you know. That potion will mend bones if you take enough of it."

She turned to Liliol, then back to Yacovi. "So...if I remove the stitches and he unmasks, it shouldn't reopen?"

"Odds are good," Liliol replied. "Do you want a hand?"

"Uh…you know, I think Taug would prefer to limit the audience. Just need my scissors…"

"How about a little something to numb the area? Just in case," she offered.

Tabitha accepted the potion and a syringe, and returned to the bathroom.

We'd just started a pool as to how long it would take her to remove the stitches from the spot below Taug's rump when Maya called back. "Hiya," she said when Connor turned on the video feed. "Got a twofer for you."

We crowded around Connor's phone as Maya flipped hers to face the laptop screen. On the other side in a split frame were Kabno and Pateme, both of whom seemed to have been pulled from…well, not bed, but perhaps a nap on a cot. Kabno's white hair rose in odd clumps, while my director had forgone his usual sleek brown ponytail. His hair fell over his shoulders, uncharacteristically greasy and snarled, and the puffiness beneath his dark eyes told me he'd just been roused.

"Interrupted your beauty sleep, Teme?" Yacovi teased.

Pateme groaned. "I heard you were bothering my niece."

"Visiting."

"*Crashing*, more like," said Liliol. "Hello, Uncle. We won't keep you. They wanted to check in."

Taking the phone from Connor, I said, "Evening, Directors. All accounted for. Hoska's ill, but Keppa seems to be all right. They've been fed, medicated, and put to bed."

"Excellent," said Kabno. "Fantastic news."

"Please tell me the portals are open again."

The two winced. "Not yet," said Pateme. "They're working on it, but for now…"

"We're stuck, I understand," I finished. "I'm not sure where we're heading next, probably Richmond or Whitford, but we needed potions, so we stopped here."

He frowned. "Liliol stores potions outside of her greenhouse?"

"Of course not," said Liliol, taking the phone from me. "My brew room's in there—I'm not stupid enough to hide them in my *home*."

"Then how—"

"My greenhouse is open. Stuck, actually. Probably Sally's fault, but—"

"It's *open*?" he cried.

"Whoa, it's okay," she said, talking him down. "I've put up a spell to camouflage the area from the street, and I've closed the nursery. This group is the first company I've had in a week. Come on, now, I'm no novice."

He didn't comment on her protective measures. "And…*Sally* is responsible for this?"

"She had a vine out the door when the Pactlands closed, I think. That's my best guess, anyway."

"Remind me to buy her a box of mice," said Pateme. "Give me ten minutes, then go to the greenhouse."

"Why—"

"Just try for me, please."

"As you like," said Liliol bemusedly, then handed the phone back to Connor to end the call. Turning to the rest of us, she said, "Shall we?"

Once Taug and Tabitha returned, everyone but Ermonir trooped after her down the trail back to the nursery area, then paused outside the cracked greenhouse door. "All right, listen closely," said Liliol, switching to English. "Yacovi, I know you can handle yourself. Gentle Breeze and Connor, this isn't your first time in a greenhouse, but don't get cocky. Taug…"

"I've never been a plant guy," he said.

"Then this is for you as well. For the humans among us, ever been to a botanical garden with a cactus greenhouse? Look, don't touch?"

The Humphrieses and Tabitha nodded.

"Same principle," Liliol continued, "but take it up a notch. Ever heard of the Poison Garden?"

That time, only Tabitha followed along. "In England,

right?"

"Exactly. Everything growing in there is toxic or intoxicating, and you don't touch or sniff anything. Pretend that's where you are. Not everything in my greenhouse is harmful," she said as Maggie and Dave shared an uneasy glance, "but you don't know the difference, and some of the plants in there are *very* unpleasant. Also, there's Sally."

The vine currently lounging in the doorway rose and waved.

"She's an Amazonian slithertrap. Raised her from a seed," she said proudly. "Sally is a combination security measure and pest control. Now, since you're with me, she should leave you alone, but if she comes exploring, gives you a tap, maybe encircles an ankle, just be still and let me know if you're uncomfortable. *Please* don't stomp her—she bruises. Any questions?"

Dave lifted a finger and coughed. "This Sally, uh…she understands you?"

"Quite well."

"You've got a plant with ears?"

Liliol wiggled one hand. "Not that you'd recognize as such. Their biology is fascinating, and the assumption is that they're the result of magical experimentation during a preliterate era, but that's a *long* talk for another time. Right, then, follow me, hands to yourselves."

We trailed her into the building, moving carefully between the rows of flourishing plants, accompanied by a rustling beneath the benches that was *almost* not menacing. "I'm not sure where we're meant to go," said Liliol as we reached the relative safety of the back counter, where she kept her mailboxes and her packing materials. "Yacovi, any clue?"

"None," he began, but then Connor's phone rang.

Taking it from him, Liliol greeted Maya, who turned the phone to the laptop screen. Looking over Liliol's shoulder, I could see that Pateme had changed locations— and considering the proliferation of green behind him, I thought I knew where he'd gone.

"What are you doing in the agency greenhouse?" Liliol asked.

"Yeah," Yacovi quipped, "that's my turf, Teme. But is it open?" he asked, sobering. "It's anchored not too far from here…"

"Unfortunately, no, the greenhouse closed off like everything else did—it was locked up in the middle of the night," Pateme explained. "But do me a favor. Someone turn the phone toward a blank section of wall."

"Uh…very well," said Liliol, and held it in position in front of a spot blocked only by a pair of plastic buckets. "Now what?"

"Just wait…"

I couldn't see what Pateme was doing on the other end, but in seconds, the wall began to glow blue in the shape of a doorway. A moment longer, and it popped into existence: an ordinary door, institutional gray with a metal handle—and a white half-sphere set just beside it, a badge lock.

"*Uncle?*" Liliol sharply asked, flipping the phone to face her. "What is this?"

I heard Pateme sigh on the other end. "After you were hit with a chaining potion—"

"I took the antidote! Gave DPP a full account of what I sent to those assholes! If you want to see my books and don't believe Yven's reports—"

"No, no, I believe you," he interjected. "Your integrity was never in question, girl. I, um…you had to run off, you know, and I worried, and…in case," he finished lamely. "If you needed help, I could get to you."

Liliol wheeled on me. "Did you know about this?"

"No," I replied.

"This was a solo project," said the director. "Don't be cross with Gentle Breeze—she had no idea."

"And have you used this…this back door of yours before?" she demanded.

"*No.* As you just saw, the door must be triggered on your end first…and I'll teach you the spell, it's not difficult—"

"So, you're *not* spying on me, Uncle?"

"Absolutely not. Only a fool would wander in there without your leave," he muttered.

I cut my eyes to the nearest bench of bushes. If it were possible for a vine to look smug, the mass of green tendrils lurking beneath it managed the trick.

"Let's see if this works," said Pateme. "A moment longer…"

The lock on our side of the door flashed red, and the handle depressed. Liliol gestured the buckets out of the way and stepped back as the door swung open into the greenhouse…and on the other side stood my unusually rumpled boss, phone still in hand. He hung up and tucked it into the pocket of the faded jeans I could barely imagine him owning, then waved. "Hi."

"Hello," said Liliol, giving Connor his phone back. "I'm still not sure how I feel about this—"

"No offense," Taug interrupted, "but that's a door *home*, if I'm not mistaken. Director," he added with a nod to Pateme.

Pateme stepped aside and gestured to the foliage behind him. "You're not. This is the Beukal side of the greenhouse."

"Is it safe to cross?" I asked.

No one had a ready answer for that, so Liliol improvised. "Catch," she told Pateme, plucking a rubber-band ball off the counter, and underhanded it through the door.

Nothing happened. The ball was unharmed when it landed in his hands, and he gave it an experimental toss in the air before throwing it back to his niece. "It seems stable," he allowed. "Do you want to try something living…*oh*," he said, seeing that Sally had already taken the initiative and was winding around his ankle. "Well, that works…"

"Let him go, Sally," said Liliol, and the slithertrap obeyed. "So," she said once her plant was safely home, "do we want to keep experimenting, or—"

"Nope," said Taug, and stepped through the doorway.

I started to grab him, pausing in the nick of time. "Are you okay?"

"Fine," he replied, then examined himself. "Mask held. Nothing feels unusual." He stepped back to Liliol's greenhouse without incident and grinned. "Looks like we've got a way home."

But considering the ongoing threat to the stability and integrity of the Pactlands, Pateme wouldn't let us cross quite yet. He made a few quick calls, pacing the greenhouse and running one hand through his hair in agitation, and while we settled in to wait, Liliol gave Tabitha and the Humphrieses a walking tour of the less dangerous portions of her facility.

By eleven-thirty, the sorcerers had arrived, all hopped up on stimulants and armed with diagnostic devices I couldn't name. They poked and took readings, and after fifteen minutes, their leader stepped back and folded her arms. "It's a fluke," she declared. "This connection is open and solid."

"Can we bring them home?" asked Pateme.

She nodded. "I think it's safe for now, but let's take it slowly, eh?"

Taug and I shared a look, and he raised an eyebrow. "Younglings first," I said, making an executive decision. "Could someone wake them and Hoska?"

A few minutes and one rapid explanation later, Galibe and Keppa were escorted into the greenhouse, kept from touching the plants on either side of the aisle by Sally's living guardrails. "Keppa, you first," I told them, and one of the sorcerers squatted, beckoning them on.

The child looked back at Hoska, who was making his

slow way toward us, but Hoska waved him forward. "Go," he called. "I'm right behind you."

Reassured, Keppa walked through the door, and the sorcerers checked their instruments as a DPP healer from the overnight shift took the youngling into his care. "I'm going to alert the parents and do a quick evaluation," he told Pateme. "Where's the contact information?"

"I'll bring it to you," the director assured him. "Do you have help tonight?"

"They're on their way."

We waited until the rest of the medical team arrived, and then, with last hugs for Maggie and Connor, Galibe crossed. "Wait," he said before a healer could lead him out of the greenhouse, "my pendant! I borrowed this—"

"You keep it," Connor told him. "You'll need your clothes to fit until your family arrives, right?"

Chattering at the healers in the manner of overexcited children, Galibe was whisked away, but before Hoska could follow, the sorcerers asked us to hold on. "I'm not loving these numbers," said their leader, scowling at her computer. "It's stressing the system, and with the localized strain…"

Around midnight, she deemed the stress tolerable, and Hoska took his turn. But as he shuffled toward the healers, Tabitha approached the door and said, "Hey, can anyone understand me?"

Two of the healers nodded, and the more senior, an earth nymph who'd gotten his start in Interdiction long before my time, drew nearer. "You're the local healer, I take it," he said.

"Pharmacist out of my depth, but close enough. I just wanted to debrief whoever's looking after Hoska."

We had time—once again, the sorcerers called a temporary halt—and the healer took notes while Tabitha ran through Hoska's symptoms and treatment. "What about the younglings?" he asked.

"Both were hungry and dehydrated when we found

them, and both had been exposed for several days," she replied. "Minor abrasions, but they seem otherwise intact. I've only had to stitch up Gentle Breeze, Taug, and Ermonir thus far."

He glanced past her at the rest of our group. "Anything life-threatening?"

"Not that I can tell, but I'll feel better once someone else takes over."

"And...*three* with such injuries, you said?"

She nodded. "Ermonir would be my choice to go first. She can't walk."

"She's injured that badly?" he asked, his eyes widening.

"She's a naga who's never had to mask before," I explained. "I second that."

"Third," said Taug, and headed for the exit. "Connor, with me. I'm not carrying her all the way down here by myself."

They returned a few minutes later with Ermonir floating above the aisle, observed from beneath the benches by several of Sally's many curious tendrils. Connor sat her on the back counter, and while we waited for the sorcerers' approval, Ermonir asked, "Can I unmask now?"

No one saw the harm, so the men turned their backs while the women helped her remove her unfamiliar clothing and lowered her to the floor. After a last check for plants in her proximity, Ermonir disengaged the pendant, then released a massive sigh as her tail curled around her once more. "Here," she said, unhooking the necklace, "I don't think I'll be needing this."

Connor took it from her for safekeeping, and Tabitha crouched to look at her wounds. "They're closing," she announced after having carefully peeled the tape from Ermonir's scales. "That potion's good shit."

I conveyed her message, and Ermonir said, "Please give her my thanks. I know I haven't been the easiest of patients..."

When I did so, Tabitha scoffed, then squeezed Ermonir's hand. Ermonir hesitated for only a second before hugging her, and Tabitha returned the embrace.

By twelve-thirty, the sorcerers weren't much happier. "The strain's not easing as quickly as it did," said their leader. "The system's absorbing it, but locally…"

"Can we try?" Pateme asked.

She made a face. "I suppose…"

Ermonir started to slither toward the door, then stopped, wincing. Connor stepped in and floated her through, and as Pateme and a healer caught her, the doorway began to shake.

"All right, that's it, no more," the sorcerer snapped. "Not unless you want to dump the whole tower into Virginia." Looking through the doorway at Taug and me, she said, "I'm so sorry, but we can't risk it tonight. Can you stay where you are for now? In a few hours, perhaps…"

"They'll be safe here," Liliol told her. "Leave the door open?"

"Close it," said the sorcerer.

"I'll reopen it in the morning," Pateme promised us. "Liliol, are you sure you're—"

"I've been living here for decades, Uncle," she interrupted. "And this isn't my first time with company. Go to bed."

"I just—"

"*Goodnight,*" she said, and firmly shut the door.

Even with our numbers diminished by four, there still weren't enough beds in Liliol's house. Yacovi and Connor shared the vacant bed, while Taug took the couch, leaving the rest of us to bunk in the RV—Dave and Maggie in the bedroom, Tabitha in the sleeping area above the cab, and me, too tired to fool with the convertible booth and table, sprawled on the couch beneath a spare blanket. The night was pleasantly cool after the day's storms, and we left some of the windows open to catch the breeze while we slept.

I curled up and closed my eyes, watching Pateme catch that rubber-band ball over and over until I slipped off, hopeful that I'd be in my own bed—and with any luck, in my boyfriend's arms—in just a few more hours.

CHAPTER 16

Though I didn't budge when the morning light began to fall on my face, my nose awoke to the smell of coffee—French roast, I groggily deduced.

"Easy, hon," said Dave as I struggled to untangle myself and sit up. My stitched wound *ached*, and I stifled a yelp when I moved too quickly and sent a bolt of pain up my side. "Take it slowly, let me help," he coaxed, pulling the blanket out of the way, then handed me a steaming mug once I was sitting. "Black, right?"

"Perfect," I replied, and took a long sip. Yes, definitely French roast…not a high-end bean, but not too shabby. "Has Pateme called yet?"

"No, and sit down," he said, pushing me back onto the cushions as I started to stand. "No need to get up yet. You've been going hard for the last week, lady."

"So have you."

"I'm not the one with a chunk missing. But look, there's no hurry," he said. "We're in a safe place, we found everyone, and now you can kick back and let those drugs and potions work until the door's ready. By the way, are you due for a morning dose of anything?"

"Antibiotics," Tabitha mumbled from her cocoon. "Ask Yacovi about potions. I don't know shit about that."

Dave and I lowered our voices, and he took a seat beside me as I drank my coffee. "Thank you again for throwing in with us," I said. "I don't know what I'd have done without you and Maggie."

"Eh, it's nothing—"

"No, it's not," I insisted. "You two have been taking care of me for a week, and I owe you more than I can repay." After another sip, I added, "We're not that far from Richmond. You two can get back to your lives now, though there's still the issue of how Maya's getting home…"

He shook his head. "Maggie and I talked it over, and we decided we're not going anywhere until the Pactlands is open again and we know Annie's safe."

"What about—"

"I have plenty of vacation time banked, I can work from the road if needed, and honestly, this has been the most excitement we've seen in ages."

I regarded him doubtfully. "Even more exciting than visiting the Hunt?"

"Oh, sure. Wylan promised they'd be on their best behavior, so where's the fun in that?" He nudged me in the shoulder, though not hard enough to jostle my mug. "Anyway, I've already extended the rental on the RV, so don't y'all worry."

We were interrupted then when the side door opened, and Connor climbed into the vehicle. "Hey," he whispered, "Maggie's making breakfast. How does everyone want their eggs?"

"Scrambled," said Dave.

"Plentiful," I replied, and pushed myself up from the couch. "Someone should probably give her a hand, right?"

Maya might have been the restauranteur, but Maggie could hold her own in the kitchen. She used every egg and slice of bread in Liliol's stores while Dave went to town in search of bacon and replacement groceries, and in all honesty, I was going to miss her cooking. Tabitha, who was also no slouch, chopped a fruit salad and made a dressing from scratch, though she moved like she was still half asleep until her first cup of coffee took effect. The rest of us offered to help, but Maggie politely but firmly shooed everyone else out of the kitchen, including Liliol, though our hostess loitered near the coffeepot to keep it full.

We ate at the table, at the counter, and in the den with plates on our laps, saying little. After a week outside, Taug and I were feeling it, and while Maggie and Dave were troopers, they were dragging. Yacovi grunted as his joints limbered up, Tabitha nursed her coffee, and even Connor seemed weary. Days on the road and a nonexistent sleep schedule had taken their toll on all of us. No one had bothered to check in with Maya that morning, and as I claimed the last of the bacon, I hoped she was still in bed.

"You know," Liliol suggested as breakfast wound down, "assuming that Gentle Breeze and Taug are able to go home today, there's no reason that the rest of you should immediately hit the road. Stay another night, get some rest."

"That's kind of you," said Maggie, "but Dave and I are just over in Richmond. The Georgians, now…"

"Oh, we'll be fine," said Yacovi. "We can take the drive in shifts."

Liliol eyed him, her mouth tight. "The younglings are exhausted, and you're no spring chicken, Hewt."

"'Younglings'?" Tabitha murmured to Connor, and lifted one of her thin braids. "Did she miss the gray?"

Overhearing her, Liliol waved her off. "Relatively speaking, dear. You're what, forty?"

"You're my new favorite," Tabitha replied, chuckling. "Forty-seven."

"Ah. I have shoes older than you."

It was a fool's quest to try to guess an elf's age. I'd had some practice and could usually get within a century, and in Liliol's case, I had a reference point: I once worked with her younger brother, Fradin, who was born in the 1670s. But to the untrained eye, Liliol seemed the younger of the two women, nary a white hair nor a wrinkle in sight. Immortality carried with it certain undeniable perks.

Moonless Night surely knew them all too well.

I'd just risen to refresh my coffee when Connor's phone rang, and he fumbled it out of his pocket. "Maya," he announced, and opened the line. "Morning, sunshine. Did you get any sleep?"

"Eh, a few hours," Maya replied, her voice gravely.

I glanced at the microwave clock—nearly ten a.m. *Someone* had slept in.

"Your couch ain't bad," she continued, "but I could really do with a mattress. Anyway, Rose is here. Says there's a group at the greenhouse door, so y'all should head down that way."

My heart leapt as I abandoned my mug on the counter, and I led the pack out the door, mentally cataloguing the few belongings I'd acquired in the last week. The clothes wouldn't fit me once I unmasked—my ruined outfit from the previous day was testament to *that*—and I wouldn't need my toiletries once I was home. Taug, similarly eager to depart, actually made the trek to the greenhouse barefoot, and he almost jogged toward the rear of the building once Liliol unlocked the door.

The door into DPP had remained unhidden overnight, and so Pateme was able to unlock it from his side. As it swung open, I took stock of the assembled in the larger agency greenhouse: my director, who'd had perhaps a nap since we saw him last, plus Kabno and, to my surprise, Diriem, both of whom seemed to have been pulling all-nighters of late.

It was, in my experience, seldom a great thing when Intelligence came around, especially not when the director put in a personal appearance.

The team of sorcerers handling the portal crisis had returned with their instruments, but accompanying them were ten or so Forum representatives, including Keppa's mother's sibling, Galibe's grandfather, Ermonir's boss, Hoska's sister, and Taug's cousin. Sunlight Breaking Across a Foggy Lake, one of my representatives, waved at us from the rear, and I waved back, grateful to see familiar faces.

From the shadows beside him stepped Wylan, who, though considerably shorter and slighter than Foggy Lake even when his antlers were factored into the calculus, carried a peculiar aura that hinted at carefully contained power and the potential for bodily harm. "Hi, Chief!" he called, his almost boyish smile disguising his true nature for a brief moment. "Are you all right?"

"I'm fine, thanks," I called back. "We all are."

From behind me came Maggie's voice: "Hey, sweetie! Is Annie with you?"

Wylan, not missing a beat, slipped into English for what little privacy it could offer him in that group. "She's back at the lodge. I put her to bed late last night, and with any luck, she's still there. She's been trying to keep an eye on Rose, and...well." He grimaced. "Have you seen Rose of late?"

"Not pretty," said Maggie. "But Annie's safe? You're okay?"

"Yes, ma'am. Hey, Dave," he added, lifting a hand as he spotted Maggie's other half. "You two send Annie the bill for the RV, at *least*. We want to repay you."

"Oh, no," Dave began, "that's not necessary—"

"It is," Wylan insisted. "And it's not just these representatives who concur," he continued, gesturing to his colleagues. "Some of these folks wanted a word with you in person."

Evapi Shilg, brushing a brown curl behind one of her horns, looked back at Wylan and asked in Pactish, "Are these the ones?"

"They are," he replied in kind. "Those two are my wife's parents, and that's...yeah, that's Tabitha. Hi!" he called to her as she carefully threaded her way up the aisle, and switched languages again. "How did you get roped into this mess?"

"Connor and Yacovi, who else?" said Tabitha, and

groaned. "Y'all, I know we should save the pain potions for the ones with actual injuries, but after a night in the RV, I *really* wouldn't say no to a nip."

As Liliol patted Tabitha's arm, Evapi asked Wylan, "Can they understand us?"

"Uh..." He paused, considering our group, then said, "Everyone but Tabitha, I believe. I haven't set you up with Pactish, have I?" he called through the door.

Tabitha shook her head. "Might have helped, man."

"Yeah, sorry about that." To Evapi, he said, "Dave and Maggie understand. Go ahead."

The faun—who, unlike the agency directors, had bothered to put on a formal robe that morning—took a few tentative steps toward the door. "Thank you," she said, focusing on the Humphrieses. "My brother told me everything, and..."

"Is he feeling any better?" Maggie asked. "Poor fellow was sick as a dog."

She paused, considering the idiom—which didn't entirely translate—then nodded. "Yes, much. He's been hospitalized, but he'll probably be released this weekend. He said he was dropped in a forest?"

"A national park. There are trails and such, but from what we'd gathered, he and Keppa had a rough time of it. How's the little one doing, do you know?"

"Perfectly fine," said Tennel Peolid, the nymph representative, drawing closer. "A few good meals and some sleep, and they'll be no worse for the experience."

Maggie's brow knit. "I'm not trying to overstep or anything, but is therapy in the picture? This last week has to have been traumatic for Keppa, and, uh...well, it helped us once," she said with a slight smile.

I noticed Dave squeeze her hand. That the grieving parents had sought assistance after the loss of their son didn't come as a great surprise.

"Their parents are considering all options," Tennel replied, "and if I know my sister, she'll do whatever's best for the youngling. They send their sincere thanks," they continued, looking over our group, "as do I."

"As do we all," said Vinnorit Yentera, Galibe's grandfather, who'd been almost hidden behind Pateme. "If you hadn't found our boy…"

"He seemed to be on the mend," said Maggie.

"*Oh*, yes. Talking our ears off. I pity his teachers once he returns to school," he added with a little chuckle.

"Has he taken that pendant off yet?" asked Connor, grinning.

The representative rolled his pale eyes. "*Very* reluctantly. He was enjoying the extra height, but then we pointed out that he wouldn't be able to sleep in his own bed or wear anything in his closet, and he surrendered it. His parents took it for safekeeping, but…" Eyeing Connor more closely, he said, "Galibe spoke of a young man who looked after him, took him for a drive…Connor?"

"Yes, sir, that's me."

"Dare I ask how you came to speak Pactish?"

He pointed through the door at Diriem. "That guy. I made an appeal to the Forum about a year ago when half my family was massacred—"

"*Oh*," said Vinnorit, surprise crossing his face, "from East Branch, yes? I'm sorry, I didn't recognize you…"

He waved it off. "Left my uniform at home. Connor Willow," he said.

Diriem pointedly coughed into his fist and muttered, "Lord ti'Catama."

"That, too," said Connor with a grunt. "Anyway, is the door stable? I'm sure Gentle Breeze and Taug have had enough fun over here."

At that, the lead sorcerer stepped closer, clutching her tablet. "So…bad news," she began.

Taug groaned.

"It's less stable than we thought. Still unsafe after last night, and we don't want to make matters worse."

"How long, then?" Taug demanded. "Are we going to

be stranded here for another few days? A week? A month?"

"We don't know," she replied. "I assure you, Agent, we're working as quickly as we can, but you need to understand that this problem is *massive*."

"So massive that you can't stabilize one measly portal with a week's work?" I groused, my soreness and sleep deficit manifesting as crankiness.

"It's an all or nothing proposition, unfortunately," said the sorcerer, not rising to my bait. "And if you want to get into specifics, the issue is a hex key."

"A *what?*"

"A hex key," Yacovi repeated. "They start or break hexes."

"Like...what sort of key?" asked Dave. "Is this a 'true love's kiss' situation?"

"I'll kiss anyone I need to in order to go home," Taug offered. "Deeply, passionately, tongue—"

"I *sincerely* doubt this is a kiss situation," Yacovi interrupted, and the sorcerer on the other side of the door nodded. "What are we talking about?" he asked her.

"It's a physical object," she explained. "We've mapped it, but we can't get the internal parameters correct—"

"So, you can't duplicate its effect," he finished.

"Correct. And whoever built the hex was smart about it. The key *stops* the hex—without it, we're stuck trying to dismantle this thing, and it's thorny."

"And if you were to find the key?" I asked.

"It would synchronize with the hex and shut it down."

As she hugged her computer like a shield against our disappointment, I cut my eyes to Diriem. "Does DOI know where to find this hex key?"

He smiled wearily. "Thought you'd never ask, Chief."

"Well?"

"One of the sorcerers still outside is in possession of the key. If we gave you coordinates, could you bring him in?"

Considering our group, I said, "I, uh…I'm willing to try, but you're asking a lot of Taug and me."

"And me," Yacovi protested.

"Hell, I'm in," said Connor.

"Okay," I said to Diriem, "one troll, one centaur, a decently trained sorcerer, and one quasi-elf."

Liliol sidled closer. "Can I help?"

"You don't have the training, my dear," said Pateme.

"Neither do they," she countered, pointing to the Humphrieses, "but I assume they're part of this mess."

"Oh, absolutely," Maggie chirped, and Dave nodded along before whispering a translation to Tabitha. "And I suspect Maya won't mind helping for a few days longer," she added. "Someone needs to babysit that computer, after all."

I turned to the human contingent and switched to English. "You really don't have to do this—"

"Stop," said Tabitha. "We're in, okay? For whatever that's worth."

"More than you realize," I murmured, and turned back to Diriem. "How do we do this without getting any of them hurt? Maggie and Dave have been attacked once already."

The corner of his lips twitched. "I can't give you a foolproof plan."

I started to argue, but before I could do more than open my mouth, Moonless Night appeared at the back of the crowd and began pushing his way toward the front, gym bag over his broad shoulder. "What's going on?" he demanded.

Pateme stepped back, balking. "How the hell did *you* get in here?"

He pointed to Diriem. "Director sent a picture to Annie, and I used that to lock on to this place. My thanks," he added, and as Pateme sighed, he asked, "Why is Gentle Breeze still out there? I thought this doorway was stable."

"Not as stable as we'd thought, uh…" The lead sorcerer looked him up and down, bemused. "Um…you're *Moonless Night*, aren't you?"

"Yes."

"From Channel 1?"

"The same," he rumbled in his polished bass.

"Sorry," she said, glancing past him at the directors, "but when did you decide to involve the media?"

"We didn't," said Kabno, her arms tightly folded across her chest. "Certainly not the sports team." She turned toward Wylan, who raised his hands and shook his head, the message clear: *I had no part in this.*

Ignoring the others, Moonless Night moved closer to the doorway. "Come on, sweetest," he said, extending his hand. "I'll catch you."

"It's not that simple," I said, slipping into Trollish for near privacy. That the directors understood my mother tongue, I had no doubt, but most of the Forum and the sorcerers surely didn't. "The key to breaking the hex that's crippling the system is apparently out here, and DOI thinks they've figured out which sorcerer has it. We find him, we find the key, we fix the problem."

One eyebrow rose. "*We?*"

I tilted my head toward Taug. "He's with Laws, Yacovi over there is retired DPP, Connor is, uh…trying…"

"And the rest? What about that elf?"

"This is her greenhouse, and good old Uncle Pateme doesn't think she needs to be involved more than she has been. The others are human, and before you say anything, they've actually been lifesavers—"

"I don't care," he said. "Are they giving you no one else? What about your second?"

"Emarae? I suspect he'd help us," I mused, "but you heard that sorcerer—the door's unstable."

He grunted. "Looks stable enough to me, and I'll be damned if you do this alone."

And without further ado, my boyfriend ducked through the doorway.

Alarms began to blare on the sorcerers' instruments, and their leader stared at Moonless Night, aghast, as the walls on both sides began to shake. "What were you *thinking?*" she yelped. "You can't just—"

"That's it, no more," said Pateme, grabbing the handle. "We'll call," he told us, and slammed the door before anyone else could get a wild idea.

I stood there for a moment, taking a long breath to center my thoughts, then turned to the others. "Uh…everyone, this is my, um…boyfriend…"

"Hey," said Connor with a jerk of his head that spoke of recognition. "Welcome to the party, man."

"Yacovi Hewt," said the sorcerer, extending his hand, and Moonless Night took it carefully. Most of us had grown up with the admonition to be gentle with smaller people's fingers, and someone must have conveyed the message to him along the way.

"Hi, there," said Dave, taking his turn. "Dave Humphries, and this is my wife, Maggie."

They knew who he truly was. They *absolutely* knew, but they were playing along. I caught Maggie's eye, and she winked.

The bigger question was what we were to do about Tabitha. Morial could speak English—Wylan, apparently, had thought it a good idea for at least a handful of his brethren to understand the language, considering how often they came outside to hunt—but what about his alter ego?

Before I could begin assembling a cover story, Tabitha stuck out her hand. "Sorry, not sure what's going on, but I'm Tabitha Bradley," she said. "Can you understand me?"

He nodded and took her hand. "Moonless Night," he said, using the Pactish rendering, then switched tongues. "Thought you might need a little backup."

"Hell, I wouldn't say no, big guy." Nodding toward me, she said, "The boyfriend, I take it."

"Correct," he replied.

"*Ah.*" A knowing glint lit her dark eyes. "Well, then,

pleasure to meet you."

Taug, who'd been standing by, gawking, finally had his turn. "*Wow*," he said, "I've been watching you for years, but…hi. Taug Berek, Laws." Shaking Moonless Night's hand, he chuckled, then asked, "When the heck did you get a language potion for *English*?"

Moonless Night grunted and rolled his eyes, playing it up. "Some years ago. There was a thought that we might send a multi-station team outside to give a little undercover peek at…what's it called, those international games…"

"The Olympics?" Tabitha guessed.

"*That*. A few of us took the potion while our bosses tried to convince the Forum, but alas, by the time we were on our feet again, the idea had been vetoed. Probably the right decision, all things considered," he added, and adjusted his grip on his bag. "So, what's the plan?"

"Let's start with getting you masked," I said, grabbing his arm. "Folks, could you give us the RV for a few minutes?"

He followed me out of the greenhouse, muttering as we exited, "Is that vine on the floor watching us?"

"Very much so."

"Is it *friendly*?"

I glanced back, and Sally waved.

"I think we're in her favor for the moment, but don't push your luck. She's *huge*."

My boyfriend followed me into the RV, hunching to fit inside a space clearly not designed with the troll physique in mind, and took a seat on the couch as I closed the blinds. Once I'd locked the door to ensure our privacy, I sat beside him and released a long breath.

"Hi," he murmured.

"Hey, you."

"I've missed you."

"Likewise," I said, rubbing my face, "but…"

He watched me briefly, and when he spoke again, his confidence seemed to have faltered. "I've embarrassed you, haven't I?"

"No—"

He swore under his breath. "I'm sorry, I didn't...that is..." Fumbling, he managed, "I didn't intend to insult you, I just couldn't sit by and keep watching while you're in danger..."

I took his hand, which dwarfed mine at that moment. "It's okay," I said, and smiled. "If you were thinking we'd get a second chance at date night out here, I hate to tell you, but the odds are *not* good."

"Forget date night. This is enough." He looked me over briefly, then asked, "Are you okay? I've been asking Wylan for updates, but he's not the most reliable."

"Because his updates are surely coming from Annie. She's been with Rose, and that looks like a full-time job right now," I replied. "I'm fine, mostly intact—"

"*Mostly?*"

"Nothing life-threatening. I fought off a sasquatch last night, and he got a good bite in," I explained, lifting my shirt to show him my bandages. "Gored him in turn, and he ran, so I think I won that one."

"You were bitten by a *what?*" he demanded, staring at me.

"A sasquatch, they're called. About my true size but thicker, covered in hair, long arms, prominent brow ridge—"

"*Oh.*" He looked impressed. "I haven't seen one of those since I rode with Father. They're rare—you found one?"

"He found us, and I don't know who was more surprised. Most humans think they're a myth, so..." I rolled my shirt back down, wincing. "Tabitha sewed me up, and Liliol's being generous with the potions, so I'm all right. Now," I said, eyeing him, "how am I meant to explain to Taug how the sports guy has preternatural reflexes, hmm?"

"I wouldn't go that far..."

I snorted. "Close. But listen, I think everyone here with

the exception of Taug and perhaps Liliol knows your secret. If you don't want to reveal yourself to those two…just don't give it a hundred percent out there, yeah?"

He sighed. "I managed to complicate things for you."

"It's fine," I murmured, patting his cheek. "And I know you meant well."

"If you want me to go home—"

"And further risk the stability of the Pactlands? Absolutely not. So, here's what we're going to do. Connor brought some of Jane's homemade masking pendants. They're not flashy, but they do the trick. We'll find one that fits you, and you can pretend you're using it while you work off that ring."

"Why don't I use yours?" he asked.

I chuckled. "Because *some* of us ended up out here without our masking jewelry—"

"Which is why I brought your pendant," he said, pulling it from his pocket. "Thought you might want it."

The silver locket glinted even in the low light of the shaded RV, and a sense of deep relief came over me as I took it from him. "Sweetest…"

"I figured you wouldn't mind if I let myself in to get that for you."

"*Thank* you. I love you," I said, rising, "and now, if you'll excuse me, I'll switch pendants."

He frowned. "Where are you going?"

"The bedroom. The pendant I'm wearing doesn't adjust my clothing, so I need to remove it between masks unless I want to shred it."

"Is that so?" His eyebrows waggled, and I waved him off as I retreated to steal a moment's privacy.

When I returned, locket in place, I found that he'd already altered his mask, bringing him closer to Morial than Moonless Night. "How's this?" he asked—and in Moonless Night's deep voice, I noticed.

"Good, but…" I looked him over: a little shorter than me, with an olive complexion, a square jaw, and loose brown hair that fell past his shoulders. He'd remembered to mask his eyes, hiding the Huntsmen's telltale amber with brown, and there was no trace of his antlers...

"Ears," I said. "Round them off."

"*Right*," he muttered, and I directed him into the bathroom to use the mirror. When I started to hand him my pendant, however, he refused. "How would you like to explain my clothing?" he asked, gesturing to his neatly tailored charcoal pants and thin blue sweater—which, thanks to the modifications DPP had made to his old ring, had shrunk with him.

I swore under my breath, then countered, "How do you want to explain the ring?"

He held up his hand. "Family heirloom, borrowed for this particular emergency."

"You planned this out."

"Once you've spent a few centuries under an alias," he replied, "you learn to adapt on the fly. But if you don't like that story, I've got spare clothes in my bag."

"Well," I said, "since the number of trolls I know with heirloom masking jewelry is roughly zero..."

"Yeah, yeah," he said, and took his turn in the bedroom. When he emerged, he'd traded Moonless Night's shrunken clothing for jeans and a green Henley, which he filled out *nicely*. Like Wylan, Morial was built like a swimmer, leaner but muscular. By sorcerer standards, the man in front of me was handsome, and while it wasn't my favorite of his looks, he wore it well.

Besides, I loved him regardless of the mask he sported.

"So," he said, making a show of adjusting Jane's pendant, "what can I do to help?"

I had just pushed open the door to Liliol's cottage when Connor's phone rang.

"They've got you working this morning, huh?" he said, opening the video chat.

"Hey, someone's got to play switchboard," Maya replied. "Is everything okay? I heard Moonless Night joined the party…"

"And the Pactlands is still intact, I'll have you know," he said from behind me, then latched the door.

She chuckled. "Hey, there."

"Hello, yourself. You have news?" he asked, moving closer to the phone.

Taug caught my arm and whispered, "How does *Maya* know Moonless Night?"

"Later," I said, and joined the cluster around Connor as Maya flipped her view to the computer screen.

"*Rose*," I snapped when I got a look at her, "kid, what the fuck have you been doing? You look like you haven't slept in a month!"

"I'm fine," she protested, though her heart clearly wasn't in it.

"Gentle Breeze is right, honey," Maggie interjected. "Sleep for a bit, then call us back, okay? We're not going anywhere—"

"Heavens, Rosie," Liliol insisted, elbowing her way into view, "*listen to me*. This isn't healthy, baby. You've got to rest."

"Hi, Aunt Lily," she mumbled. "I'm okay, and they're still trapped out there—"

"They're with me! We're just fine, little one. Look, I'm not even masked," she pointed out. "This is a safe place. Please, sweetheart, you've got to rest. Come off the Happy Juice and try again in a few hours. Yven?"

He popped up behind Rose's chair, his eyes nearly as baggy as hers. "She won't listen to me."

Liliol huffed a frustrated sigh. "Rose Lea, I know you all too well. Heed reason, baby. You can't keep this up."

But Rose shook her head and pressed on. "We've got a problem. Remember that sorcerer you left chained to the wall in Tennessee?"

"Yeah…" said Connor.

"His name is Ergal Faln, and he's the one carrying the hex key—"

She turned at the sound of a door opening, and I saw Pateme and Kabno enter the room with Wylan—their ride, I assumed. Just behind them was Canna, her healer's kit slung over her shoulder.

"What's going on?" Rose asked.

"You're being put to bed for your own good," Canna replied. "Sorry, friend, but this is the only option."

"I can do this!" Rose insisted to the unyielding directors. "Yven, tell them—"

"Rosie," he interrupted, kneeling in front of her chair, "you haven't stopped in days, and you've taken *way* too much Happy Juice. They're here to help—"

Her eyes flashed. "Did you orchestrate this?"

"No, he didn't," said Pateme. "But you really should have, ti'Ansha."

"This is coming from DOI," Kabno explained.

Rose scowled at them. "Pop's not sleeping, either—"

"More than you are, and he's *slightly* more experienced," Pateme said, cutting her off, then looked at the screen and the rest of us. "Apologies, but your eyes here need to go dark for a while."

"They'll be fine," said Liliol. "Do what you need to do."

Seeing no help, Rose began to fight, trying to force her way out of the chair and past them, but she was no match for her intervention team. Screaming curses, she was pinned in place, and Canna muttered an apology as she slipped a needle into Rose's arm. Within seconds, Rose slumped over, unconscious, and Wylan scooped her out of the chair as Yven led the way to their bedroom.

"Sorry," said Connor, "but is that really necessary? She's going to be pissed once that stuff wears off…"

At that, Diriem, who'd apparently been lurking outside the doorway, stepped into view. "Absolutely necessary," he said, and yawned into his fist. "We all have our breaking point, and the younger the farseer, the earlier it tends to be. Rose has pushed past all safe time limits."

Tabitha, who'd been watching, unable to follow the conversation, asked, "Did they just sedate her?"

Diriem nodded and switched to answer her. "You know what happens if you go too long without sleep, yes?"

"Hallucinations and death?"

"Exactly. An overly exhausted farseer tends to hallucinate, and that makes Rose a danger to herself and all of you right now. I understand the impetus," he added, folding his arms. "She wants to protect you and fix this place—"

"But she said she identified the right sorcerer," Taug interjected. "Did she?"

"She may *believe* that she has, but having seen her, I don't fully trust it. Stubbornness won't stave off the hallucinations."

"Do *you* know?" Taug pressed. "Surely you've seen something!"

"Nothing as specific as you need—not yet," said Diriem. "And as I'm nearing my limit as well, be careful," he told us. "I've got a sedative with my name on it in my room."

"So…we're to wait?" I asked.

Pateme stepped back into the camera's range. "Precisely. Rest and replenish your supplies."

Taug tried his luck with another director. "Rose said our target is a sorcerer we encountered in Tennessee, the one who'd coordinated Emonir's kidnapping…"

He could only shrug. "I don't know. You saw the state Rose was in—I'm not sure I'd trust her to give you her name at this moment." Scanning our crowd, he said, "Surely you could do with a day off the road, couldn't you?"

CHAPTER 17

With Rose out of commission and no clear indication of our next steps, we spent the rest of the morning preparing for the likely course ahead.

Dave and Maggie drove the RV to a local mechanic to have the vehicle inspected. They'd put quite a few miles on it in the past week, and we couldn't afford a breakdown. While they saw to our primary transportation, Liliol loaned Yacovi her brown pickup truck, and he took Tabitha with him in search of groceries. As for the rest of us, we loaded into Connor's SUV and headed for the distant Walmart by the Interstate. The superstore wasn't my first pick when it came to shopping—I much preferred the smaller, more specialized businesses of home—but when one was stuck outside and in need of basics, the place had a certain utilitarian charm.

Our task was to arm ourselves. Connor, who'd carried his four pistols and rifle with him from Georgia, wanted more ammunition. Taug suggested that we purchase additional guns, but Connor nixed that idea, as he didn't want to have to explain why he was buying weapons so far from home. Instead, while he bought his ammo and some pepper spray, Taug was to purchase knives, I was tasked with duct tape and nylon rope, and Moonless Night was told to find a selection of ski masks. We stopped by an ATM on the way to the store so as to make our transactions with cash, and then we split up in the Walmart parking lot and staggered our entrances—a trick Connor suggested after having watched his share of security cameras.

We worked quickly and checked out separately, and around one, we returned to Eden's Bounty to find the RV fresh off an oil change and both the kitchenette's fridge and Liliol's pantry restocked. She protested that Tabitha and Yacovi didn't need to spend the money on her, but they insisted, and I mentally added her groceries to my running tally of funds to expense from DPP.

As Maggie and Dave worked an assembly line of sandwiches, the rest of us sat around the den to strategize. The only lead we had was Rose's declaration just prior to her forced sleep. Could she be trusted? When *had* that girl last slept, anyway? But if we assumed she was right, then our first stop had to be Crossville—a six-hour drive, though we'd gain an hour with the time zone change. Since Connor had called the police, then this Ergal Faln couldn't still be in the house we'd raided...could he? Had he been released? Had he run? Was he chained to the wall where we'd left him?

We'd need to check the house, we decided, and if he wasn't there, we would need to look for him at the county jail.

Liliol suggested that we stay with her another day. "Wait until Rosie is back on her feet," she urged. "I don't mind. It's just Sally and me here."

But Yacovi, Taug, and I were restless, and a possibly bad hint was better than none at all. "There's no telling how long that girl will be unconscious," Yacovi explained. "I don't know what sedative Canna gave her, but we've got some strong ones in the agency refrigerators. She might be out for a few days, depending on the potion and how tired she is. So." He looked around the den, and seeing no objection from anyone but Liliol, he called into the kitchen, "Dave, Maggie, would you be up for a drive?"

We ate quickly, and with a hefty stash of potions from Liliol and promises from us to check in with her once we heard from Rose, we set off. As usual, Dave drove with Maggie as his copilot, and Tabitha, Taug, and Yacovi piled into the RV. Connor started his SUV, then smirked in the rearview mirror as Moonless Night and I climbed into the back together. "You know," he said, "one of you could ride shotgun."

"We're fine," I said, squeezing my boyfriend's hand.

"Uh-huh. Just keep the canoodling to a reasonable level, eh?"

"*Canoodling?*" Moonless Night muttered. "You realize we've been separated for a week—"

"As have my fiancée and I," said Connor, following the RV down the hill. "I get it, man. Just…it's a long way to Crossville, so let's not make things awkward."

Slipping into Trollish, I murmured, "He's a decent kid. Be nice."

"You think he understands any of this?" Moonless Night replied in kind.

"Nope."

We continued on, enjoying our stolen privacy, while Connor searched the dial for music to keep him company.

When we pulled up to the house that evening, we found it was much as we'd left it but for the addition of a ring of yellow police tape at the perimeter and more over the front door. Seeing no one around, we carefully let ourselves in, then headed downstairs to look for Faln…but Connor's call to emergency services had worked. The shackles were still hanging on the wall, but they were empty. It took only a few minutes more to clear the house, and we reconvened in the den, empty-handed.

"Sorry," said Connor, unkinking his back. "I didn't want them to die down there…"

Yacovi patted his shoulder. "You did the right thing, son. Any scent trail?" he asked, turning to Moonless Night and me.

He and I conferred with a brief glance, and I shook my head. "No. I can smell him here, but it's fainter than it was.

Give us a moment outside…"

But that proved useless as well. I could trail Faln to the edge of the road but no further, evidence that he'd been taken away in a car. Frustrated, I informed the others. "*Maybe*, if it had been the same day, I'd have been able to track the vehicle," I said, "but after this long, and with the rain…"

"It's not your fault, hon," said Maggie, and folded her arms as she surveyed the property. "Well, we're not going to find him in the woods around here tonight. Let's get a hotel, okay? We don't want to try to sleep eight in the RV."

We found a Hampton Inn closer to Crossville after Maggie and Tabitha vetoed several questionable establishments. Taug, Moonless Night, and I had offered to stay in the vehicle—after all, none of us had cash, a fact that my boyfriend had realized too late and was kicking himself over—but the others insisted that we come inside. The Humphrieses got a room, and Tabitha rented one all for herself for some much-needed privacy. Connor and Yacovi suggested that Taug could stay with them, leaving Moonless Night and me with the fourth double.

"Don't have too much fun without us, okay?" Connor murmured, handing me the key envelope.

But there would be no fun for anyone at first. After we'd unloaded, we searched the quiet hotel for a space large enough to accommodate our group, then slipped into a meeting room to strategize when the bored desk clerk didn't look up from her phone.

As Tabitha checked my dressing—Taug's would have to be examined in private—Connor sipped from the cup of coffee he'd snagged in the lobby and rubbed his forehead. "Okay," he said, keeping his voice low, "since Faln's not in the house and we left him pretty securely immobilized, he was probably arrested on Sunday."

"Four days," said Taug. "Where would he be by now?"

"Well, when I called 911, I claimed that I was a hunter

passing through who saw a nearly naked woman outside the house and stopped to investigate. When I saw she was cuffed, I broke in, overpowered the guys we left in the basement, and found the keys to release the rest of their captives. They probably picked up those assholes for human trafficking, but since we took their hard drives and the victims fled, the DA's going to have a hell of time making their case. Still, the condition of that house would raise red flags, so I'm guessing they're still in custody."

"Whose?" I asked.

Connor grimaced. "I don't *think* the house is in Crossville proper, and I don't recall it being on federal land, so probably the county jail, which is in…"

Yacovi beat him to it with his phone. "Crossville's the seat of Cumberland County."

"Hoo, boy," he muttered. "At least it's close."

"How do we get to him?" Moonless Night asked as Connor returned to his coffee.

"I don't know," he said, pushing his paper cup aside. "I have no contacts here, and I'm not exactly in the business of jailbreaks—my experience is with putting people *into* lockup, not sneaking them out."

"We've got knock-out potions in the RV," said Taug, and Yacovi nodded. "*And* several vials of the antidote. Went through Liliol's stash during the drive," he explained. "What if we waited until nightfall tomorrow, let things calm, then hit the place with knock-out and grabbed him? With any luck, the dampening potion we gave Faln will still be working."

Moonless Night considered that briefly, then said, "I've heard worse—"

"Slight problem," I interrupted. "There's bound to be cameras everywhere around the jail."

"True," said Taug, "but what if we stole the cameras? Or their hard drives? You know, like we did at the house."

"Which would work unless the feed's going to the cloud," said Connor. "We have no idea what the security situation's like in there."

The group fell quiet for a moment, mulling over our predicament, and then Connor cleared his throat. "I've got an idea."

"Oh?" said Taug.

He nodded. "Extradition. We'd have to bluff our way through it, but we might be able to pull it off."

Taug's brow knit. "Extra...what?" he asked, fumbling over the unfamiliar term.

"Extradition," Connor repeated. "Y'all only have one jurisdiction, right? Everything is handled by Laws?"

"I mean, unless it's a plant issue or something—"

"Crime in general. There isn't a separate police force in Beukal, is there? Or out in the sticks?"

"No," I said, seeing where he was going. "Law enforcement is centralized. It's all one jurisdiction."

"Well, we've got our tiny fiefdoms out here," Connor told Taug. "I can't just go to these guys and claim to be from the next county over—they probably know all the local cops. But what if we had extradition paperwork from, say, Atlanta? If it looks official, if we pass the smell test, then maybe we can get somewhere."

"*Can* you pass the smell test?" Yacovi asked.

"I think I know enough to fake it. We'll still be on camera, right, but things should seem nice and legal until we get out of there with Faln."

Yacovi seemed unconvinced. "Not to rain on your parade, Con, but have you ever dealt with an extradition? What's the process? Should there be lawyers involved?"

"I haven't had one," he admitted, "but let me do some research tonight. There's a business center off the lobby, and I'll see what I can find. Do a little light forgery."

It was far from a foolproof plan, but it was the best we had that night, and so we ended our meeting and went our separate ways. Moonless Night and I headed to our room, but had our fellows known what we got up once we were alone, they'd have been sorely disappointed.

"I've had a crazy thought," said my boyfriend, cupping my face in his hands.

"Mm? And what's that?" I asked, smirking at him. The scent profile I was picking up from him was subtle but unmistakable, and I suspected I knew *precisely* what he had in mind, even if I wasn't raring to go.

But he surprised me. "You, me, a satisfactory bed, and at least a solid six hours of sleep. What do you say, beautiful?"

"Well, now, that's tempting, but you're not even going to try your luck?" I teased.

"Under other circumstances, absolutely, but the responsible part of me insists that sleep would be ideal before we try to sneak into a facility where everyone's armed and cameras cover all corners."

"Fair." I slipped forward to kiss him, and his hands migrated behind my head, pressing me close to him as I wrapped my arms around his back.

Judging by the state of his anatomy, my nose had absolutely not deceived me.

I rested my forehead against his and sighed, then murmured, "That feels so weird."

"What does?"

"Kissing with an overbite and no tusks."

He chuckled softly. "Not terrible, is it?"

"Hmm. Let me take another shot at it, and I'll get back with you."

Yes, it was strange, being so intimate with someone while masked, but then Moonless Night did it all the time…

And as I bedded down with him, adjusting the blankets while he spooned behind me, I understood.

Perhaps Moonless Night was ready to roll, never mind the morning's mission, but *Morial* knew I wasn't comfortable, stuck as I was in a false skin. Though I'd been masked for more than a solid week, I still wore this other woman's body like a tight, somewhat itchy sweater. I didn't feel like myself, much less sexy.

I tightened my grip on the arm that had snaked over my waist. "Goodnight, sweetest," I whispered, and let sleep take me.

It didn't last.

I woke two hours later, and when I closed my eyes and tried to will myself back to sleep, my mind refused to shut off again. Gently extricating myself from my boyfriend's embrace, I grabbed a key and rode down to the lobby, where at least I could watch television without waking anyone. I grunted a greeting at the night clerk, then made a cup of tea at the lobby bar and wandered to the business center to check on Connor.

He was hunched over the lone computer, and I said, "Hey, Chief. Need a refill?"

Turning, he spotted me and grinned wearily. "If you're offering."

"Sure." I left my drink, got him a fresh cup of coffee in the lobby, and returned. "How's it going?"

"Slowly," he muttered. "Go back to bed, I've got this. No need for us both to be miserable."

"Uh-huh." I pulled out a rolling chair and joined him. "So, what's the problem?"

"Which one? My general ignorance as to the nuances of how extradition works in Tennessee or my craptastic Photoshop skills? Which I'd show you if this computer were actually equipped with Photoshop. As it is, I've tracked down some of the documents I think we'll need, and I'm looking for the right names to fill in the blanks. It'll be a little messy, but if you squint..." He shook his head, then sipped. "Not like they know they've got the Unabomber on their hands. If we make a compelling case, then we might pull this off."

"How about a less than compelling case and some potions?" I suggested.

"Cameras…"

"We can deal with them. Drink up, you need the caffeine."

He did as I ordered, then leaned back in his chair and rubbed his face. "You know, I never thought I'd be trying to fuck over fellow officers. It's, uh…it's not a great feeling, to be honest."

"You're not fucking them over—you're taking a problem off their hands," I replied. "Besides, once Faln's dampening potion wears off, do you really think he'll stick around in custody? And do you think he'll hesitate to leave casualties in his wake if the cops try to stop him?"

Connor sat up and stared at me. "Oh, *shit*—"

"Didn't think they'd keep him this long, did you?"

"I mean, there wasn't much evidence to go on once we got the hard drives out of that house…" Closing his eyes, he groaned. "Do you think his local buddy turned on him? Blabbed to get a deal? Or the women, did they go to the cops?"

"Hard to say without a farseer," I replied, "but that doesn't matter now. We'll get him out for the police's safety."

"I'm a fucking idiot," he muttered.

"No, you're not. You've been in an ongoing crisis, you haven't slept well, and you opted not to leave those two chained up down there to die, which was more than decent. Were you my agent, I wouldn't count this against you." When he reached for his coffee again, I said, "We can't always be forthright with law enforcement out here, you see? I know that goes against your instincts, and I respect that—I do," I insisted. "I'm sure it feels like betrayal on some level. But if you strolled in there and told those cops they've got a sorcerer in a cell, would they work with you or run you out?"

"Or get a psych hold."

"That, too. You've got integrity," I said, holding his gaze, "which is almost certainly another reason that Kabno is wooing you."

He frowned. "She barely knows me. How would she…"

"*Diriem*," we chorused.

"Look hard enough in any agency, and you'll find his fingerprints," I said. "I suspect you frustrate the hell out of him because you're not playing along yet."

"Yeah, well," he said, lifting his cup, "Oz the Great and Powerful doesn't know *everything*."

I snickered. "That's what you and Jane call him behind his back, eh?"

"To his face, too." He smirked, then sobered. "Wonder if there's someone at DOI who could find all the forms we need to pull off an extradition pick-up."

"Don't know," I said, "but we could ask Maya to put in a request."

He glanced at the computer screen. "Quarter of twelve. She ain't going to be happy."

"She'll get over it," I replied, standing. "Make the call and go to bed, kid."

Eyeing me, he said, "You, too, now."

"Yeah, yeah," I muttered, heading for the door.

"Go on! Go find Romeo!" he called after me.

I waved him off and called the elevator.

Someday, I thought, I should really get around to reading that damn play.

I jolted awake again around four Friday morning when Connor pounded at our door.

"Hey, sorry to wake y'all," he said when I flung it open and blearily stared at him, then held his phone toward me. "Got Kabno on the line."

I let him in, and while Moonless Night muttered a vague approximation of a greeting, I took the phone from Connor and sat on the end of the untouched bed. "Yes, ma'am?" I asked.

The director looked better, somewhat more rested, though the tiny black DOL sweatshirt she sported that morning wasn't her usual work attire. "Sorry for the early call," she began. "Maya left a note in the system last night, and DOI has been trying to get the information you've requested, but there are still gaps. Are you sure Faln is in custody? Or that he's even the one with the hex key?"

"That's what Rose said—"

"And Rose was on the brink of a breakdown when she made that pronouncement. Why not wait?"

"Because," I replied, rubbing the grit from one eye, "even if Faln isn't the one we're looking for, if he's in the county jail, those officers are about to be in trouble. Dampening potions don't last forever."

She swore under her breath. "That could work in the Unity Plan's favor. A show of true magic in front of a bunch of cops…"

"Assuming he doesn't just kill them all and go on his way. So, no, we can't wait. We need DOI to get us that intel, and we need Rose now—we don't even have Faln's alias."

"DOI is doing their best," said Kabno. "As for Rose, I'm really sorry, but that's impossible. She's still sleeping under healer supervision—"

At that, Connor leaned over my shoulder and said, "Get Ganti ti'Van. Wake him, I don't care. We've got to have eyes, or this'll turn into a shit show."

Her mouth twitched. "You do realize he's not my agent, yes?"

"Then wake Diriem's ass up and tell *him* to get Ganti on the line. Blame me if you want. But I'm not sitting here and getting a bunch of officers killed because of some fucking sorcerer, understand? In fact," he continued, "if you want to be sneaky about it, tell *Annie* what's going on, and I know damn well she'll find Ganti."

A solid plan. As a formerly human victim of a sorcerer herself, Annie was understandably *touchy* about such matters, and locked doors presented little impediment to her if she knew what was on the other side.

About an hour later, as Connor and I were loitering in the lobby, waiting for the breakfast buffet to open, Maya called back, and we kept her on the line while we retreated to my room. Warning Moonless Night to stay in the bathroom unless he wanted to give Connor an eyeful, I sat on the nearer bed and watched the laptop screen come into focus, revealing a baggy-eyed elf with a messy blond ponytail and a gray zip-up hoodie. "Agent ti'Van?" I asked.

He nodded, and his eyes flicked toward my right, where Connor had pressed close to be visible in the phone's camera. "Connor."

"Ganti."

"I was told it was an emergency...sorry," he mumbled, and stifled a yawn. "Been up for two days, just got to bed around midnight. What's going on?"

"Are you *capable* of helping us?" I asked.

"I'm not delusional right now, if that's what you mean. It's Gentle Breeze, yes? I know we've crossed paths, but—"

"The mask probably isn't helping," I said, and disengaged it—and fortunately, my clothes shifted with me. "Better?"

"Ah, *yes*. Hi. All right, tell me what you need."

"Ergal Faln. Where is he, what's his alias—"

"We think he's in the county jail in Crossville," Connor added. "What's he being held on, what's happened to him since last Sunday—"

"Faln, okay, I get it," said Ganti, cutting him off. "Yeah, uh...sure. I thought there was another farseer working on him..."

"Rose," Connor muttered. "Who's been benched."

"They had to sedate her," I told Ganti, who grimaced at the news.

"Oh, *someone's* not going to be happy when she wakes," he said, "but that's the boss's problem, isn't it?" He yawned again and shook his head briskly. "Right, yeah, let me see what I can find. Back soon."

I shooed Connor out so my boyfriend could dress, but he returned barely twenty minutes later with Ganti, who appeared no less fatigued but had armed himself with a large, steaming mug since we'd last spoken. "I love the easy cases," Ganti said. "Recent events, good pictures of the target, no blinding potion—"

"You found him?" I asked.

He smirked. "You sound surprised."

"I mean, my investigations tend to take a *little* long-er…"

"Different tools, Chief. Here's what you need to know," he said, then paused for a long sip and winced as the hot liquid went down. "Faln's not in Crossville. He's in what appears to be a drunk tank in a tiny jail…White Hill? I think it's close."

"I'll look it up once we're off this call," said Connor. "Why's he not in Crossville?"

"County jail has an electrical problem, and the city jail is at capacity. Plus, they wanted to separate him and his human buddies, seeing as no one's talking. They've been calling in favors." After another bracing sip, Ganti said, "The humans are Joseph Crewe and Samuel Gore. Your sorcerer is now in the system as 'John Doe.'"

Connor grunted. "Dumb alias or lack of ID?"

"The latter. He won't give them his name. They finger-printed him, incidentally, but since his don't match any-thing on file, they're out of luck. They were arrested on suspicion of human trafficking, but the other two have bonded out. Since Faln won't give a name and has nothing to prove his identity, he's being held as a flight risk. Looks like his friends are leaving him to fend for himself."

"Uh-huh." After a moment's consideration, Connor asked, "This jail—how's the security?"

"From what I can tell, meh. It's not designed for long-term housing. White Hill has a police force of three or four, I think—"

"I know the feeling," he muttered.

"The same faces rotate in and out, at least," said Ganti. "There's barely more than a kitchenette in the jail. One of the staff brings in meals from outside, and I suspect they're homemade."

The kid nodded. "Yeah, we don't exactly have catering in Whitford, either. I've brought in takeout a few times when we have overnight guests." Again, he paused to think, then nodded and grabbed a notepad from the room's desk. "Okay, man, I'm going to need everything you've got about this place and the staff. And I mean *everything.*"

"You think we can get Faln?" Moonless Night asked.

Connor glanced up and grinned. "Might could. I'm going to need a posse."

Just before ten that morning, Connor's SUV—masked with Atlanta markings, thanks to online reference photos and Yacovi's artistry—parked in front of the White Hill police department, a tiny, whitewashed brick building with barred windows and a faded metal sign proclaiming the place a fallout shelter. Connor, who was six inches taller than usual, about twenty pounds more muscular, and bald, climbed out from behind the wheel to release Yacovi—who looked like Connor's junior partner, tall, lanky, and blond, with prominent acne scars—from the back. I'd altered my mask only a little, giving my hair more body and enhancing my fake chest and hips, and we'd made sure that my uniform was perhaps a bit tighter than regulation dictated.

Sure, it felt cheap as hell, but it wasn't the first time I'd amped up the sex appeal.

Connor led the way inside, folder of phony paperwork in hand. A leather strap of brass bells jangled on our entry, and I'd barely had a chance to notice the lone camera mounted in the corner of the cinderblock room before a brown door opened and a chubby man with a mop of boyish red curls appeared. "Morning, y'all," he said, quickly taking stock of us. "Can I help you?"

"Morning," said Connor, his voice artificially deepened to the neighborhood of Moonless Night's bass. "I'm Lee Creswell. Atlanta PD," he said, flipping open his masked badge. "My colleagues, June Perkins and Ryan Brown," he continued, nodding to us. "Sheriff said I should ask for Chief Galagher."

"Oh, gosh, he's gone to Crossville for a breakfast prayer meeting," said the officer. "Those things always go long. Buddy Hornsby," he added, shaking Connor's hand. "Can I help y'all?"

Connor, who was admittedly better than I was at reading the insignia on human uniforms, didn't miss a beat. "Well, Sergeant, I hope so. We left home early this morning to get here." Holding up his folder, he said, "Seems y'all have someone we've been trying to run down for *several* weeks."

Buddy's head cocked. "That so?"

"Yup. You got a Doe, don't you?"

"That we do…"

"Well, we finally got some fingerprints into the system yesterday, and wouldn't you know it? Hit." He glanced around the lobby, which was empty but for the four of us, and lowered his voice. "Mind if we go somewhere a little more private? This is a bad business."

The sergeant led us into his cubby of an office—a small room with nary a camera in sight—and Yacovi closed the door as Connor opened his folder on the cluttered desk. "You seen this guy?" he asked, flipping to a grayscale security photo of Faln approaching his apartment building. Ganti had sent several such pictures through DOI's system to Maya, who was skilled enough to download, crop, and mail them to Connor.

Buddy bent to peer at the photo. "*Damn.* Yeah, that

looks like our Doe." Straightening, he asked, "What's Atlanta want with him? We're holding him for the sheriff on human trafficking charges."

Connor's mouth pulled into a tight line of distaste. "Child exploitation. Son of a bitch produces."

"Fuck," Buddy muttered, his expression suggesting a sudden desire to spit. "He got a name?"

"Julian Terrance Grimaldi," said Connor. "And I'm grateful that all I've been asked to do on this case is retrieval. The poor bastard who's had to watch Grimaldi's movies is going to get therapy for Christmas."

"Hope y'all's insurance covers that."

"Union's got it under control. But hey," Connor continued, flipping the papers, "the folks above your pay grade and ours don't mind if we take a crack at him first. That folder's an extradition packet. So…mind if we get him on the road?"

At that, the sergeant balked. "Oh, uh…jeez, I haven't dealt with extradition before."

"It's not hard," said Connor. "I'll show you where to sign—"

"Appreciate that, man, but my chief would have my head if I did this without him. I hate to make you wait, but can you stick around until he's back? There's a diner in town, DeeDee's Kitchen—it ain't *great*, but the biscuits and coffee will do you."

"Yeah, sure," Connor replied, closing the folder, "no problem. I get it. Guess we'll get some breakfast and wait for the big guy, eh?"

"Again, I'm sorry about this," said Buddy.

"No, no, you're just doing your job. Come on, y'all, I'm starving anyway. Let's get out of his hair—"

"Um, sorry," I interrupted, giving Buddy my most apologetic eye flutter, "but before we go, could you show me where the ladies' is?"

Yacovi grunted. "Perkins, is your bladder the size of a thimble, or what?"

"Shut up, Brown," I snapped, and gave Buddy a look of what I hoped was sexy desperation. "Been a long trip. Do you mind?"

"No, ma'am," he said with a smile, and squeezed past Connor to open the door. "Come right this way, let me show you—"

That was as far as he got before I jabbed the syringe I'd been concealing into his neck. I clamped a hand over his mouth to stifle any yelp of surprise, then guided his dead weight to the floor as the sedative potion quickly took effect. Pocketing the spent syringe, I straightened and nodded to Yacovi. "All yours. Got a cover story in mind?"

"You two get Faln and leave Officer Friendly here to me," Yacovi replied. "The stuff you just gave him should be good for ten minutes. I'll handle the memory adjustment once he comes around."

Connor frowned. "Ten minutes? That's all?"

"Modified sedative," he explained. "When you only need to subdue the target long enough to get him restrained. Get to it, now. We'll still need to handle the cameras."

With Yacovi babysitting the sergeant, Connor and I headed for the back of the jail, where we found a pair of barred cells behind a metal door, each equipped with a bunk and toilet. One of the pair was empty, but in the other sat Faln, who scowled at us as the outer door swung open. His blond hair was dirty and hung in his face, and he wore old-timey black-and-white garb that I wasn't entirely convinced hadn't come from a costume shop. A pair of blue flipflops completed the ensemble.

"Hiya," said Connor, holding up the ring of keys. "Ready to go for a ride?" When Faln didn't answer him, Connor slipped into Pactish. "We can do this the easy way or the hard way, bud. Your pick."

That got his attention. "Who the hell are *you*?" Faln demanded, jumping off his bunk.

"The guy taking custody of you right now. So, what's

your preference? Easy or hard?" As Faln glanced around his cell—looking for a weapon, I guessed—Connor said, "Let me give you a little more information. The easy way is that you cooperate, we give you a nice sedative, and you take a nap until we're out of here. The hard way is all of that, except my colleague will unmask first, and I don't think you want a tusk in you, right? Those things probably make nasty flesh wounds."

Faln eyed me, and I cracked my knuckles.

"What's it going to be?" Connor asked him. "Make up your mind."

The sorcerer seemed to shrink back into the corner of the cell and glared at us. "You think I can't take a damn troll?" he muttered.

"You couldn't the last time we met," I retorted. "And I know your power's still being dampened."

He stared at me, his eyes narrowing in challenge. "Want to bet your life on it?"

As I started to answer him, a blast of force cracked Faln's head against the unforgiving wall, and he fell to the floor with a groan. Before he could rise, Connor had jabbed a loaded syringe in his shoulder, and he was unconscious seconds later.

"I did have him, you know," I said, slinging the sorcerer over my shoulder.

"I know you did," Connor replied, "but why waste a good cheap shot?"

CHAPTER 18

Luck was on our side that day. We'd fled before the chief returned from his prayer breakfast, Faln securely bound and gagged in the back of Connor's SUV and every camera and computer we could find fried beyond repair.

It was Connor who'd come up with the plan. With a bit of work, he and Yacovi had planted evidence of a massive electrical surge, destroying computers, exploding light bulbs, and leaving burn stains around the power outlets. No one felt *great* about the idea—the White Hill PD surely didn't have the budget to cover the damage—but we banked on their insurance and hoped for the best. As far as the hapless sergeant knew, he'd been answering a call on the land line when the surge hit, throwing him from his chair and leaving a knot on his head. The blow had knocked him out. Somehow, their John Doe had escaped in the aftermath, but with the cameras gone—and no outside security cameras facing the police station except the one we'd destroyed by the door—there was no telling what had happened to him.

By the time Faln came to, we'd rendezvoused with the RV and parked behind a decaying gas station several towns away. Faln struggled as he began to wake, then shook off the sedative and saw what had happened to him. We'd taken no chances, injecting him with a fresh dose of dampening potion, duct-taping his hands into useless fists, gagging him with more tape, and shoving him, firmly tied, into the dinette booth. His eyes widened as he realized his predicament, and he squirmed and grunted until Moonless

Night took the bench opposite him, grabbed Faln's chin, and rumbled, "*Don't.*"

Faln might have been brash, but he wasn't stupid, and his movements calmed.

"That's better," I said, having traded the morning's disguise for my usual mask. "I didn't introduce myself to you last time, Mr. Faln. My name is Gentle Breeze. I'm the Interdiction chief at DPP, and while this isn't strictly a case within my agency's purview, we're assisting. My colleague from Laws, Agent Berek," I continued, gesturing to Taug, "my former DPP colleague, Agent Hewt, and the fellow over there is on loan to us from, uh—"

"Whitford," said Connor, folding his arms as he stared Faln down. "Georgia. And not to put too fine a point on it," he said in English, "but you done fucked up, son."

While Faln was trying to figure him out, I said, "Now, I'm going to ask you a question, and then I'll remove your gag. I want a truthful answer, understood?"

Warily, he nodded.

"Where is the hex key?" I asked, and ripped away the tape.

He screeched, then sucked on his lips and whimpered.

"Where is it?" I pressed.

"You're crazy," said Faln.

"The key."

"I don't know what you're talking about," he insisted. "*What* hex key? I don't have any key—"

The rest of his answer turned to muffled protestations as Moonless Night applied a fresh layer of tape to shut him up.

I looked toward the front of the RV, where Dave and Maggie sat out of the way. "Could someone call Maya, please? We need to put in another request."

At least DOI was on standby, as Ganti called not ten minutes later. "Boss told me not to go far," he told me. "What's up?"

"We've got Faln," I replied, turning the phone's camera

to show him our unhappy captive. "But we've frisked him, and there's no sign of the hex key."

"Or anything that could pass for one," said Yacovi. "No jewelry, no small objects. I didn't feel anything embedded under his skin, either."

"Rose believed he was holding it," I told Ganti. "Of course, she might have been hallucinating," I allowed, "but assuming she was right, can you find the key?"

Ganti made a face. "Not knowing what it looks like...I mean, I can *try*, but this may be pointless. How far back do you want me to look?"

"Rose identified Faln yesterday morning. If she's right, he can't have done much with it—he's been locked up, and that cell was empty when we left."

"*If* Rose was right," said Ganti, and sighed. "Okay, I'll poke around again. I was tracking Faln's movements between jails when I looked before, but I'll attempt a closer inspection. Bye."

The video feed on the laptop screen cut out, and Maya turned the phone around. "So...someone's cranky," she said, switching the conversation to English. "Where are y'all, anyway?"

"Middle of nowhere, Tennessee," said Connor.

"Huh. Well, seeing as you've got a guy tied up in there, might want to lie low..."

Yacovi nudged me aside and took the phone. "Dear girl," he said with a little smirk, "the day I can't hide a body, just put me out to pasture."

Maya gnawed her lip. "Was that supposed to be reassuring? Because that was actually kind of creepy—"

"Amen," called Maggie from the front.

"Oh, uh..." Yacovi cleared his throat, suddenly flushing. "What I meant was that I can mask him—"

"Yeah, I got that," said Maya, "but the execution needs work."

He looked at Taug, who shrugged, then at Tabitha, who nodded emphatically.

"Look, y'all," said Connor, taking the phone, "you hang out anywhere Pactlands-adjacent long enough, and the weirdness bar moves."

"Totally," Maya concurred.

I grunted. "We're not *weird*. You're just sheltered."

"Except now I'm calling Yacovi if I ever kill someone," said Tabitha.

When he glanced her way, she winked.

"You want that body buried or vaporized, hon?" he asked, and then considered our prisoner. "We *should* stick him somewhere in case of nosy cops."

"There's storage bays under the RV," Dave suggested.

"Yeah, but those aren't as secure as I'd like...ah, bin-go."

A few muttered syllables sent Faln rising into the storage and sleeping area above the cab, and our bags followed. Another spell silenced the prisoner's muffled protestations, and as Yacovi dusted off his hands, he turned to Dave and Maggie. "I told y'all a few days ago that there's a lot I can do, yeah?"

"Something like that," Dave replied.

"Well, *that* is reserved for idiots," he said, pointing to the pile of bags. "Now, until we hear from Ganti, does anyone want to play Hearts?"

The impromptu tournament was off to a good start, with Tabitha and Maggie the players to beat, when Maya called around noon with Ganti on the feed.

"There's an Americanism I've come to appreciate," he said by way of greeting. "*Brain bleach.* Know what I mean?"

"Oh, boy," Connor muttered. "What'd you see?"

"Does Faln have the hex key?" I asked.

Ganti chuckled mirthlessly. "*Yeah.* Rose gave you good information, thank heavens. You've got the right sorcerer."

"And the hex key?" Yacovi interjected. "What and

where?"

"I'm not entirely certain of its contours," he replied. "It's small, maybe half the size of your thumb," he estimated.

Yacovi frowned. "You haven't seen it?"

"I've seen its *wrappings*." With a resigned expression like that of a man on his way to the firing squad, Ganti said, "It's well wrapped in protective material. Faln swallowed it on the night he got out there, and, um…matters have taken their course."

Connor grimaced. "You mean…"

"Please don't make me draw you a picture."

"Yeah, *no*. Jesus," he muttered, and glanced at the loft. "Uh…how recently did it, um…go down again?"

"Two days," Ganti replied. "It's working its way toward the terminus, but you might be able to chemically speed it along."

All eyes flicked toward Tabitha, who straightened in her seat. "What's he saying?"

"Sorry, I didn't realize," said Ganti, switching languages. "Is that the healer?"

"Pharmacist," she corrected, and took the phone from me. "Hi. What's up?"

"Without going into detail, what do you have in there with laxative properties?"

She thought briefly. "Not much, just a bit for travel discomfort. Why?"

"Can you *acquire* a strong laxative?"

"Sure, but…" Slowly, her head tilted toward the storage area, and her face creased. "Oh, *no*. What we're looking for, it's…"

"In there," Ganti finished.

"And he can't vomit it up?"

"Too far gone."

"*Shit*," she muttered, then turned to Connor. "All right, you heard him. Let's go find a drugstore."

The two returned about an hour later with sacks of fast-food burgers and three plastic bags from the nearest pharmacy. Before Tabitha unpacked, she said, "Bring Faln down here. We need to get a few things straight."

Yacovi did as she asked, plopping him on the couch, and Faln watched anxiously as she began removing items from the bags: a selection of small boxes, a bottle of liquid, a plastic bottle with a long tip, a bedpan.

"Here's the deal," she said in an almost conversational tone. "We're not waiting for nature to take its course. Now, I've got a selection of products here that will unstop just about any pipe, some of them more harshly than others. We can do this in one of two ways. Be a good boy, and you can take some pills and drink this lovely magnesium citrate," she said, holding up the bottle of liquid. "Fuck around, and we're going up the back door," she continued, pointing to the long-tipped bottle. After giving him a moment to consider his choices, she asked, "Want to start with pills?"

Faln nodded vigorously, then let out a silent scream when Moonless Night ripped off the tape gag again. Still, he didn't fight Tabitha, swallowing the pills she gave him and sipping as directed from the bottle.

"It's not an instantaneous process," she warned us, giving Faln a drink of water as a chaser. "Unless there's a potion around here that'll do the trick…"

"Not on hand," said Yacovi. "It's not difficult to brew something that'll practically make your intestines gleam, but I don't have the ingredients, and it takes a good two days, anyway."

"Figured. So, here's the plan," she said, looking around the RV. "We've got to babysit him while the drugs work. The…*result*…will come in waves, hence this," she continued, lifting the bedpan. "As I assume no one wants to go digging through the waste tank of this vehicle. Gentlemen, I'm going to leave that part up to you."

"Aw, come on," Taug protested, "that's gross—"

"Man, I stitched your ass back together," Tabitha interrupted. "You owe me. Just take him in the bathroom and position him over that, then...see if anything emerges."

"Like the world's worst Cracker Jack prize," Dave muttered.

"Mm. Fair," she allowed, "but look at it this way: he's going to be *miserable* in the near future."

With that modicum of consolation in mind, I adjusted Faln's binds, keeping him tied hand and foot but undoing some of the earlier taping and trussing. Yacovi removed the muting spell on him, and since there wasn't a soul around to come to his aid, Faln seemed to sink into the couch, resigning himself to his fate as his stomach emitted the occasional gurgling portent of the unpleasantness to come.

The Hearts tournament resumed, but as I had been eliminated, I took a seat beside Faln and stared at him until he faced me. "What the hell were you Unity Plan idiots thinking?" I murmured. "Grab a bunch of innocent, unsuspecting people, dump them out here with the clothes on their back, leave them at the mercy of the humans who find them, and...what? How did you actually see this playing out?"

The current game paused as the others turned to Faln, waiting for an answer.

"We had no choice," he finally said. "Our proposals are always shot down in the Forum, and no one there has the vision to see what we're trying to accomplish."

"We're listening," Taug muttered.

"It's simple," said Faln, shifting on the couch. "If we all just left the Pactlands and showed ourselves, *really* showed what magic can do, then the humans would be scared enough to cede us land. We could rebuild here—"

Yacovi chuckled. "They might be frightened into retreat at first, but we'd never survive the counterattack."

"*Please*. Magic is stronger than anything they could muster—"

Connor's full-throated laughter cut him short that time, and Faln glared at him in annoyance. "You're nuts," he said in English, then glanced at Tabitha, explaining, "Their grand plan hinges on humanity just running away and leaving them with whatever land they want."

She snorted. "Unlikely. Even the cosplayers wouldn't go for that."

"You think you're any match for me?" Faln retorted, switching tongues. "At my full power, I could crush you."

"And right now," she calmly replied, "I could put a gun to your head."

"This is different—"

"Dude, stop," said Connor. "You're not going to win this argument."

"Oh, yeah? What do *you* know?" Faln spat.

He put his cards face-down on the table and smirked at the angry sorcerer. "Ever heard of East Branch?"

Faln frowned. "Yes…"

"I'm the last of us out here. Hi," he said as Faln's expression shifted toward surprise. "And I didn't grow up on the compound—I lived in town. Nothing but humans. No clue that there was an alternative to 'human.' My family, all the folks at East Branch—they had no idea that we were anything else. We just had some freaky abilities and the occasional birth defect, see? And East Branch kept to itself."

"Which proves our plan would work—" Faln began.

"You didn't let me finish. East Branch was beyond impoverished, and if the county had come in and seen how the community actually lived, they'd have taken the kids. The community didn't last as long as it did because of *magic*," he said dismissively. "It endured because generations of us fought off our neighbors with guns and knives and such, and after a while, they let us be. But that only lasted because cleaning out East Branch would have been more trouble than it was worth, not because it *couldn't* have been done. East Branch endured through the apathy of its neighbors, not because of fucking magic." Shaking his head, Connor said, "I grew up with humans. Work with them. Culturally, I'm closer to them than anyone else, see? And I've got a *pretty* good idea of how this grand plan of yours would play out. Sure, your average human might be scared off with a show of magic," he allowed, "but when humans get scared, they regroup and *fight back*. Call in reinforcements. You think you've got what it takes to fight off, like, bombs? Drones? Tanks? Chemical weapons? Enough good old boys with guns? Magic doesn't make you bulletproof, bub. And seeing as there are more than eight billion humans you'd need to convince of your might—"

"Come again?" Faln squeaked.

"Eight billion," said Tabitha. "There's a lot of us out here. Connor's right," she continued, staring Faln down. "And believe me, if word were to get out to the general population that the sort of beings we know only in stories and legends exist..." She shook her head. "Some would want to make peace—we're not all bloodthirsty, you know. Some would want to study you, lock you in labs and pick you apart and make sure you weren't going to start a pandemic. And then others would want to neutralize the threat. See, it doesn't matter that you held land out here once upon a time and humans took it from you—we have a *long* history of doing that to each other. You ain't *that* special."

"And again," said Connor, "bullets are mighty effective."

"Sure. Hell," said Tabitha, giving Faln an odd little smile, "you're practically human, anyway. A bad flu might put you all on your asses."

I tensed. Did she not know those were fighting words? Quickly, I looked at Yacovi, preparing to diffuse a brawl, but to my surprise, he seemed unbothered.

Faln was a different story. "*What* did you just say?" he growled.

"I brunch with a healer," Tabitha told him. "She knows

the biology. You're just weird humans—*maybe* a freaky subspecies, but we're kissing cousins at worst."

As Faln sputtered, Yacovi coughed. "She's not wrong, kid," he said quietly. "If you look at the genetics—"

"*I* am nothing like *that*," he snapped, glaring daggers at Tabitha.

"No," Connor interrupted, "you're a fucking monster who snatched children from their beds and dumped them in the goddamn woods. Not to mention the shit you put poor Ermonir through. Taug's hurt, Gentle Breeze is hurt, Hoska was sick when we found him—"

"All in furtherance of the greater good," Faln protested. "Besides, the ones we dropped off wouldn't have been any great loss."

I wondered then if the drugs Tabitha had given him had affected his thinking, and from the look in Taug's eye, he shared my sentiment.

"Oh, do tell," said Connor, his voice dripping with sarcasm.

Faln snorted. "Lesser species, all of them. Barely talented, if that. Now, nymphs can be useful in a limited capacity—"

He yelped as I singlehandedly pulled him off the couch and held him dangling above the floor, kicking and squirming but unable to land a blow.

"A thought, sweetest," said Moonless Night in his accented English. "We could just kill him now and dig the hex key from his entrails. You wouldn't mind, would you?" he asked Taug.

The agent's nose wrinkled. "I mean, *technically*, that's murder, but under the circumstances…"

Faln ceased wriggling like bait on a fishhook and stared at my boyfriend for a moment, then at me, the pieces clicking into place. "You…*you're* that Huntsman, aren't you?" he asked, his face blanching to a satisfying pallor.

"May I, dearest?" Moonless Night asked, smiling, then took Faln from me and wrapped his hand around the sorcerer's neck. "It would be very simple to cut out your tongue," he murmured. "I will not dignify your question with a direct response, but it would behoove you to remember that if I am who you think I am, then I am *very* old, and I have killed many, *many* times. That person you're thinking of could snap your worthless neck before you knew death was upon you. So, just to be safe, perhaps you should offer a sincere apology to these agents for the words that have slipped from your fool's mouth and the shit you've put them through…and if you're coward enough to piss your trousers, you'll be sitting in them," he warned.

I won't say that Faln's apology was particularly *sincere*, but as it was fueled by terror, it was sufficiently heartfelt.

But as Moonless Night tossed Faln back onto the couch, Taug considered the pair of them, his brow furrowing. "Um…sorry, am I missing something?" he asked. "What was all that about a Huntsman?"

No one said a word for a moment, and then Moonless Night sighed and plopped onto the other end of the couch. "You tell this to no one," he warned Taug, "and before you ask, Erenani is very much aware, so you're not keeping secrets from your director."

"Keeping *what* secrets?" he pressed.

He glanced up—checking for clearance for his hidden rack, I assumed—then disengaged his masking ring. As Taug gawked, my boyfriend said in his suddenly higher voice, "'Moonless Night' is an alias I assumed eight-hundred-odd years ago. Technically…" He waved one hand toward his antlers. "My father and I didn't see eye to eye, hence the new identity."

Taug said nothing for a few seconds, absorbing this, then glanced around the RV. "Am I the only one surprised?"

"Sorry, hon," said Maggie.

"*Huh.* And…you two?" he asked, pointing at Moonless Night—well, Morial—and me.

"Want to make something of it?" I retorted.

Taug held up his hands. "No, *nope*, not looking for a fight, just, uh…" He cleared his throat.

"It works. Leave it at that." While Taug stewed, I turned my attention back to Faln. "What's the Unity Plan's connection to Gerem Aniap?"

He stiffened, clearly having not expected the enquiry. "What do you mean?"

"Don't play dumb with me," I said, then pointedly looked at my boyfriend, who cracked his knuckles. "The handful of people in the agencies who know about *him* aren't the type to spread secrets. That leaves a Forum leak, and there's a *very* likely contender. So, with that in mind, I'll repeat myself once: what is the Unity Plan's connection to Aniap?"

Perhaps having finally come to terms with his predicament, Faln caved. "Jorval Haldin."

"Who?"

"He's an aide," Faln explained. "Used to work for Aniap before…you know—"

"Before my fiancée got him shipped off to a prison farm?" Connor interrupted. Faln's head whipped toward him, and Connor smirked. "Oh, please, go on. Janie's grandpa is such a *lovely* piece of work."

Uneasily, Faln continued. "Jorval works for the new guy now, the replacement, Taliam Recett. Aniap wasn't one of us, but he was sympathetic. Recett's useless. Jorval stayed on because the money is good, and he still has access to all of the Forum's files. That's how we found the targets—pulled names, did our research. Everyone in Aniap's office knew about *him*," he added, glancing at Morial,

"And that's why I'm out here?" I asked. "A backdoor way to prod the Hunter into desperate action?"

Faln hesitated, then nodded.

"Unfortunately for you, I've worked with Wylan. He's smarter than that. All you've done is piss him off."

"Him and the rest of the family," Morial muttered.

I grinned at him. "Some more than others?"

A grunt and an amber-eyed glare at Faln answered *that*.

"Are you going to kill me?" Faln murmured.

"Not if you cooperate," I replied. "You have my word."

"And *him*?"

"Are you implying that I would dishonor my girlfriend by making a liar of her?" asked Morial.

Faln swallowed hard.

"Much as it pains me," I said, "much as I'd love to wring your neck for the mess you idiots have put us through, I'm an agent. We do have internal regulations, and generally, it's frowned upon for us to kill suspects in custody."

"Oh?" said Faln. "Because I know what happened in Central."

"What, your little buddy?" said Connor. "We didn't hurt him. Just gave him a chance to think about life and his choices."

"Though I suppose it's a good thing someone found him," I grudgingly allowed. "He *was* alive, yes?"

The sorcerer nodded. "That trick you people pulled with his phone didn't work as well as I'm sure you'd hoped. We just followed his tracker."

My guts clenched. "*Tracker?*"

"Yeah, we've got trackers so the others can find us. A search party freed him that night—"

"You've got a tracker on you?" Taug interrupted. "Or *in* you?"

Faln's mouth snapped closed.

"Sorry," said Maggie, "but what's a tracker?"

Yacovi took the lead. "You know those things you can stick on your luggage or your keys or whatever and find them with your phone? Trackers work by the same principle, albeit with magic. Depending on the tracker and how the spells are set up—"

"Liliol ensorcelled a compass for Jane and me," Connor offered.

"That's a bit different," said Yacovi. "Similar idea, right track, thaumaturgical divergences. Generally, trackers are made into jewelry. You can actually set up a phone to find them if you're comfortable working with the tech."

All eyes fell on Faln, who said nothing.

"If he's got one on," I said, "then his friends didn't break him out of jail…"

"But they'll know he's been moved," Taug finished, and swore. "How many sorcerers are out here, again?"

"I don't think Rose ever got that far. So," I said, folding my arms as I considered our prisoner, "where do you think his tracker is?"

With a sigh, Tabitha rose from the booth and dug in her bag until she found a pair of disposable gloves. "Hold him still," she said once her hands were covered, and produced a penlight. "Let's see what we can find."

Her search, mercifully, was brief. "*Paydirt,*" she said, peering into his nose. "Septum piercing."

"Huh?" said Taug.

She pointed to the cartilage separating her nostrils. "That's the septum. He's got a horseshoe, and he's hidden it by tucking the ends up in there. Fashion or tracker?"

He made a face. "Tracker, almost certainly. I don't know of anyone who willingly pierces *that*. Can you get it out?"

"Shouldn't be a problem. Gentle Breeze and…uh…are we going by Moonless Night, or—"

"That's fine," my boyfriend told her, and joined me to immobilize Faln's head. "Is this a good angle?"

"It'll do. Let me get this ball off the end…"

With a moment's work, she'd disassembled the jewelry and pried it from his nose. "Okay," said Tabitha, wrapping the tracker in a paper towel, "what do we do with this?"

Connor grabbed his keys. "Guess I'm forfeiting the tournament. Let me take that little thing for a ride."

She handed it over, and Yacovi told him, "Flush it, toss it in running water, throw it down a well, whatever you like. Easier to get rid of it than to try to break the spells on it."

"Roger that," said Connor, and hurried out to his SUV.

Once the sound of his engine had faded, Morial masked again, then asked me in quiet Trollish, "How long do you suppose he'll be away? Until the first evacuation, or…"

"I don't know," I replied in kind, "but you, Dave, Yacovi, and Taug can figure out who's got the first shift."

"I didn't sign up for this," he muttered.

"None of us did, dearest," I said with a peck to his cheek. "But since I believe you're scaring the crap out of Faln, perhaps this will be a short wait. And besides, surely Tabitha has more gloves."

Perhaps suspecting the ill will that would await him at the RV otherwise, Connor worked quickly, driving only as far as Crossville and disposing of the tracker in a gas station waste can. "If they're tracking him, they'll think he's been moved back to county lockup," he explained. "By the time they're close enough to realize the problem…"

"We'll be on the road," I said. "Hopefully."

But it was a long, unpleasant afternoon and evening before the hex key made its appearance. By then, Faln was miserable, cramping and sore, and the men who'd been drafted into retrieval duty had all seen battle. It was Yacovi who found the prize, and once he'd cleaned it up in the kitchenette with hot water and plenty of soap, he showed the rest of us what we'd been waiting for: a piece of silver-colored metal curled into a strange, irregular, looping figure no larger than the penicillin tablets Tabitha had been passing around all week. Yacovi muttered over the hex key until it began glowing blue, then grunted. "Protected against stomach acid—that's good. Means it should be functional," he said. "So, let's wake Maya."

Connor did the honors, and DOI was quick to respond, asking her to stand by while one of the portal sorcerers was brought in. Around eleven-thirty that night, Maya called us with the video feed, and I saw the lead sorcerer's eyes light up as she spotted the hex key in Yacovi's hand. "That's it!" she cried. "*Where* did you—"

"You don't want to know," he muttered. "Tell Pateme we're heading for Liliol's place."

The sorcerer glanced at her wrist. "How soon should I be at DPP?"

"Just a moment," he said, and looked around the RV. "Who's got the directions?"

"Six and a half hours," Maggie called from the front. "Maybe seven."

"I can push it—" Dave began, but was interrupted by a chorus of *no*s from the rear.

Yacovi turned back to the phone and the waiting sorcerer. "Early tomorrow. I'm sure the director won't mind."

With a warning call to Liliol, we were off for Briardale. Dave took the first shift, then surrendered the wheel to Connor at our fill-up stop, conceding that it was long past his bedtime. Tabitha took the SUV, an easier vehicle to handle, and Maggie jumped ship to keep her company while Dave crashed on the bed. Armed with slim cans of energy drinks, Connor powered on toward Virginia, leading our two-vehicle convoy parallel to the spine of the Appalachians. The sun rose Saturday over the mountains to our east, far larger than the ones we'd left in Tennessee, until finally, a little after eight, we pulled up the long driveway to Eden's Bounty and came to a stop in the gravel parking lot.

Liliol hurried down from her cottage to meet us, masked and seemingly ready for customers in dirt-stained jeans and a black windbreaker, though the greenhouse was still visible past the illusion blocking it from the road. "I've got coffee," she said in greeting. "*Strong* coffee. Who needs it?"

"Thank you, but let's deal with the priority first," I said, adjusting Faln where I'd thrown him over my shoulder. "Someone alert Maya."

"You know they'll be a few minutes," said Liliol. "Drop him in the greenhouse and come up for breakfast—Sally will keep an eye on him."

Sally did more than that. By the time Pateme was in place in the DPP greenhouse, the slithertrap had coiled herself around Faln, keeping him cocooned several feet above the floor. All I could see in the layers of green vines were the tip of his nose and a pair of frightened eyes, and I gave Sally's nearest tendril a pat. "Nice work," I murmured.

The vine vibrated with what I dearly hoped was pleasure.

Liliol convinced Sally to drop her prize, and then she floated him toward the back of the greenhouse as the door began to open. "All yours!" she announced cheerily, letting the trussed-up sorcerer drop to the floor. "Do you want him now, or shall I ask Sally to hold him for you?"

I looked through the doorway to see Pateme and Kabno waiting, along with the lead sorcerer, several of her team, and about twenty DOL agents.

"Hex key first, please," said the lead sorcerer. "Toss it gently, eh?"

Yacovi stepped close to the door and underhanded it to her, and she caught it in her cupped palms. After passing it off to her underlings, who hurried away, she consulted her computer and said, "I *think* we're stable enough for one crossing. No more than that. If you'd like to send our problem child home…"

Before we could maneuver Faln closer to the door, a thick vine shot out from beneath a bench, wrapped around his ankles, and slung him through the opening. He screamed as he slid back into the Pactlands on his belly, and the agents immediately descended on him like carrion birds.

"There's a mole for the Unity Plan among Aniap's old staff," I told the directors. "Jorval Haldin. Might want to cut off his access to Forum files, know what I'm saying?"

"On it," said Kabno, walking away, which left only Pateme and the sorcerer at the edge of the door.

There was home, mere footsteps away…

"So, what now?" I asked.

The sorcerer's mouth tightened as she reviewed her readings. "It's not stable enough for more to come through. I'm sorry, I really am, but with any luck, we'll have the Pactlands stabilized shortly after we activate the hex key. You *should* be able to come home in a few days."

I looked at Pateme and cocked an eyebrow.

"Rest," he told me, and glanced at Yacovi. "Make her take it easy, won't you?"

Yacovi snorted. "I work with magic, Teme, not miracles."

"They can stay here," Liliol interjected. "Really, it's no trouble," she insisted to our group. "I mean, beds are limited, but other than that…how many of you are there now?"

"Eight," I told her. "If we could borrow the guest room again, we can make do with that and the RV…if Maggie and Dave don't mind."

"Or if you two want to head home, no hard feelings," said Yacovi. "We're not that far from Richmond, after all."

Maggie shook her head. "We're staying until this mess is straightened out. My little girl's stuck in there, remember."

"Your little girl is tough," murmured Moonless Night. "I wouldn't be overly concerned, Maggie."

"You say that, but you're not the mama," she replied primly, then turned to Liliol and folded her arms. "*So.* I'm thinking we might need to make a grocery run."

CHAPTER 19

Dinner Saturday night was only for seven of us and Liliol.

"Poor Maya has been stuck in my house for days," said Connor as he checked his tires around noon, having caught a few hours' sleep. "It's high time we relieved her."

"What if there's a message?" I protested. "If DOI calls—"

"Then someone can damn well open the greenhouse door. Y'all ain't going anywhere, right?" he countered. "And if I know Sally, she'll find a way to alert you."

He had a point.

"I'll be back with Maya tomorrow," Connor promised, climbing into his SUV. "Don't have too much fun without me, now."

He'd offered to take Tabitha and Yacovi home with him, but the two had declined. Yacovi insisted that as an agent, even a retired one, he was obligated to stick around, while Tabitha just pointed to Taug and me and said, "I don't trust them to take their meds if I'm not here to nag them."

Thus it was that dinner that evening was for seven, but Maggie and Liliol went all out: three roast chickens, enough mashed potatoes for a dozen humans or perhaps two hungry trolls, several steaming bowls of vegetables, an entire bag of frozen rolls, a few pounds of trout that Maggie had thought looked nice at the market, a bean salad, and finally, some slices of tomato layered with mozzarella and basil and drizzled with a balsamic reduction, which Tabitha swore was also a salad but I deemed an unorthodox vehicle for cheese. There was a chocolate cake from a bakery in what passed for downtown Briardale, tubs of ice cream, and more of the strong coffee Liliol had offered that morning, and by the time I put my plate in the dishwasher, I almost felt stuffed.

At the rest of our group's insistence, the Humphrieses took the guest bed, while Yacovi landed on the couch. The four of us remaining eyed the options in the RV, none of them superb, and then Taug sighed. "You two should take the bed," he said, pointing to the rear of the vehicle. "Tabitha, do you want the couch or the dinette?"

Moonless Night and I helped them rearrange the furniture and passed around pillows, and then my boyfriend and I retreated to the bedroom and closed the door. The bed wasn't great, but after our long night's vigil, neither of us complained. The last thing I remember was the warm, comforting weight of his body spooning behind mine, and then exhaustion won.

I woke alone Sunday morning and groggily took stock of myself: rumpled clothes I'd worn the day before, funk in my mouth, desperate need of a shower. When I emerged into the RV, I found Taug and Tabitha still buried in blankets, and so I quietly lowered the shades to keep out the light and slipped outside.

The coffee was on in Liliol's cottage, and most of a pan of blueberry muffins remained on the counter. "Morning," said Maggie, waving me in with her mug. "How're you feeling?"

"Kind of disgusting, not going to lie," I replied, making a beeline for the coffeepot. "You?"

She chuckled. "Our hostess has offered the use of her washing machine, and that might not be a bad idea. I'm going to run a load for Dave and me—want me to chuck yours in as well?"

"Oh, thanks, but don't bother—I'll see to my clothes

later. What little is left of them," I added, glancing down at myself.

"We should have found you something stretchier—"

"Unmasking in my condition would test the strength of any fabric. It's my own damn fault," I assured her, and took a sip. "She's got good taste in coffee."

"No complaints here. We're going to need to send her a gift basket or something once we're home…"

"I'm sure she'd say that's unnecessary," I replied.

Maggie gave me a *look*. "My mama raised me better than that."

Before I could respond, the front door opened again, and in came Liliol, dressed and chipper. "Ah, Gentle Breeze, you're awake," she said, going to the sink. "That's two."

"Two?" I echoed.

"From the RV," she explained, and began scrubbing her dirty fingernails. Someone, it seemed, had been repotting already that morning. "Your boy's restless. Are the others still sleeping?"

"Yes, and where is he, anyway?"

She grinned up at me. "Well, I found him sitting out here around dawn, and then he helped me with the watering, and last I saw, he was over in the greenhouse, making friends with Sally."

I paused, considering that. "How *does* one make friends with a slithertrap, anyway?"

"He found a dead mouse under a bench of mums and brought that to her as an offering, so I think he's off to a good start. Get some breakfast," she added, nodding to the muffins. "Maggie made those."

"Yes, from the finest of boxes," Maggie teased at the table.

"If you have to add vegetable oil, it counts as baking," Liliol replied, then turned back to me. "I don't have much experience with the Hunt, but something tells me *he's* not very good at just sitting. Right?"

She knew about Moonless Night, then—and considering the people in her orbit, I wasn't shocked. "Not when he's unsettled."

"You and Annie should probably compare notes," said Maggie, nodding knowingly. "Does he need to blow off steam?"

"Probably," I allowed, "but organizing a melee game or, like, a *sparring* situation wouldn't be easy here…"

Liliol turned off the water and reached for a towel. "Please don't destroy my stock." She thought briefly, then said, "Why don't you shower, dear? Use my bath. And then…I know a few decent hiking trails in the area."

Truth be told, I was almost as prone to pacing as my boyfriend was, and waiting around was never my strongest skill. Once I'd cleaned up—and Liliol had gestured my clothing into a fresher state—I found Moonless Night in the greenhouse, sitting on a pile of mulch bags with vines covering his lap like a living blanket, and shared Liliol's suggestion. He was amenable, and Sally allowed him to leave once he promised to come back.

"Thinking about a plant for your desk?" I joked. "I wonder if those things will grow from cuttings."

"That'd be one way to keep bugs out of the newsroom, but no," he replied, waving to Sally over his shoulder.

"You two seem attached."

"My boss would probably consider it a safety hazard. No need to put the weather team in mortal peril."

Seeing as no one else was up for a hike, Liliol drove us to a quiet nearby trailhead and gave me her phone, preprogrammed with the Humphrieses' numbers. "Call when you need a ride back," she said. "You have water?"

And sunscreen, bug spray, a knife, and a small first aid kit—Liliol hadn't let us leave the house without the pack. "We'll be fine," I assured her. "Thanks for the lift."

I flinched as I began to shoulder the bag, and Moonless

Night took it from me. "It's not heavy," I protested.

"It might rub your stitches."

I huffed and followed after him into the woods. "I'm *fine*. Been through worse."

"Understood."

"So, you needn't baby me. I'm entirely capable—"

"I know you are," he interrupted, pausing while I caught up. "I also know you're in pain and probably shouldn't be out here, so won't you let me *try* to help?"

Much as I hated to admit it, he was right—I'd swigged a pain potion on the way out the door, but my healing side complained nonetheless.

"I don't think you're weak," he murmured. "Or incapable. And since there's no one but us to see…"

I sighed. "Slow down, okay? This isn't a forced march."

"Sorry." He let me set the pace as we continued. "I wasn't thinking…"

"You don't have to be so nervous," I said, taking his hand. "I've been to Liliol's place before, and it's safe. There are no trackers on us to lead any Unity Plan sorcerers who want to be heroes to Briardale—and even if they attacked, it's not like we're defenseless. You, me, Connor—once he gets back with his guns—Yacovi's well trained, and I suspect that Liliol can hold her own. *Plus* the giant slithertrap."

"Sally would eat well," he mused.

"*Very* well, I'm afraid. So, try to relax, yes?" I said, and gave his hand a squeeze. "It's a nice day. Birds, squirrels," I said, gesturing toward the canopy. "There might even be deer in here."

He grew momentarily pensive. "If we did encounter deer—"

I could see where his mind was wandering, and having watched his little brother training, I had no doubt that he could run down a hapless doe and dispatch her with the knife in our kit. "You know, I could be wrong, but I don't think Liliol would appreciate fresh venison today. Not like that."

"You're probably right."

On we walked over the mostly gentle terrain, dodging the occasional low-hanging branch and avoiding roots. The trail was nearly empty and well-manicured, perfect for a stretch of the legs, but even as I fell into the easy rhythm of the hike, Moonless Night remained tense— superficially pleasant, but I could smell his nervousness. After half an hour or so, when we were alone but for the birds, I pulled him down with me onto a fallen log. "Tired?" he asked. "We can call Liliol—"

"What's on your mind?" I demanded. "I know you too well."

He hesitated, clearly wrestling with his thoughts, then surrendered to my insistent stare. "I just want you to know that I'm damn proud of you," he said softly, "and I didn't mean to insult you by jumping in—"

"*Dearest.*" Shaking my head, I said, "If I were angry, you'd be very much aware. I'm not."

"But that *was* insulting of me, and—"

"It's forgiven. Don't let it bother you. But if, someday, I were to run onto the sidelines while you were covering a match…"

"You'd make the shot much prettier," he said, smiling, but I could still see the anxiety beneath the veneer.

"I'm damn proud of you, too," I told him. "Hope you know that."

Again, Moonless Night was quiet for a moment before he spoke, and when he did, the words tumbled out in a rush. "What I said to Faln the other night about kill-ing…that was a long time ago. I mean, yes, I hunt on occa-sion, but I haven't hunted any*one* since I was young. Back when I was with Father."

I waited, letting him get it out.

"It wasn't right, I know that, and I have no great ex-cuse other than…*Father*," he muttered. "But if that makes you uncomfortable, if there's something I can do…I'll swear off the hunts going forward, if that's what you want. Wylan has already said I'm free to go or not as I choose, and if you'd prefer—"

"Dearest," I said, gripping his arm to silence him, "no."

"I mean it. Just tell me—"

"That's part of who you are. Who you were. *What* you are," I said. "I'm not afraid."

His anxious eyes searched mine.

"You know, I've done shit in the line of duty that I'm not proud of," I told him. "Followed some orders I probably shouldn't have when I was younger. Things I'd rather forget."

"Not like I did," he whispered.

"But you stood up to the fucking Hunter," I said. "How many of your brothers can say as much?" When he didn't respond, I slid closer on the log and hugged him. "I love you, okay? Moonless Night, Morial, whatever you want to call yourself. I love you. I'm proud to be with you."

His grip around me tightened, and I rubbed his back until he released me.

"Honestly, though," I said, grinning, "you must think I'm such a child sometimes."

"*No*," he insisted, vehemently shaking his head. "Never."

I arched a brow. "Are you calling me old, then?"

"Of course not! I…" He struggled briefly, then said, "Look, once you're dealing with immortals, age gets…weird. Technically, yes, I've lived your life several times over," he admitted, "but looking back…it's almost like seeing the lives of different men. I barely recognize myself at some points."

"I'm pretty partial to this version of you."

"Yeah, well, I'm not always sure of what I'm doing, even now," he replied, "but I know I'm in love with you, The Joy in the Spirit at the Scent of Rain on a Gentle Breeze, and I…I've never felt for a woman what I feel for you."

"Good enough for me," I said, and kissed him.

When I sat back, though, he still seemed uncertain. "Is it, truly?" he asked.

"What do you mean?"

"Good enough. *This*," he said, and patted his chest. "You…"

"I love you," I said, holding his gaze. "What are you worried about? Think I can't handle a bunch of guys? I mean, deep down, Wylan is probably still a *little* scared of me."

"I don't doubt it. But…you're young."

"By some estimations," I replied, wondering where he was going.

"You, um…you might want a family someday. And you know I can't give you that."

"*Sweetest*—"

"Perhaps Wylan can find a way now, but that's him. I'm still incapable. None of us can procreate, and even if species weren't an issue—"

I cupped my hands around his face to quiet him. "Hear me: *I don't care*. I've never been firmly decided on the idea of children, and if the tradeoff is children or you, then I choose you."

"Gentle Breeze—"

"Every time."

Releasing him, I sat back and waited, watching his expression shift. "Anything else you need to clear up?" I asked. "I'm not upset, I'm glad you're here, I love you—"

"Would you marry me?" he blurted.

He froze, a look of sudden horror crossing his face, and I laughed until my stitched-up side ached.

"I'm sorry," he mumbled as I wiped my eyes, "that—"

"Of course I'll marry you," I interrupted, taking his hands. "But we've got to work on the romance, dearest."

"I had this planned out!" he protested. "Dinner in the Edolis, candlelight, mountain ambiance…"

"Well, you got the mountain part," I said, glancing at the uphill trail ahead of us.

He closed his eyes and groaned, and I hugged him again. "Sorry I ruined your nice proposal by getting kidnapped."

"Want me to wait and redo it properly?" he mumbled into my shoulder.

"No. No takebacks."

We held each other until I felt the tension in his arms subside, and then I stood and stretched. "Come on, let's keep walking. I'm not ready to go back just yet, are you?"

He fell in beside me, and when the trail flattened out again and his arm snaked around my waist, I didn't complain.

"So," I said, "you're going to have to meet my family eventually."

"I suspected as much. And I should probably take you to the lodge, eh?"

"At some point. But I've already met a few of your kin—the next big step is visiting the extended family in Vengoti."

"Mm." He pulled me closer into his side. "Are they aware that we're dating?"

"Word's gone around. One of my cousins saw a picture of us—you remember the youth melee league gala?"

He chuckled. "Prettiest woman in the room. No wonder the cameras found you."

"*Ha.* Anyway, she asked me what I was doing with *you*, of all people, and I explained that we were kind of a couple, and...well, then the calls started, since she can't keep her mouth closed."

"Do your parents object?"

I paused before answering that. "They'd surely prefer that I marry a nice, normal farmer, move home, and raise a family, but my cousins who've moved away are excited. Besides," I told him, "my older siblings are all back in Vengoti with farms and babies, so my parents can deal with it."

We walked on for a time, and then I asked, "What do you want to tell them?"

"About…"

"You. Are we sticking with the cover story or giving them the truth? You tell me," I insisted. "We can play this however you think best."

He considered the question for a moment, then asked, "How do you think they would react to the truth?"

"Not…well," I admitted, "at least not at first, but I want you to be comfortable. Besides, if Dave and Maggie can come around, then surely my parents can be convinced."

"There's no need to make matters difficult," he replied. "I can be Moonless Night for them."

"That's fair. But would you still be Morial for me sometimes?"

He held me so tightly that I yelped, then apologized profusely and called Liliol to retrieve us before he could further exacerbate my injuries.

I had always imagined that were I to get engaged, I'd immediately call my parents—that's what one did, after all. Instead, Moonless Night and I celebrated that evening with our weird crew in Liliol's home, gorging ourselves on another pot of Maggie's spaghetti and half a dozen cakes and pies. Left to her own devices with only the television for company, Maya had passed the time at Connor's house baking, even calling a delivery service to bring her more eggs and flour when his limited supply ran out. She talked like she was being paid by the word that night, so happy was she to be around people again.

Even without our engagement, the mood was festive. Maya was personable and dying to befriend Sally, Dave and Maggie were well-rested, Taug was healing up well, and Yacovi had spent the day with Liliol in the greenhouse, examining her plants and comparing brewing notes. While Connor was weary after his long drive to Georgia and back, he and Tabitha chatted amiably while they washed the dinner dishes and Maya poured champagne— well, sparkling white, she admitted, but no one minded.

Had I been in Vengoti with my family, there would have been aged liquor, the bottle my parents laid aside the day I was born. The toasting would have been formal, the same wishes for health and life and children that I'd heard at other dinners. This was different, yes, but...*nice*. The toasting was more freestyle, the beverage effervescent, the company odd, but at least my boyfriend—fiancé, that is— could drink in celebration. That lovely old troll-strength bottle in my parents' cellar would have surely put him under the table, if not in a hospital.

Moonless Night *never* drank, but Morial seemed to be having fun.

When we finally retired to the RV, I kicked off my shoes and sat on the bed, listening. Emerging from the tiny bathroom with his toothbrush, he cocked his head and asked, "Is something wrong?"

"We're alone," I replied.

He jutted his thumb toward the cottage. "Uh…"

"I overheard them trying to be sneaky before we left," I murmured. "Sounds like everyone else is camping in the house tonight."

"Why…" he began, and then the realization pierced the wine fog. "Oh. *Oh.* Well, now, that's courteous of them."

"I suppose we shouldn't let this go to waste."

"Definitely not."

He locked the bedroom door, just in case, and changed his mask. There was Moonless Night, hunched over to avoid the ceiling, toothbrush in hand and eager smile behind his tusks, and I chuckled as I reached for my pendant. "Just let me slip into something more comfortable, okay?"

I removed my mask and slid out of my clothes, grateful to be back in my own skin. After giving my jaw a test wiggle to readjust to an underbite, I glanced up and caught him staring at me...and if I'd been confused about what I saw in his eyes, my nose didn't lie.

"You really don't mind this?" I asked.

"You're beautiful," he said as he joined me on the bed. "Why would I?"

"You wouldn't prefer someone who looked...I don't know, more like Maya?"

"*Maya?*" He snorted. "She's cute enough, sure, but she's not you. *This*," he said, running his fingers through my short strip of hair, "is what I want."

"Is it, now?" I teased.

"Mm-hmm."

"Well, then," I said, "why don't you turn off that light and come and get it?"

He needed no further encouragement, and when we curled up afterward, spent and satisfied, I slept better than I had in a month.

We knew the hex key had worked on Monday morning when we awoke to find the greenhouse missing.

Liliol brought it back and checked inside, then announced all was as it should be. "And I have an absolute *glut* of mail," she said to Yacovi, "if you wouldn't mind giving a colleague a hand."

The two worked steadily for several hours, but the hidden door at the back of the greenhouse never so much as cracked open. Still, we remained hopeful, doing laundry and tending to the nursery's daily watering schedule, and Maya, decreeing that she'd had far too many carbs of late, prepared a ratatouille for lunch.

The master gardeners had just come inside to wash up and eat when Liliol's phone rang. "It's my uncle," she said, and quickly took the call on speaker. "Good to hear from you. I see the phones are working again."

"They came online ten minutes ago," Pateme replied.

"Your greenhouse is stable?"

"Back to normal. So, what's the plan? And how's Rosie?"

He laughed low in his throat. "Your darling great-niece is sulky but on the mend. She was discharged last night, and I suspect Diriem and the poor ti'Ansha boy have had an earful, but that's not my problem, is it?"

"Until she returns to work," Liliol countered.

"Perhaps she'll have vented her anger by then. Now, as for your guests, if they'll head to the Oilville portal, they can come home."

She frowned at the phone. "Oilville? Why not just send them through my greenhouse?"

The director sighed. "Because the Forum and the media are making a big deal out of this, and frankly, I don't want that many untrained people in the agency greenhouse. Can you imagine what would happen if someone stepped into the wrong plant?"

Liliol and Yacovi grimaced in unison. "Point taken," she muttered. "All right, then. I'm sure they'll be on their way soon," she said, and we nodded.

But I drew close to the phone before she could end the call. "What about the Unity Plan members still out here?"

"Laws is organizing retrieval teams," said Pateme. "DOI is working with them, and if I know Rose, she'll be involved. Come home."

"Are you sure—"

"You've done more than your share, Gentle Breeze," he said firmly. "Come home, yes? You've earned it."

"He's right," said Liliol once she'd ended the call. "DPP should give you a bonus for this last week."

I snorted. "For what? Staying alive? They're the ones who saved my sorry ass," I said, pointing to Maya, Maggie, and Dave. "Connor gave us a base, Tabitha *literally* held us together, Yacovi—"

"Did my duty," he interrupted. "As did you and Taug. But Teme's got the right of it—let's get you home."

Our goodbyes that afternoon were brief. Maya left the ratatouille with Liliol—"This ain't car food," she said when Liliol halfheartedly tried to protest—and within fifteen minutes of Pateme's call, we'd loaded our two vehicles and set off for the Oilville portal, Dave at the wheel of the RV and Connor in his Hyundai. Around two, we took the Oilville exit, then pulled onto the side of the road at the break in the trees that marked the trail to the portal.

"You can drive all the way down that path," Taug told Dave. "It'll be tight, and there appears to be a fallen tree in the road, but that's just to keep people out—"

"Not enough room to turn around," said Maggie. "I've been in there, and if we drove down, we'd probably have to reverse the RV the whole way back. Is it going to be too much of a problem for y'all to walk from here?"

Taug frowned. "You're coming with us, aren't you? You can turn around in the portal building."

"Oh, uh…" She and Dave traded uncertain glances. "Well, with everything, we'd kind of assumed this was goodbye."

"What? No," he said, "absolutely not. Gentle Breeze is right—we might be dead right now if not for you. The *very* least you deserve is thanks."

"We don't want to cause trouble…" Dave began.

"What *trouble*? Come on," he said, smirking, "if they want a show, then let's give them something. We're pretty boring otherwise," he said, nodding to me.

"Besides," said Moonless Night, "if anyone gets aggressive with you two, Wylan *will* kill them." That hung in the suddenly silent RV for a moment, and then he cleared his throat. "Too much?"

"Want to get back in character there, buddy?" Taug muttered.

"Yeah," he said, rubbing his neck, "I should. But what I'm getting at," he told the Humphrieses, "is that my little brother is *quite* fond of you, and no one with half a brain is keen on provoking him. Come with us. Aren't you just a tiny bit curious?"

Again, they exchanged looks, and then Maggie said, "Well…yes. If you're sure…"

"Absolutely," I said. "Someone call Connor, eh?"

Five minutes and one bumpy ride through the woods later, I stood behind the front seats of the RV with Maggie's phone and dialed the portal number, then held my breath.

The line clicked as the call connected, and then I heard a woman's voice in calm Pactish: "Name and location, please."

I almost laughed with relief but managed to maintain my composure. "Gentle Breeze," I said. "I've got Taug Berek with me. Two vehicles to come through at Oilville, one oversized."

To my surprise, I heard muffled cheering on the other end of the line. "You have priority," said the attendant. "Welcome home. Portal will open in approximately one minute, and we'll keep it stable until both vehicles are through."

I thanked her and passed the phone back to Maggie. "You heard her," I said. "So, has Annie mentioned how these work?"

"Not the specifics," said Dave.

"Okay. See that pinprick of light?" I asked pointing to the bright spot that had materialized in front of the RV and was rapidly widening. "That's about to become what looks like a hole in the fabric of reality."

"With rainbow lights," Taug offered.

"*Right*. It'll be a gateway into the Pactlands," I continued. "These dump into the external portal building. Just drive through slowly, and there will be a security checkpoint up ahead—a booth. Let Taug and me do the talking, yes? And don't panic."

Maggie laughed softly as the portal spread. "I think we're past that point, dear."

I sat down and removed my mask in preparation, and

Moonless Night switched his, though Taug demurred, explaining that it would be a pain to navigate the narrow staircase on four legs. Once the portal had grown sufficiently to accommodate the RV, Dave inched forward, bracing himself for a shock that didn't come—the portals were painless, if perhaps somewhat intimidating to those unaccustomed to magic. But as he approached the booth and my eyes adjusted to the light of the portal building, I saw why Pateme had been so adamant that we not return via the greenhouse.

The place was *packed*. I picked plenty of Forum representatives out of the crowd—particularly the ones who'd spoken to us from the greenhouse—plus Pateme, Kabno, and Diriem, as well as a slew of familiar faces from DPP and Laws. There were camera crews pressing toward the front, and flashes began going off before Dave had come to a stop.

"Hey," said Taug excitedly, pointing through the windshield at a trio of centaurs, "there's my family! And...is that Hoska?"

The faun was back on his feet, and he waved at us. Beside him stood Keppa and a pair of nymphs—the youngling's parents, presumably—and a whole cluster of gnomes, one of whom held Galibe back by the shoulder. A male naga had staked out a spot nearby, and safely huddled against his side, looking healthier than she had in days, was Ermonir, who grinned as the green-clad portal attendant, a middle-aged sorcerer, approached the driver's window.

Dave rolled down the glass and lifted a hand in greeting, and she frowned bemusedly up at him. "Um...hello," she said. "Any credentials?"

"Taug and I were dumped with the clothes on our backs," I said, leaning over Dave to address her. "Yacovi Hewt is in the SUV behind us, and he should be in the system for DPP."

"And there's Lord ti'Catama," Taug reminded me.

"*Right*. I think Connor has creds—probably through

DOI, but don't hold me to it."

"I see," said the attendant. "And, uh…you, sir?" she asked Dave.

He held out his driver's license. "All I've got, ma'am."

Her eyes widened, but I said, "He's with us. Better lift the bar before you get mobbed, eh?"

"But he's—"

"*With. Us.*"

Maybe it was the crowd, maybe it was the tusks, but she surrendered and raised the mechanical arm, and I directed Dave to a clear spot near the assembled. He rolled up the window and parked, then looked back at us and asked, "What now?"

"Let us go first," I said, and, hunching over, exited the RV through the side door.

The applause began before my feet had hit the ground, and I looked awkwardly at the crowd as cameras flashed. Taug followed me, unmasking as soon as he was clear of the vehicle, and ran to greet his wife and kids, leaving shredded trousers in his wake. Next came Moonless Night, who, having been able to actually *pack* for the trip, looked far more presentable than either Taug or I did. I glanced at the SUV to see Yacovi exiting, waving…and then a blonde pushed through the throng and ran to hug him. Jane, I realized, as she plowed into her father, then into Connor, who picked her up off her feet and spun her around.

Several of the representatives began to approach, but I lifted a hand to stop them. "We didn't come alone," I said, raising my voice to be heard in the domed building.

The nearest representative, one of the fauns, furrowed his brow. "Who else did you bring?"

"The people who kept us alive out there. Who owed us nothing but dropped everything to rescue us. Humans— and we want that to be known," I replied, then poked my head back into the RV. "Maggie, Dave? Want to say hi?"

I heard a few gasps from the back of the crowd as the Humphrieses stepped out, but those were quickly drowned out by an emphatic shout: "*Mama! Daddy!*"

Annie practically vaulted Galibe's family to get to her parents, and the three embraced. Wylan followed on his wife's heels, along with the other Huntsmen on the Forum, and there were more hugs and back slaps strong enough to almost knock poor Dave off his feet.

I spotted Tabitha sticking close to Connor, Yacovi, and Jane, taking in what she could without being able to understand the language. She was in good hands, I reasoned…

And then Maya climbed out of the SUV, spotted the DPP group, and waved. "Hey, folks!" she called. "Missed me?"

Jaws dropped, and then Emarae, my second, yelled, "I thought you had your memory altered!"

"Roulette's a hell of a potion, man. The memory wipe didn't *quite* take…"

With that, she was rushed. "Are you coming back?" another agent excitedly asked. "Mangia Due's still running, it's all there."

Between hugs from some of DPP's most caffeine-addicted employees, Maya said, "No, this is just a quick trip. I've got my own place in Richmond, yeah? Original Mangia—which you're all *cordially* invited to visit the next time you're in the area. Don't tell me no one ever comes through."

"We didn't want to risk affecting the implanted memories," Emarae explained.

"Well, that's not a problem, is it? Stop by! There's almost always cheesecake."

I looked away when Moonless Night took my hand and murmured, "Incoming."

The Channel 1 team was quickly approaching, ready for a comment from their colleague. Before they'd fully cleared the knots of Forum personnel, Moonless Night was camera-ready, as poised as I'd ever seen him—his old self, the one Beukal had been watching for decades.

"We're here live with Channel 1's own Moonless

Night," said the nymph with the microphone as the cameraman jogged after her, "and we have *so* many questions. How did you get out there? Were you recruited? And are those *actual* humans with you?"

He chuckled, a deep rumble with his familiar masked voice. "I made a request once I realized this lady was outside," he said, turning to me, "and she was kind enough not to rip my head off when I crashed the party."

The reporter quickly took me in. "You are—"

"Gentle Breeze, DPP Interdiction," I said. "And to answer your other question, yes, they're human. We wouldn't be here without them."

"I, uh...well," the reporter replied, and cleared her throat. "This is...certainly unexpected. Any other surprises?"

I looked at Moonless Night, who arched an eyebrow.

My nod answered that.

"Actually, yes, Vallit," he said, pulling me closer. "Even after all this, she said she's going to marry me."

Kissing him on live television was, I decided, one way to quickly break the news to my family.

That kiss was deep, the product of comingled relief and joy and love. Even through my closed eyes, I could see the camera flashes. Reporters around us pressed closer, asking questions. I could smell their shampoo, their aftershave, their sweat and hairspray and soap. I could smell the tell-tale scents in the crowd that signaled anxiety and shock, and more than a little fear. Gnomes were approaching— probably Galibe dragging his parents nearer to greet us— and when I opened my eyes and glanced over my fiancé's shoulder, I spotted Diriem standing alone, a knowing grin on his face.

It could wait. All of it could wait.

I kissed Moonless Night again in front of the cameras and the representatives and seemingly half of DPP, and I didn't care.

This was home.

ACKNOWLEDGEMENTS

Hello, friend! Thank you for joining me for this next Pactlands trilogy. Stick around—I think you'll like where we're heading. (And if you're so inclined, a review on your favorite reading platform is always most helpful!)

My thanks go to the Novel Chicks, a wonderfully supportive group of ladies. I sincerely appreciate Adam Domby's excellent feedback.

And yes, here's to you, Mom and Dad.

ABOUT THE AUTHOR

When not writing fiction, Ash Fitzsimmons is an appellate
attorney and an unrepentant car singer.

Find her online:
www.ashfitzsimmons.com

www.ingramcontent.com/pod-product-compliance
Lightning Source LLC
Chambersburg PA
CBHW051528250626
47156CB00001B/271